THE LAST STRAND

V R BHARDWAJ

Title: The Last Strand by VR Bhardwaj
Published by: Self Published
Printed in India
ISBN: 978-93-5408-323-5

M.R.P. : ₹ 499.00

FIRST EDITION
Cover & Design Layout – MS Dot

ACKNOWLEDGEMENT

This book could never have become the reality if Neha, my wife had not stood up to provide the financial support for the months I was engrossed in writing this book. Big thanks to the fan emails (some unknown) on my first blog, which motivated me to write more and better.

Thanks to Rupamala and Saumya for their dedicated editing efforts right from the first draft of the manuscript. A hug to Abhisht, my brother and Saurabh, my friend for being the first readers of the whole manuscript and providing me with the honest & encouraging feedback that made me believe in my work.

Finally, thanks to my mother for bestowing me with her fabulous genetic make-up, all I am, is simply a product of genetic engineering and I owe it to her. ☺

July, 2020 V R Bhardwaj

ABOUT THE AUTHOR

"V R Bhardwaj" as he wishes to be known in the world of books, is the author of the story. He has been an avid but selective reader for more than 25 years. He has a Master's degree holder in Consulting Management from one of the premium institutes of India called BITS-Pilani. He is currently based in Melbourne and has been a globe-trotter, having traveled to more than 15 countries for his various consulting assignments. He hails from a humble background, born in a small town in Haryana to parents who are retired government service officials. He was brought up hard-wired to become an obedient son, following the footsteps of his parents, studying and then getting married to a woman of his parent's choice to finally settle in his hometown. As a born rebellion, he took his chances to find his own truth. This story is evidence of the fact that if one desires intently, then every obstacle on the path of dreams and aspirations becomes nothing but just a small hurdle.

DEDICATION

My special friends,

So you know that you were always on my mind when I wrote this book. Those who know us would immediately understand where the enchanting tale of friendship comes from in this book.

I dedicate this book though to you both, now the young boys, Aarnav and Eshaan. As I know that one day you would pen down several stories, better than mine, as I see the magic flowing through your writing and story-telling. While you, Eshaan, the younger boy trying to understand the alphabets, still create wonderful stories, you, Aarnav, the older one are blessed with your penchant for carving words on the notebook. Whenever you miss some self-belief, remember my belief in you both, for I know that you both are born to achieve the grandest splendour, mother earth has ever stored for the humankind. And don't forget that when you reach that point and marvel at your own worldly accomplishments, look back and re-ensure that there is no blood on your footprints.

I have always loved you and can't stop loving you my sons till the end of this lifetime.

THE LAST STRAND

PART 1

PART 2

PART 3

PART 4

PART 5

PART 1

GOLDEN VOICE

SOMEWHERE IN THE LUSH GREEN MEADOWS of Northern India, year 1998, mother nature had thrown its abundance in countless ways. While the view pacified almost everyone who looked at it, some were still unaffected by the serenity. There was a group of young boys where a conflict seemed to be growing.

"Please give me back my pebbles," the youngest of the boys implored while the other two, a bit older than him stood there laughing.

"Let's see your guts. Try and take them from us, you moron," one laughed.

"This has happened so many times. Why do you always pick on me?" The young boy attempted to reason with them.

"It is not us who pick on you. God Himself has picked you to be thrashed by us." The bullies guffawed. The young boy looked at them for a few moments.

"Look at yourself, you bastard. You look into our eyes, you are beaten by us all the time, but you still don't comply. Lower your eyes now," one of the boys shouted.

"Alright, leave it. I don't want to make it ugly again. You keep my stuff and I will leave." The young boy answered politely but without any hint of fear.

But the troublemakers refused to accept this. "Where do you think you are going? We have to teach you a lesson now," one of them snarled. The two boys caught hold of the young one and fell upon him with punches and kicks.

The passing villagers did not seem to pay any heed to the confrontation. It was so mundane that no one paid attention any more.

The village was Chandan Nagar, beautiful and small, nestled in the lap of the great Himalayas in Himachal Pradesh. The young boy lying in the dust getting beaten up was Shankar. Carrying the innocence of his teenage on his diamond face and reflecting the maturity of an adult in his large brown eyes, Shankar watched the boys leave the scene.

He was worried that his scars and injuries would make his mother stressed, and he wouldn't be able to do anything to make it better. His mother, Mandira, was his best friend and his connection to the world, and the only soul he could share his grief with.

Shankar had lost his father, Karambir, when he was one year old. Karambir had died in a skiing accident. He was known to be the best in the sport in the neighbouring villages and towns and even represented his state in the national level games. Sadly though, the sport gave him no means to earn well. As a responsible head of the family, he started participating in the local events for the prize money. The local events with their limited budgets had much-reduced safety arrangements. The participants rode more on their lucks than the safety measures provided.

Karambir was certainly not immune to fate and one day, after strenuous training for a competition, he felt an excruciating pain in his upper thigh. He chose to ignore it as he needed to earn for the family, he loved the most. The injured hamstring gave way and Karambir plummeted hundreds of feet to his death while skiing. It had snowed so heavily after the accident that Karambir's body could be recovered only three days later.

A local priest had predicted that Shankar's birth would signal catastrophe for his father and those closely related to him. While nobody could react in front of the extremely protective parent Karambir, the incident changed it all. The villagers took the soothsayer's words for truth and started keeping the distance from the toddler. Some went even further & held him responsible for everything wrong that happened in his proximity. An innocent child faced admonition and shunning from the society for no fault of his own. Treated as a bad omen, Shankar received the poisonous gift of wrath and humiliation from the people around him.

It is said, you can change the people around you but not their habits. It had been more than thirteen years since the unfortunate accident that killed his father, but Shankar still felt the apathy of the villagers. The long time span, instead of wiping the bad memories from the hearts of the village folk, had dug deeper welts instead.

Shankar made his way home, a small cottage with yellowish-grey walls made of teak wood and a thatched roof. As he opened the main door, came running their pet, Sheru, the dog picked up by Shankar from the street when it was just a puppy, wagging his light brown furry tail. His large ears were relaxed and he panted softly running around his master on his wide and strong paws. The house had a small but fenced compound where the dog was sometimes tied in the night. The backyard , a place for the home-grown vegetables had a fence longing for mending. There was another point just near to the rear entry of the cottage where Sheru was sometimes kept as and when required depending on the position of the Sun in the ether. Shankar touched his dog's head softly acknowledging his affection for his master and then went in. Inside the house was Spartan, furnished with just a wooden bed and a couple of stools. His mother draped in a green Salwar Kameez, sat near the small stove cooking the day's meal. Her hair neatly tied together in a thick braid touched the floor.

As Shankar entered, his mother noticed the bruises. She stood up and walked towards him. Her triangle face carried the expression of love and pain. "Not again." She sighed.

"Sorry Ma, I tried to move out but....Sheru stop it, go out." Shankar looked annoyed at his dog as the dog licked his bruises on the feet.

"Hmmm, try to do better next time son.....Sheru, you go out." She addressed both calmly and took Shankar to the stool checking closely on the bruises on the arms and legs. Sheru lowered his head and went out silently.

"It is okay Ma. It doesn't hurt much. Seriously"

"I can see that son." She said and lowered her large watery eyes, inherited by Shankar. "See, you are crying again. I told you that it does not hurt. But you never believe me."

"Just like his father", she thought to herself and continued examining the bruises without saying anything.

"And now you won't even say anything." Shankar said sharply

"Well, just don't hurt yourself again please, if you can." She retorted and then went inside to bring the medication.

"You know me. I never start the fight Ma." Shankar yelled

"I believe you,son. But that does not help either. I want you to stay safe and fine. That is, it." She replied calmly and came back with the medicine box.

"That is okay, Ma. I don't need any ointment. I am fine, seriously. I just don't understand why am I being treated this way. Am I really cursed as the people say?" He looked pained now.

Looking at her son, she stopped for a minute. The question she had always avoided had confronted her. After a few more stressful moments, she regained her composure and said, "I know it doesn't seem to be fair."

"Yes, it is not fair Ma."

"Forget about it now son. Calm down. We will talk about it in the night. Right now, let me put the ointment and then let us have some food."

"Ok." A terse reply followed by Shankar

A few minutes later, Shankar sat on the ground beside his mother who served Rotis & Aloo Gobhi to her son.

"Ahaaa, love you Ma. I just thought of Aloo Gobhi in the morning and here it is." Shankar sounded suddenly elated.

"Hahahaaa, mother knows everything, my boy." She said and then thought, "the brain always works better when the stomach is full."

Soon after the food, the night was on its way.

In the night as they lay in bed, the boy asked his mother again.

"Now tell me Ma, why does it happen so often to me? I am calmer now and will understand what you say."

"Life is a mystery my son....and only he knows what is in it for us?" She said

"That can't be true....tell me something else Ma....please."

Mandira noticed the curious eyes of her son. She looked up remembering her husband and then looked at him. Then she said, "There must be some greater plan, son. The strongest of souls and sturdiest of characters emerge from sufferings. You see, even a stone, when under tremendous pressure, turns into a precious gem. Those who are exposed to such transformation are lucky and you, my love, are a lucky person to undergo this process so early in life. Don't forget that, deeper the scars in the heart, the more love it can contain."

"Hmmm, I hope what you say is true Ma. I believe you and that is why I wait for the moment when things change for good." He sounded hopeful.

A few moments later he remembered something and gave a scowled expression. "What happened?" Mandira quizzed

"Still don't understand why anybody hates it?" He asked.

"Hmmmm, prepare yourself to listen, son. Interestingly, ever since, the first human walked on earth, love and hatred have always shadowed each other. Generally, people need a driving force to live and since loving somebody is not under their control --they tend to hate somebody which can grow on itself. Surprisingly, they don't know that the same hate has given them reasons to live. Both love and hate are forces of life but come in different forms." Mandira stopped and looked quizzically to her son trying to know if she made any sense to him.

"But is it necessary to hate someone to give your own life the force it needs? Is it not true that what we offer to others comes back to us?" Shankar removed any doubts, if his mother had, with this question.

"Your question makes sense. It is not necessary to hate someone to set off one's life forces, but as I said, the haters don't even know about this phenomenon. It begins on its own and then one day, it is solidified in their system. And yes, we certainly get back what we offer to the world. Life is like an invisible, rounded, unbreakable and bouncy glass shell; each of us lives inside that glass ball. Whatever we offer to or throw at the world, it actually comes back to us in an amplified form." She completed her thought.

"Oh. That is an interesting thought Ma. The world is a round glass ball.....whatever we throw, comes back in an amplified form. Wow." Shankar seemed enchanted.

"Hahahaa, thanks, my son. But these are not just thoughts, these are the ways of life. Today if you remember these, tomorrow you will be able to practice them too. A good thought has no value if it can't be inculcated in real life." She smiled. He smiled back and then snuggled closer to her, resting his head on her lap. She touched her son's curly dark brown hair. "Exactly like his father," she thought.

THE COLOSSAL LOSS

(I)

AS THE BIRDS DECLARED MORNING WITH their loud chirps, Shankar woke up & heard some noise in the neighborhood. He came out, Sheru following him, to see his mother standing there with the other neighbors. He sat there on the hedge outside his home. The wind blew towards him so he could hear and understand some parts of the conversation.

"So, what shall we do now?" One of the neighbors questioned.

"I don't know. Should we talk to Girija on this?" Another neighbor replied.

Girija was one of the most respected people in the village. He was one of the very few ones in the village who had seen the city life so closely. He was very fond of fighting in his childhood. His parents, who were the biggest landlords in the village, sent him to his uncle in the city where he studied and learned martial arts. After he achieved the top honors in his fighting skills, he wanted to open a school dedicated to the martial arts. However, his father got seriously ill and he had to drop all the plans. He came back to the village and took over the responsibility of their vast lands and farms. His father very soon succumbed to a major heart attack. Not too long from there, his mother also died of a grave injury on her head when she slipped on the river bank. After that tragic incident, emotionally broken Girija gathered himself around and started a small martial arts school on his parents' name.

"I think we should speak with the government department that takes care of the wildlife. I have seen their office on our way to the main town Kishnagar." It was Mandira who spoke this time and everybody nodded.

"I am down to do anything but just cannot afford any more losses. Already the leopard has taken away the live-stock of five families." The neighbor who spoke first, spoke again. He seemed to be gravely concerned.

"Ohhh, the beast has reached this far this time. This is close." Shankar said to himself and then turned to his dog, "Come on Sheru, let's go inside". As he went inside, he took out his pencil and started sketching on a white sheet.

In a few minutes, Mandira came back and saw Shankar busy in carving his imagination on the paper.

"You will be late for the school son." She came forward and leaned to have a look at the picture.

"Will be ready in two minutes Maa. Look what I am drawing." Shankar noticed his mother trying to have a look

"This is brilliant, son. But be careful about what you show. The leopard may not be as much a demon as you are trying to portray here." Mandira noticed the demonic eyes of the leopard in Shankar's drawing. Sheru, who had been watching the conversation for some time, came closer to have a look at Shankar's art and then started barking.

"Hahahaaa, this is not real you stupid. Stop it" Shankar laughed looking at his dog. Then he looked at his mother and asked

"Why Maa? What is wrong with that?"

"Son, this is a fight for survival for both, us and the animals living around." She replied with her usual calm.

"Hmmm, I will think over it. Anyways, it is far from the completion." Shankar said and stood up to get ready for his school, still startled on his mother's response. "Come Sheru, let's have a bath".

"CN Primary School" was the only option for early education for the kids in the village. It was a small campus covering around six hundred square meters, just enough for the number of the kids. The campus was based around three hundred meters from the bank of river Chandrabhag. The river was formed after the meeting of two streams "Chandra" and "Bhaga" and was the largest river in terms of the volume of water in the whole region. During the rains, the river water level reduced the distance between the bank and the school by another fifty meters. If silently observed, the sound of the river could be heard distinctly from all the fifteen rooms in the school.

Shankar had to walk two kilometers downhill to reach the school. He often started late to avoid any encounter with other kids and often was the first one to come out of the school after school hours.

Shankar was ready for the school in no time. Mandira kissed him on his forehead and wished him for the day. Sheru, as always, ran with Shankar for a few meters before Shankar asked him to turn back for home. Dressed in the white and blue school uniform, Shankar paced himself up to make it in time. He covered three fourth of the distance pretty quickly when he heard a loud synchronous shout. He stopped & looked towards the direction where the sound emerged from. An even louder sound followed. He didn't look perplexed. He knew the source of the sound. Stopped for a few seconds as if planning his next move and then he started moving in the direction of the sound. He walked a small street that opened into a bigger one. He crossed the bigger street to reach the façade of a very large mansion. Pushed the gate slowly, opened it & showed no hesitation to enter inside. As if he was well acquainted with everything, he straight away headed towards the backside of the mansion. As he reached the backyard, the source of the sound was clearly visible.

"Heeeeyaaa"

"Heeyaaaaa" The synchronized louder sound followed.

A bunch of young boys were following every move of a large man standing in front of them. He quickly hid behind the wall such that he could still see everything.

"Ready for Combination two; Right Cross, Upper Cut, and Straight jab. Start"

"Heeya, Heeya, Heeya", The synchronized shout followed with each move.

In a few minutes, Shankar had also taken the stance and had started copying the moves of the large man.

A few more minutes passed and then suddenly he felt a shadow behind him. He turned back and saw another boy of almost his age, body and weight but slightly darker in complexion behind him.

"Who are you?" Shankar snapped

"Ohh, I should ask you this question. Who are you?" The other boy asked authoritatively.

"Umm....I am his nephew." Shankar hinted towards the large man with hesitation.

"Ok, then why are you hiding from him. I will take you to Girija Sir.....I mean your Girija Chacha ." The other boy said sarcastically.

"Oh no, no, please. I am rushing to school. Some other time please." Shankar picked up his bag and started to move but the other boy stopped his way.

“You can’t go just like that.”

“Why? What is the matter?” Shankar sounded nervous.

“Look, I have seen you here watching the classes several times.”

“Ohhh” Shankar stopped for a moment and then asked, “What do you want?”

“Just follow what I say or I will tell Girija Sir about everything.” Shankar looked embarrassed as the other boy ordered him.

“I don’t understand. What are you upto?”

“Nothing much. You just have to fight with me.” The other boy winked.

“Fight? But why? And Who are you?” Shankar was surprised now

“I work here in this school and just like you, I also watch these boys. But I don’t have anybody to try or test my learning onto.” The other boy replied with a confident smile.

“Hmmm, that sounds interesting. But I really have to attend school now. Let us meet after school. I hope that is ok” Shankar looked relaxed now.

“Alright. It is evening, then. I will see you on the riverside of your school straight after your school time.” The other boy replied and left the area.

“No time for negotiations, crazy boy he is,” Shankar said to himself.

(II)

In the evening, Shankar reached the riverside of his school. He found no one. As he started to move after waiting for a few minutes, he saw a boy hopping and running towards him.

"That must be him"

A few seconds later, the boy reached the point.

"Sorry, I am late"

"That is ok," Shankar replied

"So, shall we start?" The boy seemed eager

"Easy. At least tell me who you are? Have never seen you here before." Shankar said

"First you tell me your name? I will decide then" the boy replied with a naughty smile.

"Okk, if that helps. I am Shankar."

"And I am Javed", the boy replied

As Shankar nodded acknowledging, Javed jumped forward and shouted, "Don't waste time, get ready to take the first hit."

Shankar quickly took the stance and stared into the eyes of his opponent.

Javed looked at him and then checked on his own stance. He corrected himself a bit and then threw a side-kick on Shankar's left thigh.

"Ouch, that hurts." Shankar stepped back a little.

Javed came forward and quickly threw a combination of two side-kicks from his right leg and a straight kick from his left leg.

"Aaaahhhh." Shankar bent forward and then sat on the ground holding his groin. The straight kick had worked for Javed.

Javed looked down at Shankar with a sense of victory. After a few seconds, he extended his arm towards Shankar to lift him.

"Hang on, I am not done yet." Shankar pushed back Javed's hand and then looked up at him.

"Ok, your wish." Javed stepped back and took the stance.

Shankar erected himself up and took the stance again.

"Heeya" Javed threw the right side-kick on Shankar's left leg but Shankar lifted it for a shin guard.

Javed stepped back and quickly came forward with the same right side-kick. Shankar, watchful, lifted the leg for the Shin guard again. Javed, irritated, got back, and came forward to hit the straight kick with full power. Anticipating the move, Shankar turned his body to dodge the kick and in a moment got back to hit a straight kick on Javed's chest with his right leg.

Down came Javed with a strong blow. Surprised by the moment, Javed paused for a while and then looked back at Shankar who stood over him extending the arm to help him stand.

"It is going to be fun, Shankar. I am also not done." Javed laughed and pushed back Shankar's hand.

Shankar laughed back and soon both were back on their feet facing each other once again.

(III)

Next day, Shankar and Javed met at the same point once again. The trees had shed their leaves preparing themselves for the winter season ahead. The river water level had reduced but still flowed close to the danger level. The year had witnessed the highest rainfall of the 1990s.

The young boys sat on the grass facing each other soaking their bodies with the outgoing sunlight.

"It has already started getting colder for these days," Shankar said. "Is it? Don't know much of the years gone by." Javed confessed "Hmm, so you are new to the village. I thought so."

"Yeah, I am."

"Where did you come from?"

"Several places. It's a long story, some other day" Javed turned his head away from Shankar while staring at the sky.

Shankar looked at Javed and then turned his head too away from Javed as if giving him his personal space.

A few seconds passed, Javed lowered his head and said, "I was born in Kanpur." Shankar turned his head towards Javed and waited for him to continue speaking.

"My uncle once told me that they wanted a girl. It is the profession they were into. I perhaps understand that now."

"Ohhh, where was your mother?" Shankar asked hesitantly

"It was due to her that I have some good memories of my childhood. And then she died when I was six."

"Ohhh, I am sorry Javed." Shankar lowered his head again disappointed with his question.

"That is ok Shankar. I have heard much tougher questions." He replied and started uprooting the grass.

"Leave it. So, how was your relationship with your uncle? I guess he was the one who brought you up. Right?"

"Yes, he did. He was not a bad person but unfortunately, he was half paralyzed. Practically, he was not capable to take care of a kid so he made a deal. He bargained for his life-time food and gave me away to Aseem." Javed said and looked up at Shankar

Shankar was further dismayed at his question. He looked at Javed's suddenly turned fiery eyes and said, "Leave it, Javed. Somethings are better not spoken about."

"Hmmm. Let's fight then." Javed said

"Not today, you don't seem to be in a forgiving mood," Shankar replied with a smile. "You bet, I am not." Javed too smiled back.

"That is better now. Ok, let's have another friendly match." Shankar got up.

"Right, a friendly match between friends." Javed too stood up.

Both looked at each other and another zealous duel followed.

(IV)

Mandira sat outside in the porch on a thin chatai rug, knitting.

When Shankar came in, he jumped near his mother.

"You seem to be very happy today." She exclaimed

"Oh yes Ma. I guess I also have a friend now."

"Wow, that is great. Who is he?"

"You may not know about him Ma. His name is Javed."

"Javed?" Mandira paused for a little while and lowered her head.

"What happened Ma?"

She raised her head and noticed the gleam in her son's eyes.

"Nothing son."

But he had sensed the changing eyes of his mother, so Shankar insisted

"Even if there is, it is not important really. Everybody has his opinion." Mandira retorted

On hearing this, Shankar became even more curious and insisted further.

"As I said, nothing important Shankar. Infact, what I have heard, if it is true, makes him a really commendable boy."

"Okk, so what is that Ma?" Shankar was now eager to hear.

"I have heard that he has come from nowhere and has survived where no one could survive." She said

"Means what Ma?"

"Means that nobody really knows about where he came from. He perhaps has been to many places. And the world where he has come from is famously notorious to swallow its inhabitants. His uncle had sold him to a gangster. This boy miraculously escaped from those people and landed into the custody of an orphanage. Luck didn't favor him much as the head of the orphanage too was a very cruel man. The boy didn't only survive the ordeal but also one day injured the head of the orphanage badly to flee away from there."

"Wow, that is heroic. But how do you know this?"

"Well, the police had followed the boy after he assaulted the orphanage head. The boy though by that time was provided shelter by Girija. Girija, true to his words and promise, took control of the situation. He managed the policemen and got the report of his death filed. So, as per the world,

the boy called Abdul Hameed is dead. The boy you met is somebody else, called Javed." She smiled at him.

"Ohh…" Shankar almost transfixed heard with abated breath.

"Most of the people have not supported what Girija did. They just could not say it openly. They have many reasons to not support him. Religion, background, police charge, and what not. That is why I said, it is unimportant." Mandira said conclusively.

Still Shankar kept looking at his mother. He remained silent for a few more seconds and then he lowered his gaze and scratched his head, "You are right Ma. It is unimportant." He whispered slowly. Then he again looked at his mother and aasked, "He is a tremendous boy. And we are almost the same age. Can I call him home someday?"

"Yes, my son. Sure, you can." She smiled looking at her son.

"Thanks, Ma. And don't worry, when I grow up, you don't have to do any work to earn money. You will knit the sweaters only for your son." Shankar said with his chin moved upwards. Mandira looked at him with love, caressed his hair and murmured, "God bless you, my son"

It was a sunny Saturday morning the next day. The schools were closed. Shankar and Javed had promised to practice in the morning itself. They both reached the same spot near the riverside of the school.

Both wore lose clothes fit for the body's movement during the fighting.

Both friends hugged each other before starting their practice. After a little bit of body stretching exercises, they stood together to face each other. Both took their stances. Shankar said, "Before I forget, you are invited to my home. We will have lunch together."

"Thanks. But it doesn't mean that I will leave you today" Javed smiled and then jumped at Shankar who was fast enough to frisk away and stand at a distance, laughing at Javed.

"You are so slow, Javed. You will be the easiest kill for the leopard. You should also forget the village girl. They are much quicker than you." He teased Javed once again and started laughing. Javed suddenly sensed the moment and leaped towards Shankar to catch him as he stood laughing. This time he could not respond as quickly and Javed caught him by his neck. “So, my chimpanzee friend, now where will you run?”

“Ahh, Javed, sorry.... sorry. I won’t say it again. You are quicker than the girls.” Shankar said and then laughed louder. Javed too could not control and joined him laughing. In a few moments, they got ready again for a serious session. The friendly duels started and ended with sore legs and arms.

Both of them grinned at their pain. There was no feeling of animosity, no hint of aggression. Both relished their games.

While the friendship developed, it didn’t go unnoticed. The passersby had noticed the camaraderie. But that day there was another man who had noticed them practice. A keen observer with a special interest in the art they practiced, stopped, and observed them for long. After the boys were done, unaware of a third presence, the watcher made himself visible from behind the big oak tree.

“Girija Sir,” both the boys were taken aback at the sight of the man. They quickly stood up and folded their hands wishing their idol.

“I can see that I have been closely followed,” Girija spoke sternly. His creased head was prominently visible on the large balding head.

Both the boys kept mum, looked at each other, and then looked down at the ground.

“So, that is where you come every day Javed,” Girija said once again in the same tone but a question in his long black eyes.

“Yes sir” Javed answered sheepishly.

“Why do you want to learn this art, Javed?”

"Ummm, it feels good Sir." He replied again sheepishly "And what about you Shankar?" Girija lowered his tone a bit

"Oo, I don't know, just feels good" Shankar was pleasantly surprised to know that the big man knew his name.

"Hmmm, ok, both of you choose one reason out of four; Influence, Fitness, Power or Honor?"

"Sir, can you elaborate please?" Shankar requested slowly, still scared of the large hands of the person, he had seen several times in action.

"Ok, since you asked. Influence or you can call Fame, is to be better known in the world; Fitness is to feel and look good; Power is to dominate others and Honor is for your self-respect. Does it make sense?" Girija replied looking at Shankar

"I will choose Power," Javed interjected.

"Well. And you Shankar? Have you made up your mind yet?" Girija turned his head back to Shankar.

"Honor sir," Shankar replied

Girija paused for a moment, looked straight into Shankar's eyes, and then nodded in acceptance. Then he spoke, "Power and Honor. Alright then, let us see how successful you both will be. Tomorrow morning at 6, both of you, in my class."

Both the boys looked at each other amazed at the sudden twist in their fates and then replied together, "Yes Sir."

(V)

It was raining the next morning. The clouds had extended the darkness. The birds lay inside their cozy nests hearing the sound of raindrops, silently. The roosters preferred to halt their hoots. Shankar draped himself with a long plastic sheet and set out for the walk. His mother, well aware of her son's stubbornness, didn't make any effort to stop him. He made it to the premises of the martial arts school just in time. As he reached the wall behind which he had clandestinely viewed the training several times, he paused for a moment, looked at it and then moved ahead to step in the spacious backyard with a smile. Girija stood there facing six boys, who stood in a shoulder to shoulder queue, under a shed. The weather had done its trick as five students were marked absent already. A couple more were expected to not make up that day. Javed who stood last from right, turned his head back to see the newcomer. He nodded on noticing his friend's presence. Shankar moved towards Girija.

"Namaste Sir."

"Namaste" Girija replied and noticed the drenched and disheveled Shankar.

"Stand in the queue Shankar."

A thin murmur started suddenly as all the boys but Javed started talking with each other.

"All of you, listen to me." Girija commanded

"He is your new classmate. His name is Shankar."

Shankar moved towards the left corner of the queue looking at the boys he recognized well.

"Good one. Now I can break his bones." The second boy from the right murmured as Shankar passed by. He didn't seem to notice though and went straight to stand besides Javed.

"Mark my words boys, I don't want to see any kind of indiscipline here. Be careful before you think or plan anything." Girija commanded once again. The warning seemed to work as the boy who stood second from right shuddered on hearing the words and stood straight quietly.

"Let us start now." Girija said and started directing the boys. One long and physically draining hour passed.

"Alright boys, the session is over. You can leave now. The two new boys, Shankar and Javed, you both wait here." Girija commenced.

"Yes Sir." The boys replied.

When the rest of the boys had left, Girija came closer to Shankar, "Don't let it worry you son." Shankar on hearing this looked at Girija emotionally. "Right Sir. I have been trying."

"Good. Ask Javed, he has felt the same. Now, he is much more at peace." Girija hinted towards Javed, who stood there looking at both of them.

"And yes, come a bit early tomorrow." Girija asked. "Right Sir."

When Shankar reached home in the evening after attending the school, he found people gathered outside his neighbor's house. He noticed his mother also present there actively participating in the discussion.

"Write to them one more last letter. Write this time that if nobody comes forward to help us from the government's side then we the villagers will do whatever possible we can to help ourselves." Mandira said strongly

"But do you think it will work? We have sent three letters already." The neighbor replied.

"It may or may not Shambhu bhai. But we need to cover ourselves well before you and other villagers angrily destroy that beast." She replied

"Yes, she is right. What if the police catch us for killing a protected wild animal?" Another neighbor raised the concern.

"Hmmm, so let us do it one last time." Shambhu replied.

"Yes. And even if we need to put in some money in the pockets of those government officials, let us do that. We need to be heard." One woman said.

"Yes, we will collect the money for this." Shambhu echoed the sentiment of everybody else. The people started to disperse as the discussion was concluded.

Mandira turned back and noticed Shankar at a distance. She reached to him, hugged him tightly, and then asked, "Must be hungry my son."

(VI)

The next morning, Shankar reached the martial arts school before time. It was still a bit dark. The sky was clear and a gentle breeze blew from the North. Girija already stood outside carrying a small box when Shankar reached. Javed too joined in a couple of minutes later.

"Namaste Sir"

"Namaste." Girija replied gently and then extended the box towards the boy. "What is this Sir?"

"You will see."

Shankar opened the box and found a new pair of blue color sports shoes.

He looked up at Girija confused, what was that for, and then he looked down at his feet. The threadbare old shoes which had changed the color from brown to a dusty grey were crying in silence for long.

"Thank you, sir, but my mother will not like it." He replied with a suddenly restored calm.

"I know. Don't worry this is not a gift. You will earn it. As you learn the art, you will help me along with Javed, teaching other kids after your school hours. In return, I will take care of your needs." Girija replied

"Done Sir." The joy was clear in his voice.

"One more thing, Javed will also start his school next week. I have been teaching him as much as I could at home but now it's beyond my capabilities. I have spoken to the principal. He will be in the eighth standard, one level lower than you. If he does well in the first six months then he will be promoted to ninth grade with you. I have heard that you are a bright student, you help him study. Whatever may happen, you both take care of each other."

Both the boys looked at each other while listening to what Girija just said. Their amazed eyes widened a bit and smiles gleamed on their faces. Then both replied together, "Yes Sir."

The week went by quickly. The two boys got themselves ready for the school after the martial arts class in the morning. It was a short walk from there. The mornings had begun to be colder. The days were pleasant. The trees were naked and the earth was covered with the leaves. The air was filled with the aroma of crushed leaves and the rustling sound of walking over the dead fronds. The breeze continued from North and the water level in the river Chandrabhaag had reduced slightly.

The boys reached the school much before the bell went on. Just before entering the school, Shankar halted and looked at Javed.

"What happened?" Javed quizzed

"Nothing" Shankar still stood there contemplating

"Hey, let us go in." Javed said impatiently

"You go. I will come in a few minutes." Shankar replied

"Why? What is the problem?" He asked

"Nothing much. Just haven't entered the school through the main gate and that too at this time ever." Shankar replied with a feeble smile

"It will change now, my friend. Now it is the two of us." Javed raised his thick eyebrows and looked at him, inviting to stand by his side.

Shankar looked back at him and said, "Right, the time will change. It has to." And he moved forward. Javed followed him and started walking by his side. Both friends entered the premises together. A murmur followed them, it became loud. The boys were unfazed, they turned back and stared hard at the sound, it faded. They both looked at each other and moved towards their respective classrooms.

It is said that the Devil feeds on fear. A hard & fearless stare right into the eyes of the devil can shake his very existence. It happens and it happened that day too.

The days seemed to pass swiftly after that, the martial arts classes adding a unique sheen to the time & personalities of both of the boys. Both boys worked hard under the mentorship of Girija and warm affection of Mandira. Javed got promoted to the ninth grade and from there both got promoted to the tenth grade. Within the last one year, both had shown a massive change in their appearances. While Javed was growing to look broader in size, especially from the chest and shoulders, Shankar had suddenly become taller than any average man in the area. Both showed strong arms and a light line of mustache on top of their lips. They had just achieved the Brown belt in their martial art and were totally focused on the next advancement to attain the black belt.

March 1999, a few more months rolled on and Shankar was about to turn fifteen in one week. The cold weather had finally given way to let the warmth of colors be felt as the flowers bloomed everywhere. The trees drooped with the abundance of new green leaves. The squirrels chittered, wagging their bushy tails.

For the boys, the schools were coming to an end. Only the final tests were pending. The state board exams for the tenth standard were due in four weeks and the "Black Belt" test for their martial arts was due immediately after the school exams. The boys were present at their favorite spot. It was a pleasant afternoon. The river Chandrabhaga chortled often when the fishes jumped in and out of its blue streams. The anglers were frequently spotted catching their favorite Trout and Mahseer. The boys, witnessing nature's grandeur were sitting on the grass bed under the big Oak tree in the company of their books.

"I do not like History. Why do I need to know what happened in 1920?" Javed complained pulling the hair of his newly appeared beard

"Hahahaaa, you won't stop complaining about History ever." Shankar laughed. His broad jawbone visible prominently

"No, never. And not only History but Geography and English as well." Javed said showing a tight fist to the books lying in front of him

"Hahaaa, but I find the languages very interesting." Shankar continued giggling

"Hindi is fine but English.... God save me. Do not understand a bit of it. Thankfully you were there to help me, otherwise I could not have been promoted with you ever." Javed spoke irritatingly.

"Always with you brother. You also helped me in Mathematics. Remember?" Shankar asked, his long index finger pointed towards Javed

"Yes, I do. It was the Logarithmic tables you were struggling with." Javed smiled with his broad chin held upwards

"Soon, the exams will be over and we will have to think of our life ahead. People go out to study Medicine and Engineering." Shankar said

"Tell me about it. I will stay here and work on my martial arts. Really looking forward to get the Black Belt now." Javed seemed suddenly happier

"Whatever, I will still beat you." Shankar giggled

"Crap, as if you are some Akshay Kumar." Javed said funnily

"Yeah, the Khiladi man. Love watching his movies whenever I can. Solid action not like your dhai kilo wala Sunny" Shankar said sarcastically

"Forget it. Your Khiladi man can't even come close to Sunny. He has a fist of iron." Javed exclaimed, his fist even tighter.

"Hahhaaaa, look at yourself. Control your emotions and focus on studies. Show this anger when we get the leopard." Shankar said calmly. He knew when to stop making fun of Javed

"Oh yes. What happened to the hunter the Govt had sent? I heard he was attacked last week but he survived somehow?" Javed asked

"Yeah, that is true. The leopard left the hunter injured. The guy hasn't recovered as yet from the shock. He has just been muttering about the two fiery eyes of the animal. The situation has become much more dangerous than ever. Each one of the villagers need to be careful now." Shankar sounded worried

"That is scary brother." Javed was tensed

"It is." Shankar too felt the shiver. Then he took a big sigh and started reading his book. Soon, both got engrossed into their books.

(VII)

The next afternoon, the Sarpanch called for an emergency meeting and asked all the young and experienced men to come together in the meeting area of the village. It was a plain area almost in the centre of the village under a large banyan tree. The sun was going down fast and it was just a matter of two more hours for the darkness to surround everything physical. The villagers were gathered soon. The anxiety was notable and the fear palpable. The Sarpanch took the elevated spot right under the Banyan tree to be able to be heard and seen well. He took a seat and so did everybody on the ground facing the Sarpanch. The Sarpanch indicated towards the gathering of more than a hundred men and boys, some of them quickly stood from their spots including Girija, and walked towards the Sarpanch to take the seats beside him. Shankar and Javed sat at the rear left corner of the crowd.

"My fellow villagers, you would already know the reason why we are here. It has been a very long time since we have been struggling in this situation. Many of you have lost your animals to the leopard. The Govt did fail us several times. Finally when somebody came from their side to contain the wild cat, he too had to run for his life. The matter finally lies with us. I don't believe that anybody could help us but we ourselves. I have spoken to the govt. authorities also and they have given us the permission to do the needful, on the grounds that the leopard has now tasted the man's blood which makes it a grave situation. I propose that we form a special team and hunt the leopard. How many of you are in favor? Raise your hands to support this." The Sarpanch spoke with conviction, his thick white mustache wobbling with the air gusts coming from his nostrils. The long scar on his creased forehead clearly visible even under the white turban made a strong case of his valor, wisdom, and experience. The crowd generally in line with what their leader said, raised their hands and cheered enthusiastically. The Sarpanch looked attentively at all of them for a few seconds and then raised his right arm asking the people to settle down. He then looked at Girija and signaled him to speak.

Girija stood up and then spoke, "Good to know that you all support your Sarpanch. But one thing everyone must know that this is a dangerous mission. One could lose their life as well. Everyone should think about it, discuss it with their families and then those who still are prepared to go for it should come back tomorrow here at the same time. We will be here waiting for you. The next plan will be discussed only then." He then turned back to look at his fellow advisors, the silence in the crowd soon turned into a murmur and then into a loud chatter.

Girija's warning had a visible effect as the turn out of the people reduced to a half on the following evening. Girija and the Sarpanch along with other few respected people of the village decided to choose two separate teams. One "Main" and the other as the "Backup" team.

The main team from the village consisted of sixteen men led by an experienced Girija. The backup team consisted of twenty people and was planned to be led by the Sarpanch himself. Girija had kept Shankar & Javed a part of his team as the extra two as they were too young to be fully involved on the front in a dangerous mission like that.

Once the team was decided, Girija addressed his people standing under the big Banyan tree. It was almost dark by then.

"Thanks for being a part of this mission. I am sure we together will honor our village. Har Har Mahadev"

"Har Har Mahadev." The men reverberated the dimming sky with their loud thumping while chanting the name of their warlord. Shankar and Javed too joined their fellow teammates with high energy cheer.

"It is a blessing to see my men with such energy. It leaves no doubt now that we will come out victorious." Girija spoke, his exuberance clearly visible after he witnessed the enthusiasm of his team.

"Yes, we will come out victorious." The team echoed the words of Girija with the same astounding energy.

"Now, any task needs a good plan to be well executed. So, I have a plan for us. Are you ready to know that now?"

"Yes, we are." The team supported with another loud thump.

"Great. The main team that consists of sixteen men has two extra boys who need to remain available to address any emergency. Those two boys as you all know by now are Shankar and Javed." Girija pointed at the boys who stood at their place on Girija's indication.

It was the very first formal introduction of the two boys to the village and the boys soaked in the vibrancy of the newly found recognition, were overwhelmed. They joined their hands and bowed showing their respect to the others. The men in return nodded their heads acknowledging and accepting their presence.

"The boys are well trained to fight with a dagger and spear. I am sure that if needed, they can prove their mettle." Girija continued while looking at the boys.

"Both of you remember that you will not be directly at the front. And since your final exams are near, you don't need to be involved in the preparation of other arrangements."

The boys nodded in acceptance of Girija's decision. After a brief pause, Girija turned towards the rest of the men and continued.

"We will have three days to collect as many weapons as possible. Knives, Swords, Daggers, Guns, etc, everything you can get your hands on to is welcome. The plan seemingly simple is not easy to execute. We will prepare Machaans on the trees in the jungle. The location will be decided based on the information we have got from the Govt hunter when he followed the trail to reach the leopard. We will need a goat to be used as the bait for the leopard. Ideally, we should be able to execute the plan in five days." Girija stopped and looked at the team expecting any question.

"What is the purpose of the back-up team and when will that be used?" one of the men from the back-up team asked

"Good question. The back-up team will ensure the safety and security of the other villagers. They also need to be prepared to replace any member of the main team if and when the situation arises." Girija answered looking at others waiting for any other question.

"Anybody else?" He asked again the men

"Alright then, let's start preparing for the big day. Har Har Mahadev." Girija roared

"*Har Har Mahadev*" a louder roar followed

The next five days went quickly. Everybody tried to contribute as everyone wanted to be a part of the biggest ever story in their village in the whole decade. Each one of them wanted to be able to tell a tale at the end of it. Shankar and Javed not much unnerved sharpened their daggers and the spear. Javed relied more on his strong arm to take the long shot by throwing his spear at the beast, if required. Shankar, relying more on his agility and strong limbs fit for a closer fight, chose for the pair of six-inches long daggers arched towards the tip. One last meeting was held that afternoon to re-evaluate the preparations between the two teams. The teams were dispersed before the dark so everyone can prepare for a very long day ahead.

(VIII)

The clock had struck six in the morning. It was still dark outside. Shankar still in his slumber smelled something. He opened his eyes and looked around. He noticed some movement in the kitchen. Rubbing his eyes, he came out.

"Happy Birthday my son." Mandira spoke looking at his son as he came towards her.

"Ma, what are you doing so early in the morning?" Shankar asked yawning.

"You know better my boy. Didn't you smell?" She asked surprised

"I did. In fact, that is how I woke up? My favorite *Halwa.*" Shankar smiled at his mother

"Yes. I thought before you go out on your mission, you should have enough store of energy. And moreover you turn seventeen today."

"Thank you, Ma. I will quickly brush my teeth and then will dig into the *Halwa*." Shankar re-energized by now spoke enthusiastically and stood up.

"But don't eat all of it. Save some for Javed too." Mandira ordered,

"Sure Ma, will do so." He replied while walking towards the toilet.

In one hour, Shankar was ready to leave for Javed's place. He packed his bag, put the box of *Halwa* in it, and then touched the feet of his mother.

"Bless you my son. Do well and stay safe." She said while looking at her son.

"I will be fine Ma. When I come back, will repair the backside of the house as well. The broken fence is an invitation to the wild animals. Keep Sheru in the backyard.....just in case" He fumbled a bit towards the end.

"Ok my brave boy. Do whatever you want." Mandira kissed her son's forehead and then gently caressed his hair.

Shankar let go of his suddenly emerged ominous thoughts & was filled with calm as he looked at his mother's smiling radiant morning face. He halted for a moment and then turned back to start a very important day. Sheru followed him once again but this time walked with him much longer than usual. It was the point where Javed waited for his friend.

"Arr... What is Sheru doing here?" Javed asked loudly as he saw them approaching.

"God knows. I told him so many times to go back but he does

not listen. And look at him, he is barking at me....... at his master." Shankar sounded annoyed

"Hahaha, perhaps he too wants to join the party today....or perhaps he is asking for your birthday party." Javed giggled

"Hahaaa.....whatever, he has to go now.... Sheruuuu, go back now." Shankar yelled at his dog. Sheru paused for a moment, looked at Shankar and Javed, and then turned back to go home.

"See this stubborn animal, look at his speed.... even a tortoise will be faster than him. I will...." Shankar picked up a pebble from the ground and threw it at Sheru. The pebble hit Sheru on the back, he whimpered a bit, looked back at his master for a moment and then started running slowly towards home.

"Calm down my friend. Save this anger for the big cat." Javed giggled on Shankar's behavior.

"Ahhh, it gets annoying sometimes. I don't know why but I am worried about Maa." Shankar said worriedly.

"Why is that?" "I don't know.... just had this strange vision in the morning...."

"Ohh, that is why you are so disturbed. Don't worry, it will be alright. And yeah, happy birthday my friend."

"Thanks brother. You always remember that and I don't even know when is your birthday?"

"Big deal. Even I don't know the exact date. It is someday just before our Independence Day as I was told. Come, let's move on." Javed smiled.

"Hmmmm....do you have some memories of your birthdays?" Shankar asked while walking.

"Not much, never got to celebrate. When my mother might have celebrated, I was too young to remember that and when I came into senses, she....she had left. Just one thing though I remember.....my mother told me that I was born on a stormy thunderous night just a few days before *Rakshabandhan.* It rained like hell that day.....no wonder, here I am....hahahaa" Javed gave a dry laugh.

"Never mind, we will celebrate our birthdays together today. Maa has sent *Halwa* for you as well." Shankar said with a smile

"*Halwa*....aahaaa, and here is our destination also." Javed pointed towards the meeting place which was already swarming with people.

The two teams met at the meeting point at eight in the morning and started walking towards the jungle. Their first task was to build the *Machaans* before the night sets in. The point decided to set as the hunting point was very close to the Chandrabhaag river. It was the same spot where the Govt. hunter was attacked by the leopard when he followed the trail to reach the leopard. With a favorable weather and enough hands at work, the *Machaans* were built well before the time. Girija asked the back-up team to leave from there and stay together at the central meeting place of the village guarding the villagers and staying alert in case of an exigency.

It was a full moon night. The main team was all set to hunt the hunter. They had made three M*achaans* on top of the trees, where all the eighteen people from the team were comfortably placed. A goat was tied to a rope and left out as a bait.

The night, as expected, was cold. The silvery moonlight falling on the moving water created several faces in the river. The moon must have been astonished at the sight of such weird & sometimes scary images of his own in the clear water. The eerie sounds of the jungle bestowed those faces a language, much understood by the emotion of intrigue and fear. Anxiety levels seemed to rise with every moment. The team was ordered to keep absolute silence. As the night grew cold and the sleep started to sneak into their freezing brains, the fear crept into the tricky minds.

It was around three in the morning. The goat had stopped whining and the hunting team was half asleep in their Machaans. Suddenly, a shadow emerged from behind the tree to which the goat was tied. Before Girija could pick up and load his gun, the wailing of the goat was cut short. The team leader suddenly saw a glimpse of the leopard and shot at it. The bullet hit the target but did not injure any of the vital organs. The leopard ran uphill towards the east and was out of sight in a flash. The moment everyone waited for so long was lost in a whiff.

Girija, not much pleased with his shot, addressed his team, "It is over for today. We will have to come back with another plan."

"Should we wait for the morning now?" One of the teammates asked

"I don't think we should. Soon it will be misty. We can fire up the torches and start moving back to the village in a closed square formation. We will cross the jungle within two hours before the visibility drops badly." Girija replied.

The team nodded and followed the instructions to set

themselves back on course to the village. A group is as fast as the slowest person in it. The younger and faster people which included Shankar and Javed, thus formed the rear side of the square, while the slowest formed the front part. Girija leading the pack placed himself on the right arm of the square. The group moved and with them moved the eighteen somewhat defeated, bit scared but angered flames.

After the initial few tentative minutes, the group soon found its rhythm and moved speedily. They reached the foot of the hill in around one hour and took a brief halt to rework on their group formation and the burning torches. The route to be traversed now had a dark narrow steep gorge on its way, that could accommodate only one person at any given point of time. While the others still thought of the way out, Girija already had a plan. He opened one knot of the long jute rope tied around his waist and addressed his team.

"From here, we will walk in one long queue. All of us will hold this rope keeping a distance of a minimum of thirty meters from each other. Make a knot for yourself at your position."

"But how will we carry the torches if we have to hold the rope also in one hand? We need at least one hand to support the hike as well." One of the teammates asked

"You won't carry the torches now. I will carry one torch with me and will be on the front. The rope is tied to my waist; others just hold it easy to not pull me back and keep on following me."

"Can we also do the same?" Javed quizzed

"No. One person's mistake can lead everyone into danger." Girija cautioned; then he continued, "It is almost five hundred fifty meters long pass. So when the first person crosses, the last person would still be entering on this end. I will raise the alarm by waving my torch rapidly from one side to the other along with the shouts if I find anything on the other side. The person on this end who still would have his torch burning if, does not hear me, will definitely notice the moving torch. He would stop the movement at his side immediately & light up all the other torches."

"So, who would be the last one?" Shankar asked in anticipation "Being the fastest, it would be you and Javed next to you." Girija said softly "Right Sir." Both affirmed, the sense of pride visible. "Let us begin now," Girija ordered.

The team was quick to follow the instructions. Girija went into the gorge and the others started following him up. The stars had started dimming, the moon had begun fading. The darkest hour of the night had conquered them all. The flames of the torches started to extinguish one by one as more men slipped into the ravine one after the other. Soon, the third last flame blew off and with that, a gust of wind blew from the north. A dark cloud hovered and covered the fading moon. The wind caused a big splash into the river that could be heard till long distance, following which the crickets suddenly muted themselves, the mysterious silence enveloped the region. Javed looked at his friend and said in a trembling whisper, "See you on the other side"

"I hope all is well on the other side. By now, Girija kaka should have reached and given us the signal." Shankar said worriedly still looking in the direction of the other side, anticipating to see a stable burning flame. Javed moved forward and turned his torch upside down to push into the ground. The stubborn flame, however, refused to die, he pushed the torch deeper to cut off any oxygen but the flame resilient than ever did not doze off. He stopped for some more time trying to put off the flame completely while looking at the darkness into the gorge. Better adapted to the darkness, he turned his eyes to the extinguished torch. Suddenly he moved his eyes back to the gorge and paused on the way. The two stars appeared to be very close.

"Shankar, what is that?" He whispered

Shankar still waiting for a signal from the other side, moved his gaze to Javed and asked surprisingly, "What, where?"

And then his eyes moved up following Javed's gaze. The two tiny stars still present suddenly disappeared for a fraction of second before getting visible again. "Was that the eyes blinking?" Javed quick to notice murmured & left the rope to move his hand on his back to grip his spear. His heart thumping and feet shaking. Shankar looked further into the direction suddenly noticed the two stars moving fast towards them, in a sudden reflex, he aimed for the direction and threw the burning torch towards the stars. The eyes disguised as stars of the dark night, erupted angrily through the fiery images of the flames in them. The yellow skin with the black spots, visible for those couple of seconds announced the presence of the ghost with white whiskers. Suddenly taken aback by getting its presence disclosed, the leopard took a step back. Javed in better control of his breath now took out his spears and shouted to inform the others of the leopard. Shankar still astonished with the sudden turn of events and his eyes still trying to adapt with the complete darkness, took out his daggers and pointed them in the direction where he had sighted the wild cat. The evil is said to have an eye to pinpoint the vulnerable among the hundreds. The beast stepped back further to be fully absorbed by the darkness. The teammates in the gorge, however, could not be of any help as there was no way back for them in the dark. Javed and Shankar back to back, their pulses racing, the earth beneath their feet quivering, eyes refusing to even blink in the dark, hands holding the weapons firmly, brains anticipating an attack from any direction, moved slowly in circles. It went for a few more seconds when another gust of wind blew. The dark cloud drifted away and the last fading rays of the moonlight brought the region to an unforgettable visibility. The leopard had pounced from the top of the gorge aiming for Shankar's back, Javed sighting the beast leaping towards them from his left, threw his spear with full force in the direction. The spear missed any vital organs again but pierced into a tree tearing the left front limb. The animal wailed and disappeared into the woods. Shankar realizing the situation handed over one of his daggers to Javed. Then he knelt on the ground looking for the rope to find their direction of exit from the area quickly. The region lit with moonlight showed the rope and the entry to the gorge. Right then, Shankar found hope as he sighted a flame appearing on the other side, burning proudly and stably. The boys slipped into the gorge immediately.

Soon the boys met with their team. Everybody anxious to know the story kept the boys in the middle of the group and they talked as they walked. "Two extremely close encounters in one night and both sides still surviving" Everybody had the same thought.

Dawn was breaking when the team reached the meeting point of the village. The back-up team waited for them eagerly. The teams met each other and shared their sides of the stories. The highlight though was the confrontation of Shankar and Javed with the leopard. After a couple of hours, the teams dispersed as everyone needed to rest after the long night.

Hungry and drained, Shankar & Javed, left for their homes as well.

It took fifteen minutes for an anxious Shankar to reach his home. The Sun had lit the pale blue sky. The eastern side of the house fence was deprived of the green color paint under the bright sun. The long shade of the full-grown *Peepal* tree outside the fence, covered almost whole of the front yard of the house.

Shankar opened the main door and noticed the absence of their dog in the front yard. "Maa would have kept him in the backyard so it would be less cold there" He thought. As he stepped in, he heard a sharp noise coming from his left. He paused to turn to his left, the shriek became louder. He stood there looking at the tree for a moment. Suddenly a black image emerged out of the top branch of the tree flapping the two large wings and took a flight towards Shankar. The flight was quickly cut short as the large creature struggled to keep the wings open & fell on Shankar's feet. "Oh, poor boy. Seems the bat has injured itself." Shankar thought while looking at the fallen mammal. "What a radiant skin this bloodsucker has? I should get something to lift it and put it back in a safe place before the predators notice it." Shankar started moving towards the backyard straight away from the narrow side-walk on the right side of the house.

When Shankar reached the backyard, the first thing he noticed was the loose rope tied to the rear side of the cottage. Their dog was not where it should have been. He moved his gaze to check for anything unwanted. The red spots, perhaps blood shone vividly in the sunlight. He frowned and turned to get inside his home but what was that. The rear door was wide open. His chest pounded suddenly and nerves pulsated. He held his breath and stepped inside.

There was blood everywhere, already drying in the morning sun. Mandira's torn body lay on the ground. Shankar, not willing to believe in what he had seen ran towards his mother and shook her rapidly calling her. The screams went louder and louder and then it started fainting. Tears started rolling down, he had finally realized, though had not accepted what had struck him. Unstoppable tears, demolished spirit, loud sobs, and a scarred soul, altogether gave way to the anger. Enveloped in the grief, he suddenly heard a feeble sound to his right. *Sheru,* whimpered in his tears. Soaked in blood, he came closer and started rubbing her face on Mandira's feet. He then turned back and sat in Shankar's lap. Shankar looked at the extremely bruised body of the animal. His anger grew. He sat still for a few moments and then tried to move his dog. *Sheru* did not respond, Shankar tried again and then he noticed the motionless body. Broken down, he stared in the oblivion for very long. A few days later, Shankar stood before the funeral pyre. "Son, put the fire to your mother's pyre," the old Brahmin requested. After the body was burnt to the ashes, he continued to sit there. By now, his tears had dried and his sorrow was being transformed into a wrathful ire. The anger had turned into rage. In the hour of twilight, suddenly, Shankar rose from the earth and murmured, "The search is on, the hunt is still on." Javed still standing beside his friend put the hand on his shoulder and said softly, "Let's go home."

Something had changed irrevocably.

BATTLE OF EQUALS

IT HAD BEEN TWO WEEKS SINCE THE TRAGIC day. The young boy had his head shaved as per the Hindu rituals. After completing all the ceremonies and religious rites as advised by the old *Pundit,* that went on for thirteen days, he stood on the elevated place addressing the crowd on the evening of the fourteenth day. "We need more people. We will be divided into six teams with eight people in each team. The teams should carry weapons, nets and drums. The beats of the drums will make the leopard restless and it will run away from the source of the noise. It will fall into a trap and we will surround it from all sides. Leopards usually hunt alone and have their territories marked up to several miles. So, it seems unlikely that we will face another threat of this kind. Just beware of cobras and other snakes while walking and stay calm. We will succeed this time." With Girija standing right beside him in his support, nobody could intervene and protest Shankar's abrupt emergence. Seventeen years of hard physical labor was visible in his muscular legs and shoulders. His chest was pumped and the blood veins could be seen bulging out. When he spoke, his large forehead became creased complementing the rage in his eyes. "So much like his father," Girija thought and patted Shankar's back.

The story of a Himalayan man-killer had made very quick rounds in the media circle and the small village was host to several journalists from various newspapers, magazines, and TV channels that day. The story of a young man's vengeance and his sudden emergence as the de facto leader of the hunt was very appealing. When the media tried to approach him, Shankar was tacit as usual but Javed was keen to give his view and provide a few stories of their friendship and martial arts training. He discerned this as a perfect moment to gain the attention and envy of the people and the admiration of the village girls. Shankar was pre-occupied with his planning for the hunt. He was tormented by the eyes of his mother, and the sapphire eyes of the crouching cat staring at its prey.

They had to move very early the next morning. Two separate teams were ordered to keep a watch during the night.

The teams were out in the jungle at the first hint of the sun at the horizon. They had to be divided into six groups and then start the movement as per the plan. Shankar and Javed were in the same team with three other young men and one man in his early forties. Girija was leading the charge from the west while Shankar's team was on the right side of Girija's. They all spread out and settled in their respective positions, now waiting for the signal to start moving. As soon as Javed blew the whistle they started beating the drums. It was a strident and brazen call to the tormenter, a foe who had dared enter their arena. The birds started shrieking and the monkeys jumping from one tree to another. The sound waves made sure that the snakes moved away from the hunters. The beating of the drums went on for two hours and soon the radius formed by the six teams had shrunk from the initial six km to two km. They were approaching the place where the beast might be seen at any time. At the shrill sound of the whistle, all the teams ceased beating the drums. It was a sign to take some rest before heading deeper into the woods.

After fifteen minutes, another whistle was heard from Girija's team, followed by one more. Shankar knew the leopard had been spotted. He sped up, hurrying into the jungle. He could hear the birds and the monkeys, the clamour surrounding him. "You can't remain hidden anymore. I will kill you today!" he thought. Javed had caught up to him. Shankar sliced at the grass and bushes, cutting himself a path. Javed was not too far behind when he saw Shankar's feet slip in the slimy mud, and then his friend fell into a deep valley. In a flash, Shankar was out of everybody's sight. The dense trees didn't allow the sunlight to enter but there was enough light to illuminate the yellow-spotted skin of the large animal, staring at Shankar, a hundred meters away.

Shankar's hands were bruised due to the fall and he could feel some pain in his left leg. His daggers were still held in a tight grip as he lifted both his hands. The gleaming yellow body of the animal began its slow watchful movements towards the lad. Perhaps the leopard remembered their last weighted confrontation and was gearing itself for this probable last face-off. One of them had to die that day, and both of them were aware of it. In such situations, the fear subsides.

Shankar sprang on his feet. He limped a bit but so did his opponent. So it was a duel between equals. Each watched the other for a couple of minutes gauging their strength and then the leopard took its turn to charge at Shankar. It jumped to take him by the neck, but Shankar jumped to the right and saved himself from the clutches of the deadly animal. The leopard immediately turned back and charged again and this time came on at a vicious speed, and almost caught its adversary. Shankar threw himself onto a big tree and climbed up to save himself again. In the event though, the leopard's left paw injured Shankar's right arm badly. The scent of human blood, the anguish and pain of the injury, and the babel of loud drumbeats, now coming very close were making the beast frenzied. It hurriedly tried to climb the tree but only slipped back, scratching the bark due to a wounded limb.

"Shankar, don't worry, I am here," Javed yelled. The leopard turned at the sound. Javed came running towards the leopard with his spear pointed at the target, not realizing that the distance between them had become too short and the animal's wild and raw energy made it too spontaneous and quick for human beings to pinpoint. The leopard roared and jumped on Javed, the spear once again missed the heart but injured the front, right limb. With the spear gone, Javed took out his hunting knife standing right below the tree.

The animal moved forward, its speed slowing. In a last-ditch effort, it summoned its strength and pounced on Javed, not realizing that Shankar had also taken the leap at the same moment, gripping the two daggers and landing on the beast. His daggers pierced deep into the flesh of the beast's neck. The thunderous last roar was heard across the jungle, all the way up to the village. The drumbeats suddenly stopped at a loud whistle from Javed. The other teams rushed to the site.

Shankar was half-conscious and drenched in blood. "Oh, I never knew that revenge could be so gratifying. Revenge, sweet revenge," he said, and rose to his feet and roared like an animal. The sight could incite fear in anybody but there was Javed, a true friend, who held Shankar's hands to subdue him. The villagers came closer and then an old man spoke. "It was a female leopard. She was pregnant. Not good, not good."

Suddenly everybody went silent "So that was the reason why she reappeared much sooner than expected." A lot of thoughts were now echoing in Shankar's head. He looked at the leopard, her eyes wide open fixed on Shankar. The agony seeping through the animal's eyes, he could not bear to look into them for an extra second. He moved away his eyes and saw the old man standing over the animal's body looking at him and his lips continuously moving. On a closer look at the lip movement, Shankar heard the silent words, "Not good, not good....this is a curse." Shankar moved his eyes again, stood up and started walking. His shoulders drooped, head down, feet heavy but the chest pounding.

Javed came up to him. He held his friend's hand and started walking back to the village, leaving the others, astounded, behind them.

NEW HOPE NEW HORIZON

THERE WERE NO CELEBRATIONS IN THE village; the Sarpanch had merely acknowledged the bravery and the gallantry of the entire team, with a special mention to Shankar and Javed, but had also requested the villagers to stay away from bringing the fore the killing of a pregnant animal. He tried to work out a plan according to which the villagers would not be drawn towards the jungle anymore and such confrontations could be avoided.

Despite all this, the media still caught wind of the story and the village was soon swarming with those professionals. They were taking pictures, went to the point where the animal had been killed and within no time the media had painted the two men as warriors.

Shankar, apathetic towards anything laid still in his house on the ground. Javed sitting beside him said, "It has been five days Shankar. You need to get out and feel better."

"I am fine Javed." Shankar answered still looking at the ceiling pensively.

"Ok, then don't ask me to stay in the night with you. Face your demons yourself." Javed stood up.

Shankar looked at Javed and then spoke in a low voice, "Ma was wrong.... death is more mysterious than life...."

"What are you saying?" Javed stopped and turned towards Shankar who once again stared at the ceiling.

"I will have to die to find out the answers...." Shankar said in the same low tone

Javed came forward and shook him strongly. Unperturbed by the impact, Shankar said softly, "Don't go brother. I am not feeling good."

"Of course I won't go, you idiot. At least come to Girija kaka's home. He came in the morning also to meet you but I told him that you had just slept after the long sleepless night."

"I understand but I don't feel like going out." Shankar pleaded

"Then speak to me."

"I don't know how to explain. Just don't feel good. Especially because I know that Maa would have never liked what I did......and I miss Maa." Shankar said with the last three words as a whisper.

"That is true Shankar but don't punish yourself anymore. It all just happened. Even I don't feel good about it. Just let it go." Javed perhaps didn't hear the whisper.

"Yeah, you are right. I will try brother". Shankar continued staring upwards into the nothingness.

"Hey, what is the matter with you?" Javed quizzed as he saw tears in Shankar's eyes....." Oh, I know......" a sharp silence prevailed for a few minutes suddenly broken by a bicycle bell.

"Sheru would run and bark on any such noise around the premises and Maa......she would reach for Sheru's head and calm him by her touch." Shankar spoke, still looking up blankly.

"The perfect guardian of the house....I remember Sheru never let me in for the first time until *Mausi* asked him to." Javed said softly while looking outside the window.

"Yeah, I remember. She loved him a lot. When she cooked, the first *Roti* always went to him." An evanescent smile appeared on Shankar's face as he remembered the moment....and then it faded promptly. "I know the feeling, my brother. I wish I could help." Javed looked away from Shankar realizing his helplessness.

"Hey, don't worry. I am fine my friend." Shankar turned his head towards Javed and wiped his eyes.

"Good. Then we have to get ready for the final school exams also." Javed extended his hand asking Shankar to join him.

"Ok, so let's go to Girija *kaka's* first." Shankar held Javed's hand and stood up.

There was one person in the attention-seeking world of media who had seen the intensity in the young eyes of the two boys. Mani, a reporter from Delhi, was covering the story for his employer. But unlike other people, he wanted to know and understand the inner worlds of Shankar and Javed. He was intrigued by the deep silence of Shankar. He tried to speak with him a few times but Shankar showed no interest. After a couple of days, he followed Shankar to the riverside and then announced his presence. The sunny day was on the verge to touch the silky presence of a delightful evening. Drowned in his thoughts, when Shankar realized that he is not alone, he turned to Mani.

"Oh hello, Sir. I did not realize that you were here," He politely accepted his presence.

"I hope I have not disturbed you in your private moments," Mani sought permission from Shankar.

"No Sir, that is fine," Shankar replied.

"Don't call me Sir, my name is Mani. You can call me by my name," Mani replied with a warm smile.

"You are older than me and Ma always asked me to respect experience," Shankar replied.

"Your mother must have been a very honorable woman. As I can see with my limited knowledge, she did a commendable job bringing you up."

"Thanks, sir. I wish she could hear those words," Shankar said in a low voice. "She certainly can. Wherever she is, she must be proud of you today, my young friend."

"Or maybe not. The night perhaps will stay with me forever haunting my sleep.," Shankar prompted

"Why is that Shankar?"

"Nothing Sir, just a slip of tongue....is there something I can help you with?" Shankar tried to change the topic

"No, not at all. I was just passing by. I will leave now." Mani prepared to turn back

"Sure."

"One thing though I would want to say...." Mani halted and continued, "Your mother will not like you to bear the life-long burden of the incident as well. She would want you to learn from those mistakes and stay happy."

"I agree. But, I can only feel the questioning eyes of a hungry animal who was soon to be a mother at me. And when I turn my head, I see my mother with the same questioning eyes looking at me."

"I understand Shankar. Give yourself some time. Nothing happens for nothing. You will know it in the future. Anyways, I didn't come to bother you. I shall take your leave." Mani finished and turned to leave but then suddenly Shankar spoke.

"You don't have to Sir. Stay if you want." Mani halted and then smiled at Shankar.

"Come on, let's have a walk here. It is such a beautiful riverside."

"It is," Shankar replied looking at the river.

"Where is your friend, Javed?"

"He liked you media guys. Must be busy telling somebody the story of his bravery" Shankar laughed

"Hahaha, but that indeed was brave."

"I don't think so."

"And why is that?"

"The moment did not give us any other option. We just survived the moment." Shankar stopped walking and spoke while looking at Mani.

"I am glad you have this realization. But just to add one more thing, it is not many who could survive to tell a tale, the way you both did."

"Perhaps you are right. But it does not change the fact."

"It changes everything, Shankar. Because along comes the fact that your time has come. This is your moment, live it. Become like the Sun; don't care about the darkness covering you. The tide of time will take that away and then it will be your time to glow. It always happens."

Shankar suddenly had no words to express the gratitude he felt towards him. He tried to speak but his voice became heavy and he could only utter these words: "Thank you, *Kaka*." Feeling the same way as he felt for his mentor Girija.

Mani smiled, patted Shankar's back affectionately, and then turned away.

The next day, Shankar appeared to be a different person, much more open to talking, and easier to approach. Javed loved this change in him, and the villagers found him admirable while the media had their hero. Before leaving, Mani hosted a dinner for Shankar and Javed. He invited them to Delhi to meet him whenever they decided to leave the village.

It was a strange morning. The night had just passed with a heavy downpour and the after effect caused the sun to stay away for much longer. The air had come to a stand-still and the fog had covered the surroundings. While Shankar slept covered in a dark brown blanket, he heard a strange voice, Shankar woke up with his head ablaze with thoughts. He looked around and saw Javed standing at a distance, smiling at him as welcoming his friend to his place. Once sure about his location, Shankar started thinking about the voice he heard. It was not the first time that he had heard some strange voices in his dreams but it was different this time.

It is said that these are the voices of your soul; in a special state of mind, the soul is trussed with the soul of the cosmos and then the union brings forth a message for you from the universe. If you force them to cease then one day, the process also cuts off and one loses a great connection.

"I think I should leave this village," Shankar whispered to himself, but he was loud enough to be heard by Javed.

"What are you saying?" Javed suddenly was taken aback "I don't know, just felt it very strongly" Shankar was visibly perplexed. "What happened exactly? Tell me." Javed asked

"Nothing brother. I don't know what is it.... some strange voices in my head, some blurred visions....Am I really cursed.....forget it, I should just go out of here." Shankar still had the same confused expressions.

"You are being extremely strange, forget about it for now. Just focus on tomorrow's exam. We will talk about it later." Javed changed the topic.

"Yeah, right." Shankar stood up and walked towards the washroom.

"By the way, whatever the plans you had, don't ever think of deciding without me. If you leave, I leave with you." Javed asserted

"No, not at all. You don't have to. You are finally getting all settled here, don't unsettle yourself for me. Moreover, I don't even know where will I go and what will I do." Shankar turned back and spoke

"Huhh... doesn't matter. We will figure that out." Javed shrugged

"We will talk."

"No talks, it is decided. If you go, we go together, period."

"Ma often said that life is a mystery.... for me you are a bigger mystery, you stubborn boy." Shankar smiled

"Don't worry, we will solve the mystery together." Javed winked

"Only if we could..." Shankar looked at Javed and then looked up getting lost in his own aching thoughts.

PART 2

CITY OF HOPE OR CITY OF DESPAIR

IT WAS A WARM MORNING, WARMER THAN usual. Mani, the reporter, was still at home, getting ready for his office at a relatively slow pace. As he took out his shoes from the shoe-rack at the entry of his apartment and started whistling, rejoicing another day of getting ready for work, he heard a shrill sound.

"Don't whistle, the baby will wake up....and listen, please come home early today," she said.

"Why? We just bought groceries this weekend," Mani answered calmly while tying his shoelace.

"You forgot again? Next Sunday is my cousin's wedding and I have to buy a new saree for it," she replied.

"New saree? But you just bought one last month?" Mani sounded a bit annoyed.

"So what? All my cousins have been married into such rich families that they never bother about such matters, but you always keep my hands tied!"

"Manju, dear wife, don't fight with me in the morning. I have a limited income and you know it pretty well. So please, not again today." Mani tried his best to control the growing conflict but to no avail.

As she heard this, she rushed out of the kitchen and yelled at him, "Yes, it is me who is always fighting. When I demand something, it always appears illogical to you. Even our neighbors have bought themselves a new car but we keep pulling the same old car. Why can't you earn like them?"

"Just shut up, please. I do this job because I love it. Money is a by-product for me. I never chase it and you knew that well when we got married. Right now, my objective is to save something for our daughter, so we must not splurge on unnecessary things," Mani said, his voice firm.

"Pallavi is just a year old. You can think of her later. God damn it, you just don't care about me." She frowned and turned her back towards him hiding her resentment.

"Manju, she will not stay that young forever. Once she grows up, we will need all the money for her education. We need to manage our finances wisely."

"Ohh, is that so? Let me see how wisely do you manage the money now. If you spend anything on those outsiders, then you see." Manju turned back and pointed her finger as a warning signal.

"Don't worry, they are self-respecting boys. Even I offer them any financial help, they won't accept that. And yeah, they may not remain outsiders either. When you meet them, see it yourself." Mani calmly responded

"I am not meeting them. Why should I?"

"Whatever, I am leaving." Mani was getting ready to leave when he heard a baby cry. He stopped and went back inside to reach the dark yellow colored cot where a little girl lay with her eyes open. When she saw him, she stopped crying. He smiled at her and took her in his arms. Then he started playing with her and thought, "Pallavi, my baby. You are like your name, 'new and fresh'. So oblivious to the complicated world outside."

As the girl responded joyfully to her father, he started talking to her. "You have such large eyes like your mother and your face is just like mine." The more Mani looked at his daughter, the more he desired to be like her, bearing the smile of an innocent child, untouched by the worldly worries sabotaging his happiness. His wife watched him play with their daughter in silence. Her anger had disappeared. Completely won over by an affectionate smile, she spoke, "What are the names of the two boys?"

Mani turned back and looked at his wife. He smiled and said, "Shankar and Javed."

"Hmmm, bring them over. They can stay here till they find another place to live." She too smiled back and came closer to her husband and then continued, "I too get frustrated but I am proud of you. You go now and leave Pallavi to me." She extended her hands to hold her daughter from the man, she just felt love for.

Manikaran was an experienced reporter. He was in his early thirties, with wisdom in his small dark brown eyes that seemed to belong to a much older man. He was short and stout and his head was rapidly balding from the front. He had a mustache which he was proud of and which he combed with great enthusiasm every day. His concave spectacles came down to rest on the tip of his nose and he looked at people over the top of the glasses as if questioning them all the time. Manikaran could instantly connect with people and commanded great respect.

Mani always looked for fresh stories from the masses. He had such an eye for them that he could see through the outer membranes of an incident and directly into the motivation of the people involved. Once he published an inspiring story of a folk dancer who could pick up the beats of the music even though he was deaf. That man was now in his late forties and had lost his ability to hear in his teenage years when a series of bomb blasts ravaged the historical city of Jaipur. He was practicing for his first day of being a tourist guide in a local market near a historical palace. After the accident, though he lost his hearing, he developed an ability to feel the vibrations through his bare feet. He developed the senses further and gradually one day his body started moving to the rhythm of old Rajasthani folk music. He understood music before the accident but he had never felt it so deeply. He started creating rhythms by beating objects and became so proficient that one day he could dance along to his own drum beats. He became a proficient dancer.

In another article, Mani had written about a poor but courageous girl who testified against her powerful rapists, withstanding several/multiple threats and obstacles that came her way. Mani helped her in her pursuit of justice for three years before eventually quitting the story when his daughter was born. The imminent danger to Pallavi's life made him decide to take a step back but he could never forgive himself as evil won the case. After losing the court trial, the girl committed suicide. Mani was heartbroken and guilt-stricken.

Mani's stories always gave his readers a sense of optimism and hope and he was widely adored for his passion for work. He went far in search of truth and often emerged successful. In a single glance, he had seen the hungry but honest eyes of the two boys, Shankar and Javed. And that day, he was anxiously waiting for their train to arrive. The train station, swarming with people, was in full action at its usual pace. Mani bought the platform ticket and reached the platform no 5. The train was running late but so was Mani. The train was expected to reach in another five minutes. Mani made himself comfortable under the shade of a small kiosk. The kiosk sold tobacco products and the cold drinks over the counter. It had two large red and white colored signboards of the soft drink Coke, re-launched in India just four years ago. Under the scorching sun, too early for the season, there won't be anybody else but only the soft drinks producers who won't complain of global warming. Mani stood there and hummed the song he just heard on the radio sitting at the kiosk counter..... *"Ud jaa kale kawaan tere munh vich khand paavan.........".* A few moments later, the sound of humming was broken by a sharp whistle. Soon, the whistle reached much closer and the train was seen approaching the platform. The rhythmic rumbling sound of the train got distorted by its screeching brakes. Momentarily/Soon, the train hissed and came to a stand-still. The doors of the over-crowded train opened and people started moving out of it. Those who fought for the last one-inch square space in the train, happily jumped down to get a firm foot holding/ground. Mani, out of his musical thoughts, was in action. He started looking for his guests. In a jiffy/Soon, he saw a familiar face in the crowd. As he looked further, he recognized another face as well not far from the first one. As he walked towards them, Shankar and Javed too recognized him, so they both gave back a familiar smile.

"Welcome, welcome boys."

"Thanks, Kaka." Both the boys replied,

"How was the journey?" Mani shook hands with both of them.

"Fine Kaka, though Javed was annoyed." Shankar smirked,

"Hahahaa, what happened, Javed?"

"Nothing Kaka. He is just making fun of me." Javed sounded annoyed.

"Oh yeah, I am making fun. Everybody in the coach heard his complaints. First, it was the mosquitoes, then the flies, later it was the long journey and now it is the heat." Shankar giggled.

"Hahahaa, I can understand. Let us go now. Give me this bag

Javed." Mani responded and proposed to help.

"No kaka, let me. Otherwise, this bugger would get a chance to throw some more jokes on me." Javed said while looking at Shankar.

"Alright, let us move then." All three of them came out of the station and took the green and yellow colored auto-rickshaw to reach their destination, Mani's home.

The auto-rickshaw, honking continuously at everyone and everything, making its way in the serpentine motion, reached the destination quickly. Manju heard the sound of the engine of the automobile stopping outside her home, anticipating the guests, she came out for the welcome.

Mani settled the auto-rickshaw payment while the boys unloaded their stuff from the vehicle.

"Welcome...you must be Shankar and you would be Javed, right?" Manju took a guess pointing at the boys as they followed Mani to the main door.

"Right...how did you make a guess?" Mani sounded pleasantly surprised.

"Ohh, as if you have not talked about them a million times since you have met them." Manju said with a pinch of sarcasm.

"Well, boys, she is my wife Manju at her usual sarcastic best." Mani introduced his wife to Shankar and Javed with an affable smile.

"*Namaste Bhabhi.*" Both of them did a hand fold *namaskar* to Manju. "*Namaste*....welcome." She responded with a warm smile.

After taking a shower, the boys reached the dining table. Mani helped the baby sleep and Manju prepared the meal. In a few minutes, Mani came out closing the room's door and pulled one chair to sit alongside Shankar.

"Good job Kaka. You seem to be good at making people sleep." Javed quipped.

"Hmm, and now it is your turn, Javed. The music anyhow bores you." Mani replied and picked up the cassette player from the table.

"No problems Kaka. Music has kind of stopped bothering me for some time now." Javed quipped back.

"Yeah, only when the song is filmed on your Sunny Deol." Shankar who was listening to them joined the banter.

"Well, let's see which cassette do we have...Aaaa, sorry Javed, it is my favorite one." Mani inserted the cassette back into the player and pressed the play button. As the song progressed, Shankar too hummed along, "*Radha kaise na jale, aag tan man mein lage...*"

In a few minutes, Manju called in from the kitchen, "Listen, the food is ready. Please get it there." Mani immediately stood up and moved towards the kitchen. Both of the boys too stood up and followed Mani to help him get the food.

In a few minutes, Manju too joined them on the table and all of them served the food to themselves.

As they ate their meals, Manju asked, "How were your exams Shankar and Javed?" "Good but not better than the *Paneer masala* you have cooked." Javed prompted "Haaha, thanks for the compliment. What about you Shankar?" "Very well *Bhabhi.*

But Javed is right as well." Shankar replied with a warm smile.

"Thanks. Feels good especially since your *Kaka* has never known about this fact." Manju side glanced at Mani and spoke sarcastically.

"Oh come on Manju....anyways, so what is the plan boys?" Mani looked up at Shankar and Javed while swallowing the food.

"First of all, we need to finalize our stay arrangements and then look for some job." Shankar replied

"Hmmm, do you have some money arranged?" Manju interjected.

"Of course they have." Mani replied while looking at Manju.

"Yes, *Bhabhi.* We have some arrangements. We both had worked for our martial arts teacher for a couple of years. He has paid us up enough so we can survive this initial period." Shankar replied instantly calming Manju.

"Yes, and considering the same I have arranged a place for you both to stay. We will get the keys within two days." Mani told.

"Great. That was quick. Is the place far from here?" Javed asked excitedly.

"Not far but not too close either from here. I have a friend in the printing press who works in the same publishing house as me. He has found a place where one of his junior workers live. You three will share the rent so it would be quite easy on your pockets."

"Excellent *Kaka.* Thanks." Shankar spoke.

"Don't mention. Enjoy your food and take rest to prepare yourselves for a new start." Mani responded looking at both of them and then everyone/the four of them ate their meals silently while the song played in the background, "*Main koi aisa geet gaaoon, ki aarzoo jagaoon, agar tum kaho...*"

The next morning, Shankar and Javed were all set to reach to their new place of stay. They all came down with their bags packed and waited for an auto-rickshaw to be hired. A yellow colored school bus carrying the children to their school just passed through. Just then an auto-rickshaw stopped in front of them offering the services. After a quick few seconds of negotiations, the three of them made themselves comfortable on the back seat of the vehicle. The driver soon started following Mani's directions on the busy morning roads. Nearly forty-five minutes had passed when Mani asked the driver to stop on a side. The boys moved their heads out from the side curiously to see the area they would live in. It was a narrow street with all the three-storey houses occupying the two sides of the street. They all came down the vehicle and picked up their luggage on their shoulders. The morning had already shown a glimpse of how hot the day was going to be. Shankar rubbed his forehead with the sleeve of his red t-shirt to clear off the sweat. A vegetable hawker stood next door bargaining in a *cigarry* voice with a buyer who lived in one of the floors of the house next door.

"Let us go in." Mani ordered.

"What is this area called *Kaka?*" Javed raised his curiosity.

"This is Pratap Ganj, a part of East Delhi. Most of the buildings constructed here are still waiting to be legally approved; the reason why the real estate is still affordable."

Mani replied while opening the main door that was already unlocked by someone anticipating the visitors.

"Ok, and which floor will we live on?" Shankar asked "The top floor." Mani replied. "Exactly what I prefer." Shankar smiled

The three of them climbed up the stairs and reached the top floor to stop in front of a dark brown wooden door. Mani gave a knock which was immediately answered by the dweller inside by opening the door wide open welcoming the visitors.

"Imtiyaz?" Mani asked looking at the short & thin man in his late twenties, who opened the door. "Yes Sir. You must be Mani Sir and these two would be the boys who will live here." The man replied "Yes." "Please come inside."

They entered a small hall room and looked at the off-white painted walls all over. Five plastic chairs lying in a disorderly fashion somewhere in the center and one chair laid upside down looking at the dusty brown ceiling fan. On the left wall, there was an iron trolley stand carrying a small but heavy for its size, color television. Javed and Shankar looked at the TV and then looked at each other. The sparkle in their eyes had already endorsed their liking for the house. Further, as they walked crossing the small hallway, the kitchen on the left and the large room on the right faced each other. The boys did not pay much heed to either of them and rather followed Imtiyaz's directions to see the room where they would make themselves comfortable. Further straight was a smaller room. Imtiyaz indicated the boys to come in and have a look.

"This would be your room. There is a fan, a wooden almirah, two cots, and an attached bathroom." Imtiyaz narrated the scene. Shankar looked at the same colored walls, same dusty brown ceiling fan and the bathroom with the toilet. Then his eyes fell upon the view outside the room through the window. Imtiyaz noticed what Shankar would be wondering so he came forward and explained.

"We are at the top of the building and this is the rooftop where the water tank is placed. The water in your taps comes from here."

"Can we go outside?" Shankar asked

"Yes. The way is from outside." Imtiyaz took Shankar outside and then pointed towards a narrow slipway to the rooftop from the stairway.

"Excellent. Let's get back in."

Seeing them back, Mani spoke, "you guys start settling in and I leave for my work. Everything else has been discussed with the owner of the place so you need not worry. I have some work in the evening at home so shall/will meet you tomorrow evening."

"Ok *Kaka.* Thanks for everything." Shankar said.

"Don't worry about it. Manju had packed food for you both, so don't worry about cooking also, as of now. See you both soon." Mani said and rushed to the exit. Shankar and Javed too rushed behind him to see Mani off. When they came back, Imtiyaz handed over a set of keys to both of them and then took their leave to set off to work.

It was almost silent at that time of the day in that corner of the street, much away from the noisy roads of the big city. The sporadic noise of the hawkers was faded at the height and was further suppressed by the whirring sound of the ceiling fan. The white noise and the warm wind outside made the boys feel sleepy. They moved their cots a bit and then laid down feeling the tight nylon straps beneath touching their bodies. Both of them still wondering about the road ahead, soon fell asleep. Both woke up with thirst after a few hours. The room had become much hotter and both were sweating. They came out of the room, into the kitchen and filled up their glasses with cold water from the clay pitcher. After quenching their thirst, they opened the lunch box they got from Mani's home, on the floor of the hall room, and in less than twenty minutes they emptied the box that was supposed to last at least two meals. No words were spoken and then Javed said, "Good food."

"Yes"

"Nothing left for dinner."

"We may not even feel the need after such a heavy lunch. We will get some milk from outside."

"You go; I plan to sleep again. Never knew that doing nothing could be so much fun." Javed responded carelessly.

"Hahaaa... don't worry, I will also sleep now. Will go out in the evening."

"Good. For now, I can go only up to the washroom." Javed stood up to wash his hands giggling and went to the washroom.

"Shankar, how do you sit on this seat?" Javed spoke loudly from the washroom.

Shankar came in curiously and then started laughing... "This is extremely high.....my god...something to learn immediately..."

and laughed again looking at the western-styled toilet seat. Soon after, both once again laid on their cots silently. Lost in their thoughts, they didn't realize when it was dusk already. When Shankar looked out of the windows, he stood up and asked Javed, "Let us go out"

"What happened suddenly?"

"The evenings always make me restless. Maa knew how to calm me down but not anymore. I can't stay indoors."

"Ok, wait a minute." Javed calmly replied.

In a moment, both of them were out on the street. The silent and orphaned street of the day was suddenly alive in the evening. The women were chatting, standing on the doors. Children played on the streets. Stray dogs moved from one place to another looking for food and the children patted them without any fear. As the boys moved further down the street, the street corner was abuzz with a few young boys and men circling a fruit juice vendor. The building on the right corner carried a big blue signboard of a gym and health club. The street had opened to a wider road; the boys took a left turn. After walking for around a hundred meters, they found a milk shop. They bought some milk to be consumed for the dinner and then continued their further exploration of the area. They identified two local grocery stores, one tailor, one tobacco vendor, one alcohol shop, and one primary school, all within a radius of five hundred meters from their place of dwelling. After a long walk, both came back to their new home. It was already dark by then; Imtiyaz, also back from his work was watching T.V. seated on the white plastic chair. When he saw the boys back, he waved at them and asked, "How was your day boys?"

"Not much eventful." Javed replied.

"Yeah, we somehow managed to sleep for the whole day. How was your day at work?" Shankar asked, grabbing another plastic chair just beside Imtiyaz.

"The usual day for me. Not worth talking about. In fact, life starts after work only." Imtiyaz raised his hand and brought the two fingers close to his lips. A thick puff of smoke followed.

"Ahhh, this feels terrible." Javed grunted flapping his hand to push the smoke away. "Hahhaaa, don't worry, soon you won't feel it. It is easy to get used to." "We won't." Shankar spoke softly but strongly. "Too soon boy. Anyhow better to smoke than drink." Imtiyaz looked at Javed "And why is that?" Javed asked

"Don't you know? It is prohibited in Islam." Imtiyaz sounded surprised "Is it? I didn't know." Javed replied "Strange. You haven't read our scriptures?"

"No." Javed gave a terse reply.

"Ohh, so you are that spoiled type... Anyways, that is your problem." Imtiyaz said and switched his eyes from Javed, back to the TV. Shankar the silent spectator went inside the kitchen, opened the milk polybags and served in three glasses. He came out with the tray holding the three glasses and served to the three of them. Imtiyaz silently picked up the glass and consumed the milk served to him.

After watching the TV for almost an hour, Imtiyaz stood up and switched it off. Without looking at anybody, he said, "I sleep now" and he went straight into his room. Javed and

Shankar looked at each other, confused, and then in a few minutes, they too went inside their room.

After changing the sides several times in their beds, finally they fell asleep.

It was an early morning for Shankar. He opened his eyes and sat still in his bed for some time. He looked around perplexed trying to recognize his surroundings. Then he looked at Javed, still sleeping in his bed. Relieved by his sleeping presence by his side, he got off his bed. Recalling everything, he opened his room's door and went straight to the main door. He opened it and entered the outer balcony that connected the building floors through the stretched spring-like stairway. From there, he turned right and walked up a few stairs to reach a black colored iron gate. He opened it to see the big rooftop and felt the air on his face. He moved further and stopped at a point from where he could view large parts of the constituency, Pratap Ganj. The air was already warm even in the early hour of the morning. He tried to hear but no birds were singing the morning song. The sky was dry, showing no remorse on the heat reflected. The Sun was leaning over the hedge of the buildings in one horizon, slowly coming up and radiating its bright red face to the city. Shankar looked up at the sky and noticed some vultures already taking a flight. Lost in his thoughts, he didn't notice when the iron door had opened and Javed had come very close to him that he could almost hear him speak to himself. He patted on Shankar's shoulder and asked, "Did you even sleep?"

Shankar turned back amused and then replied, "Yes, I did." "A very different morning." "Yes, much different from our home." Shankar said.

"Missing home?"

"Home?... Missing everything. In the morning, I almost forgot that I am not in my home. It took me almost a minute to come back to reality."

"Haaa, I too miss all of it. Sometimes I really ask myself if our decision is right? Anyways, leave it, I know there is no answer... Did you see there are no birds around? How strange."

"Yeah... No birds. I hear that only migratory birds now cross these skies."

"Migratory birds...like us, huh..."

I think we should go out for a jog. That will help us settle our minds." Shankar recommended

"Perfect. Let's do that. We will come back after Imtiyaz had left." Javed complied and both went straight into their rooms. In a few minutes, they were out on the road wearing their shoes.

They came back after a couple of hours with some grocery stuff in their hands. Imtiyaz was nowhere visible. They made themselves some tea and then sat together in the living room, switching the TV on. The whole day passed quickly watching magical moments in the Bollywood movies. In between, they made themselves some tea and ate the eggs & bread they had purchased in the morning. As the sun dimmed, the wait for Mani had started. After a while, Imtiyaz arrived but no sign of Mani. The boys moved inside their room and Imtiyaz turned on the TV. Not much spoken but the wait continued inside the room. The night grew soon, the TV turned off, Imtiyaz went to his room, the wait continued. Soon the boys also slept. The next day, the same routine was followed. Morning started with the jog, the day continued watching Bollywood cinema and the night reeked of the wait getting longer. Deciding to make a phone call in the morning, they slept again. The next morning, after the jog they reached a paid phone station and made a phone call to Mani's home. The phone went unanswered. They waited for a few minutes and tried again but the result was not altered. After one last failed attempt, they left back for their home. On the way home, Shankar asked Javed, "Do you have his office phone number?"

"No.....but won't Imtiyaz know?"

"Yeah, he should. The printing press he works for is a part of the main company Mani kaka works for."

"He must have left for work by now. Let's wait for him till evening." Javed opened the main door of the home speaking to Shankar.

"Yeah, it may not be easy with him though. We will have to come out stronger else he won't budge." Shankar entered.

They entered the place they have learned to call their home and made themselves seated in the living area. Shankar went into the kitchen and started preparing the breakfast while Javed turned on the TV. It was an even hotter day but it passed again swiftly and soon the Sun was going down. Imtiyaz entered. Contrary to the automatically established protocol, Shankar and Javed did not leave the living area. Both looked at him and greeted him. The TV was still turned on. Imtiyaz looked at them and then at the TV, and then replied to their greeting. Then he straight went into the kitchen. Shankar stood up and followed him into the kitchen. Imtiyaz stood there preparing his food. Shankar asked him, "Brother, could you please give us the contact number of Mani kaka?"

Imtiyaz paused for a moment and then without looking back, he said, "I have nothing do with him. He is your acquaintance. You should have his contact details."

"Yeah, we have his home phone number but that went unanswered today. We need his office phone number." Shankar replied, Javed also reached there and put his hand on Shankar's shoulder. Imtiyaz turned his head, looked at them, and after a brief pause he said, "I may be able to get that....but Mani is not here.....ohh, didn't I tell you that?"

"No", came a terse reply from Javed.

"Ohh, must have forgotten. He had to go out suddenly for some work. He will be back in a week." Imtiyaz lowered his eyes and then turned back doing his work.

Shankar looked at Javed and gestured to calm him down. Both turned back and sat in the living area, their legs stretched placed on another chair. Javed increased the volume of the TV. Imtiyaz took the meal to his room and slept soon, the TV still turned on.

The next morning, both slept till late. Imtiyaz had left by the time both woke up. Shankar turned on the TV and Javed got into the kitchen preparing breakfast. With both engrossed in the world of the small screen, the day passed very quickly. It was late for Imtiyaz to come back home

in the night. He reached home and went straight to his room to sleep. Soon after Javed and Shankar fell asleep as well. The next two days passed the same way. The third morning, Shankar woke up first and sat quietly in the living room. He didn't switch on the TV. Javed too came out after a while and sat in the chair opposite Shankar. After a few moments, he looked at the black screen of the TV, then looked at Shankar and asked, "all well?"

"Yeah, all well. Why?"

"You didn't turn on the TV..." Javed blinked at Shankar

"Hahaaa... yes, just for a change. Guess it's the time to do some reality check now."

"Hmmm, so what do you suggest?"

"I think instead of just sitting here and waiting for Mani Kaka, we should rather move out, explore the city and if possible then look for some job as well."

"Great. I agree. Bored with the TV now. Let's get ready and go out."

"Perfect." Shankar confirmed.

Both of them got ready and moved out of the building. The sun was seething hot and the earth felt like a hot iron plate. After a long walk towards the outskirts of the constituency, they decided to hire a rickshaw. As they reached the rapidly drying river, they felt an astringent smell. Such smell of death was until unknown to them. Moved by the view around, Shankar spoke to the rickshaw puller, "The river in our village is so much full of life."

"*Babuji*, I have been watching this river for the last twenty years. It wasn't like this always." "So, what happened?"

"Look at the number of people around, all want something from the river but they never return the favor."

"Ohh, that is very unfortunate. It seems as if people have dumped all of their waste into her."

"Not only us *Babuji.* Those businesses are the actual culprits. My wife washes clothes on the river bank. By the end of every month, the water that flows is so black that we can't even wash the clothes. Now, that is not us. I have heard that some chemical factories somewhere on the riverside, dump all of their chemical waste at that period/time. Anyways, we are used to this life but we don't want our children to live in the same atmosphere." The rickshaw puller said firmly.

"But doesn't the government take any action against this?" Javed quizzed this time

"*Babuji*, these issues will never be resolved because these are the money-making machines for them... what do we call them...yes, the ATM machines" the rickshaw puller turned his face back and smiled at both of them. A big drop of sweat curled down from his wrinkled forehead to his long beaked nose.

"You are so right. Everyone is so absorbed in making their present good that the future is not at all cared about." Shankar responded with a sad smile.

"Your destination has arrived *Babuji.* This is the industrial area with several offices around." "Thanks. Here is your money. What is your name by the way?" "Moinuddeen. Ok *Babuji*, I leave now."

The boys could not have imagined that the filthy area they had just stepped in was one of the major hubs of the economic activities in the region. Suspicious, careful, hesitant, with a handkerchief in their hands, they started moving in one direction. The encroached land by the pavements of the buildings had reduced the area of the drivable road, turning it into a street. The wide street seemed even narrower with the number of people occupying the space at several street-side hawkers. The tea stall with a red board and the tobacco stall on the corner of a parking area was swarmed the most with people. They looked at each other with surprise after watching two women holding a cigarette in their hands. After walking further, they stopped in front of a building. The board hanging on the gate read, "Delivery boys needed". They entered the door and went straight to the front office. A bald man passing through stopped and came closer to them. He lowered his spectacles and asked suspiciously, "...you waiting for someone?"

"No. We just saw the board outside." Shankar replied tentatively. "Ohh, ok. How old are you both?"

"We are seventeen, Sir."

"Hmm, have you done any delivery work before?" the man now was completely facing the boys.

"No sir, but we will do good." Javed stepped forward.

"Time will tell that. Do you know the area well?" the man seemed disinterested in the eagerness shown by Javed.

"Sir, let me tell you straight. We have just arrived here and we have never done such work. But we need a job urgently for our survival. We can only promise that we will put in our best efforts." Shankar took the charge and spoke.

The man looked at him and asked, "Do you have any means of transport...at least a bicycle to start with?"

"We will manage that with the first month of income Sir." "I doubt if I can allow you without even a bicycle, sorry."

"Sir, believe us. We will be faster than your bikers." Javed came forward again. The bald man this time seemed to pay attention to what he came up with.

"Hmm, are you ready then? Because in that case, you will have to prove today. Our everyday target for each person is to distribute five hundred pamphlets in the residential areas. Collect the pamphlets now from the inside, go to your area and finish your work before the day ends. None of your transport expenses will be borne by the company. So, are you ready?"

Both of the boys looked at each other and then said together, "We are, Sir."

In the face of adversity but with aspirations on their side, some do not fail easily. Their nimble hands moved fast, the legs even faster. By the end of the day, the boys were back in the same building. "How did it go?" The bald man unperturbed by the emphatic look posed the question.

"The job is done, Sir." Shankar exclaimed

"Well, I have my ways to know if it was done properly or not. For now, go back to your homes and come tomorrow morning.

"Right Sir. We will see you tomorrow."

Deprived of their lunch, low on energy, boys smiled at each

other and started running again. They were soon home. Sitting on a chair in the living area, Mani waited for them both.

"Ahh, welcome back Kaka. How are you doing?" the boys asked "I am fine. How are you both doing? And where are you both coming from?" "We got a job Kaka!". "Oh, excellent! That was quick." Mani pleasantly surprised, made no effort to hide his feelings. "Yeah, it was the first day today" "Very well. Where is the office and what kind of work is it?" "It's a marketing company. The job is to distribute their promotional material to the houses." "Ok. But how will you manage that without transport?" "We will buy bicycles with the first salary."

"Hmmm, no need to wait that long. I will bring money tomorrow and you return it to me when you have it. Get yourselves the bikes immediately." Mani spoke with such authority that the boys could not deny.

Mani left soon after. The boys quickly prepared the meal and ate it off.

The next day, filled with a new energy of hope, they finished the target in time and ran off to their home to see Mani. With his help, the next day they bought the new bicycles. They continued their job for next the three weeks when one day the bald man, Rajeshwar Rupani, called them in his cabin.

They saw his cabin for the first time. It was their first time to step into that rear side of the building. There were six more cabins adjacent to each other. The biggest of them all, situated at the left corner, was firmly occupied by the man, they had to come to see. On seeing them outside, Rajeshwar pointed at them and waved his hand calling them in.

"Good morning sir."

"Good morning" Rajeshwar replied without looking at them.

"You called us?"

"Yes, what are you guys doing? Why are there so many complaints?" Rajeshwar sternly asked, his eyes still glued to the computer.

"Complaints? What complaints sir?" Shankar asked while Javed stared at the bald man.

"You are not doing the job properly. Tell me where did you throw all the material we gave to you?"

"What are you saying Sir? Somebody has given you the wrong information." Shankar replied reluctantly, Javed still staring at the man who is yet to make eye contact.

"My sources never lie, it is you who are lying. You are terminated. No need to come here again."

"That is not true Sir. We can prove it that we have worked sincerely." Shankar asserted with a slight tone of anger.

"Too late for this." Rajeshwar spoke, still hooked on to the computer screen. "But..."

"It's ok Shankar..." Javed interjected and then continued in a rough tone, "It's ok Sir, just clear our payment and we leave".

Rajeshwar raised his eyes for the first time and yelled, "Get out of here right now."

"What is wrong in that Sir? Don't you intend to pay us?" Shankar by then had regained his composure and asked Rajeshwar looking straight in his eyes.

"You have made the company lose much more than you earned. There are no dues." Rajeshwar reluctantly said.

"We won't. Either you prove it now or pay us." Javed almost fumed.

"Ohh, so here comes your actual self. Go away right now or I will call the police."

"Do whatever..." Shankar stopped Javed. He held Javed's hand and pulled him out of the cabin and then out of the office.

"What is the matter with you? Are we scared of this rascal?" Javed asked annoyingly.

"There is no point brother. He is possibly one of those bloodsuckers. The time will come when we will teach him a lesson. But not now. Let's go."

"Perhaps you are right, but right now I feel like a total loser. I don't like this feeling."

"I know how you feel. My feeling is no different either. Come on let's go back home."

Both rode their bikes and started paddling slowly. The day emerged to be hotter than ever, the path occurred to be stretched than normal and the legs appeared to be giving way to the weight carried by the young hearts.

Mani came to their dwelling in the evening. On seeing the two long faces, he remarked, "What is wrong with my heroes?"

"We lost the job...." Shankar said.

"...and we didn't get paid" Javed continued.

"Ohh, that is a disaster." Mani smirked.

"What... you so casual about it?" Javed asked angrily.

"Hahaa, I am because I know that it happens in this city. It was not this bad when I was young but now it is horrible. Don't worry, sooner than later, you had to learn this lesson."

"That is ok *Kaka* but what do we do now?" Shankar asked

"Well, this is not the end of the world. Go to a telephone booth, call up Girija. He called me up asking about you both, he was worried for you. You haven't called him for over two weeks. Then you come with me to my home. We will have dinner together. Then you both reach my office tomorrow morning. I have spoken with someone in a printing press which happens to be our subsidiary company. They might be able to get you in."

"Ohh, you already seem to have a plan for us. Well then, we have to make that phone call first. By the way, *Kaka,* what is that thing in your belt that often makes those beeping sounds?" Shankar asked.

"This is called a *Pager.* People can send me a direct message on this. I use it to receive story feeds from my network."

"Amazing. Never knew that such a thing existed." Shankar marveled.

"Yeah, it is the era of technology. You are witnessing a world that is changing at a pace never seen before. Keep watching." Mani said.

"I will remember that...let's go Javed. We need to call Girija kaka."

That night, the boys stayed at Mani's home itself and got ready for their morning meeting set up by Mani.

Mani referred both Javed and Shankar to Isaq, the supervisor of the printing press. He had a dark complexion and seemed even darker in the uniform, which was of a deep blue tint. He was a short but robust man with broad shoulders and tiny eyes. He might have had problems with his eyesight, as he had to squint at everything. His greying hair was sparse and seemed to stick to his skull. The long scar at the corner of his forehead had given rise to several rumors.

During the meeting, Isaq didn't ask much from the boys and called them in to join the work from the following day itself. Pleased with the quick outcome, they went back to their home and started preparing for the new chapter of their lives.

On the morning of their first day, the boys pedaled their bicycles for forty minutes to reach the workplace. Isaq, who was already present, reached to them as they parked their bicycles in the compound. "You are late," Isaq said angrily

"Sorry, Sir. We do not have a wristwatch to keep a track of time." Javed spoke softly while putting on the stand of his bike.

"No excuses. It is the first and last warning. Get inside fast." Isaq spoke sternly.

After parking their bikes, they both quietly entered inside. As they entered, they looked at the clock which read two minutes past nine. Surprised boys looked at each other. Noticing this, Isaq spoke from behind, "Here, nine means forty-five past eight. By nine o clock, you should be in front of your machine with your uniform on. Is that clear?"

"Yes Sir."

"Aseem, hand them over the machine manuals. Study them properly and get back to me before lunch."

"Right Sir."

Sitting in a corner, Shankar and Javed were flipping the pages of the manuals.

"How can one read such heavy books in these few hours? This man is crazy." Javed whispered.

"I know, especially when the books are in English" Shankar teased Javed.

"I don't think if I can do that. Let's go and talk to Mani kaka to find out some other job for us." Javed whispered again.

"You lazy, don't quit, so soon. Remember what Maa always said...*Keep on trying till you succeed.* Come on, focus on your page." Shankar said.

"Hmmm, I am trying. I will try harder." Isaq called them in at lunch time. "Did you finish?" "Not yet Sir, but we are very close." Shankar replied "Hmmm, finish it by the time I finish my lunch. No further extension after that. Go."

They went back to their corner. Javed hungry and furious over Isaq's response said, "What the hell? I am starving and this man wants me to read this crap."

"Easy. I am sure we will get our lunch break a bit later. Come on now, we don't have much time."

They started reading the books once again. The other workers were soon back to their jobs after finishing their lunch break.

One of the older men passed through them slowly and whispered, "Don't worry much. You will get used to such treatment. This man is a scumbag."

"See I told you, this man is no good." Javed quipped to Shankar after hearing the old man whisper to them.

"Whatever, it does not matter. We have to face it now." Shankar responded coldly.

In a few minutes, Isaq reached them and asked them in his usual stern tone, "Done?"

"Yes Sir." Shankar replied.

"And you?" Isaq pointed at Javed.

"Yes Sir, done, I mean nearly done." Javed said hesitantly.

"Hmmm, come with me." Isaq started walking and the boys followed him till he reached in front of a machine.

"Tell me now, what is this part called?" Isaq asked Javed "Ummm... this part... I read about it... sorry Sir, can't remember." "What about you?" Isaq pointed at Shankar "Sir, this is the carriage." "And this?" "This is the foot assembly"

"Can you tell now what are the safety features for this machine?" Isaq once again pointed at Javed who once again had only a few sounds to mutter in response. "Ok, Shankar you have ten minutes to finish your lunch and Javed, you have to study again till you really know the things." Isaq concluded and left from there.

Javed looked at Shankar and said, "Well you go and let me try once more."

"Not needed. I am not hungry anymore. Come on, let's do that again together."

They together started walking towards the end corner where they had spent most of the day. The old man who had whispered to them after the lunch break was watching all of this. He came forward and addressed them both, "Leave those books. Come with me. I will show you how it all works?"

"But *baba,* that could cause you trouble." Shankar raised his concern.

"I am already too old to be of anybody's use now. I could be soon kicked out of here. Let me feel happy to be of some use. Come on." The old man emphasized. He then started walking, the boys following him, he stopped in front of a big machine.

"This machine is an auto-platen and that smaller one is the hand-fed platen. Most of the accidents occur from being drawn into in-running nips of rollers or entanglement with the rotating parts..." The old man spoke at length while moving and demonstrating the things to the boys. In less than an hour, they had seen every machine and had a much better understanding of the press. Satisfied with himself, the old man asked the boys, "Go to him now. And always stay the way you were today. It will be tough for him to break you both if you are together."

With a regained confidence, the two of them marched towards Isaq. Perplexed to see them walking towards him, Isaq sitting on his chair, lowered his head and feigned to read some papers.

"Sir, I have finished it all. Ask me the questions." Javed said confidently facing Isaq. "Hmmm, ok, you can have your lunch now." Isaq answered still looking at the papers.

Surprised on the reaction, Javed asked again, "Sir, can we both go? Shankar didn't have his lunch either."

"Ok. Go and come back in fifteen minutes."

Isaq watched them go. As they left, he stood and moved towards the main printing area where all the workers worked. He stood in the upper corridor from where he could see everyone working in the area. He looked at everyone and then his gaze stopped at the old man. The old man was smiling, unaware of being watched, he worked and he smiled. Isaq turned and went back to his office. His face turned red and stern.

Isaq didn't say anything to the boys after they were back from lunch. An hour passed and the working hours were over. The first day had ended. The boys thanked the old man when he came out of the building and then took his leave.

The way back home was easier. The sun had cooled down and there was moisture in the air. "Looks like the monsoon is arriving soon." Javed said while pedaling slowly "Ahh, waiting for that. Remember how much did we love the rains?" Shankar replied "Oh yes. I loved watching the river during the rains. It looked so powerful and dangerous." "Ohhoo, the first time I heard you so philosophical." Shankar giggled

"Hahahaaa, what did you remember the most about rains?"

"The food, Maa cooked." Shankar replied slowly. A silence followed, pedaling continued and soon both of them slipped in the memories of the past.

The next morning, Javed and Shankar reached much before

time. They tried to find the old man but to no avail. Isaq put them in two separate teams that worked on separate machinery. He did not say much but gave a tough side glance to the boys. The two teams worked separately, even had their lunch breaks at different times. Isaq kept a close watch on the work and as the tough taskmaster, did not let anyone chat with each other. Shankar and Javed met when the day ended. Tired with the hard work, they soon pulled out their bikes from the stand. Ready to move, Shankar spoke to Javed, "Strange, we didn't see the old man today. Wonder, what happened to him."

"He has been kicked out of the company", a passerby worker who had parked his bike near Shankar's, interjected.

"What? How come and why?" Shankar turned and asked the worker.

"This is what happens here. Anyone who challenges Isaq is thrown out of the company/this place." The worker replied.

"But what did he do?" Javed came forward and asked.

"Don't you know? He helped you both yesterday. Isaq doesn't like anyone helping each other, especially without his permission."

"But what is the problem in helping others?" Javed asked perplexed.

"Don't know, but he is very insensitive about other's problems. He never helps anyone either, simply says… handle yourself." The worker replied.

"This is crazy. What will happen to the old man?"

"Don't worry about him. He did this intentionally. He has

worked here for many years but he never got his dues ever since Isaq came in. He wanted this to happen."

"But where will he work now?" Shankar asked

"He will be fine. It is time for him to relax now. He is going back to his state Bihar to join his family now. He has been promised to receive all his payments and dues by the *bade sahib* himself."

"*Bade Sahib*...who?" Shankar asked

"The in-charge of two of the three such Presses. He knows the old man very well. When Isaq fired the old man, he immediately called up the *bade sahib.* I don't know what did they talk but eventually *bade sahib,* himself, promised him to clear all his dues properly."

"This *Bade Sahib* seems to be a good man." Javed said

"He is. I leave now before somebody notices me talking to you both. *Bade Sahib* doesn't even know me. People like us can defend ourselves only by getting into a shell, just like a tortoise." He giggled and started to leave.

"Thank you for telling us all of this. We meet tomorrow. Bye"

"Bye"

The boys also retreated for their home. They felt a shell around them. Was it right for them to go under the same shell? The air was once again dry. The moisture could not withstand the heat. The timing of an event is crucial for its survival. The moisture in the air was felt perhaps too soon, so it faded away quickly. Perhaps it was the time to hide in the shell.

For the next three weeks, the boys followed the same strict daily routine. They rarely spoke at work, reached well before time, and slowly pedaled themselves back home. The Sundays brought some respite for them as they worked for the rest of the six days but even those flashed away very fast in the preparation of the upcoming week. On the first day of the fourth week, during the lunch break, both heard from their team members that the *Bade Sahib* will visit the office the following day. In fact, he always visits during the salary week, takes a round of the facility, has a little chitchat with the workers, and have a review meeting with Isaq. On their way back home that evening, Javed spoke to Shankar, "We should complain about Isaq to this *Bade Sahib* tomorrow."

Puzzled Shankar replied, "About what Javed? What is there to complain about? There has to be a strong reason."

"But he is extremely insensitive. He deals with us as machines and not humans."

"It might be true but why would the company worry about it? Do you really believe that no one so far would have complained? It might not matter to them. They are all the same."

"So what is the way out? I don't know how long can I work like this?" Javed protested.

"I understand. Even I don't know how long, and I often think about this. Sometimes, I think if it was the right decision to leave the village and come here? This was not what I imagined to do throughout my life." The pedaling slowed down while Shankar spoke.

"Should we speak with someone? May be Mani *kaka*?"

"I don't know brother. I don't know if he can help us. He has done enough for us. He got us this job, a job where we are earning finally to meet our daily needs. Finally, it is our battle. We will have to fight ourselves."

"You are right. Thankfully, you are with me here in this unknown world. I would have perished alone." Javed said with a sad smile as they reached home.

"We are each other's strength. Remember that old man? His words still echo in my ears when he said that always stay together. About this world, yes, it is still unknown. I feel nervous often. Even Maa is not there to guide us... well, leave it, what is the plan for dinner?" Shankar asked shrugging off a stream of thoughts.

"Well, let's cook some *Matar Paneer* today. What say?"

"Excellent idea. Let's do that. One more experiment today in the name of the shitty day today. May this experiment be not as bad as the last one with *Shahi Korma*" Shankar replied with a smile while putting his bike on the stand.

"Amen."

"Amen". Both giggled and entered the home.

The next morning, they reached the office again on time. Soon after they had started working, they heard the whisper of the *Bade Sahib* reaching the office. Curious, they too kept an eye on the front corridor looking for the man. A few minutes later, Isaq entered the corridor and just behind him another person emerged. The boys still looking there suddenly jumped with surprise as they watched and recognized their *Bade Sahib*. They looked at each other from a distance and their eyes said it loudly, "What the hell... Mani kaka, The *Bade Sahib*...??"

The *Bade Sahib* reached the workers and addressed them about some changes in the management policies. He looked at Shankar and Javed who greeted him with a feeble smile. Mani, in turn, nodded his head lightly acknowledging the greeting. Pretty soon, he left for a quick review meeting with Isaq, and soon after he left from there. In the evening, as the boys pedaled back to their home, they had the same question in their minds. When they reached home, they waited eagerly for Imtiyaz to also reach home. When Imtiyaz entered, Javed asked him from the kitchen, "Is Mani *Kaka* the in-charge of your press as well?"

"No, is he the in-charge of your press?"

"So, you didn't know?" Javed was surprised.

"No, ohh, so he is the in-charge and he never told you...." Imtiyaz replied with a wicked smile.

Javed looked at Shankar who sat there on the chair in the hall room busy thinking in his head and then said to himself, "Forget it".

The next day was Sunday. Shankar woke up Javed and said, "Let's call up Mani *Kaka*. We have received our salaries and it's time to return his money."

Soon after talking with him, they set off for his home. It was still morning when they reached. They could hear the sound of the TV, coming from inside the home. Javed rang the bell which was soon answered by Manju as she opened the door. "Welcome boys. Come in."

Well acquainted by the surroundings of the home, they helped themselves to be seated on the couch.

"I will get you breakfast. Mani will join you soon after he finishes his extra-long Sunday special bath." Manju smiled

The boys tried to say no but the aroma of *Aloo Paranthas* broke off any such possible efforts. The boys ate off the *Paranthas* as those appeared on the table and soon after they had finished their meals, Mani too reached the dining table. "How are you, boys? Working hard...huh." Mani pulled his chair and took the seat "Trying to... how are you doing?" Shankar replied.

"Can't complain. Manju cooks the best *Paranthas*, didn't you like them?" Mani looked at his steaming plate and smiled. He didn't wait to hear the answer and devoured the food. After he quickly finished the first *Parantha*, he looked at the boys who sipped tea silently and then asked, "Why are you so silent today? And even you Javed? Ok, ask me."

"Why didn't you tell us?" Shankar asked

"Well, first it is no big deal. The Director of the organization asked me to fill in for the other manager who quitted a few months ago. Second, I wanted you to feel that you got the job based on your own merits."

"But that is not true. You got us the job." Javed said.

"No, I helped you get the job but you got it by yourself. I didn't put any strong recommendations for you both in front of Isaq. He had a complete choice to accept or reject you both. If he didn't reject you, that means you have done really well."

"Well, Isaq is also another story." Javed sighed "I know what you mean." Mani said softly "But then why doesn't anybody take an action against him?" Javed asked again.

"On what grounds? He is dictatorial, he is ruthless and sometimes almost atrocious, but he delivers the results. The management, which is not entirely me, wants to see only the results. And my young friend, the world you have already stepped in is full of such people who will often test and challenge you."

"It's ok to be challenged but not fine when someone calls you names for one extra minute of lunch break." Shankar spoke and finished his cup of tea.

"I agree, it is not ok and it should not be. But I can't make a decision based on our personal equation. This has to come as a written official complaint from not only you but all others. And even later, the complainants must stand by what they say without the fear of losing the jobs."

"Hmmm, I understand what you mean *Kaka.* Thanks. Well, here is the money we owe you." Shankar extended his hand with a pile of banknotes.

"Don't worry. Keep it with you. I will ask when I need." Mani smiled.

"No *Kaka.* Anyhow this is our first salary which must be given to an elder at home. Who else we could offer this to. Please accept it."

"Hmmm, you reason well. On these grounds, I accept it. I wish you both always have enough money to offer the people in need."

"Thank you ,*Kaka.*"

"One more thing, don't leave your studies as yet. Join an evening school or the correspondence program to continue your education. The world is changing fast and the future beholds plenty of opportunities for the wise and educated. Don't miss the bus."

"Alright *Kaka.* We will give it a proper thought."

Soon after having some more chitchat with the family, the boys left for their home. The force in the right direction can move the mountains. The boys lost in the afterthoughts pedaled swiftly and silently on the noisy roads of Delhi. They had the force but now what they needed was some direction.

Still perplexed over what the future beholds for them, the young boys decided to continue with the same routine until the wave of time brings a change for them. Due to the paucity of time, while their lives oscillated between the highs and lows from one Sunday to another Sunday, they could not get themselves enrolled for further education. The clock never stops, moving at its constant tick-tock, the boys received their tenth salary in the job. That evening, they didn't feel the usual happiness, they used to feel every month on that specific day. While pedaling back to their home once again, the more vocal of the two, Javed, expressed his concern strongly, "I don't think I can survive like that for long."

"Humm." "What hummm, I said something expecting an answer." "As if I really had one..."

"What to do? I feel like a machine working from Monday to Saturday and then preparing myself to work again on Sunday. We could not even go out for our morning running sessions for the past two weeks... did you realize that?"

"Of course I did. In fact, I miss that too Javed. But what do we do?"

"Do what you do better than me, think...think hard."

"That is what I am doing? Mani Kaka also could not suggest much. He believes that we need to study further to ensure that we are relieved of such hardships one day. But what he doesn't understand is that it's not the hardships we care about... it's the actual life itself which we are worried about."

"True, it is not the hardships we care about, in fact, it is the actual life which we are worried about." Javed repeated as he missed the last line that got lost under the abrupt honking of the traffic on the light signal which just turned green.

"I think let's call up Girija *Kaka.* He might be able to advise something."

"Ok, that is a good idea. Anyways, it's been two weeks since we last spoke with him."

The boys straight away reached the telephone booth near their home. The booth owner knowing them well by now, greeted both of them. The boys replied to his greeting and sat on the dark brown wooden bench waiting for their turn. While they waited, the booth owner, a clean shaved big man with a fat belly, sitting on his dark brown wooden chair asked them, "How are you both doing?"

"Surviving so far." Javed smirked.

"I understand, it's the same everywhere nowadays. First, it is difficult to get a job, then it is even more difficult to work consistently and then people like us who are self-employed are facing complete unpredictability."

"Why...what is happening to your business? I think you should be doing well." Shankar said.

"Ahh, don't ask. After the pagers, now mobile phones have come. I don't know how long this business will survive. One person who came yesterday calling someone was saying, that just in a matter of a few years mobile phones and calls will be so cheap that these booths will no longer be needed." The booth owner sighed.

"Ohh, that is going to be serious. Keep a close watch brother. Take a timely decision." Shankar said with concern.

"Yes, you too, keep an eye on the timing of what you do. Well, here is your turn now. Go into the cabin and make the call."

The boys went inside and dialed a phone number which they remembered by heart now. Just after a couple of bells, they heard a familiar voice from the other end. "Hello" "Hello *Kaka.* Shankar and Javed here." Both spoke together on the receiver.

"Hahaha, who else would call me *Kaka* but you both. I was expecting your call since it had been a few days. Although I expected it to be on a Sunday, since you called during a weekday, it must be important."

"Hahahaa, you already know... Well, it is important *Kaka.*" Shankar said

"Go ahead then. Phone calls are not so cheap."

"Well, *kaka,* I don't know how to explain.... We seem to be doing everything we could but the life ahead seems to be very tough. As we had discussed once that we have a very difficult boss to tackle and an extremely demanding job which leaves no time for anything else. So, to keep the pressure level down, we live from one Sunday to the next and don't think of anything else but when the thought comes, we both feel so helpless and sometimes even stupid to have taken such a decision."

"Boys, first of all, what you decided only the brave can execute. You both have grown up now so you might understand it better. Life is nothing but a series of choices you make and then how well do you hold on to the choice you had made for yourself. Leaving the village was your choice. Good or bad, it doesn't matter, holding on to that choice and making it work for your betterment is what matters now. Now continuing with the same job or quitting it to search for another or revolting against your boss are again some choices in front of you. You have to decide. Option three doesn't make much sense to me as I always believe to focus more on the opportunities than the problems. See the positive side."

"Great, so option number three eliminated." Javed smiled as he also heard Girija's thoughts on the phone's speaker.

"Now, do you remember the first time I met you both, I asked you one question?" "Yes, you asked what is it that we want to achieve in life." "Good, and do you both remember your answers?" "Yes, I said "Respect" and I said "Power." Both replied

"Excellent. Now what do you need to do to gain respect, Shankar?"

"Ummmm... I think gain more knowledge?" Shankar replied with a hesitated question mark in the end.

"Ok, I agree with you. And what do you need to do Javed?"

"I... I think I need to gain more strength."

"Ok. You know the answers. Now use your natural talents or skills to gain what you need to, so you get the results you want for yourselves. I will give you an example, when you both learnt martial arts, Shankar, you focused more on the technique of your hits and Javed you focused more on the impact of your hits. These are your natural flairs or you can say your talents. Understand them and focus on them. Perhaps, had I been in your shoes, I would have decided to look for the next job that fits my natural flair the most."

"And what kind of jobs could those be?" Javed quizzed.

"Well, I am not much apprised of the current job situation in Delhi but, how I see you both, is; you- a strong-headed, forceful, aggressive person doing something good in high energy stuff like Sports, Managing the events or even politics and Shankar, you – a calm, strong and artistic person strategizing the actions for others, perhaps even leading them to the right direction. Think more and you will get an answer. Even if you don't, keep thinking and you will get the answer. Perhaps, just take a break for some days, sit back, and then think."

"Break, definitely I need a break." Shankar said

"And me too." Javed agreed.

"That is it then. Perhaps come here for some time and meet everyone. There is a wedding next month. People will be very happy to see you. Your village misses you." Girija said softly.

"Not now *Kaka*. I don't think I am ready as yet to enter the home where my life was catapulted... though we may use the wedding as an alibi on our leave application"

"Hahaha, that is a good idea. By the way, try to forget about what had happened. All such major events happen for a reason, Shankar. You will it realize one day when your curse will transform into a boon for others." Girija said.

"Don't worry about him *Kaka.* I will take care of his stupid thoughts. I think for now we just need a break. Then we will decide what happens next." Javed replied

"Sounds good. Be like that always, both of you. Stay together, stay strong." "Yes, we remember that *Kaka.*"

"Good. Now don't spend so much on the phone. And keep calling regularly. And yes, Shankar, hope you still sketch."

"I am not sure but I will try *Kaka.* Bye for now. Regards to everyone there in the village." He said while looking at the call meter, before putting down the phone and disconnecting the call with just one second to go before the meter would have read a higher amount. With a sense of victory, both looked at each other and came out of the cabin. They paid to the booth owner who once again reminded them of the fast-changing times, this time more out of curiosity on what lies ahead than the call for an urgent action to be taken.

The next day, they both applied for a two-weeks leave stating their visit to the family and friends in the home village to attend a wedding. In one week, the leave got approved. Sans any strong and valid reason, Isaq had to approve the leave.

The boys started their vacation with an early morning run. The exhausted and sweating bodies felt alive again after a two-hour long running session. When they reached home Imtiyaz still getting ready for work, announced about his wedding taking place in a month. He had started the search for another place for himself and his would-be wife. Until then, he requested Shankar and Javed to keep his belongings which they happily agreed to. After Imtiyaz left, the boys fed themselves with a high protein diet of eggs and milk. Then they turned on the TV. After a couple of hours, Shankar stood from the chair and said, "I want to sketch. Let me quickly buy some stuff for that." And he went out. Javed, still sunk into the chair and engrossed in the Bollywood movie in his usual position, the legs stretched out on the table, didn't budge at all.

Shankar came back home in thirty minutes, went straight inside their room and started sketching. When Javed finished the second movie in a couple of hours, he felt hungry. Wondering what Shankar is doing, he entered the room. Shankar still absorbed in his sketch didn't realize the door opened. Javed looking at the sketch from the top of Shankar's ahead, stood still for a couple of minutes before uttering, "Wow, it looks so real."

Shankar, out of the oblivion, looked back and gave a faint smile. Then he spoke, "I could never forget the last look in those fierce but helpless dying eyes of the animal I murdered and I can never forget the calmness in the eyes of Maa." Shankar pointed at the two faces he was about to finish sketching.

"No wonder, you really needed to express to let it go" "Yes, I don't know how successful would I be to really let it go but I certainly feel a bit lighter now." "Good, so what is the plan now?" "Just a few more minutes till I finish the sketch and then let us go out." "Cool. I have an idea." "What?" Shankar asked "I think it is time now. Let us try some beer." "Well, maybe. And you can buy as well as you look like an adult."

Shankar gave his consent.

A couple of hours later, a friendship blossomed further as the two friends gave in to the flow of emotions under the stupefying effect of spirits. As the first-timer, one bottle of beer had opened the floodgates for them. Their conversation started from the stumbling rhetoric on why their current job sucks, then reached the philosophical tone on what lies ahead for them before they cried as they entered the darkest and deepest corners of their minds. "Maa always said that the world is a huge glass ball. Whatever we throw at it, it boomerangs back to us stronger. What did we do to get to this stage? What should we do now to get better from here?" Shankar muttered as their conversation came to an end with Javed dozing off. Soon after they slept. The next morning, both woke up and found their hearts lighter. They went for a run and came back after almost two hours. After the breakfast, they decided to enroll themselves for further education. They spent the next three days arranging the information for the few options they had to pursue further education. They zeroed in on an option that had a mix of evening classes and distance learning. The admissions were going on so they got the enrollment easily in the eleventh grade with the main subjects chosen as History, Political Science, Economics, Mathematics and English. They spent the next two days in arranging the required books for their studies. Once it was all set, another session of beers followed. This time joined and sponsored by Mani.

The next four days flew and soon they were left with the last two days before they had to rejoin their jobs. That evening, Javed, seemingly stressed, chopping the onions in the kitchen spoke first, "Do we really need to go back to the same life once again?"

"I too feel the same stress brother, but what should we do?" Shankar, standing beside, watching at the oil heating in the pan, replied with the question.

"Don't ask me. As I always say, you have to think it out."

"Hmmm... I have been thinking about this and you may not believe, I have some thoughts....but don't ridicule me if you don't like it." Shankar spoke cautiously.

"What are you saying.... Of course, I will." Javed smirked.

"I knew it, that is why I was not telling you."

"Oh come on. Say it." Javed said anxiously.

"Hmmm....ok, I was wondering what if we start our own Martial arts school?"

"What...?? Oh yes, of course, we can teach it to the kids around. That is a fantastic idea. When do we start?"

"Hold on, it is not that easy. First, we are not left with enough money to last for more than a month or so. Second, the people here don't know us well to send their children to us for the coaching and third, we can't spend money on any promotion."

"Hmmm, I am sure you would have some plan for that as well in your naughty mind." Javed smirked again

"Hahahaaa, well, if you like the idea of teaching martial arts to the students and children then we can talk about a plan as well. And the plan is to start with a single coaching session in the morning and then continuing with the job. Once we get ten regular students then we can possibly quit the job and focus completely on our school."

"Hmm, looks difficult but doable. Also, don't forget we have to study as well."

"Yes, that is why we have to get the ten regular students within the first three months so that we can focus on our studies as well."

"Alright, let's do that."

Within the next two days, the boys got their pamphlets designed, printed and circulated in around one thousand homes. They woke up early on the following Monday morning and reached the spot in a nearby park expecting some students to come over. No one arrived on the first day. They practiced the stances and some sparring among themselves during the one-hour session. Later they reached their job on time and completed the day with a hope to witness a better response the, next day. The next four days produced the same result. On Saturday, a 12-year old boy reached the spot. He sought permission to pay later after one session which they agreed upon. The next day, he was absent and was never seen thereafter. One month passed without any favorable results. In a desperate attempt, they re-worked on the pamphlets and put forth an introductory offer for the first seven free classes. It worked this time, the very first day after they had distributed the pamphlets, five candidates appeared for the class. Within six days, they had fifteen prospective students. After the completion of the month, they were left with four serious students who had paid the monthly advance fees for the coaching. The positive, though not-so-great results motivated Shankar and Javed to keep on doing what they had planned for. They invested every penny they earned in getting new gear like the punching gloves, pads etc. They also got themselves ready for another round of promoting themselves. As suggested by the owner of the telephone booth, apart from the distribution of the pamphlets in the homes, they also put them in most of the shops in and around the area. There is no substitute for the hard work, it always pays off, one day or the other. The continuous planned and dedicated efforts earned them reach their first benchmark within the timelines they had defined for themselves. They had exactly ten students who paid their advance fees at the end of the first three months.

As per the plan, they quit their jobs and started working on their two primary goals; Studies and Teaching Martial Arts. The very same month, one large organization in the country launched mobile phones at extremely cheap prices. It was mayhem in the telecom industry but that gave millions of people an opportunity to connect with the people easily. Javed and Shankar booked the two CDMA mobile phones for themselves. They borrowed the telephone directory from the phone booth owner, Durgesh Bhati, who was visibly upset and uncertain with the change in the telecom industry, sought some participation in other businesses as well. He offered some monetary support as well on the condition of keeping some part of the profits to himself. The prevailing circumstances in middle-class India didn't favor the children much to participate in the extra-curricular activities. In the form of Bhati, who was quite unequivocal about rejecting the popular belief-system and mind-set of the country's middle class, they gained a strong boost for their business. Bhati also lined them up to organize the classes in the compound of the local govt. school along with a banner and a signboard for them. The new phones were used extensively to call up the people and ask them to join the Martial Arts school. In the following six months, the signboard bearing the name of the coaching school, "Girija Martial Arts School" in the honor of their master, had become a landmark.

As it always happened, it was 2004, once again Shankar's birthday coincided with the school exams. Javed organized the gathering with the small coterie of their people that included Mani and the new entrant Bhati to celebrate the twentieth birthday of his friend. The home appeared fresher with a new rectangular glass table surrounded by a new three-seater light brown colored couch, aptly placed in front, and the old wooden chairs on the two sides. Mani and Bhati sat firmly on the couch while Javed and Shankar occupied the two chairs. The almost empty table-top still had the circular imprints of water left by the chilled beer bottles. Mani donning his usual Sunday dress, the white Kurta Pajama, looked at Shankar from the top of his specs and asked, "One beer is enough for the celebration. I hope you are fully prepared for your exam in the next two days."

"Yes *Kaka.* I am. Don't worry."

"And what about you?" Mani turned towards Javed.

"Should be done, don't worry." Javed carelessly replied.

"Hmmm, I was told that some of the boys here called you in for their help in a fight. Is that true?"

"That is ok *Kaka.* No big deal. Those boys wanted my help and I wasn't much busy at the time."

"It is ok to help but don't get too much involved in these things. Don't lose your focus. Remember, with strength comes a greater responsibility to use it wisely."

"Yeah, I know. Come on, leave it for now. It is party time." Javed once again said carelessly.

Surprised on Javed's response, Shankar came forward and interjected, "Don't worry *Kaka.* It was ok and he will take better care, the next time. You know him, he is Javed only from outside, inside he is Sunny Deol."

"Hahahaaa, I know but this is real life, not a Hindi movie. So, be careful please." "Right." "Right" Javed too followed as Shankar agreed with Mani. "What is the plan ahead?" Mani asked.

"After the exams, Girija *Kaka* is arranging a meeting for us with the National authority of Mixed Martial Arts. The idea is to be able to provide proper certifications and belts to the students that are recognized all over the world."

"Good idea." "And what are your plans Bhati? How is the business going?"

"Not much left in this business. I am now planning to start a cyber café. Everyone needs the internet these days." Bhati replied with a usual grin on his face.

"Ok, still be careful. I hear that computers are also going to be very cheap soon which will badly affect this market as well."

"Ohh, the same problem again."

"Why don't you use your space for a computer education course? If computers are going to be so cheap, then everyone would want to learn computers." Shankar intervened with his idea.

"In fact, you can use your cyber café itself for computer

training program as well. So, if the internet business goes down, you will have another business model to fall upon." Shankar continued.

"True. That is a very good idea. Where do you get these ideas from? I remember you used to be such a silent person and I thought you will never have anything to talk about." Bhati giggled.

"I don't know. I think it's just that I am spending much time reading these days." Shankar said politely.

"These days? Ever since we have started the studies again, he is always reading something." Javed said to Bhati.

"And you picking up fights with people." Bhati said in a funny tone.

"Ohh, for god's sake, not again." Javed clearly annoyed said while scratching his stubble.

"Stop scratching that, it sounds irritating." Shankar complained

"Ahh, don't be jealous. You still have the baby's facial hair. Who will say that you are few months older than me." Javed joked.

"And you have hair all over like a bear. You already look like a father of two kids." Shankar replied back in the same witty tone.

"Hahaha, you both are exact opposite of each other!" Mani exclaimed.

That evening everyone talked about their aspirations and future plans. Bhati had several moments of epiphany as he realized how myopic his ideas were about his business and how fast the world was changing. He offered Javed and Shankar to learn computers so that they both can assist him in setting up his cyber café cum computer learning center as well. Both too, in complete realization of the need to learn technology, quickly consented.

The days flew much quicker from that day onwards. Their transformation from the naïve boys to the know-all men was quite quick and smooth. With the right people around them, engaged in the constructive tasks of learning and teaching, they were soon out of the dark memories of their past. Much adapted to the big city life and without much baggage to them, they moved swiftly and in four years, they were both graduates and the owners of two businesses, Girija School of Martial Arts and Benchmark Computer Centre, which they co-owned with Bhati. They had people under them who could take care of general routine matters of the business so the three of them could focus on the more important matters. They also often took the weekend breaks to meet their friends and acquaintances. Amidst their growth to achieve the same results, they never realized how different they have grown individually. The two words they once uttered, "Respect" and "Power" were becoming a reality, a reality which was fast forcing them to two different destinies.

AND THEIR EYES MET

IT WAS A MOIST LATE EVENING. MANI LAY ON the couch facing the TV that played a video song... *Maujan hi maujan, sham savere hun maujan hi maujan.*

"Any words can be a song now and anyone can sing. This technology has changed everything." Mani spoke looking at the TV.

"Hahaa, you bet, Javed still cannot." Shankar teased sitting on another couch.

"Have two more pegs and you will find me suddenly in tune and by the way, this is a great song with superb music." Javed responded.

"You are right, even I love the energy of this song. And the movie was brilliant."

"Hmmmm, love is in the air my boy. Our saint is impressed by a romantic movie... not bad." Javed teased back.

"Of course, unlike you, I believe in true love and I don't salivate for every girl." Shankar defended himself. By the way, it is over." Shankar pointed towards the bottle.

"You kidding me?" Javed snapped back.

"What?" Mani asked.

"The fuel to our imagination. It is finished. It is over," Shankar replied.

"Oh, don't worry, let us go out and get us some more." Mani invited.

"Are you sure?" Shankar asked surprisingly.

"Oh yes. Your Bhabhi knows that it is your celebration today. So, it is okay. Although, Pallavi will ask for a separate party from you both"

"Super, see, she trusts me so much. And yes, our little girl will have her special party. So where should we go now?" Shankar asked standing up from the couch.

"Well, I know a couple of decent places. Let us move." Mani answered.

They summoned a taxi and set off for central Delhi. Mani led them to a place tucked in the depth of the streets. It was still the early hours of the night and the street was well lit by the headlights of several vehicles passing them. They were soon in front of a lounge bar where they were frisked quite thoroughly by a guard for security purposes and then allowed to go inside. As they entered they were greeted with loud music and acerbic smell of stale smoke. They walked up the stairs and entered a big hall packed with bodies moving in rhythm to some Punjabi music beats. They made their way through the whirlwind of spinning bodies and took a seat in the right corner of the hall. Their inebriated brains and the ambiance flooded with flesh and sweat of young bodies worked together to bring them to a state of stupefaction.

Suddenly a voice from behind startled Shankar from his current stupefied state, "May I take your order, Sir?"

Shankar's head rolled in the direction of the voice and then remained there silently gazing at this wonderful creation of God. Her luscious lips wore the color of berries and those, perfectly sculpted chin and nose were placed just at the most appropriate place. The large deep brown eyes bestowed elegance to her. She was standing right behind Shankar. He could hear her breathing and the scent of mint from her breath was hypnotic. He was charmed by everything about her. She stood with dignified poise and was dressed in a red and white uniform - bearing the colors of the lounge bar.

Javed was fascinated by the young girl too, but then he noticed the change in the rhythm of Shankar's breath and the tremble in his body.

"Ummm, hi. I mean, Hello..." and Shankar promptly slipped

his hand into the girl's hand and shook it.

The girl pulled away in an impulsive reaction and quickly retracted her hand and stepped back. Shankar was embarrassed by his nervous reaction and became even more nervous and lowered his eyes. This was a strange evening; something unbelievable had happened, thanks to that nervous touch. Without him even noticing it, his eyes pierced the girl's stream of thought. In an attempt to recover from the moment, she shrugged off a bit and then stepped up once again with a renewed confidence to take their order. Javed, the most extroverted of the three, spoke. "He is my friend Shankar and he prefers to have a beer. Am I right Shankar?"

"Oh yes. Beer is fine." Shankar quickly regained his poise.

"Great, so we will have three beers to start with, Miss..."

"Sanyukta," The girl said.

"Sanyukta." Shankar repeated the name and kept gazing at her from the corner of his eyes, appreciating everything about her.

Sanyukta left. Mani came forward and patted Shankar with a smile. Shankar lowered his head sheepishly but his eyes were still looking for the girl, Sanyukta.

Though she was extremely busy, she had noticed Shankar's gaze, loaded with appreciation for him. She had possibly sensed that the man in awe of her, was not the one she needed to defend herself from. By the time the third round of drinks was served, the place had become much louder and everybody seemed to be wasted. Mani and Javed too were inebriated but Shankar, who felt very strongly for the girl, sensed an opportunity and initiated a conversation.

"Thanks," he said when she had brought another round. "You are welcome," Sanyukta replied with a shy smile and turned to leave. Shankar noticed and quickly took the conversation ahead, "Is this place always so noisy?"

"Not always. Only on the weekends." "Oh, I thought so. So do you work here only on the weekends?" "Not always. It depends," "Depends on what?"

"Depends if I have time to work, depends on my college timings that day, depends on the number of customers here in the bar...and so on."

"Oh, okay. So you are not a regular here. Which college do you go and what do you study?" Shankar wanted to know more.

"Sir, it may not be right for me to talk with customers like this. You enjoy your drink and let me know if anything else is needed."

"I am sorry for making you uncomfortable. But that is not what I wanted. I just wanted to know more about you. I don't know what has happened to me but for the last two hours I have only been thinking about you."

Sanyukta looked into the honest but troubled eyes of Shankar for a moment and then she turned away and left.

Shankar looked at Javed and Mani sheepishly and said, "Shall we leave now?" "So soon?" Javed asked "Soon? It's almost past midnight." "Well, you might want to wait for a few more minutes." Javed smiled.

"And why is that?"

"Well, hold your breath. She is coming, right behind you...

don't turn back" Javed said softly.

"Ohh, is she angry?" Shankar questioned.

"Doesn't seem to be. She would be here now." Javed culminated.

"Your bill Sir." Sanyukta put the tray on the table. She then turned around, looked at Shankar for a fraction of second and quickly left from there.

"You have obviously pissed her off and now she wants us to leave." Javed said.

"Wait a minute. Doesn't look like what you said." Mani an audience to everything leaned forward and picked up the bill.

"Well, congratulations my boy. You perhaps have got your first date. Here are the details." Mani handed over the piece of paper to Shankar.

"National School of Journalism. Tuesday, 5:00 pm, at the institute's bus stand." Shankar's voice raised as he read those words. His smile broadened as he looked at his fellow companions. They soon left the place and reached their homes.

Shankar reached the appointed place much earlier than he had to. After waiting for almost forty minutes, he saw Sanyukta walking towards the bus stand. He felt his heart beat faster at the glimpse of her and then as she was about to reach the stand, he felt a deep sensation in his body. Sanyukta smiled at him shyly from the distance. She looked stunning in blue jeans and a short white sleeveless shirt with pearl white embroidery on its deep neck. Shankar too was dressed in a similar white and blue combination. He had chosen his favorite white T-shirt and dark blue jeans. When they met, they both looked at the similarity of their choice of clothes for a moment and smiled at the quirk of fate. Several/many people stood there at the bus stop waiting for the next bus to come. Sensing so many eyes on them, Shankar moved forward towards Sanyukta to a keep distance from the crowd.

Shankar extended his hand towards her and said, "Hi" "Hi," Sanyukta responded. "Good to see you." "Likewise."

"Did you have to wait long?" she asked after a brief pause. "Oh no. I arrived just two minutes ago," he lied.

"So what were you doing for the last forty-five minutes, you liar?" Shankar and Sanyukta saw Javed walking towards them from behind the bus stop.

"Sanyukta, this man has not slept since he saw you that night. I don't know how much time it will take him to tell you about his feelings but I am telling you now that I haven't seen him act like this around anyone else, ever. Mind you, I am his childhood friend." Javed laughed out loud and put his arm around Shankar's shoulders. Sanyukta hid a smile at his outburst. Shankar was embarrassed and looked at Javed through the corner of his eye and whispered, "What are you doing here?"

"Nothing, my friend, just passing by. When I saw you here, I wanted to know why you had come here. Hahahaa. Don't worry, I am just leaving. You guys carry on. Good to meet you again, Sanyukta. Take care of my friend." Javed winked at them and then left them smiling at each other.

"Where should we go?" Shankar asked

"What do you mean? Do you want me to wear the pants, Shankar? You have to decide," Sanyukta replied with a witty smile.

"Oh, I have never been to this area before. I don't know much. Can you help me this time please?" Shankar pleaded.

"Hahahaa. Don't worry. Just follow me." Sanyukta laughed and started walking.

Shankar looked at his bike parked a bit away from the bus stop and then followed the young lady.

Sanyukta took them to a nearby café. They took a corner seat and then made their orders. "So you study here?" Shankar asked. "No, I am the Principal here." "Oh, is that so? You do not look that old." Shankar looked baffled.

"I am just kidding, Shankar. Of course, I am a student here." Sanyukta laughed and Shankar once again looked perplexed before this extremely confident girl. Then in a quick moment, he regained his composure and said, "You don't look young enough to be a student."

"Now, that is sarcastic." Sanyukta stopped smiling and raised an eyebrow.

"Yeah, I know. I am yet to achieve that sense of humor. Sorry about that. Oh, by the way, you are looking lovely. And that is an honest compliment," Shankar said.

"Hmmm, you need to clarify, Shankar. We women have an extra eye to see right through the lies of men," Sanyukta said with a smile.

"The men better be careful." Shankar smiled back.

"Oh, by the way, I have something for you. I was wondering what should I bring with me on our first date. I don't believe in plucking flowers to express my emotions, so I got this." Saying this, he extended a small envelope towards her.

She took the envelope and then started opening it when Shankar suddenly said, "Not now please. Look at it when you are back home."

"Ok, I will do that. But you have certainly made me curious now. So what do you do?" She asked.

"I work in a printing press. I have just finished my undergraduate degree. In fact, we came to that pub to celebrate our results," Shankar replied.

"Alright. So who was the third man who came with you?" Sanyukta asked. "The third man is Mani Kaka. He is like a guardian to both of us here in this big city." "Like a guardian? So where are your parents?" "I lost them both," Shankar replied in a low voice.

"Oh, I am sorry to hear that." Then after a pause, she spoke again. "I know the pain of losing somebody of your own. I lost my big brother two years ago. He was like a guardian to me. In his presence, I never even felt the need of mom and dad, though they were always there whenever needed. But for me, my brother was like a perfect sibling."

"Oh, if you don't mind, tell me more about him," Shankar asked.

They seemed to speak with ease now. "He was mad about sports and bike, and had unlimited courage and love in his heart. He loved me a lot and always protected me like a child.

He was the perfect son of our parents until one day..."

"What happened, Sanyukta?" Shankar patted on her hands curiously.

"Leave it. Let's talk about something else. So where are you from?" Sanyukta pulled her hands away.

"I come from the mountains of this land. I am from Chandan Nagar, a small village in Himachal Pradesh."

"Oh wow... you are from the mountains. I will always remember you as Shankar from Chandan Nagar". Sanyukta interjected.

"Well, it has been a few years since I came to Delhi after my mother died in an accident..." As he said those words, he was suddenly transported to his past and his eyes stared into space. Sanyukta realized that and quickly changed the topic. "Let's leave what happened in the past. I understand that it bothers us both. Let's talk about our present and our plans for future."

"You are right. So, what do you want to be one day? From the nature of your studies, I understand that you want to become a journalist someday. Is that so?"

"Yes. I want to become a journalist. Though to keep myself going, I need to work at the bar too."

"So why don't you try some other job?" Shankar asked.

"Hey, I am not complaining. I like my job. In fact, no work is small. And yes, I tried some other professions too. Working at the bar is certainly better than speaking to foreigners in fake accents and pretending to be one of them in a call center," she laughed.

"You are right. At least, here you can meet real people and sometimes a few good ones. Isn't that so?"

"Oh yes, you are hinting well, Shankar. So what is it you want to become?"

"I don't know. I have thought about it several times but cannot find the answer. Mani Kaka predicts that I will be guiding the people to their destinies. But for now, I don't know even my own destiny, what a tragedy, hahaaa."

And they both laughed together.

It is said that pain builds stronger bonds than joy. That day, as both of them looked into each other's eyes, they discovered a painful past, that made them say in their hearts, "O Pain, I have known you so well and here you reside too."

When Sanyukta reached her home after the meeting, she quickly went into her room and opened the envelope from Shankar. She found a sketch inside. "Ohh, this is lovely. Do I look that pretty? Are my eyes really that nice?" She kept on talking to herself as she looked at the sketch through her admirer's eyes. The more she looked, the more intrigued she became. Then finally, she fell asleep.

They met again a few times. Every meeting had an agitating effect as both left with a stronger desire to meet again soon. Neither could she concentrate on her studies nor could she breathe easily at her workplace. They met thirteen times in such short bursts until finally, everything fell into place one day. They both had the entire day to themselves. They reached a lake in the middle of the hills in a neighboring tourist attraction, Soorajkund. They both sat silently watching the birds swimming in the lake, feeling the bliss of each other's presence. After a while, Sanyukta placed Shankar's head on her lap. She then looked straight into his eyes and spoke.

"You know we can never escape from our pasts. The more we try to forget things, the more they haunt us. I don't want to remain a prisoner of my past. I want to say it out loud and be free."

"Then say it." Shankar looked into her eyes.

"I come from a city Bareilly, in Uttar Pradesh. My father is a banker and my mother, a housewife. My father provided us with every comfort of life and my mother ensured that those comforts did not spoil us. Everything was like a beautiful dream until one day..." She paused again and then she continued.

"That day my brother and I were driving back home from a friend's house. On the way, there was a stretch of road which was relatively desolated. My brother opened the car windows to let some fresh air come in. Suddenly we heard the cry of a woman, asking for help. My brother stopped the car. He came out of the car and tried to understand what direction the sound was coming from. Then one more cry came, this time even shriller. My brother started moving towards it. I too got down from the car and started following my brother. He ordered me to sit inside, but I refused. Then we heard the cry the third time. This time it was even shriller and louder. The source of the voice seemed very close now. I was afraid but my brother wasn't. He moved towards the voice. It was late evening and it was getting darker. Suddenly we saw four people wearing masks and holding long knives in their hands. I was horrified. The girl they had captured was bleeding profusely. Her torn clothes filled in the rest of the story. I screamed and pulled my brother back but it was too late. The masked men had seen us and were charging towards us. My brother understood that our lives were in danger. He asked me to rush towards the car and leave. I stood frozen in horror and then he yelled at me again. I ran towards the car and my brother jumped on those masked men. He might have kicked a couple of them very hard as I could hear them groaning after each blow. But the sheer number overpowered him very soon. The moment I reached the car, I heard my brother scream. I was paralyzed again as I sensed somebody running towards me. I started the car and drove for the next thirty minutes till I reached home. When my parents asked about *Bhaiyya,* I was blank. I could not answer them and then I realized what I had done. I had fled from the scene when my brother cried for my help. By the time, I told the whole story to my parents and we reached the spot along with some more people, it was too late. He could never come back. He was found dead along with the girl and one of the four men. My parents perhaps forgave me but I could never forgive myself. Memories of my brother haunted me every night. One day, I left home and came here. I decided that day that I owed my life to my brother and the only way to pay back to him was not failing him again. My parents opposed my decision, but I knew what I had to do. I await another such moment and that moment I will not be scared." Sanyukta stopped, her eyes blazing with confidence and promise.

Shankar, looking at her radiant face, embraced her. With the drizzle, embrace tightened. The drizzle took the form of rain but both of them lost in their embrace were unaffected. He kissed her, she kissed back. They kissed again and again. They remained in the same state for many minutes before she leaned back. Looking at the dark sky, she said, "We should leave from here". Shankar pulled his motorbike and soon they were off to the wet roads. Sanyukta held him tightly from behind. It didn't take them much time to reach Shankar's home or perhaps it didn't appear to be a long distance. They entered his home and found no one there. Javed was still at work. Shankar pulled out a towel from the cupboard and handed over to her in his room. He took one for himself and went inside the bathroom to quickly change. He then got into the kitchen and turned the burner on. Sanyukta came out of the room, dressed in a loose white t-shirt and black shorts. On seeing Shankar in the kitchen, she asked, "What are you doing there?"

Shankar turned to face her and after a brief pause he said, "Well, was thinking of making some tea but now after seeing you, seems like the plan has changed."

"Hmmm, I can see what lies behind this naughty smile. Carry on with what you were doing....and yes, I like 2 spoons of sugar in my tea." She turned around and went on to sit on the couch.

"Alright, Madam. The order has been taken. By the way, my clothes suit you better." "Thank you. When does Javed come?"

"Normally just around this time, but if you approve, I can ask him to stay out till late..." Shankar smiled.

"O my my... so eager ... well.. I don't know. Do whatever you want to do." Sanyukta lowered her eyes and picked up the magazine from the table.

Shankar smiled, took out his mobile phone and entered the text, "*Bhai, Sanyukta is here with me at home. Let's meet at dinner time in two hours from now.*"

The tea was ready. He poured the tea in two cups and brought them to the center table in the living area. After putting the cups on the table, he went to the main door and bolted it from inside. Sanyukta saw that but did not speak anything. Shankar reached Sanyukta, kissed her on her cheek, and said, "you look lovely."

"Thanks." She shyly replied.

He then sat beside Sanyukta on the same couch and picked up the teacups. Both sipped the tea. A few moments later, Shankar touched her hair with his fingers and asked, "Who else in your family has such fine hair?"

"My dad." "Okk, when was the last time you spoke with him?" "Been long..." "Hasn't the time come yet to bury the old matters?"

"Don't know... I think when the time will come the matters will be buried by themselves."

"Correct. Well, leave it... you tell me, from where do you get these beautiful eyes?" Shankar smiled.

"From my mum." She smiled back.

"Ohh, she must be a gorgeous woman."

"She indeed is."

"And last but not the least, what is the secret of these beautiful lips?" Shankar leaned towards Sanyukta feeling her breath.

"Ummm...these are..."

Shankar put his finger on her lips and said, "You speak a lot, sometimes at the wrong time." And then he removed his finger and placed his lips on hers. They kissed. A passionate kiss. He touched her breast, she felt the tenderness. He started undressing her, the lips still sealed. He undressed himself, the lips still sealed. The next few minutes were gone in a flash. When the lips were unlocked, they looked at each other's red hot faces. In the eyes, the inhibitions were gone.

Soon after they had dressed themselves up, the doorbell rang.

"Must be Javed", Shankar responded and walked towards the door.

"Finally... can I come in Sir?" Javed teased.

"Of course. Get in."

"Hello Sanyukta, ohhoooo, look at these two blushing pink faces." Javed teased again and Sanyukta blushed more.

"So, my dear love birds, have you cooked something to eat or were just too occupied with your boring love talks? I am super hungry."

"Ohhh, we thought you were to bring some noodles, isn't it Sanyukta?" Shankar smiled.

"Hmm, so you both are teaming up against me... well, today's dinner is on you, brother." Javed said faking the grudge.

"Hahhaaa, it is then. You guys talk and I will get into the kitchen."

"Wait, you both help me and I will be the cook today." Sanyukta stood and smiled at both of them.

"Alright then, what kind of help do you need La Chef Madame?" Javed asked.

"Not much Javed, just show me where the things are and keep talking as you both normally do." She giggled, following which all three of them chuckled.

The next day, Shankar woke up quite early. He looked at Sanyukta, sleeping on her left side beside him. Her body was curled, face silent, eyes half shut. Her hair blew with the air coming from the air cooler. He looked at her for several minutes and then placed his right hand on her face softly. He then kissed her gently on her forehead, cheeks and lips. Disturbed in her sleep, Sanyukta moved a bit. She then opened her eyes slightly and on seeing Shankar, she moved closer and cuddled him.

"It's the most beautiful morning." He whispered in her ears.

"Ummm, why?" She whispered back.

"I found you beside me when I opened my eyes... that is why."

She further inched closer to him and surrendered herself in a tight embrace. Soon they were again asleep.

They woke up with the sound of the main door opening and someone getting in. They came out of the room and saw Javed wearing off his sports shoes.

"You went running?" Shankar quizzed "Yes. As always." Javed replied.

"Ohh, completely forgot. Sorry" Shankar said. Then he turned to Sanyukta, "Every weekend, we always go for a long run. Missed today."

"Don't stress. We will go tomorrow." Javed smiled.

"Well, you guys can still run. There is not much left in the groceries. You both go and get it. I will do some work in the meanwhile." Sanyukta said.

"Ok. Come on Shankar. Get up fast." Javed invited.

After they were gone, Sanyukta stared at the number of slippers lying on the main entrance. She then looked at the golden-brown curtains which looked black at several places. Deciding in her mind, she started working. After a couple of hours, Shankar and Javed came back. After opening the door, as they were about to step on the floor, they stopped. Both looked at each other, then at their discolored and dusty shoes. They removed their shoes outside and then entered. As they walked towards the kitchen carrying several bags of groceries, they looked at everything with disbelief/astonishment. The floor seemed transparent, the lonely walls had the company of calendars and paintings, the naked and awry looking chairs and table looked new with the cloth covers and the kitchen looked clean for the first time. Sanyukta stood in the kitchen smiling. They went to the rooms, the bedsheet was neatly tucked and the cupboards were well organized. Shankar came out of his room and reached Sanyukta, "Great job my girl!"

Just then Javed came out running, "Great job! My friend, this is the greatest job ever. This is magic... Can you believe it? The toilet pot is also clean... my friend, the toilet pot is also clean. I cannot believe it, feeling like crying. Thank you Sanyukta. You are an angel." Javed spoke making those witty faces and everyone gave a hearty laugh. The day soared quickly. Sanyukta stayed there that night as well.

The next morning, they woke up again with the sound of the main door. Still sleepy in each other's embrace, Sanyukta whispered, "Seems, you again missed your running session."

"Yes, I will do it next time." Shankar replied lazily.

"We should wake up now. I have to go to my home and prepare for the next week. Tonight, I am working as well." She spoke slowly with her eyes still shut.

"No, please don't go." Shankar still sleepy pulled her face towards him. "Ummmm, now or a bit later, but will have to go." She said with a sad smile, looking at Shankar.

"But why?? You can live here with us?" He looked at her "Not so soon." She smiled and released herself from the tight embrace.

"I will make some breakfast for all of us, you get ready and then you have to drop me to my place."

"Ok, I don't think that I have an option."

"Correct, you don't have." She stood up saying.

Soon, they were all on the breakfast table. After having the meal together, she took leave from Javed as Shankar waited for her at the main door. In less than an hour, Shankar came back home after dropping Sanyukta to her place. He sat quietly on the couch and looked at the paintings on the walls. Javed came forward and asked, "What happened brother?"

"Nothing. Just thinking that how lively does the wall looks, now with the addition of this colorful painting."

"It does. Come on, let's go out."

"Where?"

"Oh, come on. You are so lost these days. We had a party planned for today."

"Ohh, yes. With the college mates."

"Yes. Come on now."

"But why didn't you remind me?" Shankar asked.

"What? Why is it needed? Come on, get back in the real world. I have been watching you for last couple of months. You have been behaving strangely." Javed said annoyingly.

"Ok, okay ...take it easy. Will get ready quickly." Shankar stood up and walked towards the room. Javed sat down on the couch and started playing the game on his mobile. In a few minutes, Shankar came out of the room. Still not dressed for the party, he came to Javed and said, "Brother, I am not feeling well. Why don't you go and say sorry on my behalf?"

Bewildered on the sudden excuse, Javed looked at Shankar angrily. "After that, we had planned to go to Mani Kaka's home also. Remember, we missed Pallavi's birthday last week just because of you?"

"Yes, I remember. I will call up kaka and will explain. Don't worry."

"I am not worried, Shankar. I feel sorry for you. You have no time for anybody else now. You have let one girl take over you completely. I feel sorry for you." Javed stood up from the couch and moved out.

Shankar looked at him walk away and then astonished on the sudden twist in their usual interactions, he turned on the TV. The channel played the song, "Saanson ko saanson mein dhalne do zara, dheemi si dhadkan ko badhne do zara. Lamhon ki guzarish hai yeh, paas aa jaayein, hum, hum tum...."

He took out his mobile and dialed Sanyukta's number.

Things went on the same way for the next few months. The heatwave gave way to some coolness when the rains lashed the region during monsoon. The season was changing once again. The chill was felt in the morning. For the first time, Shankar forgot Javed's birthday. Javed complained and celebrated his 24th birthday with his friends who often needed his muscle power in face of the adversaries. The increasingly grumpy Javed had started spending more time with Bhati in the computer center than at home where Sanyukta was often present, either physically or on phone. Sanyukta's twenty-fourth birthday was approaching soon and so was Diwali, and that year, 2007, both moments fell on the same day. Shankar deluged in the stream of thoughts had not realized that his agitated friend was not around him for the past few days.

THE RISE OF GOOD AND EVIL

AFTER A BUSY DAY OF WORK, IN THE EVENING, Shankar picked up Sanyukta from her college and drove his bike straight to his place. It was a breezy evening. The days had become shorter and by the time they reached, it was already dark. After preparing a quick cup of tea, both came out on the roof to see the starry ether. Wearing a light fleece, apt for the evening coolness in the air, they both sat on two bamboo chairs. Javed had recently bought those used chairs in good condition from an online website, when he spent a lot of his time in the computer center, improving his computer skills, browsing and online chatting. That evening as well, since he was apprised of the Sanyukta's presence in the home, he chose to stay back in the computer center till late.

Shankar oblivious to the fact, lost in his own isolated world, was thinking of proposing to Sanyukta on her birthday that fell in exactly two weeks. Watching the changing expressions and understanding the confusion behind them even in that fading light of the late evening, Sanyukta leaned towards Shankar and said, "Stop it."

"What?" Shankar asked.

"You know what. By now I know that whenever you have this confused state of mind, you start tapping your feet. Please stop that and tell me what are you thinking about."

"Haha, you got me. Is it not similar to the way you start moving your fingers in your hair in a circular motion while deep in thought?" Shankar asked with a wicked smile.

"Ohho, Mr. Intelligent, so you do notice a few things about me. I am pleased to know that. Well, don't deviate from what I asked. Tell me, what are you thinking?" Sanyukta snapped back.

"Nothing much. I was just thinking of when should I talk to Mani about a job for you at his magazine." Shankar lied.

"Hmm, I know you are lying. But anyways, keep your secret with you. On what you just said, don't even think about it. I will ask you when I need any help. For now, just let me try my best first."

"Ok, no problem." Shankar replied casually.

"And also, just so you know, I don't like celebrating my birthday. In fact, I almost despise cutting the cake. So, don't even think about it."

Suddenly caught off-guard, Shankar had no idea on how should to react, in a moment after gaining his foothold, he remarked, "What is it then you would like to do on your birthday?"

"I don't know as yet. Try a few things. Though for sure, don't plan a gathering, any party, or a typical cake cutting ceremony for me. Also, no expensive gifts. Think about an experience and not a thing you can gift me. Enough of the clues for the surprise-master." She giggled in the end.

"Alright. No more clues please and please, stop getting inside my mind."

"Hahaaa, I don't get inside your mind, you make it so obvious that I can't stop reading it."

"Ohh, I better watch it. What is the plan for dinner? Shall we go out today?"

"Whatever. But where is Javed? I don't see him very often these days?"

"Must be at the computer center. He is becoming an expert on computer matters these days. Good for him, now no one calls him to be involved in a fight."

"Hmm, I hope my presence here is not bothering him."

"Of course not. He is my best friend. He can't be bothered by such small things. Even if sometimes he does, it's only momentarily."

"Sometimes, that means something happened?"

"Not exactly. I missed a few moments of socializing so he got annoyed with me. Just that."

"Ohh, so my presence has changed something." She sighed.

"No, it's not about you being a part of my life honey. I, myself don't feel like going and meeting everyone. It bores me now."

"I don't know if you are lying to yourself or everyone else because what you said can't be entirely true. Try to balance everything."

"Oh, come on yaar. Leave the boring topic. It's all fine and in control. What about dinner now?"

"Let's cook at home, call up Javed, and have dinner together." Sanyukta suggested.

"No, I don't feel like having enough time with you alone. I will handle my friends, don't worry about them. Let's go out." He protested and ended on a decisive note. Sanyukta complied and they both got ready for a dinner date.

After the dinner, they returned to the roof under the starry sky, lit by the full moon. Javed had returned and was sleeping on the couch with the TV still turned on. Shankar turned off the TV and covered him with a blanket before climbing the stairs to the roof. The nights seem to be short when in love and the days often unbearably long. They both walked on the roof while holding on to each other. Sanyukta hummed the song, "*Lag jaa gale ki phir yeh hansi raat ho na ho, shayad phir is janam mein mulaqaat ho na ho.....*"

"You sing well." Shankar said. She kept on humming without any reply.

"You know, I often heard this song when I was younger. Maa always raised the volume of the radio whenever this song played."

"Wow, which other song did she like?" She replied this time with a genuine eagerness to know more.

"Many more. She was extremely fond of music. Many Hindi melodies from Mohammedd Rafi, Lata Mangeshkar, Kishore Kumar, Hemant Kumar and other great singers she used to listen. I think in the absence of Baba, music gave her solace so she could still smile and have a positive outlook towards the world. She loved her radio more than the food and clothes. She once even joked that if the earth starts shaking then the first thing she would pick is her radio and its batteries." He gave a slight giggle, more to hide the flow of emotions passing through the veins to the eyes.

"What is your favorite type of music?" She quickly changed the topic, ignoring the moist eyes of Shankar helping him gain control of himself.

"I like easy-going music. The *jhoom jhoom jhumroo* types. I cannot absorb the intense and extremely soulful music. Javed is good at that. He appears so carefree from outside but he is very deep."

"Hmm, so I should probably listen to my type of music with Javed than you." She teased.

"Ohhh, so you too are the same bore types..."

"Oh yes, proudly I am. Though I thought this music suits your personality better than him. I thought he would listen only to Sunny Deol's earth-shaking dance songs like *Yaara o yaara"* She moved her hands and feet from one side to another in a funny way as the actor did on-screen in that Bollywood song.

"Hahahaa, that is also his favorite... ok, tell me one thing, how do you see your life in the next five years?"

"Hmm... That is an easy question because I keep on thinking about what do I want from my life. I soon hope to get a decent job assignment, one that involves writing a research on a social cause. Within five years of getting that, I hope to make a name for myself in the world of journalism through my path-breaking write-ups on those social matters which would make everyone more aware of their surroundings and push them to be more participative to help make it a better world for everyone. What is your plan?"

"Ohh...my plan? Yours was quite thoughtful. Let me think." While he expected his name to be heard somewhere in her five-year plan, he was surprised that she didn't even talk about her parents, the idea of proposal seemed infelicitous. Consolidating her thoughts, he said, "I have never wanted much from my life. I just wanted to be happy and peaceful with little things and acts of love and care. But I like your idea of paying back to society in some way. In fact, I and Javed, have few times, provided food and clean water for the poor kids in and around this area. Only, as much as our limited resources allowed."

"Great. You can sometimes even bring them to the computer center. Those eyes have for long not seen any dream. Give them a dream so they could also try to fly. Also, since you are so much into reading books, you can help in their education as well."

"Yes true, I can. But I think for now my hands are full. Will think about it." Still despondent on the thought of dropping the idea to propose Sanyukta, he said slowly.

Thereafter, they did not converse much that night. They spent the next few hours in the silent comforting company of each other before surrendering themselves to the cozy warmth of the bed inside the house. Sleeping in each other's tight embrace, while she felt tranquil, he felt anxious. The night brought different perspectives for both. The next morning, when Sanyukta woke up, she did not find Shankar by his side. She walked out of the room in her red t-shirt and denim shorts and found Shankar on the couch holding a book in his hands. She came forward and caressed his head. He looked at her, smiled and then turned back towards the book.

"What are you reading?" She asked.

"Just finishing a novel I started months ago." He replied calmly.

"Months ago? What happened in between?"

"Nothing, just lost my focus perhaps."

"Hmmm, you seem to be much thoughtful suddenly. What time did you wake up or did you even sleep?" She looked at his eyes and raised the suspicion.

"Didn't sleep much. How about you?" "I slept well. Let me make some tea for us. Where is Javed?" "He is in the martial arts coaching center." "Tell me one thing, why do you read?" She quizzed as she walked into the kitchen. "I feel empowered." "How?" She questioned from the kitchen holding the pan.

"Well, I always had the paucity of words. That caused me a loss of confidence often. It was Maa whose words helped me survive. When she was gone, I struggled big time. After I came here and joined the studies again, I realized that whatever I read, gave me the words to speak. The meaningful words which often diffused the clouds of confusion in the mind made me feel better each time and thus, I read more. The more I read, the better I could explain and the more I gained acceptance in society. That is why I said, I feel empowered."

"Hmm, I can see that already. You suddenly are speaking like a philosopher. I like that. What are you reading now?"

"It's a political story setup in the Lenin ruled Russia. It talks greatly about Communism and Marx."

"Cool. I didn't know you like the political angles in the stories. Enjoy your book with the tea now. I will soon get ready for I have to go out for some shopping." She said as she poured the tea into the cups.

"Thanks. I will come with you and then later, let's have lunch together. I have also asked Javed to join us."

"That is wonderful."

That day after several days, the three of them had food together. While Sanyukta teased Javed on his choice of music, he appeared to be unbuttoned.

As the days progressed, Shankar spent more time reading, apart from the work on his two businesses. He made lesser phone calls to Sanyukta who objected a bit but in reality did not mind the change. Although, they tried meet at every possible moment during the weekdays and the weekends. On her birthday, Shankar gifted her a compilation of her favorite old songs in a CD along with a little CD player. Javed gifted her a headphone and together she received an experience she loved.

Soon after her birthday, Sanyukta bagged an internship offer from a leading news magazine to research and write about the change in the life of the poor with the changing condition of the rivers. Shankar and Javed, living at/along the riverside area, were now quite well known by everyone around. She explained to Shankar and Javed and sought their help which they happily agreed to.

In an attempt to understand the lives of the indigents, she proposed to visit their homes and watch them closely. For the start, Shankar decided to go to Moinuddin's place. Moinuddin was the rickshaw puller who had met them in their very early days in Delhi. After that first meeting, they had confronted each other several times as Moinuddin often found the customers in the same area where they lived.

One day, they decided to go directly to Moinuddin's place. They didn't know the location of his home but knew the area. After querying a few people, they soon found his home.

Shankar, Javed and Sanyukta reached his place on a Saturday evening. The small house unit, one of the hundreds of similar units was in a narrow street, very close to the river bank. At first Moinuddin was surprised to see them but soon he got his composure back when Shankar quickly explained what they needed. When they entered, Shankar noticed the very low ceiling as a person of height like him could easily touch the ceiling with a jump. With the door opened, the cold air moved the small ceiling fan that stared at the floor. Moinuddin, quickly closed the door to stop further cooling of the already cold walls of the home and warmly welcomed the three of them. One kerosene lamp flickered a bit from the distance and then was stabled when the door was closed. A woman emerged from a shadow in the left corner and joined Moinuddin in the welcome. He introduced the woman as his wife. The walls appearing green in color seemed to have shrunk suddenly with the arrival of them. Moinuddin offered them to sit on the old plastic chairs and occupied one by himself. The woman went inside and came back quickly with four glasses of water on a steel plate.

A few moments later when everyone was settled, Shankar asked, "Is there a power outage?" "What power *Babuji*? It's been five days since there has been no electricity here in this area." "Ohh, did you complain?"

"Yes, we did. They said that the people in the next block are stealing electricity and during one of such attempts, they had short-circuited the whole transformer. Let us see when do they correct the fault." The despondency in his voice was perspicuous.

"Don't worry, I will talk to the electricity office tomorrow morning. I will take ten people with me and then let's see how long do they take to solve this problem." Javed gave an aggressive response.

"Try that too. Don't know what will work. By the way, I hear a lot of good things about you both. You did well to leave that hell of a job. I have no other option, have to live with it." Moinuddin spoke again in a slightly hopeful tone.

"You have kids?" Sanyukta asked the woman who stood there on her husband's side.

"No." She replied and looked at her husband with her pale eyes.

"You arrange for something to eat." Moinuddin asked his wife pointing to go inside the kitchen and then continued speaking, "Earlier I felt bad for not having any children of my own but now when I see the children of others, I feel lucky to not to have one of my own."

"And why is that?" Sanyukta asked curiously

"Most of the children have some inborn lifelong diseases. Some are born crippled, some are asthmatic, some have kidney issues and those few who are lucky to not be suffering from diseases have no motivation in life to do something good. They either end up drunk in a gutter or are used by the political people for their political gains."

"Ohh, what is the reason behind so many diseases?"

"What else..... Water. What we drink is not drinkable. Furthermost of the people here have very low-end occupations. Either they are washer-men or they work in small factories like *Bidi or Patakha* factory. Only a few like me are rickshaw pullers. But believe me, I am better than them because the washer-men and women have long exposure to the toxic water and the *bidi and patakha* factories destroy their lungs badly. Javed immediately looked at his glass of water and put it down silently. Moinuddin quick to notice, pointed out, "Don't worry *Babu ji,* what we drink here is boiled at least five times. I am very careful about these things."

Shankar looked at Javed and smiled. "I am sure the local authorities won't be doing anything, isn't it?" Sanyukta asked again.

"No madam, the MLA here has won for the last two times but he has not done anything. At least something that can reduce our problems."

"So, why do you vote for him then. Vote for someone else who listens to you." She explained.

"How do I, madam? Traditionally all the Muslims have always voted for him only. Now it is about all of us, so we all have to follow the collective decision."

"That is a mistake Moinuddin. Democracy loses its power if the individuals like you don't put forth your opinions. Voting is also like putting forth an opinion, you should say what you believe in." Shankar objected.

"Maybe *Babuji*, but I am not sure. I will never go against the community. Already the life has so many other problems, cannot add one more to it."

It fell upon Shankar that there is not much he could do to make Moinuddin understand. He left it to Sanyukta to finish her interview so they could leave soon. She asked a few more questions and soon after they stood up to leave. Moinuddin asked them for the dinner but they politely refused for none of them wanted to stress the already crumbling circumstances of their host. As they stepped out of the place, Moinuddin came forward and said slowly, "*Babuji,* don't be angry. I understood what you said but I just cannot follow it as of now. Maybe when you meet the others in the area, try to make them understand as well. Even if a few understand, I will follow what you said."

On their way back to their home in the auto-rickshaw, the three of them did not speak. They looked at each other, noticed the lines on each other's forehead and decided to remain quiet. Each one of them had discovered a hidden direction leading each one of them to their aspiring destiny from the meeting. While a political dream had germinated in Javed's head, Sanyukta could see a story that had the potential to seal her fate in the professional world. Untouched by their thoughts, Shankar had found his soul troubled, and to pacify himself, he knew that he had to put in more effort. The distinct directions of their life journeys from there on had the same origin and the next landmark too was the same, meeting others in the area and trying to understand their stories.

For the next four months, the three of them met hundreds of other families living in that area almost every weekend. They saw live examples of the characters shown in the tragic Hindi movies. They witnessed the cold homes having no fuel to cook as they looked at the hungry eyes staring at the handful of raw grains. They noted the desperate attempts to satiate the hunger by swallowing the uncooked rice and they behold the effort to gulp down the undrinkable water. They befriended the men and women who weren't better than skeletons, as they held the hands of the crippled children helping them to stand straight. Was it the similarity in their fates like the red circle that had brought them together during the life-defining moments? Though, unsurprisingly the aspirations of the three of them seemed so distinct and unrelated.

After those few months, Sanyukta joined them both on a Friday evening. She had just submitted her study and was in a mood to celebrate. The spring had set in. The days had already started getting warmer than usual but thankfully, the evening still brought the aroma of some refreshing coolness in the air. She was the first one to reach their home. Shankar and Javed ran late as it was the exam day in the martial arts school. Based on the skill, the students were to be conferred with different belt certificates; a black belt certificate, the highest of them all. Sanyukta, though had an extra key with her since she was not like a visitor anymore. For the last-half year, she had spent every weekend in that place, and she fondly called it her second home, her parents' place being the first one. She knew more about the place and the place seemed to be more aware of its true master. The brass lock opened in the first attempt with the first key she inserted from the bunch of keys in her hand. The newly painted brown door too opened swiftly without making the normal jarring sound. She went straight into the room and came out in a few minutes wearing more relaxed clothes, cargo shorts and a fluorescent orange, suited more to a casual evening at home. She then sent a text to Shankar asking him to bring a few things from the market on his way back home. Once convinced of everything, she came into the sitting area and sank comfortably into the couch with the TV remote in one hand and a coke in another.

Shankar and Javed too reached the home in around thirty minutes. After taking a quick shower, they too settled down around Sanyukta. Javed opened the beer cans and Shankar opened some *namkeen* packets. The sound of music coming from the TV had dominated the few spoken, but often silent words of the three of them. After a couple of drinks, Sanyukta turned off the TV and asked, "What is it with you guys today?"

"Why, what is wrong?" Shankar snapped back while Javed still quiet as if he didn't notice.

"You tell me, you both been so quiet for the past couple of weeks. All well?"

"Yes, everything is fine. In fact, as you said, I just realized that Javed has also been quiet. What happened to you?" Shankar giggled.

"Nothing. You were lost in some thoughts so I didn't interrupt. Simple." Javed retorted.

"Haha, that is so kind of you. Well, I am fine guys, just a few thoughts crossing my mind every now and then."

"Let us be the audience." Sanyukta asserted "Don't know how to explain, I was just wondering about what next?" "What next...means?" She asked.

"I mean, after all this long exercise to meet so many people, to know them, to understand them, to relate so closely with their agony... What next? Is it all done with just one write-up of yours or is there something for us here?" Shankar sounded concerned and confused, both at the same time.

"I really didn't think that way. Javed, what about you?" She turned to look at Javed.

"I did, certainly did. But not like Shankar did perhaps. To be honest, I see an opportunity here."

"What opportunity?" She asked.

"Will tell later. First, let me hear what Shankar has to say? When he asks a question, he often has an answer to it." Javed smiled at Shankar.

"Not this time brother. The only thing I know is that I want to do something for these people. Something that can make their lives better."

"But how?" She asked, "I don't know... as yet."

"Well, I have a plan. It may not suit you but it might give you an answer to your question." Javed said as he rose from his place.

"Ok, let us hear that." He replied curiously "I think together we can win the trust of these people so much, that they would even vote for us." "What do you mean? Vote as in real elections?" Sanyukta asked while Shankar stared at him "Yes, real elections." Javed smiled

"Leave it with him Sanyukta. Seems like once again some hooligan has spoken to him and shown him grand dreams about the political world. I have always told you my friend, this filth is not for us."

"Maybe not for you, but I am sure about myself. I think I can handle it." "Well, that is your life. Do as you please."

"But I cannot do much without you and now, without you both." Javed looked at both Sanyukta and Shankar while he stressed on "both".

"Power corrupts brother. Forget it."

"Even it does, do you have a better plan to achieve what you want to? And by the way, why are you being pessimistic?"

"I am not a pessimist; I just know what works for me and whatnot. Moreover, I don't believe that any of these political parties seem real good for the people." Shankar replied annoyingly.

"Ok, if that is the case, I offer to build it from scratch. Let's launch our own party and make this region as our base. And then I assure you that as we win the local MLA seat for that area, we will do everything possible to make the people's lives better. And that is a promise to you otherwise you know me that I don't feel sympathetic easily."

"Yes, you stone-hearted. How many girls have you already left?" Sanyukta remarked in her usual witty tone to ease things up. Shankar laughed while Javed gave a side glance to Sanyukta.

"I won't leave her if I find someone like you." Javed retorted and then he looked at Shankar to continue, "So my friend, here is the deal. You help me and I help you. We will do everything, what do you say, even the name of the party will be decided by you. Just stay with me. What say?"

"It is not that easy Javed. Serious party work will need enough funds as well. How can we arrange that?" Sanyukta posed the question.

"That may not be the bottleneck. There are a few big companies now who would want to acquire our computer institute. In fact, Bhati brought one such proposal a few days ago." Shankar replied.

"See, how every piece just falls in the right place. Shankar had even worked for a business presentation to attract the investor." Javed said.

"Well, that is news to me." Sanyukta sounded disappointed as she leaned back on the couch.

"Ohh, it's not like that. We were never serious about that until this moment. What Shankar did was only on Bhati's insistence, though we had disagreed to sell our stakes." Javed replied and then asked Shankar, "So, what do you say?"

"Let me think it over. I will sleep over it and we will talk tomorrow."

"Alright. So till then, let me enjoy with my besties around." Javed came forward and moved his arms around both Shankar and Sanyukta to embrace them together.

The night went long for Shankar and Javed, for those eyes had dreams and aspirations seldom seen by the living people. Javed roamed for hours on the roof anxiously with lots of planning in his head. While Sanyukta slept like a baby in the lap of Shankar, he sat awake with the thoughts storming his head/brain. In the last few months, he could see and now could identify with the two different worlds. He himself had been vacillating between the pulls of these two distinct worlds. While his relationship with Sanyukta needed the shelter of a stable and simple realm, his own pursuit and hunger to understand the purpose of existence pointed him in the direction of the unstable and seemingly complicated world. As the night passed, Shankar seemed calmer and assured. He fell asleep in the very early morning hours. When he woke up, he headed straight in the other room looking for Javed. When he did not find him there, he came out and spotted him lying in the hallroom on the couch. He seemed to be deep in sleep as his mouth was agape. "Must have slept very late, just like me." Shankar thought and then he shook Javed to wake him up.

"What is it?" Javed asked when he saw Shankar with his half-shut eyes. "Let us do it." He replied in a decisive tone.

"That is terrific." Javed stood up rubbing his eyes in disbelief, "So what is the deal?" He raised an eyebrow.

"The deal is as you promised yesterday, it will be your thing but will be done my way." Shankar replied.

"Ok, explain a bit."

"Well, I have no political ambitions. I will just work towards the goal of empowering these oppressed people and you will support me in this. Any political benefit is yours."

"That is cool but what do you get out of it?" "I don't know. For now, the only thing I know is that it would make me happy."

"Ohh, you and your philosophical self... but never mind, anything for your happiness my friend. So when do we start?"

"Today, now." Shankar smiled, a smile that Javed recognized, a smile that was not to pacify but to challenge.

Things moved very fast from that moment onwards. The party was formed and was baptized as "Janadhikar Sangha". Shankar and Javed visited the houses in the locality to ask people to join the party. They had always done that, conceiving a dream and then bringing it to reality as a start-up, before they know it, their hard work puts the start-up on a path of growth. The same people they had met a few weeks ago, received them with open arms. The difference was that unlike the last time, Shankar spoke to them while they listened. They were all ears for they could see a torch-bearer before them. Many of them followed what Shankar and Javed had to say, a few who didn't were convinced by the believers like Moinuddin. In a matter of six months, Janadhikar Sangha had five hundred members. At the very same moment, Bhati grabbed a fine deal to sell the business as well. That evening, after the strenuous day, both of them reached their home earlier than usual. After a quick round of snacks, Javed asked Shankar, "What are you thinking?"

"What else brother? Just wonder how can we motivate these people to educate themselves? I don't think that there is any other way for them to get rid of this exploitation."

"Hmm, maybe you are right but what about the other things in your life?" "Other things?? Ohh, you mean Sanyukta... She is fine, brother." "Ohh, and how do you know that?" "Well, I spoke to her recently."

"That is exactly what you do Shankar. You spoke with her ten days ago. There is nothing wrong with speaking in ten days but it seems weird after how often you used to talk to her. Strange, being so cold in love related matters was my thing, not yours, Shankar."

"Javed, what happened to you suddenly? I will speak to her, she is just too busy with her new job now. It is ok." Shankar tried to calm down Javed who looked perturbed.

"It is not ok. I know because I have faced it. Tomorrow is Sanyukta's birthday and she is coming home in thirty minutes. I told her that you have some plans for her and you wanted it to be a surprise."

"Oh my god. How could I forget about it?" Shankar looked at Javed with his apropos puppy eyes thanking him.

"Don't worry. Here are the movie tickets for both of you." "Super. What about you... are you not coming for the movie?" "Naah, you both spend some time together. I will take care of the work tomorrow." "Hmmm... thanks again, brother. By the way which movie is it?" "A good one that should help you get your humor back as well. It is 3 Idiots."

"Thanks brother. I will now quickly go and bring a cake. We will celebrate her birthday at midnight. It's her twenty-fifth."

"Twenty-fifth? She is elder to you? Didn't know that. Anyway, I have ordered the cake and the bouquet which will be delivered at midnight."

"Okkk... that is superb." Shankar stammered a bit as the expressions on his face changed from disbelief to gratitude.

Sanyukta joined the two of them after a few minutes. As always, she first went to the washroom to take a shower before donning her casual outfit. Unlike a usual November evening, that day was extremely cold. A quick hailstorm had dampened the air and cooled the atmosphere to give a chilly effect. They ordered the dinner from a *Dhaba* nearby. As the food arrived, Javed brought a bottle of wine from his room.

"Let us open this today." He said.

"Where did you get this from?" Sanyukta asked in surprise.

"Mani *Kaka* gave it to us. One of his relatives gifted him, who got it from Germany."

"Oh wow. How is he doing? And by the way, how will we open it? This is a cork lid. It needs a special opener." Sanyukta looked puzzled.

"That is a good question. Anyways, we will do something to open it. And yes, on your second question, Mani *Kaka* is fine. We had a long conversation with him last week. He liked the idea of *Janadhikar Sangha* and is keen to join us now." Javed replied.

"That is excellent... by the way, guys, I also want to join and contribute in some way to your mission." Sanyukta looked at Shankar and pleaded.

"You are welcome my love, but won't you overburden yourself with this extra responsibility?" Shankar asked.

"I might, but do I have any other way to stay in touch with you?" Sanyukta questioned. Javed looked at both of them and then kept quiet. Shankar suddenly annoyed, quipped back, "Now don't you also start the same thing please."

"What do you mean Shankar? We have met only thrice in the past six months. I had almost given up on us, but glad you made it today for my birthday."

"Uhh... of course, I won't forget your birthday." He hesitated a bit but then said it convincingly.

"Whatever Shankar, I am scared of your over-indulgence with anything, even with me. I can't let you go away from my life just like that. Either you give me a reason to stay closer to you in your union or let me start living here with you."

"It's ok Sanyukta... you are welcome to join the union. He was just kidding. You can do plenty of things." Javed immediately barged in and then politely slipped away into the kitchen.

"Correct, you are welcome to join the union Sanyukta, I was just worried about you. That is it." Shankar continued from where Javed had left.

"Ohh, so that means you don't want me to start living with you here?" She snapped back.

"And where does it come from now?" Shankar looked perplexed.

"Forget about it. I am perhaps too demanding for you." She replied exasperated.

"Ohhh, what is it with your mood swing today?" Shankar sighed and then he turned towards the kitchen and asked loudly, "What are you doing there Javed?"

In a few seconds, Javed came out of the kitchen sheepishly holding some tools in one hand and the bottle of wine in the other. As he came closer to them, he said softly, "Opening this bottle is a bigger pain than solving your disagreements". Shankar and Sanyukta both looked at the battered cork still unwilling to lose its position from the bottle's mouth and a dozen of small tools which had left their wrath on the stubborn wooden piece unsuccessfully. Then they both started laughing as they looked at the helpless face of Javed, who too joined in. After a few torturous minutes, Javed tore through the cork with a sharp knife due to which several wooden shreds fell into the bottle. Still unwilling to give up, he brought a tea-sieve from the kitchen and started pouring the wine into the glasses using the sieve. Once the three glasses were full, they all lifted their glasses and toasted in celebration. As they tasted the first sip, they made similar contorted faces. "Sour" Javed retorted. They too nodded in agreement.

THE SHOCK WAVES

THE CLOCK MOVED FASTER FROM THERE onwards. Minutes turned into hours and the hours directly transformed into the weeks. Bhati had moved back to his village taking control of the farming land his family-owned. Mani, after joining Janadhikar Sangha, had become an active part of the union and with his connections, the union found its first donation. The money was immediately lined up to start a literacy program in the area. A few capable men from the area had become active participants of the union. While one man named Ramkishen had started helping Shankar in the accounts, Moinuddin, Abdul, and Bano helped in the parts of the operations with Javed.

The growing influence had started to reveal its negative traits too. They say that even the walls have ears. Oblivious of such walls around them, Shankar and Javed had started challenging the local authorities during their several interactions with the people. To the discomfort of the authorities, the discontent had started spreading among the people.

While hundreds of those oppressed people willingly listened to Shankar, a few of them were the messengers for the local politician, Hari Lal, helping him analyze the situation. Hari Lal, aware of the growing influence of Janadhikar Sangha, had sensed the rebellion in Shankar's words.

A political wizard who had played the master-stroke of turning the tide in favor of his party in the last few days of the last general elections, Hari Lal, was the metaphor used for the political acumen. The area demographics, which comprised of five lakh voters, including more than one lakh Muslim voters, was at Hari Lal's fingertips. He knew how to influence and move them as per his commands, but the things were changing and he could see the volatility of the change. With the advent of Janadhikar Sangha, the oppressed community of Muslims, primarily employed in the *Bidi* and firecracker factories, visualized the power of their votes for the first time. Over the last few months, many of them had faced some tough questions from Shankar and Javed. In an attempt to answer those questions, they had started learning to speak freely and question more frequently. The key to change was the presence of the right questions asked by the right people and Hari Lal had started noticing the very trend.

On the quaking political grounds, another man stood with strong feet. Devidutt, Hari Lal's primary opponent, had his eyes firmly stuck on the changing atmosphere. Both had faced each other several times but it was a first for both to have to deal on a second front as well.

Javed, ignorant of the watchful eyes over him was getting anxious to see his dreams come to life soon. Every day as he spent time among the people, he felt powerful. Shankar, leading the campaign and doing the things his way, had developed an honest connection with the people. Unaware of the strong wind around her, Sanyukta tried her best to balance her demanding job and extra work at the union to remain close to Shankar. Failing several times in six months after the discussion on her birthday, she increasingly felt weaker from inside to cope up with her desires and insecurities. Shankar, in his usual tendency, got further engrossed in the union.

It was the festival of *Id-e-Milad* that day. Just a week before, the Janadhikar Sangha had finished one cleanliness drive in the area. Euphoric with the results, the union had planned to celebrate the day. Javed had received permission for the local town hall. He sent the invite to a few union members through the mobile text message and asked them to forward the invite to all others who might be interested. He also went to the local mosque and invited the Maulana from there. Bano and Moinuddin took control of the preparation of the food while Abdul took some people with him to serve. Mani and Sanyukta reached in the morning itself and took care of the mic and sound, showing their support to the union. In the evening, the town hall was filled with more than five thousand people, much larger than the anticipated number of two thousand. The food ran low after the first thirty minutes. The people with the empty plates started getting anxious. Watchful of the precarious situation, Javed selected fifty people from the union randomly, who lived very close and asked them to immediately start cooking food at their homes. Another fifty people were selected to deliver the food to the town hall once cooked. Shankar, in order to handle the situation, took control of the mic and started addressing the crowd in his natural calming manner. The anxiety was soon seen to be lowering down. After a wait of one hour, the food was again started to serve. Shankar had joined the crowd chatting with them. There was laughter everywhere. The faces were beaming with hope. And in the middle of all this, a pair of sad eyes looked at Shankar. With the situation in control, Sanyukta stood at one elevated corner alone holding a glass of water. She sipped from her glass whenever someone passed from there. Shankar, encircled by the number of people, right in the center of the area slowly shifted from one step to another greeting the people and sometimes chatting with some of them. In around thirty minutes, as he reached towards the edge of the circle, he felt tired and thirsty. He tried to look beyond and found those two eyes still gazing at him. Feeling suddenly tranquil, he smiled and moved towards her. He reached closer and hugged her. Unmoved by the gesture, she moved back a little and then offered him the glass of water. "You need this more than me." She said it a bit sarcastically.

Shankar looked at him, smiled a little and then grabbed the glass of water. With a big swig, the glass was empty. He then looked back at her and said, "Now it is your turn."

"Shut up, you naughty." Sanyukta pushed him back, hiding her bashful smile.

"Is this a rejection or an invitation?" Shankar flirted.

"Rejection, definitely. Now go back to your people. They are noticing you." She pushed him back once again.

"Ok, I will go. But I was thinking it has been long since we spent some time together. We should do that soon." He said.

"Well...and here I was thinking of leaving you." She replied coquettishly. "You won't. Even if you do, you will come back." "What if I don't." "Then I will come looking for you, wherever you are, I will get you."

She noticed the same affection again in his eyes that had lifted her off from the floor of the cosmetic world several months ago and transported to the world of her dreams, the dreams which she had never shared with anyone but him. Then suddenly she took her arms to her back and crossed her fingers before saying, "We will see."

Shankar recognized the emotions behind those words. He knew that she was despondent, he looked into her eyes once again and opened his mouth to say something when suddenly the ground beneath them shook fervently. A deafening thud rode on the shock waves. In an impulse, he covered her with both of his arms and pushed back to the wall. He remained still for a few seconds with his eyes closed. After a few moments, he opened his eyes and tried to recognize the surroundings.

The bomb blast had wrecked the area. The deluge of thick red blood, internal organs and loud cries of the people all around were yelling the twist in the tale of the festival celebration. On the first sight of his surroundings, he puked. After a few minutes, when he regained the control, he asked Sanyukta to stay there and started moving through the cloud of dust that had ceased to settle down. Amid the wails of the injured bodies running directionless and on the bloody slippery ground, he saw a familiar silhouette moving towards him cautiously. Javed too recognized him from that distance. He extended his hand to Shankar and spoke in a numb voice, "Thank god you are okay."

"Yes, I am. How are you?" Shankar asked worried to notice some blood on his hands.

"I am fine too. The blast perhaps happened inside the main room just near the food stalls. I will call up the police now. Let us find Mani *kaka,* Sanyukta and all others." Javed said with a tremble of fear in his voice.

"Sanyukta is fine. She was with me."

"Ohh, thank god. Let us find the others." They started walking together in one direction.

In a few minutes, they found Mani also walking & searching for others. He had an injury on his forehead which was not too grave a concern. The police took another few minutes to reach the spot. They were accompanied by the bomb disposal squad who started their search to find the presence of any other bomb, if present. The work didn't stop for the whole night. The area was vacated by morning and was seized for further inquiry by the police. Shankar, Javed and Sanyukta reached home after dropping off Mani to his home, in the morning.

While everyone was affected by the incident, Shankar seemed to have been exposed more than others. The sombre scene had stolen sleep from his eyes and instead, there was anguish in his countenance that screamed against the cruel forces of so-called humanity. Even after a few days, his world was facing unconquerable forces. He had nightmares of the unpleasant sight of the dead bodies, mutilated by the scavengers, lying rejected by the vultures. He spoke constantly for hours when awake and muttered in his sleep. Sanyukta stayed with him for those days and readily heard him. Another night, his worst dreams from the past crept up. He saw the same demonic eyes and heard the same voice calling him cursed. The next day, his blabbering continued and became even worse. Mani, Bhati and many others came and left but nothing he spoke made any sense to anyone. Javed himself, under pressure to work for the union and several meetings with the police got him irritated and he stormed out of the place, leaving Sanyukta with him. After three days, Shankar suddenly became silent. Everyone came once again to meet him but he did not speak. His face still looked confused but was much calmer than earlier. He slept quietly, spent the day unspoken, ate small meals and walked a little. Much aware of Sanyukta's presence around him, he spent several hours sitting away from her. Sanyukta did not force him for anything and just remained there around him. It went for another three days when Shankar stood up from his bed and went to the kitchen where she cooked food. He reached closer to her and then swirled his arms around her waist from the back and leaned his head on her left shoulder. She dropped the kitchen knife on the shelf and gently moved her fingers in his hair from her right hand without turning and looking at him. He remained still for a few moments and then whispered, "Thanks".

She did not say anything, did not move, just caressed his hair softly with long silent breaths. "I want to go back to the village." He whispered again "Do you think it is the right time?" "Can't say, but I need it."

"Those who listened to you and followed you also need you. Think again."

After a few minutes, he stepped back and went into the bathroom. Soon, he came out looking ready to go out wearing his blue jeans and a light blue shirt.

As he wore his shoes, she interrupted and enquired, "Are you ok?"

"Yes." He came closer to her, patted on her cheek, and stormed out.

He called up Javed, checked his location, and reached to his location in an hour on a tea-stall near a metro train station. The stall with a large Coke banner in the front had four wooden benches on the two sides. The area swarmed with several human figures, who appeared to be moving ghosts amid the thick dust cloud floating through several construction sites nearby. Shankar found Javed occupying one of the benches. He reached him and took a seat while ordering two cups of tea. Staring at him with an unconvinced look, Javed asked, "So are you up for it now?"

"I guess I have to be." "Well, in that case, expect much bigger problems." He still looked unconvinced "Tell me about it."

"Well, to start with, the blast got twelve people killed and left more than a hundred injured. Unfortunately, the whole scene has taken a communal angle. Last month a fight broke out between two religious communities in the vegetable market where one Hindu was killed. The bomb blast is being seen as the response to that." Javed narrated quickly in a way to test the listener.

"Ohh, that is terrible. Have you tried meeting the union

members?" Shankar replied unflustered. "Yes, I did. Could not get a better response than a cold shoulder." "Why is that?" "Don't know, probably because they are extra cautious or even suspicious of everyone."

"Hmm, let us try to meet a few today."

"I suggest not. It is almost like a curfew in that area. People are angry and are ready to believe in any rumor. I am trying to find a house these days where we could set up the union office. By the time it gets done, I am sure the circumstances will also improve. Till then, chill." Javed almost concluded.

"Are you sure? I think if what you told is true then it is a testing time for us as well. We must be there with them and not chilling."

"Brother, you may not like it but I think that the reality is harsher for you. You must take a break and attend to Sanyukta. I don't think she has really slept well since that night." Javed said in a little stern tone. "Perhaps she should stay from me. I don't have a history of people staying with me for long, most of the time they suffer or die. Anyway, I will go and meet the people in the area."

"Perhaps you are wrong, otherwise how am I still alive?"

"Alter-ego... Maybe."

"You have somehow found a reason to support your crazy ideas. I don't support that. Go and talk to Sanyukta, she deserves better than what she is getting from you right now." He almost commanded, for the first time.

"Will think, for now as I said, I will go and meet the people in the area."

"Hmm, you won't budge easily. Well, in that case, I have met the concerned police officers already. I will introduce you to them. It will make it easier for you to roam around in the area." Javed said while sipping the last drops from his tea-cup. He had sensed the obstinacy in Shankar's words.

"That will be helpful. By the way, what is Hari Lal doing?" "Nowhere seen. Although strangely, his wife, Arpita, is often seen helping the victims." "Hmmm, she must be a good lady." "Or maybe a part of Hari Lal's trickery" Javed replied unconvinced "Whatever, only the time will tell." They both emptied their cups and then left from there.

Although unsuccessfully, the two of them tried to meet several people that day. By the time, the sun went down the horizon, their morale too had reached its nadir. Shankar pulled out his mobile phone from the pocket and noticed a few missed calls. Javed noticed and asked, "Sanyukta?". Shankar nodded. "Of course, but you won't care... would you?" Javed said.

"What is the matter with you today?" Shankar asked while sitting on his bike.

"Nothing, I just know that. I felt it myself. You will know it someday too. Let's go." Javed kicked his black bike and accelerated. Shankar, perplexed, followed him.

When they reached home, Sanyukta was not seen anywhere. Shankar called her up but the phone went unanswered. He again tried her phone after an hour but the phone was not answered. After another couple of attempts, he went to his room to sleep. The hours passed sluggishly for him as he went from one side to another on his bed. He remembered the constant presence of her around him for the last few days, he recalled her aroma that filled the air around him. When he moved on the other side of his back, he felt the weight of her body missing from the mattress. In his half-sleep, his arms reached for her for an embrace but returned despondent on not finding anyone there. He missed her terribly. In the morning, he again called her up and this time the phone was immediately answered. The sound on the other end was still sleepy. Shankar prepared himself for a few moments and then he spoke, "I don't want to lose you Sanu... but I don't think that we are meant to be together."

"Why do you say that?" She asked bewildered with a sudden jolt.

"I just know that. I will lose the ones I love."

"Wow... and I hoped that you would come for me. I hoped you would ask why I left yesterday and didn't answer your phone calls. I hoped that I would show that I am upset with you and then you will make it up for yesterday by cheering me up... Shankar, don't let your past be hitched to the present."

"It's a part of my present, my love, you won't understand. There are some invisible strands that are tied to my cursed destiny. I can feel that."

"Shankar... for me it is easier to love and die, than not."

"But not for me to watch everyone but myself stand here, waiting to be left alone by the ones I loved."

"What is it you want Shankar?"

"Not to lose you, and for that, you must go away. You have a wonderful career in the making. I know about the offer you got from Mumbai, go and grow." He said slowly in a disguised positive tone.

"Is that it Shankar? Is that what you want? ....Well, in that case, I will not disappoint you. You won't see me again." The tremble in her voice was even more audible, the more she tried to hide that. A silence followed, broken intermittently by heavy breathing on both sides of the phone. After almost one minute, Shankar said, "Good luck". She responded by disconnecting the phone, anger palpable. He squeezed the phone and closed his eyes. The phone screen broke as the right thumb pierced into it. He put his left hand on his forehead and fell on the couch. Javed came out on hearing the noises. He saw Shankar lying still on the couch. He came closer and shook him. Shankar opened his eyes to look at him and said, "She will survive now."

In the meanwhile, one fine day, as if by magic, the identities of the possible miscreants were disclosed by the local police station. When the police were questioned by some reporters, the officials could not put forward a convincing reply regarding the basis of their suspicion. It seemed everybody was in a hurry as if under an external influence to bring the events to a pre-determined conclusion. And the people responsible for the investigation, it was perhaps easier to circumvent the obligations and responsibilities by using people as stooges. Some arrests were made, cases were filed, the media lauded the efforts of the police, and the local politicians led by Hari Lal came forward, grabbing the limelight and receiving more than their share of applause. Hari Lal also made a visit to the affected area dominated by Muslims. Along with his huge cavalry, he remarked upon them, "Forget about these kids from Janadhikar Sangha. They are selling you false dreams.

Those who have no faith or religion have no identity of themselves. We are the only ones who have always worked for the betterment of you, the minority. Your association with others will only result in such bomb blasts. Stay with us." The listeners took the words of Hari Lal either as a threat or a word of advice, in either of the cases, they more or less agreed with him.

Once the worst was over and the things gradually hobbled to normalcy, Hari Lal, with his political rhetoric and his tall claims, became a common sight in the neighborhood. He provided monetary compensation to the families of the deceased and injured from the government fund. The posters of his image, with folded hands directed towards his arrogant chin, wearing a khadi kurta with a matching Gandhi cap and a Machiavellian smile, were omnipresent.

It had been two weeks since that conversation between Shankar and Sanyukta. Both had not spoken since then. Javed had finalized a double-storey building for the union's office. It was right in the middle of their home and the slum sector of Pratapganj where most of their union members lived. Shankar and Javed had planned to reach straight to the building that day after the morning session at the Martial Arts coaching center, to set up the office. It took them twenty minutes to reach the white colored building, constructed on a 60-meter square land block, in the middle of the two-similar sized blocks. It faced a small triangular park located at the corner of a not so busy street, that comprised of only ten buildings out of total the thirty blocks which were yet to begin the construction. Javed opened the lock of the main door of the ground floor and they entered in. Both assessed the area and then went to the first floor of the building. The entry to the first floor was from outside, so both floors were not connected with each other. Both the floors opened to a spacious hall room with one window on the left wall. An aisle from the left wall connected the hall room with the rest of the rooms, bathroom and kitchen in a line. The ground floor had two rooms and a kitchen while the first floor had only one room with a kitchen. The hall room, therefore, was very spacious on the first floor. At the back of the first floor, there was a window that opened to the green belt declared by the govt. authorities. Shankar came closer to the window and opened it. He noticed two dark-skinned children, almost naked, playing in a sand pile. The sand was perhaps thrown in for the ongoing construction of a neighboring building. Due to some reason, the construction was stopped. However, the children, who knew what the scarcity meant, didn't mind that. He watched and smiled at them as the children innovated a small hill of sand, creating several games in no time. After a few minutes, he moved back to Javed who was busy taking some measurements. They took some mental notes there as well, and soon came out of the building. "We need to buy some used furniture." Javed said standing out on the street. "Yes, and we will need a board as well that reads Janadhikar Sangha to be put outside the office". Shankar contributed.

"Yes. What to do with the plain walls?" "I don't know" Shankar replied slowly realizing where it is getting at.

"Strange that you have not spoken with Sanyukta for so many days. She is a master of reviving lifeless walls."

"You can call her and seek her opinion." Shankar said "Why would I? Unless you want me to..." Javed chuckled.

"I just suggested, moreover, you also needed her inputs on a couple of other matters, if I correctly remember."

"Ok, so you want me to call her. Well, I will now" Javed chuckled again and took out his phone from the back pocket of his blue jeans. Shankar did not utter any word this time and rather anxiously waited for Javed to speak with her. In a few seconds, Javed lowered the phone and looked at the screen. "What happened?" Shankar asked anxiously.

"Nothing, bad reception probably." He said and then dialed the number again. After calling her several times, he said annoyingly, "This can't be a reception issue, the phone is constantly unreachable." Shankar felt a pulse racing through his heart as Javed said that. In a moment, he sat on his bike and kick-started it. "Let us go to her place". Javed complied too.

They reached her place in around forty minutes. Shankar got off his motorbike and pressed the door-bell of the house. A few seconds later, an old lady peeped out of the window and after recognizing Shankar, she started coming out. As she came out in an orange *salwar kameez*, she greeted him with a faint smile. "So, you have come finally. Well, here it is for you." She extended an envelope to him. "What is it Aunty? Where is Sanyukta?" Shankar asked worriedly.

"Don't worry, she is fine. She is a strong girl. But she left. Before leaving she just asked me to give this to you." The old lady turned back to go inside ignoring the looks at Shankar's face.

"But when did she leave?" Shankar asked loudly standing at the door.

The old lady turned back and looked at him, "You are five

days late, son. She waited for you." And then she went back inside her home. Shankar turned, holding the envelope in his hands, he reached for his bike to sit on it. "What is this?" Javed asked who had already come to some understanding after hearing the parts of the conversation between Shankar and the old lady.

"Letter for me." Shankar replied heavily as he opened the envelope and took out the letter. His hands trembled as he read,

"I am leaving Shankar. It was not easy for me but neither was it easy to just wait for you when I knew that you are so close. I was angry at you but not anymore. I believe in destiny as much as you do. So, if your state of mind is a part of a bigger plan of destiny, then let it be. And yes, don't try to find me. If we are meant to be together, the time will come.

A piece of advice for you though, what you have set out to achieve is a great opportunity to define your life, don't let it slip so easily out of your hands. I will always be watching you wherever I am... don't disappoint me...

Wish me luck as well, as I also set-out for another journey... you know what... suddenly it reminds me of the moment when I first left my parent's home... I am really gonna miss you, honey.

See you in the future till then Love S"

Shankar wiped his eyes and then started reading the letter again. "Is she okay?" Javed asked "Yes" "And you?" "Just feeling so small..." He looked at Javed handing over the letter to him.

"Is there no way to find her?" Javed asked after reading the letter.

"There would be, though not easy if she is determined not to be found. You know her, social media shy, barely responds to email, only if it is important."

"Of course, no wonder, she is just like you" Javed handed over the letter back to him "Yeah, just like me..."

He whispered while folding the letter to put back in his shirt's left pocket and then kick-started the bike to leave from there.

That day, he read the letter several times at home. Every time he read it, he went silent. He stayed like that the whole day. In the evening, he folded the letter and put that in one of the pockets of his wallet, like a talisman. He then called up Javed who was out buying some furniture for the new office and said, "We have to regain the confidence of the union members. We can't fail."

"Yes my brother, we won't fail." Javed replied back.

It was a relatively warmer evening. Sitting on his grand teak sofa, Hari Lal read some notes from his blue-covered diary. The golden sofa with pearl embroidery that gave it a look of a throne, was just one of the several embellishments in the palatial house. As he noticed a woman climbing down the stairs to reach the hallway, he spoke loudly but in a respectful tone,

"You need to attend an event with me tomorrow evening,"

"But I told you that I have an appointment with a gynecologist then," the woman dressed in a light blue top and denim jean replied.

"Ahh, leave that. You can always go to the doctor later but this is a political rally. You need to be with me, Arpita," he removed his oval glasses and looked directly at her while re-emphasizing.

“I don’t care Hari. I think you have used me enough. It’s better now that people see you and know you directly rather than a layer of you”. The lean woman with the short stature came forward and confronted the man.

“Ohh, not again. Do you really think that I have anything to do with the bomb blasts?” He turned back his thick neck and started looking at his notebook again. His thick mustache trembled as he breathed heavily.

“You know what you know Hari. I just know that I won’t be a part of your games anymore.” As she spoke with poise, her oval face turned more radiant and her sharp nose seemed to point upwards.

“Arpita, I have told you several times that these are rumors spread by my enemies. You are my wife and you should not believe them,” he tried to reason but in a lower tone.

“Forget it. For me, my visit to the gynecologist is more important, so I won’t come with you,” she answered firmly and then turned back. He, caressing her hair, waved her shoulders and the jerk was received by her slender neck.

“Why? You have been visiting doctors for ten years, but what is the result? There is no chance, Arpita. At least with me, you have some chance.” Hari Lal pleaded.

“Chance? You had your chances dear husband. It is this name of the relation between us that holds me back, otherwise, my upbringing does not allow me to be a mute spectator of the wrongdoings.” Arpita turned back to look sternly into Hari

Lal's eyes and then left the room. He kept quiet this time, perhaps he knew that he had no words to justify himself in front of a righteous woman.

Hari Lal had a small but ardent following. They saw him as a miracle man who could turn the tide in any direction if he made up his mind about it. He came from a renowned family of lawyers. He himself had studied law and practiced it in the High Court for almost a decade before being lured by power into the field of active politics.

EMERGENCE OF THE TORCH BEARER

FOR THE NEXT ONE MONTH, SHANKAR WROTE one email to Sanyukta every day from his home computer and waited for her reply. Disappointed on not being answered, one evening he sat with Javed on the same brown couch in their home. He held a glass of whiskey and took a big swig while his mobile phone played Jagjeet Singh's ghazals. Javed could see the agony in the silent eyes of his friend. "Remember what she said, do what you are set out for.

She is watching you and will come back one day." He pointed out.

The drinks continued, the bottle of whiskey had given way to fill the last two pegs in less than three hours. Shankar looked at the empty bottle, then he looked at his full glass. Then he took his mobile phone in his hand and changed the music to a light soulful old classic. He then sipped from his glass and lingered the taste in his mouth like a connoisseur. Even after the heavy drinking, both of them seemed to be sober. Soon, they both fell asleep on the couch.

The next morning, Shankar reached the union office and had a long discussion with the very few members who still believed in Janadhikar Sangha. Tired, when he came home, he fell asleep. The next day was also spent in a whiff with a busy schedule. The third day, after the day ended, he thought to have a look at his emails. Not expecting anything important, he casually scrolled down till the bottom of the page when suddenly he stopped and carefully started scrolling upwards, the speed of which slowed further as his heartbeat went faster. The scrolling stopped with the heartbeat racing like a marathon runner; the coveted reply was in front of his eyes. He clicked open the email and started reading.

Shankar,

Please do not make it difficult for me. It hasn't been already easy for me, you should know that. You made a choice and now I have made mine, it is time to stand by the choices we made. I have full faith in our destinies, we will certainly meet in the near future. Till then, let us make a promise, we will achieve what we set out for so when we meet in the future, we don't have to face our own failures in each other's eyes.

Love S.

Shankar read the email a few times and then he clicked on "Reply"... he typed, "Dear Sanu,"

He paused for a moment and then deleted what he had typed. He waited for a few more anxious moments, till he finally made up his mind. He discarded the "Reply" and closed the browser window of his computer.

The next day onwards, Shankar along with Javed, set himself out on the mission to break the ice with the people and regain their faith in "Janadhikar Sangha". Apart from the union matters, he only visited the martial arts school twice a week while Javed divided his time in a more balanced way between the union and the martial arts school. When Shankar was not doing anything at either of the places, he often read. As a naturally silent person, he grew quieter the more he read. He spoke only when it was needed, but when he spoke, people listened. Slowly but steadily, people started coming back in the weekly Union meetings. Those days, he was reading a book that he grew quite fond of. Unwilling to leave that at home, he carried the book with him to the union office. It was the weekly meeting day of the union. They had expected to see more than a few participants that day. Javed had set up the first floor for all such union meetings as it could accommodate nearly fifty people. It was an open arrangement where twenty people could sit on the folding chairs, while the rest stood, all facing the front table and two chairs for Shankar and Javed. The meetings were generally planned to start with Javed's opening remarks about the specific agenda set out for the day followed by Shankar's views and then an open session for questions and answers. That day after the opening remarks when Shankar came forward to put forth his views addressing nearly half the capacity of the premises, he still held the book in his hands and firmly placed it on the table. Before he could speak, Moinuddin, who once again had decided to stand with the union, asked curiously, "What book is it you are holding?"

"The Old Man and the Sea" Shankar translated the name in Hindi for them to understand, looking at the book in his hands.

"What is it about?" Moinuddin seemed intrigued by the book cover where an old man was shown bravely fighting with some monster fish in the high sea currents.

"It is a very inspiring story about the struggle of an old man, Santiago, against his misfortune. He was a fisherman who could not catch a fish for several weeks. His failure was so big that even the villagers almost abandoned him."

"Ohh, so what happened then?" Another man in the front queue asked with his eyes wide open with anxiousness.

"Well, so his struggle continued for almost eighty days. On the eighty-first day, he decided to go in another direction. That is where he caught a very big fish."

"Very well. So it ends well finally." Another man spoke from the middle row.

"Not yet, the fish is very big. Much stronger than what Santiago could handle. So, they both fought against each other, both for their survival. Santiago, the stubborn old man as he was, did not let go. Finally, he killed the fish. During the event though, his heart was full of respect for the valiant fish." Shankar continued effortlessly as he enjoyed the storyteller mode of his personality.

"Ohh, so he could have actually left the fish. Anyway, so did the story end?" Moinuddin asked.

"Well, he could have left the fish but he did not. He did not because he was a fisherman, so he remained who he was. So, after he killed the fish, he set himself off for the shores but the scent of the fish blood invited the sharks. So, Santiago's struggles were still not over but he did not give up. He fought back and reached the shore. But, the sharks ate off the fish. What remained tied to the boat was only the large fish-bone skeleton."

"This is sad. So, did his misfortune ever end?" Moinuddin asked in a low tone.

"It did. It ended the very same day when he fought his heart out against all the adversaries. The next morning when other fishermen saw the fish skeleton, so big, tied to Santiago's boat, they all understood what an amazing catch was that. They all felt sorry for their behavior and let their kids learn the art of fishing from Santiago."

"Wow, that was brilliant. So, do you always keep it with you?" Another man from behind asked pointing at the book.

"Not always. I just finished reading it, so felt very positive with this in my hands."

"It is a good one, but is it not just a story? Some people are doomed forever." Moinuddin remarked.

"That is not true. Yes, if you stop trying, then nothing can help you but if you don't stop then you will get your dues."

"But everything has its limitations. We tried as you said but you know what happened... at least, Hari Lal has finally listened to us." A man from behind spoke in low voice, loud enough to be heard by everyone.

"You are so gullible. Everybody can trick you.". Shankar sounded bit annoyed but then a few moments later he regained his composure and continued in a more blaming manner, "By you, I mean those individuals who form the masses and are most prone to getting tricked. You constitute the poor, the middle class and the rich because you all have one thing in common, following something or someone blindly. A Bollywood superstar makes an absolute dud and it still comes out as a commercial success because fans like you, who form the masses go out in blind support. Another day, a technology company comes in and sells another phone without any major advancement but you go out and spend your money on the brand. A politician uses his rhetoric and dissuades you from using your own logic and rationality, and you promptly vote for him. Everybody can see the chaos and destruction but the same people close their eyes like a pigeon as if the cyclone won't hit their homes. They forget that man is a social animal; whatever goes around must come back to us someday. Your rejection of revolt will seal your future," Shankar ended with a rigid calmness. Javed, annoyed by the mention of Hari Lal, stood up and responded angrily, "You are bound to suffer because that is what you want. You have chosen for weakness. If you remain this way, no one can help you."

"But what can we do? We were born this way and this is our destiny. We cannot start a fight with those powerful people." It was the new member, a young man with olive skin and intelligent almond eyes, Ram Kishen, questioning from the left corner at the back.

Startled on sudden opposition, Javed turned his head and looked at Shankar. Shankar pointed at him to stay calm and sit, and then he addressed the young fellow, "You are right, we don't have the resources to fight these powerful people. But that is not impossible. First things first; you must start believing that you were not born to be rejected by the whole world. Once you believe that, then you must realize that respect is not given until it is deserved. So, you all have to become worthy to gain respect from the people. Your belief in a cause will earn you respect and your unity will translate into your strength."

"But why do we need to put in extra effort for respect? Are we not to be respected simply as human beings regardless of any special skill or quality?" Ram Kishen retorted.

"Why should you be respected just because you are born a human? Were you dropped from the sky as a special child or were you born with a blessing from Lord Surya? Why must a man be respected for what he is? In my opinion, you should not be disrespectful to anybody, be it a human or an animal or even a non-living thing; but as far as respect is concerned, it needs to be earned. Just like the story I talked about, one is to be respected for who he is and not for what he is. The "Who" is born from the thoughts and actions taken by the person in life. The "Who" is the outcome of a number of moments experienced in life."

"Babuji, we don't understand these deep talks. These stories are made for educated people like you. My question is simple, can we live a peaceful life where we get quality food and water, and our children can progress to be in higher society?" A middle-aged woman from the middle row asked. Everyone looked at her and nodded in agreement.

"Yes, you can if you want to." Shankar replied.

"How?" She asked.

"First of all, prepare yourselves mentally that you will not quit the path till you achieve what you want, whatever it takes. Then join the path we together lay out for the union. The union will make us a part of the system that will help us to change the system. The union's success will come out of your success and there is no short cut for that."

"I and my family are with you Babuji. We trust you, don't break that." The woman promised and cautioned at the same time.

"We are also with you." A unanimous sound followed and reverberated through the premises.

That day onwards, the union's weekly meetings saw an upsurge of the participants. In a month, Javed had to arrange the meeting in the triangular park right in front of the office building as the number of people outgrew the space in the office.

Time flew. Jandhikar Sangha received a wide acceptance across the region. Mani became an integral part of the union along with Shankar and Javed. With his influence, the union got a few streams of funding. The union also got a second level of management that included Moinuddin, Fatima, Ram Kishen, Abdul and Brijwasan. The hardworking fellows with their sincerity almost dedicated to Javed more than the union, Abdul and Brijwasan strengthened the rise of Javed. Shankar read even more and grew even quieter. Sanyukta was not heard of since that email many months ago. The literacy program and cleanliness drive which the union had started had entered its second year. Several non-govt. organizations and charity associations extended their support to the union. The second anniversary of the union had arrived. As a mark of celebration, Sangha decided to introduce a uniform for the party workers. White and Bottle green were the colors chosen for the uniform as a symbol of peace and prosperity. On the anniversary day, almost one thousand people wore the uniform while traveling across the metro city. The union grabbed the attention of number of eyeballs, many more than even remotely anticipated.

It all seemed to be breezy and peaceful, until one day. That morning, the door knocked. The knock was more like an order than the permission to enter. Suspicious of the beat, Shankar, occupied in the washroom, called for Javed. The knock repeated, this time, louder and sterner. Javed lazily walked towards the door when the third knock took place. This time like a warning. Annoyed with that, Javed still walking towards the door, shouted angrily, "Who is there?"

As he opened the door, a tall man with a fat belly wearing a *khaki* uniform stood on the door. "Hello."

"Hello, who are you?" Javed asked standing at the door. "I am Sub-Inspector Brijesh Aggrawal and this is our constable." "I am Javed. How can I help you?" "We need to search your place," sub-inspector Aggrawal said. "What do you mean? Why?" Javed was even more surprised. "Well, we have information that Shankar is engaged in illegal activities," he replied.

"What the hell are you saying? And who are you to put such allegations on my friend?" Javed was livid.

"Look mister, we have the search warrant. If you interfere in our proceedings, we can arrest you right now. Better that you don't get involved. Here are our identity cards and the search warrant for your reference." The sub-inspector extended some documents to Javed.

"What is happening Javed? Who are they?" Shankar had come out from the washroom.

"I don't know what's happening, Shankar. They are from the police and have a search warrant for this place. They say that you are involved in some illegal activities." Javed quickly briefed Shankar on what was happening.

"Hmm, don't worry. Let us see what surprise they have for us." And then he turned towards the police officials and said, "Come in gentlemen. Please do your duty."

"Sure. You will have to stand outside the house." Shankar and Javed complied, wondering what would happen.

After a search of close to thirty minutes, the constable came out, carrying a bag. The sub-inspector followed him.

"What is in that?" Shankar asked.

"Shankar, you are under arrest. You are booked for dealing in fake currency notes." The sub-inspector opened the bag and showed the stuff lying inside.

"What the hell? This is not my bag!" Shankar shouted.

"Whatever you want to say, say it in the court of law." The Constable put the handcuffs on Shankar's wrists. Stunned at the way the things suddenly unfolded, Javed looked at Shankar in horror. He had never felt so helpless before. He didn't know what to do.

Shankar was taken into police custody and thrown into a cell. Javed reached the police station along with Mani but they were not allowed to meet Shankar. Mani had quickly spoken with a lawyer who had initiated the process to seek bail. But, as the lawyer said, the court hearing would not be possible for at least four days. They all felt helpless. For Shankar, the small cell was now his whole world. The two natural acts of eating and defecating were done barely a couple of feet from each other. There was no provision for taking a bath and his stomach had rejected the jail food he had been given. Hunger had overtaken his finer senses of taste and smell but the digestive system rejected the food. After the first tumultuous forty-eight hours, Shankar laid almost unconscious on the ground. On the morning of the third day, the Sub-inspector Aggrawal came in with his deputy constable Hanumant Sharma. With one hand in his pocket, and carrying his staff in the other hand, the inspector came looking down at Shankar from his pot-belly. He then chuckled on seeing the motionless Shankar and guffawed, "What happened to you O leader? Lying like a dead fish already..."

On hearing that, Shankar moved his head and looked at the guy who rubbed his mustache. He then looked at the deputy who stared at the wall.

"I haven't done anything." He screamed at the policemen.

"Everyone says so initially but later confesses when we use our third degree." The sub-inspector remarked again in his loud manner. "Hanumant, cuff his hands and bring him to the interrogation room. Let me see how strong he is." He ordered to his sub-ordinate and stormed out of the cell.

In a few minutes, Shankar was brought in another room. The

large room of around 30 square meters, was even darker. Despite the light arrangement, the darkness prevailed, perhaps deliberately, so that the room lives up to the expectations of its ghostly past. Reeking of pain and agony, the dimensionless walls seemed to be sinking into the darkness. Getting gently pushed from the back by the constable, Shankar noticed a wooden chair placed at the center of the room. He saw a large drum filled with water just behind the chair. A few meters from the drum on the right side, a large car battery was seen and exactly opposite to that near the left wall, several canes and sticks lay. He closed his eyes for a moment to calm down his heart racing after seeing the visual. He imagined the great physical pain he was about to experience. Just then he heard the sound of boots tapping on the floor. Sub-inspector Aggarwal entered in. "Make him seated on that chair and cuff him with the chair". He ordered the constable.

A few moments later, looking at Shankar with disdain, the sub-inspector came closer to him and said, "You stinking rat, what do the people see in you that they end up following you. Tell me now, since when are you in the illegal businesses?"

"That is not true. I have no connection with that bag." Shankar replied softly.

"Hmmm, so you still have not changed your mind. You don't leave me with any other option now." He reached very close to Shankar and then rotated his chair. They both now faced the water drum. He then ruthlessly grabbed Shankar's hair and pushed his face into the water drum. Numerous water bubbles erupted at the surface as Shankar breathed out in the water. The more he struggled to come up, the more the sub-inspector pushed him down. The chair trembled on two front legs as

Shankar's arms tied behind his back got tenser. After more than twenty seconds, the sub-inspector pulled him out. Shankar coughed hard and gasped for breath. Before he had barely breathed for a couple of times, the policeman once again pulled him into the water tank. Struggling very hard to keep up with life, Shankar swigged in some water. In another couple of seconds, it started getting dark in front of him. Before he was lost into the complete darkness, the policeman once again pulled him out. "Turn him back, I am sure he is ready to answer now." The sub-inspector ordered his deputy and moved away from the coughing Shankar. After a couple of minutes, Shankar could again breathe normally. On seeing his recuperated state, the sub-inspector taunted, "You needed a bath anyhow. So, are you ready to confess now?" After having a near-drowning experience, Shankar was getting prepared for the worse. With nerves in better control and a normal heartbeat, he looked at the policeman and asked, "Why don't you tell me the real story first."

Surprised on the sudden blatant reply, the sub-inspector came closer to Shankar and fumed, "Your friends outside have paid me to not hit you. But they don't know that I have better techniques of torture without actually hitting someone. You will pay for it."

"Cut the crap sub-inspector. You know that I am not guilty but I might confess if I know who is behind all this? I am trying to help you here."

"Hmmm, so you are trying to cut a deal. Very well, you are innocent and we planted the bag in your home the previous day. Also, let us say that you have made yourself some very strong enemies who will destroy you. Now, will you confess?"

"Who is it? Give me the name."

"You are not ordering me here. And yes, no names. If you were smart enough, you could have guessed it. After all, politics has never been for the weaker ones."

"No names, then no confession." Shankar replied sternly.

"You bastard, I will show you who is the boss." Sub-inspector rushed towards the car battery and pulled it towards Shankar's chair. Then he looked at Hanumant and yelled, "Where are the power cables?"

"Should be there in the corner where you are standing sir." Hanumạnt pointed.

It was the darkest corner of the large room which had an almost invisible pile of several peculiar things, the power cables one of those. The sub-inspector moved his hands in the dark to find what he was looking for. In that dark, he touched something slithery and immediately felt a strong bite on his hand. He pulled back his hand and turned back screaming with excruciating pain, "Turn the lights on, something has bitten me."

Hanumant quickly reached the light switch at the entrance of the room and turned it on. By the time, the eyes adapted to see in the light, they could only spot a long black serpent tail disappearing into the sides of the wall. The sub-inspector had collapsed on the floor. In a few minutes, other policemen took out the unconscious sub-inspector and Hanumant escorted Shankar back to his cell. When they reached his cell, Hanumant said slowly, "It was me who planted the bag in your house." Shankar looked at him in distrust. "I didn't have any option, I am sorry." said Hanumant and lowered his eyes before moving out of the cell and locking it.

Each moment thereafter, Shankar felt more restless. The unbearable moments behind the bars seemed endless. He struggled to stay afloat and then gradually sank into his own misery. Right when the situation had become unbearable, he was summoned by a constable. A visitor had come to see him. "It must be an influential visitor who could get permission to meet me," he thought.

He was right. The visitor was indeed influential, for she once did influence his life with the most memorable touch and tender love.

His eyes grew bigger with astonishment as he saw the familiar face. Before he could say anything, he noticed an expression on her face. Behind the bars, he kept quiet and waited for her to approach. Sanyukta reached closer to him and whispered, "No one knows that we know each other. Pretend that way." Then she started a formal conversation with an introduction of herself and the reason for their meeting.

Just after a minute, a policeman turned up to remind them that the time for the meeting was over.

"I will come again tomorrow for much longer. Be ready for the interview. And yes, just remember one thing, even if you are a prisoner of these walls, don't be a prisoner of your mind. Good bye, and see you tomorrow." Sanyukta quickly stepped away from there. She then thanked the policeman with a pleasant smile and took leave from there.

Shankar felt the same energy that he had felt earlier being with her. He went back to his cell with a new vision and a stream of thoughts filling his mind. He saw the same walls of the cell and thought of carving his thoughts on them. He asked for a pen and the constable, Hanumant provided him with one.

The constable, Hanumant Sharma, belonged to a very poor family from the interiors of Haryana. The price he had paid to get this job was too high for a poor family like his. His salary could barely take care of their basic requirements. The destitution and debt he incurred to get the government job were pushing him to the sort of immoralities so common in his profession. At the age of thirty-five, he was still unmarried. The eerie loneliness, financial pressure, responsibility for his parents and two younger siblings, lack of direction and purpose in life, an occupation he had no love for and the frenzy-creating effect of testosterone: together, all these reasons had slowly but steadily resulted in the loss of mental peace and the burgeoning of sleep disorders. He saw a reflection of his own innocent self in Shankar.

Shankar started scribbling on a piece of paper. He wrote, "Who am I?" This simple question made him think deeply. He remembered his childhood, remembered his parents, he thought about his struggle when he was rejected by the people around him and the day he killed the leopard and the manner in which the whole world embraced him. He remembered the serene face of Sanyukta and he remembered his friendship with Javed. "Life has not been that cruel to me. I have beautiful memories and I have people who look to me for suggestions. I must have been able to solve some of their troubles or I might have given them some hope which could bring life back to them. But what is it that I was born to do? How to understand that and what if I fail to achieve what I must achieve?

"*The soul travels*. It is not a matter of achieving something specific in this lifetime. There is no destination; instead, life is about a journey which has no final end. Death does not end the journey because the soul does not die; it travels and comes back in another body, form or shape. And with the soul, the wisdom it acquired in the previous body; also travels. So, one day the soul becomes enlightened and understands the matrix of this universe. This might happen in this lifetime or the next or the next. But it should not matter because our aim to learn and gain wisdom, and to gain real knowledge of this tricky world is only possible through experiential learning. For that matter, I am blessed as I have more experiences to relate to than at least 80 percent of the people in this world."

The thought comforted him and he stretched out, and fell into a deep slumber, devoid of any dreams.

Sanyukta had given him a time of 11:00 am. "What if she doesn't come or what if she is not allowed to see me this time?" he worried. No, she would get permission; in fact, she might have already got permission. She had probably become an influential person; because nobody else was allowed to come and see him. What had she meant by an interview and why did she want to do that? Shankar was lost in thought when Hanumant Sharma reached to take him to another room. He understood that she was there already. Suddenly, he felt a rush of blood on his cheeks. As he walked the intimidating aisles of the prison, he thought of the time spent with Sanyukta. He breezed through the hideous walls and nothing seemed to bother him. He thought of the day when they both last talked over the phone, he recalled the thirty emails, he had written to her after she had left. He remembered the one email that she had written back. "Should I be angry for she never wrote back in the last so many months... Or what if she is still angry with me? How should I react, oh, I must be looking filthy in these stinky clothes?" Numerous thoughts bombarded his head but the confusion was easily won over by the anxiety of meeting Sanyukta. Soon, he entered a closed chamber where Sanyukta sat on a folding aluminum chair. As she saw Shankar approaching, she stood at her place and smiled at him. Shankar returned a feeble smile as he reached for the chair kept opposite to Sanyukta. The constable, Hanumant Sharma asked

Shankar to take the chair and announced that Sanyukta had thirty minutes to finish her job. Thereafter, he came out of the chamber and stood at the door. Both Shankar and Sanyukta looked at each other, he with surprise and curiosity, she with pain and agony. She then asked first, "How are you?"

"Can't say much." His expressions changed as he heard the familiar comforting voice.

"Don't worry, I have got something for you." She lowered her eyes as she noticed the helplessness in Shankar's eyes. She then picked up a bouquet from behind the chair and extended to Shankar.

"Oh, is that for me? Wow, after so long?" Shankar felt rejoiced on seeing the flowers.

"Yeah, after so long. And don't worry about keeping them watered, the flowers are not real." She said with a warm smile as she passed over the bouquet to him. He took the flowers but didn't pull the hands back as his hands touched the warm hands of hers. The tender touch that had smoothened all of the rough patches on his soul was missed for months and that day he was in no hurry to miss that again.

"That is unlikely of you. You always loved real flowers Sanu." He said softly.

"Only till you got them for me. Now I like them on the branches." She replied in the same soft tone.

"Apart from that, you don't seem to have changed much. You still look lovely in your favorite white *kurti*."

"Hahaa, thanks. Though I think I have changed in more than one way. I am conscious of what I eat now." She said with a shy smile as she found the same old admiration in Shankar's eyes for her.

"Look at you, you still blush the same." Shankar pointed mischievously.

"Stop it, Shankar. We don't have much time honey." She pulled her hands back and then looked at Shankar with the pleading eyes.

"Oh, I almost forgot. So, you are the boss now. I am sure since you have come here, you would have a plan. But before that, very quickly, brief me what happened after you left Delhi."

"Ok. From here, I straight away went to my home town and stayed with my parents for a few days."

"Wow, that must have been great."

"Yeah, it was for the first few days. But after that monotony started taking over once again. To add to that, there were many memories of my brother that still bothered me. So, after a few days, I decided to leave."

"I understand. It must have been difficult for your parents to let you go again."

"Yes, it was. In fact, they had even started looking for a suitable man for me to get married to." She chuckled.

"Oh, wow. You can't beat Indian parents, can you?" Shankar replied teasingly.

"For sure. Well, after that I straight away went to Mumbai. You knew about an offer I had from Mumbai?"

"Yes, but only that much. You never revealed the details, otherwise I would have easily tracked you sweetie."

"Yes, I know. So that is it. After that, as I promised, I was always watching you. It is easy in my professional world" She said with a dignified smile.

"Lucky you, as I had no clues of your whereabouts." He sighed.

Sanyukta paused a bit and then continued, "I know honey. Anyway, I got to know about your arrest. Coincidentally, I had volunteered for a study in Delhi at the same time. The growing pollution has become an environmentalist's favorite and my boss, Mr. Swayambhu Das knew about my old study done on the similar subject."

"Swayambhu Das? I know this name. "Do you mean the Swayambhu Das who runs the biggest online portal for citizen journalism in the country? Mani often talked about that man in high respect."

"Yes, the same Mr. Das. I work for him now. What a dynamic personality! He walks faster than a teenager at the ripe old age of seventy. A huge fan of Devanand, he always hums the songs from his movies. We can really make out how he is feeling by the song being played in his office." She giggled.

"Very well, must be an interesting person to meet."

"Yes, he is. He often says that whatever we are doing right now to make this world better, the results will be seen after three decades and the best will be available for the next generation."

"I feel that he is right. I realized that nothing would change for a couple of elections as the change has to happen at the grass-root level. And all of us are responsible for such a movement and will remain responsible even in the distant future, in the same body or in some other form, because the soul will keep on traveling anyhow."

"Interesting thought... *the Soul travels.*" Sanyukta said it loud as if trying to connect with the thought. Then she expanded on it, "It has traveled through times, rough and shining, it has learned the ways of the world and has acquired un-perishable wisdom which is carried to the new body to take up the work exactly from the same point it had left off. Nice thought... In fact very optimistic as it makes me feel comfortable to know that none of my good actions will go wasted because all the wisdom I acquire remains with me for eternity... Good one Shankar, you are a better philosopher now." She smiled affectionately.

"Hahaha, thanks Sanu for the elaboration. You too have become better." He smiled and touched her cheeks softly.

"Hahaa, thanks. Well so now as we speak, Javed and other core members of your union have been trying to get in touch with you but there is massive external pressure on the police, as it seems, because of which no one could get in touch with you. As I understand, this could only be politically motivated."

"Hmm, so it is a trap. Any idea who could it be?"

"Could be anyone but given the circumstances, my first suspicion goes to Hari Lal. You have straight away influenced his largest voter section."

"Ok, I get you. Any suggestions now?"

"You bet. I have a workable plan. With the media on your side, we can build a more considerate atmosphere for you. So much that even your foes will find it difficult standing against you."

"I understand what you say but it is easy to be said than done. And this might take months. For me, even the thought of spending here another minute kills me." He groaned and lowered his head.

"I know honey but it won't take months. Just so you know, everyone outside is fighting hard for you. We have filed the petition for your bail in the high court. It will be heard this time." Sanyukta consoled brushing his hair with her pointed fingers.

"This time? What happened last time?" Shankar asked.

"As I told you, there is a massive external influence on everything related to this matter. I could come here only because Mr. Das pulled some strings. Your story will be in the media from tomorrow. With the strength of Janadhikar Sangha and the media, the judge this time will have to grant the bail."

"What would be the story?" "The story of you, as the philanthropic leader and the victim" "Ok. Do what you have to do." "Excellent. Now just tell me everything you know or recall about this incident."

Shankar told everything including what the two policemen had told as Sanyukta made quick notes. As soon as they finished, Hanumant Sharma entered and announced that the time was over.

"Please, just two more minutes." Shankar pleaded to the gentle policeman. "Ok, I am standing out. Please come out by yourself in two minutes." Hanumant Sharma granted the request and moved out.

"Sanu, I don't know when will we meet again but there is one thing I want to tell you." Shankar turned to Sanyukta and clasped her hands in his.

"When you left, I realized how much I loved you. Most of my thoughts were there in the mails I wrote but there was one thing I wanted to say in person."

"What is that...?" Sanyukta asked anxiously.

"I imagined us as the ocean and the sky. We both see the colors of our souls in each other just the way the ocean and the sky see their reflections in each other's existence. But....they both never meet. I don't want to love you like that anymore, because I want to spend the rest of my life with you and for you." Shankar said, the four eyes grew moist and the hands clasped even tighter. A few seconds passed in the embrace of the revered silence. Realizing the urgency of the time, the hands then loosened and both stood up to move out of the room. Both took small steps side by side, her head leaning on his right shoulder and the right hand on his chest, his arm curled around her back to the right shoulder.

CAGING THE SEER

OVER THE NEXT THREE DAYS, SHANKAR'S story became the most followed one on the news portal run by Mr. Das. The fourth day, it grabbed decent space in a national newspaper. The readers connected with the aspirations and agony of the common man through Shankar's character in Sanyukta's story. The story was moving and with the discontent among the youth of the nation, it turned into the talk of the nation. The story threw direct questions at the political rivals of Janadhikar Sangha and motivated people to come forward and expose the opponents.

Devi Dutt, being vigilant and extra cautious of the final outcome tried to turn the tide in his favor by befriending the Janadhikar Sangha management. He connected with Javed and Mani promising them his support. Desperate to get Shankar out of the jail, Javed and Mani welcomed any help from anyone, including Devi Dutt.

On the other hand, Shankar still waited to see himself as a free bird. Sub-inspector Aggarwal was still recuperating from the venomous snake bite and in his absence, the station in-charge gave no importance to Shankar's case. Strangely though, Shankar's appeal for the bail was once again rejected and no one including Sanyukta was allowed to meet him, despite of all the pressure surmounting the case. While it fueled the anger in the union and all the believers in Shankar's innocence, constable Hanumant Sharma increasingly felt restless, perhaps out of guilt. One morning, as he received some orders from his superiors, he straight away rushed to Shankar. Oblivious of all the happenings around him, Shankar calmly laid in his cell. Hanumant reached him and asked slowly, "How are you, Shankar?"

"I am alright. How are you?" Shankar answered calmly hiding his surprise on seeing the constable suddenly.

"God's grace. So you will be with us for some more time."
"Yes, even if I don't wish to."

"I understand. Anyway, just be careful Shankar. You are being sent to a larger cell. It will have other inmates too. I didn't understand the logic to it, but someone might try to use those inmates against you. So be careful." Hanumant hushed.

"Ohh, but how can that happen in prison?" Shankar asked in the same low voice.

"Well, prisons are the battlegrounds where a lot of wars raging outside are fought." He replied in a philosophical manner.

Soon after the quick conversation, Shankar was moved to a cell which had another inmate named Raghu. Raghu had been sentenced to ten years of imprisonment for an attempt to murder. He had tried killing his own daughter to protect the so-called honor of his family when she expressed a desire to marry a man outside their caste. He was a tall man with large hands and narrow shoulders. He hailed from the eastern part of Delhi and belonged to an affluent landowning family. His thick dense hair was very short and his small eyes had a certain coldness that iced the warmth of human relationships. His tough skin was as harsh as his stern attitude that formed the basis of his principles and caste-based sentiments. Shankar tried to converse with him but Raghu disliked him from the start and abhorred his presence. He refused to even acknowledge Shankar's presence in the same cell and continued with his activities as if he were alone. Shankar found it a bit weird and tried to break the ice a couple of times, especially because he wanted to know more about the prison. But after a few failed attempts he too submerged himself in his own thoughts and notes. Hanumant helped Shankar to keep on writing by supplying pen and paper whenever required. It went on for almost ten days and then on the eleventh day, Raghu spoke to Shankar, curious to know what he was writing. Shankar was pleasantly surprised at first but then he regained his state of mind and told him that he wrote because the activity helped him get the answers for the questions that constantly stormed his mind.

"How is it possible? How can you get replies from a pen and paper? Don't try to joke around." Raghu reacted in both anger and disbelief.

"This is no joke. I actually get answers." "Ok, how does that happen?" Raghu raised his left eyebrow and asked in a sarcastic tone.

"Well, let us first introduce ourselves. I am Shankar," Shankar saw the opportunity to break the ice.

"Shankar....what Shankar? What is your full name?" Raghu asked first time with a genuine curiosity

"I know what you mean, Raghu. These are the kind of questions, why I write and try to find out answers."

"Hmmm, so what is the answer you got?" his tone got even more sarcastic.

"The answer is that it does not matter. My full name doesn't matter, definitely at this stage."

"You are an idiot. Now I am certain of this. On this planet, your identity is of utmost importance and nothing else matters. And here you are, a moron discarding the importance of his own identity." Raghu spoke bitterly.

"Well, thanks for the adjectives. But as I said, that does not matter," Shankar said with a smile on his face.

"What do you mean and why are you smiling?" The calmness on Shankar's face was making Raghu agitated. The wind coming out of his left nostril moved the greying hair of his mustache with every breath.

"Raghu, when a new thought or idea arises, it is first insulted, then opposed and then accepted. We are still in the first stage. And I am smiling because I can see the future of our discussion." Shankar smiled again.

"Ohh, so now a fraud is talking of being a seer. What irony? What a joke of the legal system of this country? And that is why you intend to hide your identity so that people don't look down on you and your caste," Raghu jibed.

"Raghu, as far as I know, the caste system was based on one's work and occupation. Later, nepotism took over and powerful people used it to their own advantage. As far as I am concerned, by birth I am a Hindu Brahmin but I don't practice any religion. Though perhaps by occupation I am still a Brahmin as I believe in educating the people around me. If you also wish to be taught, you are welcome." Shankar said eloquently with a serious look in his eyes.

Raghu kept looking at him for some time and then went back to his corner without discussing it any further. He did not speak the next day. Shankar did not try much to initiate a conversation either because he understood that Raghu was immersed in thoughts and this was a good sign.

With the help of Hanumant, Shankar's days in prison were made slightly better and this gave him the courage to spend the otherwise torturous time. He waited for the coveted freedom while the next plea date for the bail in the higher court was still a few days ahead. Raghu's silence continued for another week. That evening, Shankar was biding his time when the door of their cell opened. The policemen were holding a dark and stout man with bulging red eyes. They pushed him inside, took off his handcuffs and locked the door once again. The silence was suddenly filled with a feeling of hatred and the smell of blood.

The new entrant was called Bala. When he entered, he looked at both the inmates and then stared hard at Shankar. Shankar looked back at him and tried to greet with a hello, but Bala ignored it. Raghu, more tacit than ever, gave no heed to the new member in the cell. He continued with his thoughts.

The lights were dimmed after dinner. Somewhere in the middle of the sky, two stars shimmered, fighting with the darkness. The blackness of the sky and the two stars together looked like a huge black serpent with two eyes covering the length and breadth of the ether with its broad fangs. The night was an invitation to all the dark forces of the universe.

Shankar, at peace with himself, was deep in slumber, dreaming of a new start when he would come out into the world, he belonged to once again. Suddenly, a shadow emerged from within the cell. It moved stealthily towards Shankar. The very next moment, another shadow emerged behind it. It followed the first shadow and soon disappeared into the darkness. A few moments passed and nothing happened. There was the same eerie silence, only disturbed by Shankar's sporadic snores. A few moments passed and then suddenly there was a hand movement, followed by a movement from the second shadow which quickly grabbed the arm of the first. Perhaps the first shadow had not anticipated this resistance and retreated suddenly, but it was held too tightly to turn back. The shadows then grappled with each other, making noises that woke up Shankar. He stood up and tried to look into the dark to understand what was happening. There was a sudden shrill shriek very close to Shankar's ears when lightning struck in the sky. In the eerie blue light, he saw the whole scene. He saw the two bodies standing, blood spilling from Raghu's body. In an attempt to free himself from Raghu, Bala plunged his knife into him again and again, wounding him grievously. Fortunately, due to the very limited movement of his tightly held arms, Bala's stabs were only wounding Raghu without putting his life in danger. Shankar shouted for help. Suddenly, with Raghu's grip loosening, Bala managed to swing his arm on one side to give a lethal stab into Raghu's stomach, Shankar leaped forward and caught his arm. The three of them grappled and fell onto the floor in a mass of bodies. The lights came on and someone came running to their cell and threw the door open.

It took a while for Shankar to adjust to the light. A few moments passed before he could see properly. To his consternation, he saw that his right hand was clasped on the blood-soaked dagger sticking out of Bala's body. Raghu was sitting on one side, his head between his knees.

The police immediately took over the place. They removed the dead body and handcuffed both the survivors. Later, both Shankar and Raghu were sent to separate cells. Both were booked with the case of murder and all visitors were once again denied any chance of meeting them.

A new investigation team was being set to investigate the fine details of that night. Hanumant, aware of the facts after talking with Shankar promised to set the things right. He went to the sub-inspector Aggarwal and sought his recommendation to be a part of the investigation team. Sub-inspector Aggarwal, still in the hospital readily honored his request. On his recommendation, Hanumant became a part of the investigation team that included three other policemen apart from him.

AN UNLIKELY HELPING HAND

THE SHADOW WITH THE ARMS FOLDED AT the back kept moving from one corner of the large hall room to the other and then there was a cold but worried male voice, "So, you mean to say that you have failed again?"

"Unfortunately, we have sir." The voice was scared.

"I don't believe it. Such a well thought out plan cannot fail just like that... Is it not possible to put the murder charges on Shankar?" enquired the first man.

"I doubt it, sir. During the investigation, Raghu will definitely be interrogated. We cannot make him disappear as he is the prime witness. He is already a murder convict who is not afraid of anything and to our misfortune, he seems to be on Shankar's side. And once he is questioned by the court, he will testify that Bala tried to kill Shankar while he was asleep and Shankar, in an attempt to save himself and Raghu from Bala's attack, tumbled over which resulted in the accident. As a prime witness, his words will be honored by the judge."

"Humm, I understand but if the prime witness is Raghu why don't we get rid of him?"

"I don't see a possibility of that. He is locked in a cell without any inmates and there is very tight security around the both of them. Even their food is tested before it reaches them. So, we cannot even poison them."

"I don't care. I want this man. Shankar must rot in prison for years to come. He is a problem that we must get rid of." The first man spoke with sudden rage in his voice.

"I understand sir, but you should not worry. This is the reason why I am here, a part of their Sangha. I will certainly get many opportunities to sort this thing out. But for now, I think we should stop pushing. Let us wait for the right moment and then we will strike back."

"Ok, in that case, let us push for the Plan B. Do not fail me this time or else..." The voice of the shadow got even colder. The other person who understood the threat nodded his head and quickly slithered out of the building. On the other hand, Shankar, all alone in his new surroundings of the new cell, with the fresh memories of the fateful night, struggled once again with his sleep. The almost forgotten demons buried under the thick layers of pleasant memories, resurfaced haunting him in his dreams. He had seen too many deaths around him and that time he was the medium and an active participant that caused the death. He felt like puking as the moment flashed through his mind. He tried to control and think about something else but the dying eyes of Bala did not leave his mind. The more he tried to think about something else, the more the image flashed through his memories. Soon enough the whole scene of that night was in front of his eyes. He saw the paling face, he smelled the blood and the fecal waste of the loosened bowels. He saw the red-hot eyes bulging out. Notwithstanding the visuals, he puked. And then he laid down on the floor. The visual had still not disappeared. He looked into the dying eyes and suddenly the eyes changed the color and the shape. He recognized those eyes. He remembered the curse in those yellowish eyes of the beast. The retribution still continued and he desired for salvation more desperately than ever.

With Devi Dutt also campaigning on Shankar's side, the media embraced Shankar's public image as a philanthropist and the recent attack on him, the court intensified the process and ordered a speedy investigation. The media invited people to come up with any evidence that could help the court reach its decision fast.

Finally, the investigation team received the forensic reports which said that the fingerprints on those packets of fake currency notes belonged to somebody else, not Shankar.

Later, while the investigation team searched for the real culprit, Devi Dutt helped with a tip through some unknown sources, that had the details of Hari Lal's international bank accounts.

On further investigation, it was brought to light that many transfers had been made to an internationally renowned money launderer who had also been booked by the international bureau of crime for counterfeiting. The team prepared a plan to gather Hari Lal's fingerprints. This was not tough. One of the team's female members met Arpita under the guise of a destitute lady. Arpita, as expected, took her to her house and gave her the job of a domestic worker. After this, the lady just had to steal a glass tumbler with Hari Lal's fingerprints on it, which was done the same evening. The forensic report reached the investigation team the next day and clearly stated that the fingerprints matched those on the packets. Within a month, Hari Lal was booked for serious offenses like conspiring against the motherland and was put behind bars.

After days of guilt of the vile night, Shankar finally had a relieving moment when he was granted bail. Javed, Mani, Sanyukta, and several others reached the court to take him with them. The memories of the night, though had enveloped his mind completely. He could not think of anything else even with Sanyukta back in his life. He stayed like that for two days. Then he started talking with Sanyukta. He talked about his days in the village, about his mother, the father he barely remembered, Javed, Sanyukta, Mani, his job, his ambitions, his dreams, his aspirations, his confusions, his weaknesses, his strengths. He had relived his past and started connecting the dots. It is said that when you kill someone, a part of the killed one seeps into you. That part haunts you till eternity and curses the very existence of the person. With time, that part only grows, putting the weight on the soul. Only a few with a soul as pure as the water from the snow glaciers of the Himalayas can have the audacity to lift such weight and throw it off one day to be free once again. Shankar was trying hard as well, it was onto his soul now to connect with the universe and show him the path. In his sleep, he started getting visions of people with the same faces but different identities associated, amalgamated in one. He tried to peep into all those personalities to see his real self.

In one vision, Shankar stood with his chin high, hissing like a vindictive serpent and pouring venom on everything around him; in another, he was sitting exhausted under the sky and watching the stars with a thumping heart and disdain towards the world. In yet another, he saw a small boy, deep in sleep, well-guarded and protected in his mother's lap. A bit farther, there stood a man with a bare torso, pale skin, long, wavy and messy hair. His eyes sparkled and the very long legs lifted his head above the clouds. There were numerous wounds on his limbs but still, he stood as steady as a rock. He could identify himself in all those visions. He longed to be the small boy curled in his mother's arms once again. Then he tried to control the anger and make the venomous reptile stop hissing; he started empathizing with the sorrows of the world and saw his own sufferings abated. Then, he tried to see what lay above those clouds. The world above was an exact replica of the world beneath. The very same people who wounded his limbs down here tried to tear his eyes with the sharp edges of blades, but somehow the sparkle in Shankar's eyes mesmerized them and their fatal blows fell elsewhere.

The last vision remained with Shankar for a long time. He tried to think deeply but could not fathom the meaning of it. As always, he wrote to solve his dilemma.

There are no different worlds and there are no different people. The world and the people in it are all made of the same thoughts and emotions. The only factor that separates them is a clear conscience. People might travel everywhere in search of happiness but all of them find the familiar melancholy around because the fact is, there is no 'there' which is better than 'here'. Your world is what you want to perceive. Foes can become harmless and adverse circumstances can become a joyride if you look into the eyes of the force opposing you and say, "Hey, I know exactly how you feel. I have felt the same. I too have complained and I have been through these dark shadows many times. But don't worry, the phase will be over soon for it is the misery we all are suffering with. Just check on what you desire because what matters most is the volition behind every act. Your volition will guide your conscience and a clear conscience will take you towards the coveted journey in the same world, right here. Just don't stop exploring; you too will be fine, one day."

In the company of his friends and his love, along with his introspective writings, Shankar transformed into a newer person free from the guilt of that fateful night after nearly two weeks. A new person who was back in his old surroundings, for he was declared not guilty by the court as well.

PART 3

EMERGENCE OF A THOUGHT

RESURRECTED SHANKAR SAW NO EVIL & held no grudges against anybody. To his happiness, Sanyukta got a longer-term assignment in the same company in Delhi. With Sanyukta back in his life as she moved in with him, his home had once again the aroma of lavender.

Javed didn't resist the move. In Shankar's absence, he anyway used to sleep in the office more than at home. The workaround arrangement in the office had become more of a habit for Javed as even after Shankar's return, he genuinely preferred to sleep in the office. His room in the house still remained intact but when for the first few days after Shankar's return, he slept in his room, he missed the cold walls of his office. Once, he had learned about his aspirations during thousands of conversations with his friend Shankar. Lately, when he missed his confidante, he carved out his dreams on the bare walls of the union's office. He used to spend most of his time in the office when Shankar was imprisoned. During those days, he met thousands of visitors, who came either to enquire about Shankar or discuss their problems, all of them showing their support for Javed and his aspirations. He had developed a strong followership for himself who wanted to stay close to him and impress him by their work. Well aware of his extrovert but short-tempered nature, the people around him contrived to keep him pleased. When alone, he talked with the walls, put the posters relating to his desires on the bare walls and felt as if he is giving his own life the direction he wanted. He regularly spent his early mornings and evenings in the martial arts school every day. Known for his fury, unrestrained in the absence of Shankar, people took him for an exceptionally strict taskmaster. Consequently, both the union and the martial arts school witnessed better results in their operations. Much more confident of his capabilities, Javed had already targeted for the next general elections.

Oblivious of Javed's yearning, Shankar started his normal life outside the prison walls with the Martial Arts School first. He decided to take it slow and started working on his physical and mental health for some time. Soon enough, he made a visit to the union office. When he reached the office on an early cold morning, he looked at the once white walls turned into a collage of the pictures. The posters ranging from the rhetorical statements of several world leaders to the beautiful sceneries covered the walls. At some places, he noticed a few pictures of beautiful foreign locations, some places were covered with breathtaking shots of amazing cars. A bit astonished on the change, Shankar looked at Javed who stood beside him and remarked, "Quite a change brother."

"Yeah, just like that." Javed chuckled while hiding the surprise he felt after suddenly seeing Shankar in the office.

"So what is the plan for today?" Shankar asked while seating himself on a chair.

"Don't worry much, you take it easy. I will handle. And yes, we are going to Mani Kaka's home in the evening. You and Sanyukta, both be ready for that." Javed said in a lighter vein.

Shankar nodded in agreement. Soon the area was buzzing with people. Everyone wanted to meet Shankar. They all came in on a regular basis and after spending a minute or two with Shankar, they moved to Javed to discuss the real matters, spending much longer with him. By lunch time, Shankar had met quite a few people. The conversation with most of them had the same pattern. He wished in his mind not to meet any more people. Just then Javed said, "You must be tired. If you want to then go home or go to the martial arts school. A new batch is starting today. I will handle here."

Relieved to listen that, he quickly agreed and left the office for the martial arts school.

He reached home in the evening and lay down on the couch waiting for Sanyukta to come. Soon she arrived. On seeing him lying on the couch lazily, she asked with exigency in her tone, "Get ready. We are going for dinner at Mani Kaka's home."

Shankar looked at Sanyukta, who still looked crisp after the day-long work, in her neatly tied hair at the back and her embroidered brown top and white jeans. He then lazily stood up from the couch and went into the washroom. In a few minutes, he was ready as well in a sky-blue collar t- shirt and black cargos. Javed had promised to reach Mani's house directly from the office so they left on Shankar's fiery-red color motorbike. On the way, they halted to get a gift for their host. Sanyukta selected a bonsai plant for which Shankar insisted to pay. From there, they soon reached Mani's house. Javed too reached at the same time. Shankar approached the doorbell and rang it. The familiar street and the surroundings had always a calming effect on both Shankar and Javed. After a moment, Mani appeared from behind the closed door, now wide open welcoming the visitors. With a warm smile, he directed them all to come upstairs. Nothing seemed to have changed since they had last visited Mani's home almost a year ago. The brown color chaise was exactly at the same place adjacent to the matching divan. The medium size wooden dining table with six chairs too was firmly seated at exactly the same place in front of the kitchen where they saw it the last time. "Exactly the same." Shankar remarked slowly.

"Yes, that is the only thing common between me and Mani. We both don't like many changes or as we should say, we resist changes." Mani's wife approached them along with her quintessential tone, studded with good and bad remarks. She looked a bit weary in her informal tone augmented by her loosely draped brown and black cotton saree. Shankar, facing her directly smiled and then greeted with a hand-folded *namaste*. Javed and Sanyukta greeted her as well. Manju replied with a smile and requested them to get seated. She then went over to Sanyukta and held her hands in hers. "Heard a lot about you but strangely it is the first time we are meeting after these many years."

"Yes, *Bhabhi.* I am very pleased to finally meet you." She said formally. Then she glanced at Mani and continued, "I have always complained Kaka to bring you over but he always skips that talk."

"Ohhh, him and his long list of things to do. I deliberately stay away from his multiple misadventures." She sighed, "When are you both getting married?" She asked.

Perplexed on the sudden direct question, Sanyukta looked at Shankar, who looked surprisingly prepared for the question. "Any time soon *Kaki,* any time soon." He replied.

"You better do that. You won't find anyone better than her. So pretty she is." She looked at Sanyukta and patted on her head softly. "Let me get you all some water now." She said and went for the kitchen leaving everyone there looking at each other.

"So how is it being back in the union?" Mani asked Shankar while sitting in his brown couch.

"Just got back Kaka. No hurry. And anyhow I may not be even needed, Javed has handled very well." Shankar replied casually.

"Why are you saying that? You are needed brother, as always." Javed interjected in an uncomfortable tone.

"Of course I am always there for you. But I think you are in full control of the things now. And anyhow, I got involved only to help you." Shankar said slowly and moved his gaze uncomfortably from Javed to Sanyukta.

"I always believed that you had your heart and soul in the union and that is possible only when your aspirations are also associated with that." Mani asserted.

"Mmm, I don't know Kaka, perhaps it was true then. Perhaps it is past now." Shankar replied hesitatingly while looking at Javed who ignored any gaze at him with his head lying low and eyes firmly set on the floor.

"What is your opinion Javed?" Mani poked

"Ummm, I can't say much Kaka. Shankar is independent to take his own decisions. I will support him. Moreover, he knows his strengths and weaknesses better than anyone else. Maybe, he is too soft for politics." He looked at Mani and quickly replied.

"Hmmm, why would you say so Javed? You know that he has always stood by you and the union. One needs ample courage and strength for what he has faced." Mani said rather annoyingly, while Sanyukta looked at Javed in distrust.

"Don't get me wrong Kaka. Shankar himself had said that he is there only to help me and he was never interested in politics. Now is the time for the real game when we prepare for the elections. You know well how difficult it was for him after that bomb blast. I had almost lost hope on him, though he came back." Javed replied in the same annoyed tone.

"He went to jail for the union Javed, don't forget it." Mani said strongly.

"I knew that you would always take his side. Anyway, what he did for me and the union, no one will ever forget. The union still belongs to him as much as it does to me. But if he is not interested, I won't push him. By the way, when I said that the real game has just begun, it meant a lot. We are almost there to join hands with Devi Dutt and that would boost our chances before the elections. Now he may not like that idea as well."

"Certainly not Javed. This indeed is a bad idea." Shankar stood and gave a fierce look at Javed.

"And by the way, whom did you discuss it with? The core team is here and none of us knew about it. The union will lose its appeal, its identity and its existence if it gets associated with the mainstream political parties. And for that matter, you will lose the elections Javed. That is not what you want." He continued.

"But..." realizing his mistake, Javed kept quiet.

Then he looked at Shankar and said in a stern tone, "The union was just a thought until I vouched for it. I will not let the thought be lost, just like that. It has to grow and outgrow everything else. We will talk about it later."

Shankar nodded in agreement and then asked Mani to put on some music. Mani, slightly uncomfortable by the just unconcluded conversation stood and turned on the FM radio channel that fortunately played their favorite old Hindi number, lightening the mood.

Sanyukta noticing the strange looks on the men's faces, stood up and went inside the kitchen to help Manju serve the food.

A few minutes later, the food was served which everyone ate off in the melancholic silence of the old Hindi songs.

The next day, Shankar did not go to the Union office. He spent his time at the martial arts school and at home reading books. Javed came very late and went straight to his room avoiding any slightest chance of discussion. Sanyukta came at her usual time and spent the rest of the evening mostly watching Shankar engrossed in the philosophical world of his books. Next couple of days passed very much the same way until one day when Shankar left the book he held in his hands on the arrival of Sanyukta. He proposed to prepare the evening tea and straight away went to the kitchen. A few minutes later he served the hot tea in white mugs with some chocolate cream biscuits in a white glass plate. Sanyukta quickly joined him on the tea. He noticed the light pink woolen jacket that she wore and asked, "Is it not the same old jacket that you brought back from your home?"

"Yes. It is." She softly replied.

"Hmm, I thought so. Missing your parents?" He asked.

She nodded.

Shankar grabbed her hands in his and said, "One promise I make to you today, I will never ever give you a chance to miss me."

She looked up in his eyes and smiled. The glint in her eyes was visible/augmented by the tiny water drops in them. Both then picked up their tea mugs and said together, "Cheers for the togetherness."

After spending the next few hours together, both went in their room to sleep. Javed was still not home. Sanyukta soon went into her slumber while Shankar could not stop thinking about tomorrow. The tomorrow, he had been planning for the past two days. The tomorrow, he could not wait for. The tomorrow, he didn't know how would that play out. The tomorrow, he was going to broach the subject of marriage. The tomorrow, he was going to put up his life's first proposal. The tomorrow when it's Sanyukta's special day, her twenty-ninth birthday, 12th November, 2012.

SOULS MEET

THE AROMA OF LAVENDER FILLED HER nostrils the moment she entered the home. She noticed Shankar uncharacteristically bothered about the ambiance of the home and his own attire. No attention was ever paid to externals - body or surroundings. But that was a special day, visibly special by the efforts Shankar had put in selecting his light blue polo t-shirt that were tucked in the faded denim jeans adorned with the black shoes, black belt and a black camel-leather jacket. Sanyukta looking vibrant in her cream color fur jacket, smiled, trying to hide her thoughts from Shankar for she wanted it to be as natural as possible. As all women do, Sanyukta too had an extra-sensory perception and ability to peep into her man's heart and mind to see what resided there. She, the intelligent and the intuitive beauty, had seen the proposal coming.

They were basking in the warmth of a beautiful evening. They had a romantic outing, spent some quality time together after many weeks, hands clasped while strolling at dusk at the India Gate, and eyes locked on to each other's as if hypnotized while sitting on a rickshaw. Now, finally, the subject of marriage was to be broached by Shankar.

Shankar was aware of Sanyukta's aspirations and knew well of the wide difference between their ambitions. His laid back and contented approach towards life was no match to the racy outlook of the world, she had and felt to be a part of. He was cautious and well aware of the fact that their journey together may not be on similar paths but he had planned to improvise a bit in order to make this union a happy one. The idea of living together as husband and wife and having a real family, his own loving family, had always tempted him, for this was something he never had.

He thought a bit more about how he would initiate the discussion and while he was gathering the courage, Sanyukta spoke teasingly. "Stop tapping your feet, Shankar, just speak out." Shankar's expressions suddenly morphed as he swam through a number of emotions and finally settled for an embarrassed look. Sanyukta laughed even louder on seeing this and then she looked away to control herself.

"Let us get married," Shankar spoke hurriedly and then he

stopped breathing for a while, as though anticipating a negative response.

"Wow, that was quick. By the way, how unromantic was this proposal? I was waiting all day for you to ask, though in a much smarter way, and here you are with one straight question. How can one marry you, darling?" Sanyukta giggled and continued to tease him.

Realizing that he was being baited, Shankar relaxed and breathed normally as he spoke. "I know, I am not very articulate. But the fear of hearing a 'no' was so strong that I lost my nerves. It is good to see you laughing and not scolding me for this." Shankar spoke with an affectionate smile.

"Oh, come on. I would never scold you for saying such lovely things. But since you said you were afraid, please tell me why," she asked with a wink. "Well, I don't know actually. The last time you left, I was a complete moron. Honestly, I am never being able to make out when I am being stupid to such an extent until the damage has been done." Shankar spoke softly.

"Hmmm, I see. Well, if you listen to me then I can almost always tell you when you are being stupid." She laughed lightly and then continued, "This is about the fears but tell me one thing, why do you think we should get married?"

Shankar looked into her large eyes, his feet not tapping anymore, in a matter of few seconds, his facial muscles relaxed and then he took a deep breath before speaking, "With you, I feel complete, I forget about my past and my earlier sufferings meet a natural death. When you are not around, I still feel strong because the memories of time spent with you make me survive one ordeal after another. I may not know how you feel about me. Women like you are not easy to see through and understand." Shankar continued after a brief pause while Sanyukta hadn't even blinked, as if not willing to let go even a nanosecond from that moment.

"But I see the deep emotions you feel for me, with me. We are two different people. But then we have many similarities too. In that sense, we both complete each other because our worlds are not limited by our similarities or differences. Our similarities make us understand each other and the differences make us understand the world. In you, I see the reason to keep breathing. Due to you, I find the world more interesting than ever. With you, I feel connected to the universe... These are just some of the several reasons why I want you to be in my life. Will you marry me to become an inseparable part of my life?" Shankar went down on his left knee and took Sanyukta's right hand in his hands.

"Now that is called romantic. I love you." She grabbed Shankar's hands and pulled them around her waist. Shankar pulled her closer and lifted her up to look straight into her eyes. Sanyukta pushed her face closer to Shankar, her mouth close to Shankar's ear and whispered, "Let's get married." And then, as if in a daze, she laid down and started undressing. Shankar removed his shirt and pulled Sanyukta towards him. As the breathing became faster their embrace became tighter, the world collapsed in the warmth of their passion.

After some time, both of them lay naked, looking into each other's eyes as if peeping into each other's souls and acknowledging the comfort of the other's presence. "Love, ably supported by sensuality is like meditation. It transports the souls into a zone of fulfillment," Sanyukta whispered before she fell asleep. Shankar saw the tranquillity on her face. "Hardships can never plunder her innocence," he thought, before he too soon fell into a deep sleep.

THE TEMPEST WITHIN

IN A WEEK, JAVED CALLED IN ALL OF THE union's senior members for a strategic meeting. He hadn't spoken much with Shankar so far after the last discussion at Mani's home but nonetheless, Shankar made it to the meeting along with Sanyukta, Mani, Ramkishen, Brijwasan and others. Javed, dressed in a long blue *Kurta* and a faded jean, took the centre-stage and narrated his vision for the union. On the first floor of the union's office, standing with his back to the new life-size poster of Fidel Castro, he emphasized openly to enter the world of real politics and gain power. Most of the union members supported the thought. In Javed's pursuit of power, their weak spirits got bolstered. Towards the end of his long but passionate rhetoric, he surprisingly made a declaration that the Janadhikar Sangha will not join hands with any other political outfit and will rather fight alone. He also requested everyone and Shankar in specific to support the union before and during the elections as they go out and fight the giants alone. By the end of it all, everyone including Mani and Shankar didn't have much to object against. Shankar promised his support to the union and so did everyone else before the meeting approached its final stage of discussion on the scale at which the Union will contest.

With the inclusion of Janadhikar Sangha in the political arena, the environment had started heating up. Javed as the face of the Sangha was pitted against the seasoned politicians, Devi Dutt as one of the heavy weights. With a thought of being cautious about their extraordinary ambitions, the Sangha decided to contest the state elections only on five seats in the areas close to their central base of operations. Together, the management committee decided that they play small for now and go full throttle in the next elections.

The state of Delhi had a total of 70 seats in its legislative assembly. The Sangha had to decide on the names of five people who would be fielded for those five seats. While Javed had already been decided upon, the other four names were still being contemplated. Mani, Shankar and Sanyukta decided to stay away from directly contesting the elections, making a straight headway for the next four Ram Kishen, Brijwasan, Moinuddin and Fatima. Though people did not know much about Brijwasan's past, they did not care either because, during his comparatively long association with the Sangha, he had proven himself to be an intelligent man. People saw him as a shrewd and sometimes arrogant fellow with strong acumen to think big, and deliver results. He and Ram Kishen had established themselves as the perfect event managers. He had developed strong relationships with the other vendors and suppliers and negotiated very well to get the best value for every penny spent. He was adept at handling operational hurdles and was very effective at managing crowds too. He had mentioned to a few close confidantes in the Sangha that he had a young daughter who lived with her grandparents, small-time traders in a village in Central India. His wife had died soon after giving birth to the girl due to excessive blood loss. He had to leave his village in search of a job, leaving his young daughter with his parents. He had not returned to the village since he joined the Sangha.

Ram Kishen was long term working partner of Brijwasan, and unlike him, his life was an open book. He had been born in the same neighborhood he now lived in and brought up by his ailing parents who had passed away by the time he finished his teenage years. He had an olive complexion, thick dark black hair and narrow, inquisitive eyes. He had a habit of moving his long arms when speaking, and he used this habit to his advantage while addressing the gathered mass of the Sangha followers.

He had always been a smart kid and was one of the few in the neighborhood who had finished high school. Ram Kishen was an extrovert and a good communicator, and always tried to make people smile with his childish pranks and sense of humor. Though he had not been able to attend college, he was naturally good at Mathematics and loved to play with numbers.

In the factory, where he had started working as a laborer, his penchant for numbers was recognized by his boss and he was shifted to the accounts department to work as a junior assistant to the accountant of the company.

Married at a young age to his childhood sweetheart, he was blessed with twins, a boy and a girl. He had a stable life with a loving family and an accounting job that he enjoyed.

The preparations for the elections had begun on a war-footing and the time seemed to be always sprinting ahead of the deadlines. A potter's wheel was selected as the party symbol, reflecting the Sangha's vision of shaping a new society. The responsibility for financial arrangements through fundraising had come on Javed and Sanyukta.

Mani got extremely involved in his task of a deeper demographic analysis of the constituency while Ram Kishen supported him. Mani also worked with Shankar to prepare a proposal to be sent to the Governor requesting a bigger place for the party. They together detailed the social and charitable events organized by the party, catering to the masses of the local community. They attached the pictures of the education program run by them and also highlighted the pace at which the people were getting associated with the party. Believing in Mani's connections and their insightful work done on the proposal, Shankar was quite hopeful for the proposal to be accepted.

In the cacophony of the preparations for elections, while everyone seemed to be up to something, Shankar struggled to find his place after the proposal was sent to the Governor. His head still stuck in the evening when his marriage proposal was accepted, he often resisted the meek attempts to come out of the intoxicated state of mind. Adding to his woes, he hadn't got a chance to share the news with his best pal Javed. He had told everything to Mani but he never got an opportune moment to have the coveted chat with Javed. Waiting for his moment, he continued drifting away from the moments of action.

Few weeks into the campaign, the working team was missing a brain that could strategically project the union to the people with an identity, they could connect with. Mani suggested the hiring of a professional to strategically create a public image for the Sangha and its leaders, especially Javed. Brijwasan rose to the moment and promised to find the right people for the job. Within a short time-span of two weeks, the Sangha had hired a professional PR company, Brijwasan had made in the roads with.

The account head for the agency was a hardnosed, introverted, reserved, pragmatic and extremely professional woman, Krittika. Her piercing stare seemed to see through people's pretense. Her natural understanding of human psychology and her flair to improvise on the fly had bestowed her so many colors that her real-self had become invisible to the world. What could be seen now was a masked woman who was independent and took complete charge of her job. It was rumored in her world that she had managed to climb the corporate ladder at a rapid pace outsmarting and outwitting many, sometimes those more capable than her. It may have miffed many people, but she calmly refused to acknowledge the resentment aimed at her. With a lit cigarette in one hand, mobile phone in the other, and the glint of a smile in her eyes, Krittika had taken giant leaps. Within a fortnight of her employment by the union, everyone was astonished by the passion with which she took control of everything and everybody to get her job done.

As it seemed, the ruthless pace at which the work had started, was merely a starting point. Shankar, in order to stay close to Sanyukta, forced himself in the union's work once again, successfully to a certain extent. In between, they got some time together when they would talk about their marriage plans. They both decided to defer the plan until the elections got over while also keeping the news only to themselves till then. As he engrossed himself more into the work, he realized how close he once was to the union and how much the people still looked up to him for almost everything. The realization slowly gave him his confidence back and he started opining more freely than in the past few months. As he started sharing his views on different subjects, the people once again started flocking near him. Very soon, Shankar and Javed, both immersed in the preparations, were often surrounded by a special coterie of people separately. He and Javed still had not spoken much, apart from the general small talk or something related to the work. While Shankar felt the difference, no one else could notice in the heat of the preparations. Javed had almost moved himself to the office, so any chance of them meeting at home was also denied.

Krittika's job demanded staying close to Javed. She always carried her laptop and was often seen making notes as she observed something. She spoke less to keep people, including Javed, guessing about her; but whenever she did, she did with authority. To Javed's relief, often during the evenings, in the relaxed aloof moments, she came out to be quite a coquettish woman full of surprises. The days briskly passed and Javed felt more and more intrigued towards Krittika. While, once again no one paid any heed to the sudden change in expressions of Javed when in the company of Krittika, Brijwasan noticed. One rainy cold evening, Javed practiced his speech in front of Brijwasan. After a couple of shaky starts, Brijwasan proposed, "I think you should practice it in front of Krittika madam. She can really help you to make it all better." "Should I?" Javed hesitated.

"Definitely Sir. She really knows how to present anything. Don't you remember how well she set-up our agenda, manifesto, the design of our emblem and so many other things in such a short span of time? I think if it were not your major and her minor but significant contribution, we would not have come this far."

"Yeah, you are right. Others have also contributed but as you said, my major and her minor but significant contributions are probably the most important ones." Javed slightly bragged. "Right, let me just call her for you. She should be here in the building, I guess." As he left, Javed leaped towards the washroom. He poured some water on his face and then wiped it with his hands looking himself in the mirror over the washbasin. He looked at his eyes and then touched his two days old facial hair. "Oh, I should have shaved today... or it should have quickly grown to fuller stubble." He thought to himself. Then he quickly moved his hands through his hair settling them down. He adjusted the collars of his white Kurta with both of his hands and then rubbed his hands over his chest downwards so as to eliminate the wrinkles from the *kurta.* He then came out and started watching the poster of Fidel Castro with his back towards the entry door. In a few minutes, he heard the footsteps approaching, which he correctly guessed to be of Krittika. He noticed his pulse getting bit faster just before he heard the tinkling voice from his back, "What are you watching there?"

Javed, after having rehearsed several times in his head, turned stylishly to his back and replied, "You know, this guy had brought nuclear missiles from Russia to Cuba during the Cold War period, directly challenging the might of America and guess what... America could not do anything against him. Now that is called true power. What do you say?"

"Well I would say, you are right. But that is not absolute power." Krittika moved her head and along with it moved her long gold earrings. "What do you mean by that? What is absolute power?" Javed moved forward, interested to know more.

"The power you are talking about is to be earned. You work for it. But the absolute power happens to you. You don't necessarily work for it." "Hmm, give me some example." "God is the perfect example of having absolute power. In human beings, though not even close to such a scale, you can see some people automatically being the epicenter of any activity even if they resist it or are not interested. They just happen to be the center of the power circle."

"I understand you now. I think I am also getting there. People are around me and I am frequently feeling more powerful than ever these days." Javed flaunted with a hesitation "Don't take me wrong but you want this power so you work for it and hence get it. Look at Shankar, he doesn't want anything and still, it's like the power begets him." Krittika jibed.

Javed completely unprepared for such a blunt answer, remarked, "Ridiculous. You clearly don't know much about him. He is the weak one who could not... Leave it." "Oh come on, don't take it personally. All I am saying is that despite his obvious resistance, he commands the things around him and he gets the best for him. He has the best girl and the best of friends."

"Best girl? If I wanted, I could have always had her. I just didn't wish for..." Javed clearly miffed, gritted his teeth and then turned his back towards her. "Sorry, sorry... my bad. Let me make a coffee for you." Krittika went to Javed, held his right arm and gently pulled a chair for him. She then went into the kitchen and brought a tray to make coffee for them. The big office table quickly turned into a coffee table with two brown glass mugs, one white electric kettle, an instant coffee jar of Nescafe with black lid, sugar jar, a bottle of milk and a torn packet of cookies.

While she made coffee, she coquettishly looked at Javed who soon had started cooling down. A minute later, as he saw Krittika making coffee, he complained, "Once again you have put extra sugar in my coffee," "Oh, is that so? Sorry about that. Anyway, you need more sugar, perhaps it will make you sweeter," She teased.

"Oh, so now you mean I am bitter as well?" Javed asked, raising a brow. "Not bitter, but bitter-sweet," Krittika giggled. "Now what does that mean? You women always tend to go beyond reason. Always mysterious and complicated," Javed tried to tease her back. "Ummm... we are complicated and that is why we are so desired." Krittika leaned back with a smug smile. "Yeah, I know. Everybody knows what men want and desire but the real question is, what do women want and desire?" Javed flung back.

"Why do you want to know? Are you flirting with me?" Krittika suddenly snapped back and Javed got embarrassed.

"No, of course not. I am just trying to understand women." "Just kidding, baba. You look so cute when you are embarrassed." Javed blushed and then all of a sudden Krittika spoke in a different tone. "I desire the man who is not a shadow of anybody, who can snatch from the world whatever he wants, who doesn't follow but is being followed and who can shower the world's best things on me." The seriousness in her voice made everything else fall silent. After a few moments, Javed broke the silence. "Oh, that is good to know. You are fortunate because at least you know what you want in life. Well, for now let's practice my speech." "Sure, let's do that." The next hour, they practiced the speech before Krittika left for her home. That night Javed could not sleep. He perpetually thought of Krittika and what she had said in the evening. That night he desired to be a different man, a man who could make the difference anytime he wants. He rolled from one side to the other on his bed till very late. The sleep had abandoned him and his dreams had begotten him. The dreams had turned into desires and the insatiated desires grew that night to clobber his mind and soul. By the time he finally fell asleep, all he could envision was himself.

Not much time was left before the elections. The next morning, still dizzy from the avalanche of thoughts from the night before, Javed lazily squirmed to the mailbox at the main door. He opened up the letterbox to see the letter from the governor's office. As he opened the letter and started reading, his eyes opened wide with excitement. Their request for the party office was accepted. The letter delivered a day before had strangely missed several eyes but still made it to the right hands just at the right time. They were proposed a place, an old govt. gucst house, that once used to cater to the high-profile visitors of the Mughal emperor. The guest house was located on the outskirts of the once dense forest spread across thousands of hectares of land in the east of Delhi and was the favorite hunting spot for the royalties. Not far from their current office, they had never even imagined to be once roaming in the open air of the Guest house that although was very old, still carried the aroma of the royalty in it. Javed immediately called Mani thanking him for his efforts and then went inside the washroom to come out ready to go and see the authorities. He then called up Brijwasan and started the process to quickly occupy the place and convert the old structure into the party office. Some renovations were needed but they decided to move in and let the renovation also take place at the same time. At a nimble speed of work, the party occupied the guest house only in a couple of weeks. Javed reserved one large room for his office and appointed Brijwasan to allocate the rooms to each one of the key members. The government-owned guest house was built in 2 acres of land. It was located on the extreme outskirts of Noida that was a part of Delhi NCR making it difficult for the commutation. No public transport was available in that area. The ailing building structure gave the feeling of an old man who still could stand erected and was willing to move without the support of staff. Despite the excessive dilapidation caused by the neglect, the structure still had strong pillars and walls. The time could embezzle its beauty but the strength still remained imbibed in its air. But with the strength, another feeling floated in very strongly... Pride. A mind full of cluttered and misleading thoughts like that of Javed was the easiest target to get affected with that. A certain sense of superiority gives rise to a lack of compassion for others. The conceited mind, when surrounded with the sycophants has the tendency to become autocratic.

Javed's behavior had been changing fast. He grew a stubble that made him look even more authoritative. He refused suggestions from others and dogmatically started forcing his thoughts and plans on the other members. While Brijwasan followed him blindly, most others were more cautious. This further agitated Javed and he openly demanded loyalty as he projected himself as the prime face of the Sangha. Mani and Shankar tried to talk to him a couple of times to smoothen the dissidence but he remained unmoved and adamant. Shankar thought the sudden change in behaviur was due to the anxiety and pressure of the situation. He counseled the members and told them that soon it would be fine and nobody would have a reason to worry. But Shankar himself was getting increasingly worried, though he did not share it with anybody else. Sanyukta too was witnessing the changes in Javed's manners and was surprised when Javed talked down to her in a tone that he had never used. She noticed how Javed behaved in Krittika's presence. She didn't think much about it but somewhere deep down she sensed the root cause for Javed's change in behavior. "Power corrupts but obsession destroys," she liked to tell herself.

One day, when Javed was sitting beside Krittika, he thought of asking her out. "Lately, you have been keeping extremely busy, Krittika. You should take a small break." "Oh yes, I want one so badly. But then I think that I should let the elections come to an end. After that, I could have all the time off to take a long break."

"Hmmm, you are right. But a small evening break to go watch a movie or visit a pub might be a nice idea. You can give some attention to your personal life too, your family, parents, boyfriend..." "Boyfriend? I don't have one, Javed. Either they could not afford me or they don't entice me... simple." She smiled.

"Interesting. Can't afford you, I understand that. But don't entice you... what does that mean?" "Well, as I told you once, I want a man who apart from being wealthy and a leader should also be highly desirable. Now look at Shankar, he has power in his hands and he has such a stunning woman beside him. He is desirable according to my standards," Krittika said calmly.

Javed was visibly perturbed on hearing Krittika's words. His voice quivered as he spoke. "What are you saying? I am the face of the Sangha. And that girl, she worked in a bar. I told Shankar to ask her out. Shankar was unable to woo her for himself, so I had to step in and do it for him. And you call him desirable...Huhh." He sounded more agitated by the time he finished speaking.

"Oooh, somebody is jealous. I don't believe it though. If you had proposed then, she could have been your woman and not his." Krittika mischievously shrugged off what Javed had said. "What do you mean? You don't believe me? I could have had her for myself any time I wanted. And I am not jealous, I am just trying to point out that Shankar is not as desirable as you think he is…"

"Calm down, dear. I was just kidding. Do you want some coffee? Let me pour some extra sugar for you to be sweeter." Krittika laughed at seeing the irritated look on Javed's face. Javed sat quietly waiting for Krittika as she went out to bring coffee. When she came back, he quietly gulped the coffee and left from there.

Krittika's words echoed in his ears the whole night. He was still disturbed the next day and didn't interact with anybody. While others just shrugged and moved away, Sanyukta could not stop wondering what was happening to him and decided to talk to him.

It was a rainy evening two days later when Sanyukta called Javed and asked him to meet her in the office. He was pleasantly surprised and wondered why Sanyukta would want to meet him alone. He left the meeting soon that he was attending and set himself up towards the guest house, now their party office, with the mind in a whirl weaving a web of illusions. It is said that purer the soul, the higher the risk for it to be adulterated, just like Gold that gets corrupted from the impurities so easily that it has to undergo a whole transformation process to attain the purity it possesses.

Javed reached the premises and walked towards Sanyukta's office room to meet her. Quite late in the evening, he took long steps under the sharp drizzle, in the open sideways of the premises. He entered the backside of the Guest House where Sanyukta had set up her office. His black sneakers almost soaked in water, didn't make any noise as he stepped on the tile floor. He soon realized that no one else is in the office. He glanced through the glass window of Sanyukta's room and saw her working on her computer. Her feet tapping, eyes fixed on the computer and the one end of the blue pen she held, under her teeth. Javed opened the door and entered the room.

"Hey, how are you?" Sanyukta suddenly jumped from her seat as she saw Javed come unannounced. "I am fine. You are looking lovely in this white *kurti,*" Javed replied with a smile. "Thank you. I am glad that you have some time to look around finally," Sanyukta said teasingly.

"Umm, I didn't understand. Is that a complaint?" "No, Javed. You are so close to us that we can't complain." Sanyukta pulled her chair close to Javed while speaking and then she continued. "But lately, we have been worrying about what has been bothering you. We care for you and that is why I thought of talking with you." "Who is 'we'?" Javed was visibly irritated. "See, that is what I am talking about. Why are you upset with everybody these days? I want to know what is bothering you. Please tell me," she requested. "Nothing Sanyukta, nothing is bothering me. And by the way, why does everybody think that I am fighting with everyone? I am just trying to be in control. Please understand that I am already aware of things and they need not be explained to me again. Period." Javed spoke with rising irritation.

"I knew that you won't give in so easily. Strange that you don't even share with your friends now." Sanyukta spoke with clear indignation. "Friend...?? Common, leave it." Javed said sarcastically. "What does that mean Javed? Don't smirk, say it out loud."

"Well, I have no friends. I have just been a follower for you and today when I try to do things on my own, it is objectionable to you. Why is it that everything good has to be associated with Shankar?" Javed spoke with a raised voice. "What are you saying? You are friends. What has gotten into your head? I don't understand. Is Krittika teaching you all this crap?" Sanyukta said angrily.

"What is it to do with her now? See, you guys can't deal with my happiness. Everything about me has to be objected to. It's not about her, it's about me. I am much more capable than what you possibly could ever believe. It's hard for you and Shankar to accept the fact and that is why you are trying to bring my progress to a halt." Javed came closer to Sanyukta and pulled her up to face him. Sanyukta was taken aback and she resisted, trying to get rid of his grip.

She cried, "You are hurting me Javed." "No, you have hurt me, just leave me alone." said Javed and pushed her back. Then he looked at Sanyukta with a certain disgust and left from there.

THE BRAVE RISE FROM THE ASHES

28TH NOVEMBER, 2016. IT WAS A COLD morning. Javed was getting ready to address a large audience just five days before the election day. Mani stood beside him like a rock to support him on this last lap before he reached the goal. Sanyukta had discussed the incident with Shankar. Feeling for his friend, it had dawned upon him that Javed could be feeling anxious and trepid before the big day. He had calmed her down and asked to give Javed enough space so he could work out the things his way, anticipating that things will get better once the elections were over.

Javed had discussed his speech with Shankar and Krittika. Deep inside, he was feeling a void after the incident but he could not muster the courage to talk about it. He believed that Shankar knew everything about his outburst that evening even though Shankar did not give any sign of it. He tried to avoid any confrontation with Shankar and Sanyukta but the work demanded otherwise. It is said that, to reach the equilibrium, the two extremities must be reached once. The humiliation he had felt and the internal upheaval he had suffered with had started making way for a better understanding in his mind. The old steadfast Javed was rising from the ashes. He had started talking with everyone once again bringing the things to ease. For her surprise though, he tried to avoid Krittika and didn't talk anything else except work-related stuff. The fall which took him to a chasm of oblivion had also produced an opposing force, leading him to a higher level. He could not face Sanyukta still and cringed as he thought about that fateful evening.

It seemed Lady Luck was on Javed's side, but destiny loses its significance if it can't catapult everything to its advantage at the very last hour. Javed, Shankar, Brijwasan, Mani and Ram Kishen were being driven in an open jeep followed by a large crowd of more than one thousand people, on motorbikes, cars, jeeps, bicycles, rickshaws and on foot. Everybody carried the flag of the Sangha and for a moment it seemed as if the world was painted in saffron. The crowd cheered and shouted slogans for the Sangha and for the motherland.

Suddenly, as if in slow motion, Javed collapsed following a thudding noise, his hands waving to the crowd as his body fell from the jeep. The whole cavalcade halted and Shankar jumped down from behind the jeep to collect a gasping Javed in his arms. Javed was bleeding profusely from a bullet wound.

Ram Kishen rushed to the driver's seat and put the jeep into the gear. Mani quickly came down and started moving the crowd, making way for the vehicle. Shankar took Javed's body in his lap and tried to keep him conscious. The jeep roared and honked, moving through the crowd and rushing to the closest hospital. It took fifteen minutes for them to reach. Mani had already called the hospital, asking them to be prepared for an emergency situation. The hospital staff was waiting to receive the wounded leader, who was still miraculously conscious. Javed was immediately taken to the operation theatre.

Everybody sat in the lobby, waiting for the word from the surgeon. The fear of losing someone close had gripped everyone.

Sanyukta got the news and rushed to the hospital. She saw Shankar sitting on a couch, staring at the floor while tears rolled down his face. She reached him and held his hands in a tight grasp and said, "He will be fine." Shankar looked up into her eyes. He tried to speak but failed. Then he pressed her hands into his face and sighed heavily. In a while, he felt a little better and raised his head to speak to Sanyukta but the words remained unuttered as a nurse approached them and gave them the news. "The operation has been successful. We are hopeful that he will survive now. We will wait until he regains consciousness."

The next day, Javed gained consciousness. He was warmly

welcomed by three people he recognized immediately. “Welcome back, my friend.” Shankar was the first to greet him. “Thanks, brother.”

“God helps the brave, my boy,” Mani said. Javed thanked him for the wishes and then he looked at Sanyukta. That one shared glance was enough to confirm it: Javed had apologized and she had forgiven him. Then a relieved Javed spoke, “You guys have not slept for ages, damn it. Look at your eyes. Go now. I am absolutely fine.” The three of them looked at each other, then they smiled at Javed and said, “You take rest. One of us will always be here for you.” And then Mani and Sanyukta left. Brijwasan, Krittika, Ram Kishen, Moinuddin and many other union members tried to meet Javed but he was asleep for most of the next two days. Finally, it was only a day before the elections when Javed was able to meet them.

Krittika and Brijwasan came together on a brief visit to meet Javed. They left quickly on the pretext of preparing for the election day.

While the election fever had gripped everyone, Shankar was anxious to get to the root of the shooting incident. Every bad moment also has something for a takeaway, just the way even a faulty clock tells the correct time twice a day. Shankar, during his toughest times in the jail had his share of takeaway in the form of the policeman Hanumant Sharma. Since the day of the shooting, Shankar had been in constant touch with him. He called him up again.

“Hello Shankar, how is Javed now?” Hanumant answered the call “He is much better. You tell me how the investigation is proceeding?” “Can’t say much. Something is bothering me. There is immense pressure from top to bury this case.

Moreover, we still don't have any clues. As I told you last time, we might only know the building where the shooter was probably positioned and we know the type of gun that was fired based on the bullets. I have asked everybody in the building if they saw anybody entering the premises. Nobody seems to have a clue." "Hmmm, is it not possible that somebody living in the building is behind this incident?" Shankar asked. "No way. Nobody would take such a huge risk. This looks like an attempt by a professional killer. These people work from the shadows." "Hmmm, well, keep on trying my friend. Let me know if I am needed and please keep me posted." "Don't worry. The most important thing is that Javed is very much among us and that makes the opponent much weaker. You must stay careful. Your lawyer has managed to get police security for Javed. So, there is not much reason to worry. Take care."

The day of the election saw a record in voter turn-out. Almost 80 percent of the voters had come out to cast their votes. A week later, the results were a clear indication of the mood, with a thumping victory for Janadhikar Sangha. It was all seven seats it had contested for. Now the other parties needed its support to form the government in the national capital because no party had got a clear majority. Devi Dutt's party came out to be the largest but still fell short of the majority. The political warfare had started.

Javed was asked to take bed rest for at least a month. The time alone in the hospital bed gave him ample opportunity to think about his mistakes and the way ahead, chalking out the best path for his future. Shankar and Mani were heading the union's stance on the govt. to be elected. In the process, they met Devi Dutt and other leaders of the state. As it was coming out, the five seats of Janadhikar Sangha had become extremely critical for the govt. formation. Devi Dutt's party was seven short of the majority mark of 36. The other two parties which were national in presence had won 20 and 14 seats respectively. The party with 14 seats was the incumbent one and had clearly struggled after their local leader Hari Lal had gone to jail for the crime he committed against Shankar. There were several offers coming towards Janadhikar Sangha's way. Devi Dutt too reached out to them with a proposal. He was ready to give out two ministry portfolios to them in return of the support. The decision had to be quick as all the parties were ready to submit their plans to the governor for his final decision. Shankar and Mani had a quick chat with Javed, Sanyukta and other team members and they decided to support Devi Dutt.

After maneuvering the way for Javed to get him Education and HRD ministries in Devi Dutt's cabinet, Shankar came back to the union office. Relieved to see Javed alive, Shankar was unable to withstand the eerie silence that had descended over the leaders of the Sangha post the shooting. He could sense danger lurking but was scared to believe that the prime danger was from somewhere within their close group. On the other hand, Mani too had some suspicions which made him extra watchful, and Sanyukta started keeping an eye on Krittika. She was always wary of Krittika, especially after the radical changes she had seen in Javed. Before discussing it any further with Shankar, she decided to clarify her doubts with Krittika on her own. She thought of talking it out with her on the coming Sunday, as that would be a relatively relaxed day for all of them.

On Sunday, Sanyukta woke up early, but felt a little off, for some reason. She was feeling dizzy and as she stood up, she suddenly felt the urge to barf. For a few minutes, she could not understand the reason for her sudden sickness and then something struck her. She immediately took out the medicine box and pulled out a pregnancy test. When she came out of the bathroom, the glow of happiness was evident on her face. She picked up her phone to call Shankar. While scrolling through the list, she halted at a number and looked at her mobile for a few seconds. It had been a long time when she had spoken to her parents. She thought for a while and then she pressed the dial button.

"Hello?" "Hello, Papa."

"Sanyukta!" There was a brief moment of silence and then before her father could continue, Sanyukta spoke. "I am sorry, Papa. I am sorry for hurting you so many times."

"How are you and where are you calling from?" "I am fine, Papa. I am in Delhi, not too far from you." She smiled.

"Not too far, then. So, when are you coming home? We have been waiting for you for a long time, my daughter." The voice became heavier.

Sanyukta sensed the sadness in that voice and quickly replied, "Very soon, Papa. In fact, I also want to meet you and tell you many things."

"Hmmm, looks like our daughter has found the prince of her dreams. Is that so?"

"Ummmm, I don't know, maybe, Papa." Sanyukta suddenly blushed and then quickly changed the topic. "I will meet with you all and we will have lots of fun together. Tell Mummy that I will be home soon. Right now, I have to go and see somebody, so I will call you in the evening to tell you about my plans. Say hello to her. Love to you both. Talk to you in the evening."

"You are just the same! Talking like an express train. Talk to you in the evening. Bye!"

She then went into her room and looked at Shankar who was still sleeping. She came closer, leaned down and planted a kiss on his lips. Shankar opened his eyes lazily and pulled her closer. They both looked at each other for a few seconds in silence and then Shankar asked, "Where are you off to?"

"I am going to Krittika's place." "So early in the morning?"

"Not early for her, she is an early riser who goes out jogging at this time. I think this would be the best time for us to have a chat."

"But what is it you want to talk?"

"I don't really know and that is why I want to catch her off-guard when she least expects me." She winked and stood up. "And yeah, by the way, we will have lunch somewhere out today, only you and me. I have to tell you something." She continued with a beaming smile.

"What is it about? Tell me now." Shankar asked anxiously.

"Not now sweetheart, just wait. I am leaving now." And she quickly left from there, leaving Shankar guessing what she was planning to tell.

She quickly grabbed her stole and took a cycle rickshaw to Krittika's apartment, which was very close to the office. It was a fifteen-minute ride to the destination, and as she got off the rickshaw to enter the apartment complex, she saw somebody coming out of the gate. On a closer look, she saw that the person was Krittika. Sanyukta was surprised to see her wearing jeans which did not resonate with the idea of going to a jog. She decided to follow her and covered her face with her stole. Krittika was completely oblivious to being followed and moved briskly down the road. In five minutes, both of them reached the road that lead to the Sangha office. This was intriguing! Sanyukta continued with the chase. In a few minutes, they reached the back door of the office where another person stood, waiting for Krittika. Sanyukta could not see the person's face clearly, so she took out her mobile phone and clicked a photo. She then used the zoom feature in her phone to see the person and was stunned to discover that it was none other than Brijwasan. Both of them moved into the office. Sanyukta could not take the risk of going inside and listening to them while they talk. She decided to wait outside. After around half an hour, both of them came out of the office.

Sanyukta saw both of them walking past her and noticed that they both looked very worried. She tried to keep pace with them and then found that both Brijwasan and Krittika had parted ways. Sanyukta was first confused about whom to follow, then started going in the same direction as Brijwasan.

In an attempt to keep up with him, Sanyukta almost began to run. After another fifteen minutes, Brijwasan took a left turn and entered the gates of a not yet operated metro train station. Sanyukta followed him in but then she lost sight of him. She kept trying to locate him till she spotted him standing with a couple of other men behind a couple of pillars in the basement parking area. The metro station was absolutely empty and there was nobody guarding the premises as it still had not started the operations. In order to identify the men, he was with, she drew herself to them. Once within the shooting distance, she started clicking photographs of the group on her cell phone. This time she almost jumped from her position when she zoomed in to discover the identity of those people. She saw Ajay Singh, while Brijwasan was on his knees before him, his hands folded as though begging for his life. Sanyukta had seen Ajay Singh standing beside Devi Dutt. Three men stood behind Ajay Singh; he was obviously their boss. Sanyukta decided to take a chance and went closer and hid behind another car pillar around fifty meters away from the men. She could now hear what they were saying. She decided to record the conversation and took out her phone to do so.

"So, now you think you can cheat us? Did you really think that if you leave us and join those beggars at Janadhikar Sangha, you will be able to live?" Ajay Singh growled.

"Nooo...no sir. I did nothing, believe me." Brijwasan pleaded.

"I know everything Brijwasan, to run such work successfully, one needs to have ten ears and ten eyes. I have twenty. You called up Krittika yesterday and told her that you want to tell her some important details. You also called up Javed two days ago and told him that you know the way how you can shut down his entire opposition. I know everything."

"How...how did that happen?" His face paled as he heard those words. Still puzzled on how this all was known to Ajay, he thought for a moment and then the image of his mobile phone came in front of his eyes... "*Keep this phone with you. It's a small gift from our side*"

"That phone... so, you always heard all of my calls. Even my private conversations with Krittika.....you bastard...." Brij, in rage, leaped towards Ajay Singh.

Suddenly, Ajay Singh raised his left hand and gave a signal to his men. The men came forward and grabbed Brijwasan's arms. The tallest of them waited for a signal from Ajay Singh and the moment he lowered his raised arm, the tall man took out a sharp dagger and slit Brijwasan's throat. Sanyukta could not stifle her gasp. The tall man heard it, raised his head and started scanning the place with his eyes. Sanyukta quickly stopped recording and settled down, hiding behind the car. But as luck would have it, her purse slipped from her hand and opened up. Several coins burst out, striking against each other and making enough noise to wake the neighborhood.

"Somebody is behind that pillar!" the tall man shouted.

The basement was getting even darker now with clouds covering the sun and fog condensing around them. Sanyukta ran but she was spotted by the tall man. The tall man ran after her and in moments, had almost caught up with her. Sanyukta sensed that saving her proof of the brutal murder was important, so she swerved and climbed the stairs to leave the basement and jumped on a side to hide behind a wall. The tall man, now joined by the other two men, was desperately looking for her while Ajay Singh decided to exit the scene and quickly sped away in his car. The three men spread themselves in three different directions and sped up their search, and soon one of them spotted Sanyukta hiding behind a car. The other two ran towards her while the first grabbed Sanyukta by her hair. Sanyukta tried to scream but a piece of cloth was inserted in her mouth, muting her efforts.

One of the men came out on the road, took a small tennis ball and a long key from his pocket, and punctured the ball before placing it on the door lock of the car parked beside them. In no time, the car door was unlocked. Quickly, the men climbed into the car with two of them in the front seat and the third pushed Sanyukta into the rear. It took less than a minute for them to start the car. The man sitting beside the driver took out his mobile phone and dialed a number. After grunting in agreement with the man on the other end, he gave directions to the driver. In minutes, the car sped down the foggy but not too busy streets of Delhi.

"What is the boss saying?" the driver asked his accomplice.

"He says that this woman could be of great value, so we should keep her alive for some time," the other man replied.

Sanyukta had her hands tied behind her and was struggling to balance in the back seat of the speeding car. The car soon left the busy roads and started cruising on the national highway. Neither of the men seemed to be in a talkative mood.

It was getting dark and after three hours on the road, everybody seemed to settle down in the moving car, including Sanyukta. She could not feel her tightly knotted hands which had gone numb due to lack of blood circulation. The men were now feeling sleepy but the driver made an attempt to swat an irritating fly and was restless.

"Why can't you forget that fly? You are irritating me with the noise. I plan to sleep now," the tall man said.

"This fly is making me crazy. I can't drive with the fly buzzing around my head."

"Perhaps it likes the garbage in your head," the second man said it with a laugh.

"Do not irritate me. Why don't you drive while I kill this pest?"

"No man, I told you I am feeling sleepy. Besides, you can't kill it now." The second man laughed.

"Don't challenge me. I can kill it even while driving." "Let's make a bet. Kill it in the next fifteen minutes and I will pay you a grand." "Done. Start looking at the watch." The driver kept swatting in the air to kill the pesky fly.

Sanyukta was now in better control of her body and heard the two men talk. She took advantage of the time to move her wrists to loosen the knot. The rope loosened a bit but was still tight enough to clasp her hands firmly. The driver kept trying to smack the fly and failed miserably in his efforts, while the second man laughed harder. Sanyukta kept up her efforts to loosen the grip on her hand. Twelve minutes had passed and the driver was nowhere close to winning the bet. With every failed attempt on the fly, his pressure on the accelerator increased. The second man laughed even louder and Sanyukta was now on the verge of getting her hands freed completely when suddenly a full-beam light blinded them. By the time the driver realized that he had driven the car into the wrong lane, he was driving headlong into a speeding truck. With no way to avert the collision, the driver swerved towards the extreme right, the car had lost its balance and was hit by the truck on the left with great force. The second man died instantly as his neck broke due to the impact of the collision. The car moved to the right and stopped right in the middle of the road. The driver was badly injured, but he tried to move the steering wheel. And then another car coming at a high speed in the same lane rammed straight into the driver's side. With bad injuries to his head and ribs, the driver too collapsed.

Sanyukta's head had struck the car's body and she was bleeding profusely. Although badly injured, she was still able to move. The car was still spinning and Sanyukta, who was now free of the ropes, reached for the back door of the car and found that it was stuck. She gathered all her energy and kicked the door with all her might and rolled out of the car. She began walking right away. After a few minutes, she saw some lights and walked in that direction. It was a roadside *dhaba* where she saw two tempos standing. There was nobody. Perhaps they had all run towards the accident after hearing the loud noise. Sanyukta was badly hurt and she felt extremely cold due to the loss of blood. Her senses were leaving her. She suddenly noticed one of the tempos had bales of cloth inside. She once again gathered her energy and hopped into the tempo to surround herself with the cotton

It soaked the blood dripping from her head and gave her comfort and warmth so that she could fall into complete oblivion.

Soon, the tempo was moving. By the second afternoon, it had entered Maharashtra where it further drove for three hours before taking a final stop in an industrial town called Madhav Nagar.

PART 4

QUEST FOR PEACE

SHANKAR'S MOBILE WAS DRAINED BY HIS desperate and incessant calling but still, there was no news of Sanyukta. Inexhaustible, Shankar dialed a number on Mani's phone. A heavy voice responded. "Hanumant, Shankar here. Any clue of Sanyukta's whereabouts?"

"No brother. I am sorry." Hanumant sounded helpless. "It has been more than 24 hours and we still do not have any idea of her whereabouts. This is so strange and disturbing." Shankar's forehead had creased as he said those words. "I know, brother. I am doing my best." "There are some dreadful and strange things happening to us and I am worried. First Javed was shot, then Sanyukta disappeared and then Brijwasan was murdered. Have you not got any clue about this from the metro station?" Shankar asked again. "Not yet, Shankar, but investigations are on and we are questioning people. We also need to wait for the forensic report on Brijwasan's dead body. I am sure that we will get some clue. All of this happening can't be a mere coincidence, there must be some connection between the three incidents." "Ok, I will wait for you to call with some developments," Shankar replied. "By the way, did you call and inform her parents?" Hanumant asked. "No, actually I have not done that yet. I am worried and scared. How do I tell them? What do I tell them?" Shankar asked hesitantly. "I understand. But this is your duty, so you must inform them. Moreover, you never know where we might find some clue," Hanumant replied. "Alright, I will inform them and update you if there is any clue. Fortunately, I found their number from Sanyukta's synchronized contacts on her laptop. Meanwhile, please put all your resources into helping us find Sanyukta." Shankar disconnected the phone to call up Sanyukta's parents.

Sanyukta's parents after hearing from Shankar immediately packed their bags and set out for Delhi. Another twenty-four hours went by and there was still no news of Sanyukta. Everyone was pitching in to either help in the search or to give support. But Shankar was getting more and more perturbed by the constant melee/katzenjammer/chaos around him. Javed was still hospitalized and now Sanyukta had gone missing and in spite of his keen desire to do so, he could find no help. In the afternoon, Hanumant walked into the office. He went straight to Shankar and found him sitting with Mani. Something in Hanumant's tense eyes and constant frown told Shankar that he has found some clues.

"What is it that you have found, my friend? Don't hide anything." "Well, we found Brijwasan's mobile lying a short distance from the crime scene. The last two dialed numbers one hour before he died belonged to Ajay Singh and Krittika." "Ok. What else?" asked Mani, eager for more information. "We also managed to get our hands on one of the cameras in the metro station. The station is still not operational but one of the cameras was set up for testing purposes. It has captured an image of a man who entered the metro station premises around the same time when the murder took place. The Himachal Pradesh police have reported that there was a car accident involving a vehicle with a Delhi number plate; there were two casualties. On receipt of the details, we realized that one of the dead in the road accident was the same man in the CCTV film. We have also managed to identify both the dead men and as it occurs both of them worked for Ajay Singh. We are questioning Ajay Singh but as you know he is a powerful person with Devi Dutt's backing, we need to find more evidence to put any kind of pressure on him." "If Devi Dutt is behind all of this then believe me, I will get to the bottom of everything and will not spare him," Shankar fumed. "We still cannot comment on his direct involvement, though the findings hint at a connection with the incident. Now, for the most important part, on inspection of the car, we realized that there was a woman in the car at the time of the accident. There was a bloodied rope on the backseat and a soiled scarf." As Hanumant spoke, he took out a small sealed polybag from his pocket which held a silk scarf. Shankar recognized the scarf straightaway. His voice broke and for the first time, it seemed that Shankar was very close to breaking down. "This means that Sanyukta is still alive."

"I would like to believe that. By the way, our team also discovered a handbag at the metro station and we are certain that it belonged to Sanyukta. There was a mobile phone in the bag but it had no records. It might be a possibility that Sanyukta was an eye witness to this murder and because of this, the killers kidnapped her and tried to take her away in the car. Sanyukta might have survived the crash. But until we find Sanyukta or her body, we can't conclude anything. Right now, all possibilities are open. One possibility is that she is alive but if that is the case, then why has she not contacted you? We can only hope she has not been abducted by someone else. But in that case, we should have received a call. On the other hand, if this is a case of revenge then there might not be a call at all. These are only probabilities but the truth is that we still are not sure of anything. In such a case, the thumb rule is that if the person doesn't appear in approximately sixty days, then it is surmised that the person has not survived."

"I understand what you say, Hanumant. Thanks a lot for your help and please keep your search on. I believe she will be back within sixty days," Shankar said. "Don't worry. We are working in close coordination with the police in Himachal. Her pictures have been sent all over the state. If she is seen anywhere, she won't go unrecognized. Let us hope for the best. We have also questioned Krittika but she is a very stubborn woman." Hanumant stood up and left after giving Shankar a hug.

Shankar and Mani decided to go to Javed and tell him

everything. Javed till now had no clues about Sanyukta's disappearance. Even though he was concerned about the visible stress on Shankar's face in the last two meetings, he had not expected the situation to be that gross. After hearing the whole incident from Shankar and Mani, the usually courageous Javed felt a chill down his spine. His body shivered for once as his mind slipped into the world of several uncertainties. Watching him getting numb, Shankar asked a bit coldly, "You worked quite closely with Krittika. Did you ever sense any conspiracy?"

"I do not know, Shankar. You know that I was not thinking clearly. She definitely cast a spell on my thinking. I never really noticed anything bad in her. It is all my fault." His face turned paler and his body shivered once again. "Do not blame yourself, Javed. You are a naïve man and some people know how to take advantage of such people." It was Mani who spoke this time.

"I really hope that Sanu is fine and I hope that she doesn't have to bear the brunt of my stupidity and faults." Javed spoke with deep concern. Shankar sensed his guilt and regret, and extended his right hand, clasping Javed's left shoulder. "We will find her," he said.

Love, such a passive force, often regenerates in extreme circumstances. When the same love appeared to have been faded in the hearts of two friends amid the chaos of life, an extreme situation recalls the old bond and infuses life with a reinforced vigor and vitality. Something similar was taking place between Shankar and Javed. The new challenges gave a new dimension to their bond. This was the day Javed stood up from his bed and sat on his wheelchair.

"What are you doing? Keep resting," Shankar said worriedly "I am fine. Let us go to Krittika," Javed pushed. "Then you don't need this wheelchair. I am still strong enough to support my best friend." They smiled at each other. Krittika was taken aback when both Javed and Shankar walked into her office. Before she could say anything, Javed spoke. "Where is Sanyukta?" His voice was hoarse and tough. Krittika tried to regain her composure but failed. "I don't know anything about her." She spoke hurriedly. "Stop beating around the bush, Krittika. This is my final warning. Tell us everything you know about this episode or else nobody on this earth can save you from me." Javed spoke with a certain sinister calm but his eyes showed cold white anger. For the first time in her life, Krittika was scared of Javed. "I... I don't know anything about it. I never knew that... that I was a part of something this barbaric." Krittika said and stepped back a bit. The tremors in her voice were clear. "Tell us more?" Shankar asked with a force in his voice. "I was only asked to play with Javed so he gets distracted and possibly it creates a rift between both of you." "Who asked you to do this?" Javed asked. "Brijwasan. I don't know about anyone else," Krittika pleaded. "Go to our friend Hanumant Sharma and tell him everything you know. Just remember, this is your last chance. If later we come to know that you tried to hide anything, believe me... I WILL KILL YOU." Javed gritted his teeth as he spoke with rage.

Then he hesitated for a bit and turned back to speak. "By the way, thanks for showing me the ugly side of this world. I couldn't be any sure of the things now. After you talk to Hanumant, you don't have to come here anymore." And then both of them left.

The days passed and the weather changed. The naked trees

grew new leaves and once again got ready to shed the leaves. Rumors ended but the base of the rumor was never found. The police conducted multiple rounds of searches but everything was inconclusive/bootless. Shankar was aching/drowning in his loss but gathered courage and asked Javed and Mani to gather themselves and get back to the business of organizing the Union for the work ahead.

Sanyukta's parents had long gone back to their home, assuming that they would never find their daughter. Shankar felt lonelier with each passing day and nearly decided several times to go away, and try to get back his peace of mind, but the faint hope of Sanyukta coming back someday did not let him go anywhere else. After the longest nine months, Shankar too started believing that he had lost his love forever. So he finally decided to go out on a journey to search for lost and detached pieces of his life and eventually find peace and solace. Javed and Mani welcomed his decision, hoping it would help him heal the wounds in his soul.

Shankar had no fixed plans, just a faint idea of going north towards the mighty Himalayas. Somewhere deep in his soul, he had a faint hope of finding Sanyukta as she was believed to have disappeared from the car after the accident in Himachal Pradesh. Somewhere in his subconscious, he was always mesmerized by the magnificence of the snow-clad peaks of the Himalayas and the caves that provided shelters to hermits. He prepared himself for the long and strenuous journey ahead. He packed his trekking bag and set himself to leave the still warm ambiance of Delhi's autumn.

The first destination was the village he had once called home. Shankar took an interstate bus to reach the village. The old bus was in a rickety condition with a jarring body and smoke-tinted window panes. He wanted to feel the wind of the hills on his face so he chose a seat next to the window. He knew that he would love the crisp chilly wind on his face. Despite all his worries and uncertainties, he was suddenly feeling optimistic and realized that in the same manner, the hustle and bustle in a bus automatically settles down after a while, so will the journey would settle his inner anguish. He had started looking forward to the journey ahead.

30th September, 2017. As he neared his village, Chandan Nagar, old memories rose/flashed before him. He remembered Girija, Raju, Biju, Sarang and the old *Sarpanch* and hoped he would find them there. He was hopeful that the villagers would be happy to see him, especially since he had regained their respect when he saved them from the leopard. He wondered if they would ask him about what he had done after he left the village. "What should I tell them? They might have news from the city and already have some idea about my life. But what if they don't know anything about it? Am I ready to be questioned? I don't want to face the people with questions in their eyes. I am really not ready for this. No, I should go somewhere else."

Shankar had reached the closest stop to his village on this route. He had to disembark and change buses. But by now he had changed his mind. He boarded another bus which would take him to Dharamshala. He wanted to go further up to McLeod Ganj, a beautiful spot surrounded by the mighty blue ranges of the Himalayas. He fervently hoped that the roads would not have been closed due to snowfall.

It was an overnight journey to McLeod Ganj and Shankar looked for an economical place to stay for the night. He discovered a backpacker's joint which offered dormitory-style accommodation. Each room was shared by four people and there was a common washroom and toilet between two rooms.

Shankar adapted himself to his new surroundings and got acquainted with his roommates. There was one couple from Holland and a young fellow from France. Though Shankar generally remained isolated from everybody in his own world, his experiences in the past had been constantly paving the way for an eternal optimism. He realized that this room was much larger than his tiny cell in the jail and another realization made him cherish his condition – the realization that he had the greatest gift in the world, Freedom. Freedom to move, freedom to talk, freedom to explore, freedom to question, freedom to dislike, freedom to love. The realization made his otherwise parched heart sense the first raindrop somewhere nearby in the desert.

Shankar just took rest for the first two days and woke up only to have food in a nearby *dhaba*.

The morning of the third day brought along bright sunshine as Shankar woke up well-rested and stretched his body. He felt as though he had been filled with new vigor. He pushed aside the small green curtain and opened the window to let the cold fresh air and sunlight into the room. He peeped through the little window and the gorgeous sight of the green valley brought a smile to his face. The snow had yet to cover the area. Right now it was feathery green all around. He felt a sense of contentment and kept on looking at the tranquil scenery for nearly an hour. Soon, the other roommates woke up and got busy with the morning routine while Shankar continued to stare outside the window.

Shankar could see a tiny wooden cube further down the hill, set beside the winding road. It looked like a tea stall and the craving for a hot steaming cup made him leave the room and clamber down to it. He found out that it was a small wooden structure, built on a raised platform with enough space for the stall owner and his utensils, some jars of sweets, cookies, cigarettes and betel leaves. The elevated platform protected its owner from rain and vermin. The stall was owned by a wizened old woman. She wore an old and torn sari and a weathered grey sweater. Her dialect confirmed that she hailed from the eastern part of India.

The woman got busy as soon as she spied her client and called out for "Bholu", maybe her son, to light the stove. Shankar ordered a cup of tea and some biscuits. As she brewed the tea, the aroma of the tea leaves, clove, cardamom and ginger filled Shankar's nostrils and gave him a sense of wellbeing. The first sip brought back images of his boyhood and refreshed the memory of the tea his mother would make for him.

He spied the foreign tourists converting their currency to rupees and realizing the advantage of conversion rates. He saw the stall owners, keen to attract the travelers for some quick selling and bigger bucks. He understood their keenness to earn as much as they could before the winter set in. He drained the last drops of the refreshing tea, ate his biscuits and paid the ten rupees due to the lady before walking back to his hotel.

When he reached his room, he washed and refreshed himself, and was then ready to start his explorations. Locking up his belongings, he dressed comfortably in a grey t-shirt and black cargos and flung a leather jacket on, just in case it got chilly. He grabbed a sketchbook, pencils, donned his hiking shoes and rushed out of the hotel. He once again wanted to draw something.

He climbed aimlessly uphill. He neither had any notion of the direction nor was he familiar with the place, but he was not perplexed. He was not looking for a particular destination, but for those days, the days before his mother died, before Javed was shot and before Sanyukta disappeared from his life. He sought for the lost part of his identity.

A FRIEND OR AN ENEMY?

2nd OCTOBER, 2017. WHILE SHANKAR LOOKED for solace in the remote corners of the world, Javed with the support of Mani escalated his efforts to corner Devi Dutt. It was a national holiday on the occasion of Gandhi Jayanti, that day. Quite early in the morning for a national holiday, Javed drove the govt. car allocated to him and picked up Mani on his way to Devi Dutt's home. The guards at the main door of the plush mansion for the state's CM in Central Delhi were first taken aback and then amused by the sudden unannounced arrival of Javed. No one was untouched by the popularity of the Janadhikar Sangha's leader who had escaped the sharp jaws of death. Moreover, after the strong victory in the recently concluded elections, Javed had amassed a very strong following for him. Dressed in the white Pathani kurta with a black half sweater, blue jeans and black leather shoes, his mesomorph rhomboid body appeared more authoritative. As he stepped up, he faced no resistance from the guards who knew the minister well. "Salam Alaikum". One guard said as he opened the door for him.

"Wa-Alaikum Salam", Javed replied as he entered the premises and started moving towards the main corridor. Mani followed him instantly. As Javed entered the corridor, his eye muscles stiffened as he fixed his gaze on the entry door and the red mark in his eye became more prominent.

Devi Dutt was completely taken by surprise as he saw Javed entering the door while he was sipping tea in the chair. He stood up and tried to come out of the shock to welcome Javed with a fake smile. After all, had Janadhikar Sangha not supported Devi Dutt's party, he could never have become the Chief Minister.

After the quick exchange of pleasantries from both sides, Javed came straight to the point. "What do you have to do with Sanyukta's disappearance?" Shocked to hear the question, Devi Dutt fumbled and mumbled before he finally replied, "What are you talking about?"

Unperturbed by the question in response, Javed repeated, "What do you have to do with Sanyukta's disappearance? Tell me everything you know or things will become much tougher for you."

By now, Devi Dutt had quickly restored his senses so he replied in a much calmer way, "I have nothing to do with it Javed. I know what you all are going through is tragic but I don't have to do anything with it." "Devi, do not think that we are not aware of what is happening inside your party? The funds you recently received from the Central Govt. in the Chief Minister's quota for education program have not been channelized anywhere. This is just an example. There are several other facts that we know and will use against you to make sure that you never ever come back to power. The bottom line is, do not play with us. You will burn your fingers." This time Mani came forward and interjected in his typical steady and deep tone.

Devi Dutt turned towards Mani and asked, "Do you mean if I had some information about Sanyukta and would give it to you, you won't come in my way on how I use the funds?" "Well, it simply means one thing Devi. If you would give us the information about Sanyukta or help us find her, we will give you some time to correct the mistakes that you have committed." Mani replied and then Javed continued with a closing line, "And that will be your second and last chance." Scared to hear the menacing tone in Javed's voice, Devi Dutt's stocky built appeared even shorter as his shoulders and neck drooped down. He gathered his senses once again and tried to assuage him, "I do not know anything about Sanyukta, Javed. And for the funds, we are actually planning to move the funds towards a sanitation program instead of the education program. I am no thief.", Seeming completely unconvinced Javed replied harsher, "I am yet to find out if you are a thief or a robber or a murderer. The day I figure it out, I will ensure that you find no chance to escape from me,"

Mani tried to calm him down and interjected, addressing Devi Dutt. "Devi, you have one week to channelize the funds in the right direction and give us a report. We do not intend any harm, but we will not tolerate any fraud or misuse of public funds. Please consider this a serious warning. On Sanyukta, the truth will come out in open one fine day and that day if your association is revealed in any form, then just remember what Javed has just promised." Mani stood up and asked Javed to come along with him. They left quickly.

"You should show some restraint in your behavior sometimes." Mani winked to/at Javed as they sat in their car.

"I know, Kaka. But what can I do? You have no idea how helpless I feel when I think of my friends and the Sangha. I know, he is behind everything that went wrong and yet I can't do anything to him because I don't have any proof." "I understand what you are saying, Javed. But when things are not in your control, just think and ask yourself what it is that you can do in those circumstances. I think you are already doing whatever you can. It may not have the desired results right now, but one day all your efforts will produce a result much better than anything you might have expected. Give it some time and stay focussed. Moreover, I am still not sure of Devi Dutt as well. He seems more like a businessman than a killer to me. Let us wait and watch."

Devi Dutt, on the other hand, was under constant pressure to perform and deliver. He had spent millions to tempt voters to his side, but now his investment was not paying him back. For some, getting elected and being appointed Chief Minister is not an opportunity for service to the nation but gratification for a well-planned business initiative. Perhaps it was the same for Devi Dutt.

THE SOUL IN TRANSIT

"AH, WHAT AN EXTRAORDINARY VIEW!" Shankar stood awestruck and nearly stopped breathing, afraid that even the sound of breath could break the ethereal silence of that beautiful space. He was standing on the side of the mountain, from which he could view the valley and the azure blue skies above. He felt he had been transported to the epicentre of the earth's beauty. The endless ranges of the mighty Himalayas seemed to form an unending staircase leading straight up to heaven. The blue-sky merging into the white snow peaks reflected back the different colors of the sunlight. And in the midst of all this glory, there stood a pair of antelopes touching each other gently, expressing their tender love.

Shankar missed Sanyukta terribly. He longed to have her there with him, sharing this moment. He wished to touch her and lose himself with her in the midst of Mother Nature. He looked down and spied a point on the other side of the mountain, a copse of tall trees in a meadow were glittering in the sunlight. He made his way there and sat on a big rock, sunning himself as the rays first warmed his limbs and then slowly seeped in, warming his core and sad heart. "I wish we could touch the sunbeams and feel blessed together, Sanyukta," he whispered, watching the grazing antelopes as they came closer to him. He was amazed at the boldness of these creatures. He looked into the eyes of the male antelope, now standing barely ten-feet from him. He saw the message in those eloquent eyes: "We are not scared of you for love does not scare us." He was lost in the moment for some time and the pain in his heart slowly dissipated; instead, he felt a breeze of happiness filling his heart. The visual of tender and innocent love amidst the spectacular view made him feel the presence of Sanyukta. He took out his sketchbook and started replicating the visual in front of him on a blank sheet. After several confident strokes of his hand, a beautiful picture emerged on the sheet. He looked at it, looked at his surroundings and then he smiled. He continued smiling for the rest of the day.

The next morning, after getting ready and drinking tea at the now-familiar stall, he rushed to the same spot in the mountains. This time he also carried his mobile phone with the camera to capture some fast-moving moments. The day flew past him. The next twenty days went by in the same way; he would spend his time at the same spot, feeling the presence of Sanyukta.

Shankar had managed to acquire a small stove, three small boxes of tea leaves, sugar and powdered milk and a water bottle, all of which he carried to his refuge. He would sit there, sketch and sip his tea, luxuriating/wallowing in the warmth of the sun. Lucky for him, it didn't rain during this period.

After twenty days, he felt the need to move on. He traveled higher up the mountain and spent beatific/ecstatic fifteen days at another beautiful location traveling every day from the lodge to there, before feeling the urge to move on again. "This is how human life works; we get bored even with the best of the things and need to move on. The familiarity with our surroundings, with a body, with anything which enters a comfort zone induces the feeling of boredom and the need for change. Thus, change becomes the essence of life. Even the best of things needs to be changed to keep the flow of life going," Shankar wrote in his notepad. Then he made a call.

"How are you, brother?" Javed replied excitedly "I am fine, Javed. How are you?" "All well. How are your travels going?" "They are going well. I am feeling much better." "I am glad to hear that. Have you found any good looking women?" Javed teased. "Ha ha, plenty of them here...by the way, do you have any updates?"

"I know what you mean." Javed paused after saying so and then after a couple of seconds of silence at both ends, he continued, "We are not leaving any stone unturned in our search for her, but it is almost certain that we have lost her forever. You know that. Even her parents have come to this understanding. Whatever happened was terrible. But now it can't be undone. You have to think of the way forward and not cling to the past."

Feeling a pinch in his heart, Shankar instantly rebelled, "She is not a matter of past, Javed. She is still in my present. When she becomes a part of my past, I will certainly move on, but I haven't felt that way yet... Just keep trying and keep me informed." Bearing no effect of Shankar's words, Javed almost reiterated, "Sure, buddy. We are trying our best. If you need anything, just let me know. Try to come out of your memories and have a real-life again. The Sangha needs your guidance."

Seeing no sign of change, Shankar took it easy this time and said gently, "Alright. But please give me some time. I will try and do as you said. Take care. Give my regards to everybody there."

"Sure, you take care." When Shankar hung up, he lost himself once again in the same aching/achy thoughts of his past. He stood still for a few moments and then cried out, "O god, I can't bear this pain anymore. Either give her back to me or give me a purpose to live." Once he reached his lodge, he thought he would try and immerse himself in something new. He started conversing with his roommates. The Frenchman, Elgor, taught him a few words in French. He taught him some Hindi in return. When both of them met, they greeted each other in the other's language: *"Bonjour, Mon Ami"*, *"Namaste mere dost"* and they smiled at each other. It was nice interacting with a fellow travller. Shankar spent the next couple of days in the main town of Mc Leodganj, wandering through the markets, streets, Buddhist and Hindu temples and meeting the monks and priests. He noticed many subtle points that he had missed earlier, the ways the different faiths and religions differed/varied from each other; as he noticed the differences, he also realized that they bore several similarities too. All of those religions preached non-violence and yet all religious fanatics spread violence in the name of their religions. They resorted to violence as they were led by the stubborn advocacy of their own worth. He observed how the priests tried to earn money from believers and disciples, mostly innocent village folks, by scaring them in the name of religion and when questioned, exposed their domineering personas and abasing the very religion they tried to dignify with their preaching and tall promises. Even religion had become a business. The temples looked like a beggar's paradise where the haves begged inside from the divine deity and the have nots begged outside from the devotees. His explorations continued in the town till his eyes fell upon a frail person with a uniquely infectious smile. He could not stop himself but to smile. He then tried to see him from a closer look only to notice the seer emanating/emitting the glow of wisdom. He was at the temple of Lord Shiva in the main market, adjacent to the very famous Hotel Clouds. Shankar felt the urge to go and meet the man, and went straight into the temple. The man was a middle-aged Brahmin, lean and fair, with a broad body frame, medium height, stern and focussed eyes, a broad forehead, round shaven head, and long arms. Even on such a cold morning, he seemed comfortable in his frugal and light clothing. "*Namaste.*" "*Jai Bhole,*" The Brahmin replied.

"I came to meet you. I was driven by a strange curiosity." Shankar spoke nervously.

"You were destined to come here. There is nothing in this universe that happens for no reason." The Brahmin spoke with a quiet dignity. "How do you know that?"

"Who am I to know such things, my friend? I am a normal human being who can see the confusion on your face. What I know is that your wait is not over yet. But it is coming to its end and soon will come the fateful day when you will understand the meaning of every incident that has taken place in your life."

Shankar remembered Sanyukta as he heard the words of the Brahmin. "Is it some hint about her or it is about something else?" he wondered. "I am flooded with loads of questions. I am surrounded by confusion. I hope I am not ruining my destiny with my actions."

The Brahmin continued in his philosophical tone. "You must celebrate if you are confused because following something blindly is very easy. Only those who are capable to delve deep can raise questions and those are the only people who reach the top of the mountain of wisdom from where everything is visible. The clouds and fog of confusion will be beneath you. That day, all your questions will be answered."

Shankar only grew more worried at hearing his words. His questions unanswered, he delved deeper. "It seems as if you have already understood my questions. Then could you kindly help me with the answers? It might be a shorter and an easier way, sir."

The Brahmin laughed at hearing Shankar's words and spoke once again without the slightest change in his tone. "Sometimes there is no direct route, my friend. Sometimes, you need to have a bad day and sometimes you need to go round and round several times till you get your job done.

These are the phases of life, and to understand their significance, you need to wait and watch."

"Why the wait? If you know what I need to understand, the cause of my angst, then just tell me. Why the presumption that I won't understand?" Shankar was still not satisfied.

The Brahmin smiled at him. "Unless you spend these days here, wandering aimlessly, you won't find a reason to go home. And until you go home, you might not find the reason for living. I know that your past scares you, but do not worry, your future holds a lot of promise. You are evolving gradually, like the flowers that blossom gradually and not instantaneously/promptly. Or better like a moth turning into a cocoon, later to develop wings and become a butterfly. You are the cocoon right now. The wings will appear but for that, this pain must be welcomed to break out of the shell."

The wise words soothed him down but then again something struck his mind, "How do you know that I wanted to go home but was scared? Do you know me?"

"Calm down, young man. It doesn't matter if I know you or not, what matters is if you know yourself. Do not believe me and do not believe anybody but your heart. Your brain and heart are the tools that can guide you to choose what experiences you should have. Depending on the experiences you choose, the wisdom will come to you sooner or later and depending on the path you take, your destiny too will appear to you, sooner or later."

Shankar listened to him and absorbed every word intently. He was more peaceful now. After a few seconds, he spoke again. "I might understand what you mean. Nobody but I can find out the answers to my questions. But for that to happen, I must have a clear insight and self-belief, which I am certainly lacking right now. One last question, how should one approach life?"

"Just keep walking and accept your fate gracefully without a grudge, building your own perspective independent of others. One day in the future, when you look back, you might connect the dots. Your present is weaving several strands that lead to your future. Out of those, one last strand will lead you into your next life. You need not to necessarily hurry up, for the nectar of the life is to be sipped slowly and appreciated. Moreover, this lifetime is only a stage, the journey belongs to the soul and not to the body. Every experience of this life will be imprinted on your soul, so the soul will be wiser in the next life." The Brahmin smiled and went inside the temple.

"That suddenly changes the whole perspective, it is so comforting now, to know that the journey belongs to the soul. Why to be restless, why to feel an urgency to do everything now." Shankar thought as he saw the wise man disappearing into the temple. He too walked out of the temple a few moments later. Regretting the fact that Shankar had not even asked his name, Shankar thought, "Perhaps that was not required. What would have changed with a name? It is one's thoughts and actions that make up a person. The name is just for convenience."

Before meeting the wise man, Shankar had been feeling suffocated by the double-faces of people. Now he was relieved and went back to the hotel. He was still thinking about the last words, the Brahmin had said to him. He was trying to understand their meaning. "Perspective", what did that mean?

He wrote in his notebook. "*It is the vision and the interpretation of the vision,*" he realized. He was encouraged by the reply and wrote further.

"So, perspective is when we see something and then interpret it. Though many people see the same thing or incident, their ways of interpreting it could be different and thus their perspectives too would vary. For example, if four people see a tiger hunting a deer then all of them might interpret the incident differently. One might say that the tiger gets his food while the second might say that the poor deer just got killed. The third might see the tiger as a cruel murderer whereas the fourth might interpret the incident as a live example of the concept 'survival of the fittest'. Same incident, but varying perspectives.

"So, even those fake religious preachers might have different perspectives regarding themselves and the people who come to them. They might be thinking that they are giving hope to the needy, even if they take money. After all, the money they take is a matter of their livelihood. But then greed can take over their needs and under the influence of greed and lust, they might cross their limits. But then the question arises: what is the limit and who decides it? The limit varies for everyone. One person's ability to take risks might be much higher than somebody else's. So, the conclusion is that everybody in this universe is different and has different attitudes, different forms of interpretation, different degrees of awakening and different colors of the soul. So trying to understand other people and their perspective is unnecessary and probably impossible. What matters is, how well we know ourselves. We perceive things as they are designed for us, our brains and our souls. It is the same way we learn in Science class that the human retina has three types of cone cells that work as color receptors. They recognize the three colors red, green and blue. That is why our eyes can see these three colors more distinctly than others. So although violet and indigo have lower wavelengths and thus are easily scattered in the cosmos by the molecules, we don't see the sky as violet or indigo, rather it

appears blue in colour. Understanding life is not easy, and our soul needs the right receptors for it. Until then, it is a long but beautiful journey ahead."

Exhausted, Shankar was thinking of taking a nap when the Dutch couple and his French friend entered the room.

The Dutch couple invited both Shankar and the Frenchman to a party in the evening. Shankar promptly accepted. He was feeling much lighter inside and wanted to have some fun now. "Perhaps it is time to accept my fate and move on," he thought. Shankar had heard of some really fun parties in this part of the country. He was ready for an adventurous evening, filled with the intoxicating and fun elements of wine, whiskey, music, dance, dope or even unleashing oneself and letting oneself into unknown arms. In fact, he anticipated letting himself go if he could.

He reached the party early. The evening was yet to rev up, the party being organized by a rich *Punjabi.* He had his own beer factory and exported beer to other South-East Asian countries like Sri Lanka, Bhutan and Bangladesh. He threw such parties once almost every three months and invited the whole circle of tourists, especially the international ones, at a very nominal cover charge. He was especially drawn towards the emancipated lady tourists in various states of inebriation and intoxication. It gave him a perverse high to be the harbinger of complete decadence to the hills.

Within one hour, the place was packed and the party had started. Shankar had a couple of beers and then watched the others dance. Initially, he hesitated to join in, but then after gulping down a couple more beers, he entered a comfort zone and mingled with the crowd. As the night drew on, the music was getting louder, the bodies moving in rhythm to the beats, eyes on the verge of losing focus and heads were spinning. The aroma of mixed body odors and stale perfumes, the close sight of women's cleavage and the soft touch of feminine flesh while dancing aroused many of his dormant fantasies. His young body had craved an encounter earlier too but his responsibilities and work pressure had taken away the pleasure of leading a sexually active life. The ambiance here had changed something and he was ready to indulge himself now. Somewhere in the middle of everything, Shankar, rather high on alcohol after a very long time, got lost in the spinning crowd. His right foot got tangled on a trailing table cloth and he crashed into a group of bodies. He looked up to find himself in the arms of a woman. A pair of sapphire eyes greeted him, badly glazed with drugs and alcohol, her breath had a confused smell of mint, vodka and oranges. Excited by the physical touch of an attractive woman, hypnotized by her looks and loosened due to alcohol, Shankar was at a point of no return. Both their bodies didn't move for a while, as though they were checking the strength in each other while readying themselves for a battle. Then the woman rose and started walking backwards, her eyes were still fixed on Shankar's. After a slight hesitation, Shankar started following her.

He entered a room to find the woman standing right next to the door. He came closer to her. Her warm breath and her radiant skin had cast a spell on him. He came forward and held her hands gently. She was a tall woman, and both their noses touched. She clasped Shankar's hand tightly in a show of strength. Shankar responded with a tighter grip.

It was a matter of moments before the heat had reached its zenith and the two were tearing each other's clothes. As the night crawled towards the day, they lay naked next to each other after they climaxed again, two souls seeking salvation in a mutual passion. After a couple of tempestuous hours, both of them fell into the deepest sleep, exhausted and fulfilled.

When Shankar opened his eyes, he saw the sunlight filtering through the window and falling directly on his bare chest. The sun's position told him that it was early noon. He must have slept for a very long time. The surroundings did not seem to be familiar. "Where am I?" Suddenly he looked into the face of a beautiful woman, still deep in sleep next to him. Her hair was blonde, she had a small nose and pink lips…

He found his clothes scattered around the room. He was eager to know the woman's identity and learn about last night, but she looked so serene in her sleep that Shankar could not muster the strength to wake her up. He decided to wait for her.

While he looked at her, he realized he had not thought of Sanyukta for a while. "So it can happen," he thought to himself. Finally, unable to deal with the tension of waiting, he came out of the room and entered the big compound where the party had taken place. It looked like a large house with four or five rooms. He opened the gates of the compound and saw a paved road leading to the woods. After walking for half a kilometre, he saw a small tea stall, similar to the one he visited near his hotel. He ordered a cup of tea and some biscuits like he often did. He didn't notice that he looked absolutely dishevelled. He didn't notice the young boy sitting inside the stall and managing the whole business. He didn't notice the dark brown snake on the side of the road trying to absorb some heat from the sunlight, lying on a small rock on his way. He didn't notice that the sun today was too bright for the season. He didn't see anything, for his head was still spinning and his brain was lost in the blurry memories of the previous night.

After a lazy thirty minutes, he finished his tea and started walking back. His head seemed to be in much better control of his body now. He suddenly spied a winding trail, leading into the forest. His curiosity got the better of him and he decided to follow it. Something was driving him in that direction, and he soon realized what was waiting for him on that path. It opened into a narrow gorge which was barely visible from afar, as it was surrounded by a grove of trees. The specific angle of the sunbeam made it visible as if it was just meant for this moment. He was very strongly tempted to go further and see the small caverns that the gorge contained. He waited there for a few minutes and then his curiosity took over and he went ahead. There was not much light within.

The opening to the cave was very narrow and one could enter only by crawling on all fours. It was hidden by vines. He didn't know what it was, but he felt incredibly safe inside. After his eyes got used to the darkness, he realized there was a small stream flowing across the ground. He noticed a small round rock with a flat top, two feet in diameter and similar in height, in the center of the grotto. As if driven by a magical force, he sat on it, crossed his legs and closed his eyes. Some special energy flowed through him and a new connection was established beyond the physical world. He felt as though he could see the deep scars in his heart. With some special metaphysical process and the complete freedom to express himself in a closed place, he felt all kinds of emotions inundating his heart and then a stream of tears began rolling down from his eyes.

After a few poignant minutes, everything stopped as abruptly as it had started. He felt no lumps in his throat and he felt as nimble and devoid of worries as a newborn child. He opened his eyes, sipped some water from the clear stream and smiled. Then he remembered his mother and recalled the way she had taught him to meditate. He realigned his body in a cross-legged sitting posture with an erect spine and closed his eyes to dive into an ocean of peace and bliss. He was transported into a meditative state and a constant smile appeared on his lips; his eyes half-open.

After a couple of hours, he opened his eyes. A message flashed in his mind: "Follow your heart". When he came out, he felt as innocent as an infant. All the weight he had carried had evaporated. He began walking again. The sunlight was getting dimmer and a mist had begun to rise over the area. He didn't know the way out but he was not bothered. He kept on moving, devoid of any fear or doubt. Two hours had passed, and the fog had grown dense by now.

In the middle of it all, Shankar saw a dim light. He increased his pace and moved briskly towards it. In a few minutes, he could see the source of the light, the street light fifty meters from his hotel. What had seemed so far was actually very close by. "This is what happens in life during difficult times. We lose hope without realizing that the solution to our problems has always been close to us and we quit without giving it another try." He smiled as he entered the hotel.

ARIA

OVER THE NEXT FOUR DAYS, SHANKAR spent his time searching for that cave, but he could not find it. On the fifth day, when he was trekking down another side of the mountain, he saw a beautiful face in front of him, emerging out of the bushes. It was the same pretty woman! He suddenly got very tensed and looked away.

But she recognized him. "Hi, I am Aria." "Hello, I am Shankar. I am pleased to meet you." "I know your name. You really talk a lot when you're drunk." She smiled cheekily.

"Oh, I am sorry for causing any inconvenience that night. I, I was completely out of my mind."

"No worries. I thought that you might want to thank me for taking you to my place, otherwise, you might have thrown yourself down this mountain." She winked.

"Ah, thanks for that. In fact, thanks for the whole night. I don't remember everything clearly but I certainly have memories of some beautiful moments spent with you."

Shankar looked straight into her eyes as if trying to analyze her feelings.

"You are welcome. I do understand your predicament. It happens sometimes. And yes, I have some lovely memories too. Thanks to you. So, let's get to know each other once again. I am Aria. It is a pleasure to meet you."

"And I am Shankar; it is indeed a pleasure to meet you too."

"So, what are you doing here? I doubt there is any rum available in these forests." She laughed.

"Ha ha... you never know. If I can find you here, I might find anything."

"So you have a sense of humor. Not bad."

"Yeah, it supports me in times of crisis. An encounter with such a lovely lady is nothing less than a crisis for me."

"Well then, you should meet me more often. Your sense of humor might stay with you forever." Aria winked again and started to move.

"Sure. If it's the destiny we would meet again." Shankar replied as he made way for Aria.

On hearing this, Aria stopped and looked at Shankar quizzically. Then she said, "The destiny has done it already, now it's in our hands Shankar. Let's meet tomorrow morning at Tibetan Mandala café at 9am." Shankar could not say anything as she left without waiting for a reply.

As Aria left, Shankar felt restless as he realized that he had not thought about Sanyukta again. He quickly took out his mobile and checked for any updates. There were none. He started thinking about the past and then the temple priest's words echoed in his mind: "One last strand leads you to your next life." He tried to shrug off the thought but then the words of Javed came into his mind too: "You need to move on." In a confused state of mind, he reached his hotel and crashed out on his bed almost immediately.

The next day, as decided, Shankar and Aria met at a point and embarked on a journey in search of the cave. He told Aria about the amazing experience he had there. Aria was full of raw energy and was eager to see it too. It was a cloudy day and the forecast was for a light shower. A usual cold morning for the month of December, both wore warm clothes. Shankar carried his stove burner, necessary ingredients to make tea and some cookies & Aria carried a small waterproof pop-up tent for any emergency stopover.

Shankar tried to use his memory to reach the cave but led both of them deep into the forest instead. It was an exhausting hike, but they were unable to find the spot as yet. After a few minutes since the start of the hike, they both had started chatting comfortably. After a few minutes of small talk, Shankar asked her.

"So, what do you do?"

"I am a biologist. In fact, I am here to discover some new species."

"And where are you from? You don't seem to belong to this country. Am I right?"

"Yeah, you are right. I am from America. Actually from a small town in Mississippi."

"Ok. I don't know much about America."

"Hmm, well, I am a descendant of the Paleo-Indians who first inhabited the America." "Alright, so you must have deep roots there," Shankar smiled.

"Very deep, though it's been mixed with the people from European settlement, hence the color of my hair and eyes. My people love farming and horse riding. My parents still plow our land every year to harvest cotton."

"Oh wow. You are a farmer. Here in India, it is not easy to be a farmer." Shankar said with a glint of concern in his eyes.

"I love my home. The land is covered with vast forests of pine, cottonwood, elm, hickory, pecan, sweetgum and tupelo."

"Well, well, I don't even know the names of most of those!"

"It comes handy for a biologist like me." She smiled.

"So what else are you passionate about?"

"I love horse riding. In fact, I had my own horse, Binni. He was an Andalusian horse. My father gifted him to me when the horse was six months old and I had turned seven."

"Great. Tell me more."

"He was dark brown and had a black mark on his forehead. It looked like a trident. He ran like the wind. Because of Binni and my wonderful parents, I never felt the need of a friend."

"So is Binni still around?"

"Unfortunately not. He died of heart failure after ten years. I was depressed for months. It was so hard for me that I had to be admitted to a hospital. I was certain that I would die of grief but then something happened to me."

"What happened?" Shankar quizzed as he walked slowly making way into the bushes.

"There was a patient in the next bed suffering from acute leukemia. He had lost his hair due to chemotherapy, and his skin looked blemished. He looked 60 years old but his actual age was not even half of that. Despite all this, he was an amiable fellow, never unhappy, and continuously writing something in his diary. After being there for two days, I stopped whining partially due to the embarrassment and also influenced by the serene soul in the next bed. I asked him his name to which he smiled and said, 'It doesn't matter now. Within a few months, I will be just a body. What matters is how people will remember me after I am gone. I often wonder what I could do in these four months which will ensure that people remember me all their lives."

"What a thought," Shankar spoke softly.

"I felt the same way. I asked him if he had any ideas yet." "So what did he say?"

"He said, 'Not yet. But one thing I know for sure is that I

won't die yelling at people. I prefer to die with peace in my heart, a champagne glass in my hand and a smile on my lips. I could not live on my own terms, but I can certainly die my way." She paused for a moment and then continued. "The dying man was actually happy with his decision and looked at peace."

Shankar kept on looking at her while walking. He was positively influenced by the calmness on her face. He did not utter a word, just let her speak.

"Those words had a great impact on me and I stopped crying. When I went home, I saw my mother and realized how beautiful she is. I looked around and found everything different. I opened the window of my car and felt the drizzle on my face. I noticed the astonished but happy smile on the face of an old lady when she was allowed to cross the road as my father applied the brakes to stop the car and let her go first. I understood that life is not only lived once. In fact, it is lived again and again and again, every day, every hour and sometimes every second. It depends on how well one understands this truth. It has been many years since that incident took place. Life is not counted in terms of days but is weighed in memories. One only has to see the right things and this will automatically happen. Sometimes, a problem does not even exist but we forget to put a full stop to the negativity all around and thus become incapable of seeing a beautiful present and a promising future. Instead, we call ourselves the victims of misfortune.

"After much thinking, I know one thing--it is not the length but the depth of life which eventually counts."

"Some people know the art of celebrating and they make sure that every

moment they live in this world gives them an opportunity to experience the ecstasy of life. Even in the face of something as terrifying as death, they are filled with contentment and serenity. They are the true brave hearts, and this world's happiness and positivity are their legacy." Shankar was drowned in his own thoughts and then he spoke. "I am glad you could come out of that zone. Sometimes, it takes many lives to understand the source of happiness."

"You are right. I was lucky in that regard. Following my renewed state of mind, I started working towards attaining complete control of my life and soon fell in love with it. This love for creation transformed me entirely." It is said that a person in love gradually takes on the same shape and characteristics of the one he is in love with. Aria, fortunately, fell in love with existence and thus she took the form of life itself, reflecting the same form of energy, vigor and vibrancy as life does.

Shankar was intrigued by her strong psyche, positivity, enigmatic persona and attitude of living life to the fullest. He told her about his friendship with Javed, his work with the Sangha, his deeply entrenched love for Sanyukta and his on-going journey of self-discovery. He felt relieved after sharing his grief with her.

After almost four hours, Shankar suddenly stopped walking. He took Aria's camera and zoomed in to the maximum and pointed it towards the north. In a minute, he was certain that he had found the grove. As he got closer, he realized that it is not the same spot but it appeared inviting for their curious beings.

In about half an hour, they reached the spot from where they were about to enter the area that had a series of very old caves.

They first entered a large cave that had a significantly wider opening and allowed two people to enter together. The inside was like that of a small tomb, decorated with beautiful limestone extensions emerging from the roof and the floor. It seemed to be an ancient cave that had numerous bats as permanent residents. Both of them quickly moved out, not wanting to disturb the winged mammals.

After visiting four more caves, they entered a space which, Aria declared, had a special energy. "I believe that every living or non-living entity had a special character and it emanates an energy corresponding to the character." She opined. Feeling a connection there, she decided to spend some more time inside. It was a very deep cavern, gradually narrowing towards the end that produced an echoing effect. Aria heeded some water oozing from a small crevice in the middle of the roof. The water dripping from there had formed a small pothole on the ground exactly opposite to the crevice in the roof. The pothole was filled with water and every drop that fell into it produced a deep sound of exhilaration that echoed through the cave. It seemed as though this were the clock of creation, which ticked and told humankind that life is slipping out of your hands every moment, take hold of it and celebrate it now. Both of them were mesmerized by the magical ambiance. Shankar chose a spot facing the falling droplets and sat down. Aria sat right next to him. Their bodies touched each other and the boundaries between those two bodies became more porous with every second passing by.

From that day onwards, Shankar and Aria spent a lot of time together. They found solace in each other's company. Shankar didn't even realize how his naughtier side had come into play in her protective company. He was as playful as he would have been in his early childhood. With the new mischief in his eyes, Aria found him even more adorable. Both of them forgot any inhibition, so in each other's company, they both saw the reflection of their real identities. Their relationship mellowed with every debate and their bond became stronger with every discussion. When they met, they saw the other's soul, naked. In each other, they found a companion, a guide, a friend, a lover. Their days together were made up of silent teasing, loud pranks, emotional tales of the past, solitary moments of meditation, hand-held excursions to the top of the mountain cliffs, rhetorical discussions of a splendid future and an invisible connection surpassing the logical understanding of the worldly wisdom flew at a rapid pace. Aria was a non-pretentious woman who was overt about her sensuality and candid about her outlook on relationships. Their relationship had evolved from a sexual encounter to an unfathomable companionship bonded by millions of invisible strands.

As is said, though that all the good times come to an end, Aria's project too was coming to a finish. The snow-clad white mountains had started appearing green & brown once again as the snow had started melting with the Sun of the spring. The naked trees were also bestowed with the new golden leaves once again by the mother nature. As this change happened in their surroundings, both of them were also getting aware of the change in their hearts. The last seventy days they spent together had created eternal memories, but now they had to be separated.

She was to take an early flight from Dharamshala to New Delhi, from where she would board a flight to America. Shankar and Aria planned to spend the last evening and night together, roaming the streets of the town. She wore a red woolen pullover and cream slacks, and a red silk muffler. She looked as gorgeous as a blossoming flower. Shankar wore blue jeans and his favorite white T-shirt and a white hooded jacket. As they strolled through the streets of McLeod Ganj, they spotted the Tibetan Mandala Café. Strangely, they had never visited the café after the first time when they had set that as the meeting point. They went straight into the café which was still open and occupied a corner table. Both sat silently for a few minutes just looking at each other when Aria broke the silence and asked, "So what will you do from here?"

"Ohh, haven't thought of that. Have little money left with me and anyhow it has been a long sabbatical. Perhaps, it is time to go back. What are your plans?" "Well for me it's simple. Submit my research, take a break for a month and then start the next project in Africa."

"Very well, so you will be off to Africa in April. Sounds great!" Shankar exclaimed.

"Yes, do you want to join me there?" She giggled

"I wish... but that is your journey. My own journey will possibly take me elsewhere."

"You are right. Our destinies are different, our worlds are different... Still, our paths intersected... it is a blessing. It is a blessing to know you, so closely....I..." She suddenly stopped speaking as she struggled with the words and the deep emotions hidden in those unspoken words.

Shankar, unable to speak anything, extended his hands and clasped her hands in his. Both of them, as strong characters they were, always fell short of words while expressing their deepest emotions, even now, when they were about to be separated. After a couple of minutes, Aria said, "Say my hello to Javed and your Mani kaka... and I wish that somehow your Sanyukta gets to you."

A bit surprised on what she had just said, Shankar remarked, "Sanyukta... no one even believes now that she is alive."

"But you believe."

"How can you say so?" Shankar was again surprised.

"I have heard you calling for her in your sleep several times; I never wanted to tell you this... you know.... I felt jealous. But then I made peace with the fact that no one could ever take her place in your heart especially when she deserves that special place."

"Ohhh, well... I don't know what to say, really. But you have once again raised the hopes in me to find her." He said slowly and then he kissed her hand. Soon they got up and left for Aria's place. The night slipped soon in each other's arms and morning announced itself with an untimely shower. Shankar came with Aria till Dharamshala airport. He wished to see her again but something in him told that this would not happen. A deluge of emotions filled her when she said goodbye, but once again she managed to hide them. All that Aria could manage to say was, "I will miss you." And then she faded/vanished in the crowd at the airport.

THE RESTLESS SOUL

AFTER ARIA LEFT, SHANKAR WAS TROUBLED and unable to cope with his solitude. He had practiced and perfected the art of living alone with his memories before Aria came into his life. But after the time spent with her, his past had rushed back to haunt him. He was now desperately looking for the way ahead. With the Sangha functioning properly, he felt no urgency to return to it. The Sangha was a dream he had once lived. But today, with no attachment to the Sangha or the days he spent there, he felt completely helpless, unable to relate with anything.

Perplexed, he sat on the banks of the Dal lake and threw a pebble in it. Lost in his thoughts, looking at nowhere, he suddenly heard the plopping sound of water as the pebble struck the water surface. Distracted by that sound, he took a bigger stone and threw it at almost the same place; this time the force was greater, the pitch of the sound produced was lower and the volume of water jumping in the air was larger. Something amused him as he took another smaller stone and threw it again. He heeded the small and big ripples generated from the point where the stone had hit the water surface. The ripples continued to the far end of the lake and then vanished away. A thought dawned upon him, "Whatever be the amount of force hitting the water surface, the ripples still get produced, affecting not only the point of contact but the whole water body." And then it made more sense to him, "*Is it not the same with us human beings? We often abstain from doing our own bit, thinking that it may not bring about any change in the current understanding. Perhaps we use this thought as an alibi to excuse ourselves from our duties and responsibilities. The fact is that however small or large an effort is, it always creates a stir in the whole ecosystem of thoughts.*"

And then suddenly his mother's teachings echoed in his mind: "Focus on your Karma without worrying about the results." He stood up and rushed back to his hotel. He packed his bags, went to the reception and checked out. He had decided to not just sit back but do what he loved, cared and felt strongly about. The results would not affect his will to act.

He reached the bus stop and the first bus he saw had Chandan Nagar as its destination. He hopped into it, took the first unoccupied seat and lost himself in the world of memories, a large part of which featured Sanyukta, and now also Aria.

THE PRODIGAL RETURNS

IT WAS LATE EVENING BY THE TIME THE bus halted at Chandan Nagar. As Shankar stepped off the bus, his childhood memories came alive in front of his eyes. He thought of his mother as he walked straight to his old home. It was already getting dark, so he did not meet anyone on the way. The little house looked bright in the moonlight, as though it were welcoming Shankar home. He pushed the weathered wooden door of the house that opened with a creak. The overwhelming pungent smell shoved Shankar back for a moment. He waited for a few minutes to allow some fresh air in and dilute the acrid smell that filled his nostrils.

He went to a corner where a broom was still lying, picked it up and with a few strokes, cleaned one corner of the main room. Placing his bag there as a pillow, he lay down on the floor and fell fast asleep.

He woke up early in the morning and looked around the house. The house was just as he had left it several years ago. Apart from a thick layer of dust and cob-webs, things were not that bad as he had assumed they would be. Without the slightest hesitancy, he picked up the broom again and started cleaning the house. The open door and the noise inside the home aroused the curiosity of the neighbors and they walked in to get a glimpse of what was happening. The number of years had had not only changed the way Shankar looked but also had weakened the eyes of people as they aged. It took them a while but as they recognized him, they instantly offered to help him out. One of the neighbors brought some breakfast. They all sat with him as he ate, asking about his life. When he finished his breakfast, a neighbor suggested that he meet with Girija. He also talked about a phone call that had come a few months ago, the caller asking for his whereabouts. Shankar was curious and rushed through the remaining chores quickly to go meet with Girija.

Girija had grown old and the toned body of yesteryear was ravaged by age. Shankar bent down and touched Girija's and his wife's feet, showing the respect for his elders who once have been his gurus. Both blessed him with a long life and hugged him. "I knew you would come someday." Girija said in a heavy tone and then he continued, "Although I was angry at you for not being in contact for so long, I am happy that you are finally here." "Don't be angry now. look at him, he has become so thin." Girija's wife said and then she started to leave saying, "I will get something for you to eat and drink."

When Shankar was settled with his snacks, Girija asked about Javed. Shankar told him about his entry and rise in the world of politics. He told Girija about the shooting as well. Girija was relieved to know that Javed had never let his fears overpower his destiny. The chat continued and soon it was lunch time. They talked about the martial arts school in Delhi, Mani, Shankar's long sabbatical in McLeod Ganj and several other things. Soon, it was just like the old times, completely informal and loving atmosphere. After the lunch, Shankar asked Girija if anyone had ever wanted to know of his whereabouts. Girija thought for a while and then told him about a phone call that had come a few months earlier. He did not remember the details, but recalled that the phone call had come from a hospital. Shankar asked Girija to try and remember more about the phone call. Girija thought for a while and then asked his wife to look for a specific diary. When she brought it, Girija opened it and started flipping the pages. After a few moments, he stopped at one page and extended the diary to Shankar.

"This was the telephone number of the hospital that called. I always thought that you would come back so I had it all noted for you. Now you handle it." Girija said.

Shankar was overwhelmed. "Thanks a lot, *Guruji.* I will call up and find out what they wanted. I must take leave now. I will be back very soon."

Girija hugged him and patted him on his back. On his way back, Shankar dialed the number of the hospital. A female voice answered the call and denied knowing anything, saying that she had recently joined. She suggested that he call back again in the morning and speak to another person. Shankar followed the advice and disconnected the phone.

He visited the house of the *Sarpanch* on his way and then finally reached home when it was already dark. He spread the cloth sheet he had borrowed from a neighbor on the ground and immediately fell asleep.

The next morning, his neighbor appeared again with a glass of milk and breakfast. Everybody was being extremely hospitable to him and he certainly welcomed all the attention.

After breakfast, he called up the same number once again. This time, another female voice answered the phone. He identified himself as Shankar calling from Chandan Nagar to the woman. On hearing this, the woman almost immediately recollected something. She paused for a while and then spoke in a heavier tone, "I had spent several hours and days trying to locate you." Perplexed on hearing this, Shankar asked again, "What is it about?"

"Well to know that you must come here once. If you somehow are searching for a woman in her early mid-thirties then this might be it."

"Sanu... are you talking about Sanyukta?" his voice suddenly quivered.

"No one knows her name. She has lost her memory. Something had stopped her from dying, otherwise, no one can survive such injuries." She breathed heavily.

"Ohhh, so how did you find me then?"

"Well, the only name we ever heard from her is Shankar and the only place she ever spoke was Chandan Nagar. I found out at least ten places in India by the name Chandan Nagar. Then I searched on the internet and found one old story on a boy who hunted a leopard in Chandan Nagar. The boy's name was Shankar. Was that really you?" The woman asked with amusement. "Ohhh... yes, I was that person."

"Umm...so I searched for someone in your village and found out one phone number and then I dialed it. The man said that he had lost contact with you for quite some time. I tried to find you somewhere else on the social media but could not. The police had sent the photo of this woman everywhere but to no avail. Finally, I am hearing back from you. It is no less than a miracle... really."

"I don't know what to say... I have no words...Umm, what is your name? And can you send me a picture of her, please? I will give you my mobile number." His voice trembled even more with excitement and heavy emotions.

"Sure. My name is Malati. I will send you her picture on your mobile. Come soon, for she definitely had more than her share of grief... By the time you come, she would have been moved to an NGO who will need all the proofs so as to ascertain that she could go with you... one more thing, when she arrived here... leave it. We will talk when you come."

Shankar was puzzled to hear the tone but sensing her predicament to talk over the phone, he did not force her. He gave his mobile number to her and thanked her several times before disconnecting the phone. In a minute, he received an MMS. As he saw the picture, he skipped a beat or two. The once beautiful face was badly scarred from the right side, the serenity of the eyes was misplaced with confusion and the once confident shoulders had drooped to give way to the despondency in the whole body. He looked at the picture continuously and then suddenly a troubled grunt erupted followed by the incessant sobs. After a few minutes as he gathered himself, he called up Javed and told him everything.

"Go friend, move fast. I will join you there. Text me the address," Javed spoke with full support. "No, you stay there. I am afraid for her safety. Please do not talk about this with anyone but Mani. Let it be a secret. Not even her parents. Will inform them once we find her. On my way, I will quickly come to Delhi and collect some of Sanyukta's latest pictures, license and other documents. We will need heaps of those to prove that we really know her, just keep them ready. I will bring her straight to our place then. I am leaving now. It might take me around a week to bring her back to Delhi. I will keep you updated. See you soon."

Shankar packed his bag and locked the old house once again. He met his neighbors who gave him their blessings. He went to meet Girija before finally embarking on the long journey, his heart full of anxious expectations.

HOPE BEGETS LIFE

HOPE TAKES A SUDDEN U-TURN ON LIFE'S track when least expected. It was happening now for Shankar, Javed and Sanyukta's parents. Everyone felt extremely relieved to know that Sanyukta was still alive but were also careful until she arrives. Javed shared the news with Mani also and they both planned out how Sanyukta's safety could be ensured. Shankar reached the hospital in just more than 24 hours. He first checked in a motel close to the hospital and then after a quick shower, he went to the hospital. It was before noon and the day was warmer than normal. He asked for Malati on the reception to which he was asked to wait. He sat on one of the few intact chairs lying there, most others were either broken or imbalanced after long time usage. The hospital's walls were a dull grey with several patches where the paint had completely come off. The floor had similar signs of aging just like the chairs had. The only ceiling fan moved incessantly at a slower speed than what it was set on the speed regulator. "Still better than most Govt. hospitals." Shankar thought to himself and fixed his eyes on one side where he expected Malati to come from. After almost thirty minutes, he saw a medium height woman dressed in the hospital uniform coming towards him. As she came close, Shankar noticed her thick wide glasses and her greying hair. She soon approached Shankar and asked in a stern voice, "Are you Shankar?"

"Yes ma'am, you must be Malati then?" He stood up and replied.

"Yes, I am." She eased herself and smiled... "Glad you have come. Anyone else with you, like her parents or someone who can prove to be in relation to her?"

"No. Do we really need someone else as well? How is she?"

"She is fine. The loss of memory is also proving to be better for her, for along with the good parts, she also does not remember the dark parts. On the need of someone else, we won't need as long as you can prove that you are related to her and can take care of her. Before I tell you any further, tell me how are you two related and what in your opinion happened to her?"

"She is my fiancée..." And then after a brief pause, he told her the entire story of her disappearance. He also took out the photographs and other documents he had brought along with him. Once convinced, Malati then asked him to sit and sat alongside. Then in a hushed voice, she said, "Did you know that Sanyukta was pregnant?"

His eyes suddenly widened as he leaned back on his chair and took a few deep sighs. Before he could say anything, Malati spoke, "Alright, I understand. So, you did not know. Well, since now you know, by the time she was brought to the hospital, she had a miscarriage. She was in her second month. The bad news is that the accident had also damaged her reproductive organs. She cannot conceive again."

"Ohh, does she know this?"

"She does not. She doesn't need to know as yet. Someone who does not even know her name, this will be a lot of information to handle."

"I agree. Where is she now?"

"She is in an NGO supported accommodation. We will have to go together to meet her. Should we leave then?"

"Yes, we should leave."

They both left immediately for the place where she stayed. A place, walking distance from the hospital, they soon reached there. Malati asked Shankar to wait in the waiting hall. His heart was thumping with the same old fierce pace it usually rose to at the sight of Sanyukta. He waited in a room, tapping his feet and with his fingers crossed in anxiety. After a few moments, the woman was brought in. His heart pounded as he saw her. He saw the scars on her face. He noticed the stitched corner of the left eye that made it slower to move than the right one. He spotted the diagonal cut on her upper lip and the cut shortened left ear lobe. He saw all of that and within a moment he could see the same beautiful Sanyukta beneath that skin. He was ecstatic to see her. He rushed forward to meet her but then immediately, he felt icy cold. Her empty eyes told him that Sanyukta remembered nothing of her past, or of him.

"You must be Shankar. Malati told me that you are my fiancé. Strange that I don't remember anything." Sanyukta spoke with a confused smile. Shankar kept on looking at her, he tried to speak but hearing her after so long, he did not want to hear his own voice. Getting no answer, Sanyukta spoke again, "Do you even speak?"

"Ohh, yes... I very much do. Just seeing you after so long. We had left any hopes of finding you ever... I, Javed, Mani kaka... ohh leave them, you won't remember them...do you?" Shankar asked with confusion.

"No..." She replied slowly with a sad smile.

"Ohh, doesn't matter. Should I show you some old pictures, it will be fun." Shankar said with a bit of exhilaration.

"Sure, let's do that." They both took the adjacent seats in the waiting hall and Shankar took out a pouch from his bag. Malati also took a seat near them and watched intently.

"Look, this is your identity card for Janadhikar Sangha; the union we all worked for... this is you again with Mani kaka, Javed and me"

"Wow...I looked pretty" She sighed

"You still look pretty." He forced

"Are you making fun of me?" She asked with a smile

"I mean it... In fact, you don't have to look pretty, you are pretty." He looked in her eyes and then continued with the pictures,"...here you go...Diwali Mela organized by our union...the day I proposed you for the marriage...."

He kept on showing hundreds of pictures, hard copies in the pouch and soft copies in his laptop, explaining almost each one of them. Though she did not remember anything, she still felt like getting transported to her past. After almost one hour, she asked about her parents.

"They are all fine. We have not yet shared your news with anyone as yet. Once we are back, I will tell them... I am concerned about your safety." Shankar tried to convince.

"Am I unsafe?" She asked with a puzzle in her eyes

"Not till I am with you and from now onwards, I will never leave you alone... even for a moment." He answered and his eyes got moist. As she saw him, she put her hand on his and then said, "I am sorry, I don't remember anything. It must be hard for you"

"Not as hard as it is for you Sanu."

"But I remembered your name... and I could feel it.... When I thought of this name, I only wanted to smile."

Looking at them from a close distance, much confident of Shankar now, Malati leaned forward and told Sanyukta, "You are not forced to go from here darling. Only if you feel confident and prepared, you should go. Anyhow it will take at least two more days to prepare all the paperwork and to verify all the documents Shankar has brought. Till then spend some time together on this premise during the day hours. There is a café at the backside where you can have something to eat or drink as well." She stood up then and asked Shankar, "You should submit all the documents for the verification. A couple of forms also need to be filled up, please get those from the reception and get it all done. I am leaving for the hospital. For any concern, you have my phone number."

Shankar nodded in agreement and asked Sanyukta to meet up in a couple of hours in the café at the premises.

After finishing the tedious paperwork, Shankar quickly reached to the café. He ran late by more than thirty minutes and the visiting hours were about to be finished. He saw Sanyukta sitting on one of the corner tables with a book in her hands. There were two women sitting on the center table and the café owner was busy counting money as he prepared to close the café in next the few minutes. Shankar rushed to Sanyukta quickly. "So, you still read books... good to know that." He remarked as he reached there.

"Did I always read?" She asked the question in a way as if she knew the answer already. "Oh yes...one common thing between us"

"Ohh, so you too like reading?"

"Well, how should I put it... Reading detoxifies me." He smiled

"That is interesting... for me... I don't know as yet but perhaps it connects me with myself. During these testing times when the whole world is unknown to me, the books have really come to my rescue."

"I can only try to understand what you have been going

through... well, so here you are in front of my eyes once again... can't tell you how happy I am. Did you have to wait long for me? Was stuck in the paperwork."

"That is ok... I have waited for months." Her eyes once again had the same sad smile.

"Hey...I will make you happy once again, I promise, even if I have to make you fall in love with me all over again... I will do every possible thing in the world to make that happen." He clasped her hands and sat close to her. Somewhere in the subconscious mind of hers, she knew this touch. And soon the familiar touch aroused a plethora of emotions in hers as the tiny droplets started effusing out of her eyes effortlessly. The droplets turned into streams and intermittent sobs became incessant. Shankar pulled her towards him and hugged tightly. After a few minutes, she felt relieved and pulled her away slowly from him. She picked up a tissue from the table, wiped her eyes and nose, and then stood up saying, "I will wait for tomorrow."

Just like old times, Shankar could not sleep in the night. The constant flow of thoughts about Sanyukta did not leave him for even a moment. "What if I could not take Sanyukta with me?" His fears had clobbered his mind and he felt more insecure than ever. On the other hand, Sanyukta slept well that night, dreaming about a new beautiful morning.

The next two days passed quickly for the both of them. They spent hours talking about their families and friends with each other. They saw the photos again and again till Sanyukta had memorized each one of the faces in the pictures by name. The third day, Malati came to them and shared the good news. The documents were all verified and the paperwork was properly completed. Now, it was up to Sanyukta's will if she felt fine to leave the place and go with Shankar. She gladly accepted to go.

Javed and Mani reached the airport to receive Sanyukta. Prepared to give her life a second chance due to her belief in Shankar, Sanyukta appeared relatively comfortable meeting them. She readily recognized Javed and Mani to greet them with a warm hello. In reply to that, Javed stepped forward and hugged her. "That is how we used to meet."

"Of course..." She replied with a smile.

"Welcome back. We are so happy to see you again." Mani said

"Thank you Kaka."

"Well done Sanu, you remember that we call him Kaka." Javed remarked gleefully.

"Hahaa...I must say that I am well trained by Shankar. But seriously, it feels great to be amongst the family."

"Well said. So, let's go home." Javed said and directed them towards his car.

Soon, he drove the car to the same old place where the three of them once lived together. Javed had rented the whole building now, which comprised of three floors, to make it safer for Sanyukta. The top floor was in the same shape as it once used to be when they all lived there. He moved first and reached the top floor to unlock the door. When he looked down at the stairs, he noticed a slight limp in the left leg of Sanyukta as she climbed up the stairs. He looked at Shankar who was right behind Sanyukta to make sure that he holds her in case of any mishap. As they entered the home, Shankar noticed exactly the same setup as it used to be. A similar but new brown couch in the hall room with the similar glass center table. The walls painted with the same off-white color. The new TV at exactly the same location. He saw everything and then he looked at Javed. He smiled at him as if saying, "Good job Javed", then he turned his glance towards Sanyukta, who looked at everything as if visiting the place for the first time. The confusion in her eyes was for some time and was replaced with the excitement to discover new things. Javed announced that he will make tea for everyone. Mani also turned on the TV and took a seat on the couch. Shankar took Sanyukta to her room and showed her wardrobe. He opened that and took out a blue suit. "This used to be one of your favorites." She took it in her hands and looked at it for some time. "This is really good. What is the story about it?"

"Well, you made me gift you this on your birthday three years ago."

"Hahaa... so I had to make you gift me. Hope you have changed now, because I love gifts. When is your birthday by the way?"

"It is tomorrow." Javed entered in and said, "Also the tea is ready, come on."

They all came out and took seats in the hall room where the tea was served with some cookies. "Try these cookies Sanu." Javed offered.

She picked up one and took a bite. "This is really nice."

"Do you remember that this was your favorite?" Javed asked

"Ohh, was it? I don't remember but I really like it."

"Excellent, problem solved then. It seems although you have

lost your memory, your preferences have still not changed. You still might like the same things you liked earlier." Javed exclaimed. "Wait, let us test this further." Shankar pointed. "Did you like your wardrobe?"

"Yeah, almost everything. What I didn't like much though was the pink tank top."

"Ok, that is good because you never liked that top. How about this hall room? What did you like and what not?"

"I like the color of the walls but not the color of the couch to start with."

"Exactly the same...see I told you, problem solved. Moreover, I think she still likes you so that says it all." Javed joked looking at Shankar.

"That means she doesn't like you even now." Shankar replied with a light laugh.

"She always liked me, remember the time when I took your proposal to her, otherwise, you had no chance..." Javed remarked teasing him.

"Well, let her decide whom she likes or not. For now, tell me what are we doing tomorrow?" Mani spoke in a loud voice looking at the three of them, while still sitting on the couch.

"What is it, tomorrow? I definitely am missing something..." Sanyukta said in a hushed voice.

"Of course, it's Shankar's thirty-sixth birthday. It calls for a party." Javed exclaimed. "Remember, we can't risk calling everyone else. Whatever happens, it happens only amongst the four of us. But...yeah, we must celebrate. It's a very special day, especially since Sanyukta is also back. I suggest that all of us gather at my place tomorrow. My daughter, Pallavi is staying at her friend's place as her board exams start next week. Also, Manju, my wife, has been asking about you all for long. I often had no answers but this will be a good time to reply to her with your presence. She really misses all the happy moments."

"It is done. It might become easier for Sanyukta as well when she meets Manju *Kaki.*"

"I wish if it were that easy though..." She sighed and then continued "But that is ok, I am absolutely fine with it." For the first time, Javed and Mani noticed the absence of her characteristic glee in her eyes. She had not only lost her identity, she was also unsure of her own interests, likes and dislikes. She had no clue about her passion and her attitude. She had even forgotten her favorite color and her favorite food. She had not just lost a name, she had lost any sense of who she actually was. The usual spark in her eyes was replaced by questions and confusion, clearly visible to the people around.

After finalizing the plan for the next day, Mani left for his home in an hour. Soon, Javed too rose to leave. When Shankar saw him leaving, he asked, "Where are you going?"

"I have to take care of a few things, brother. You take care of her and leave everything else to me. I anyhow am your neighbor. Just climb down the stairs and I can be found. This place is very safe, especially since I have got the special security provided to me by the govt. No one can dare enter the premises without my permission. Your dinner will be ready downstairs after eight, just come over. Also, I have found a very good doctor who will make frequent visits here. *Inshallah*, she will be fine soon," Javed replied before leaving the place.

After both Mani and Javed had left, Shankar noticed a slight unease in Sanyukta's eyes. It was the first time after so long that they were together, alone in a house. Once, about to be married, they stood there, face to face just like a mere acquaintance. Sensing the nervousness, Shankar proposed, "Let us watch a movie. Should we?" "Sure, which one is it?" She asked taking a seat on the couch. "Mary Kom" He smiled as he remembered that she once liked the movie.

The next day, when Shankar woke up, he heard some noise outside his room. He came out and saw Sanyukta mopping the floor. "Just like the old times." He thought. When he was about to turn back to go to his room, she said noticing his presence, "Happy Birthday". "Thanks. When did you wake up?"

"Been a while. Then I just thought to do some cleaning. I am sure you won't prefer some domestic help to come here and do the cleaning due to my security concerns." "You are right... it's better if we remain like this for a few more days. I am going to speak to my friend Hanumant soon. I told you about him...the policeman who has become a very good friend...?"

"Yes…yes, I remember that. By the way, just wondering...when are we meeting my parents?" "Ummm... I have thought about it...really. I understand what you must be feeling. Just give me a few more days and I will organize everything. Please..." Shankar nervously pleaded

"Ok. I don't think I have any other option anyhow...also, I think I trust you." She gave a faint smile.

"Thanks for that. So what is the plan for today?"

"Well, I can only follow. You have to plan."

"Ok then. First of all, we will get ready in the next hour. Then we go out for some shopping. I have to buy a few things and you certainly need to update your wardrobe, it's been a while. Then we will have lunch outside. After lunch, we will straight away go to Mani *kaka's* house. That is going to be quite a drive. I will ask Javed to arrange a car for us. How does that sound?"

"You are the boss. I am in. Just one more thing though, if you can leave me to a parlor as well for some time please."

"Sure madam. So, with the change in plan, we will first go to the parlor and then will decide on the fly."

"Great." With the decision made, the day was spent at a fiery pace. By the time, the sun went down, they had reached Mani's home. Javed had just made it before them. On seeing Sanyukta, both Mani and Javed were pleasantly surprised. After seeing her older self in the pictures, she had tried to look the closest to that. In that attempt, she spent a good four hours in the parlor. Her hair looked shiny and somewhat wavy after the blow-dry. Her skin apart from the scars looked clean and almost unblemished. Her new blue dress which she had just bought matched her earrings, pendant, sandals, and the eye shadow. "Wow, you look great." Javed was the first one to praise. "Thank you. Shankar insisted to buy this for me. It was his choice."

"Very well, the boy no doubt knows you well." Mani said smiling. Right then Manju came out from the kitchen and hugged Sanyukta warmly. She then looked at her for a few moments and then said, "You always look beautiful my darling." Then she looked at Shankar and continued, "And it is his duty to make you happy. If he ever fails, I won't spare him." Amid the smiles and frequent laughter, they all spent the evening in the togetherness of each other. When they were about to leave, Shankar thought about several such past evenings when they all made memories. He felt sad for a while but then a moment later he said to himself, "If she loved me once, she will love me again. I will make her fall in love with me."

The next morning, a medical specialist visited Shankar's place. He examined Sanyukta and studied her reports, then prescribed some medicines. He instructed Shankar not to let her feel any stress, before leaving. He also suggested that she should be familiarized with the old settings and surroundings as much as possible. Shankar worked out a plan for how to make her feel better every day. He decided to take Sanyukta to all the places they had visited together. It is said that the memories created in the time of love die hard. Now was the time to test the saying, more importantly, to test their love.

Javed came in by the afternoon and the three of them went out to have lunch. Shankar decided to go to a restaurant they had visited very often, where Sanyukta had once relished chicken biryani. A bit skeptical about the order, she later devoured the delicacy and wondered how her appetite had suddenly become so large. That day, she discovered that she loved to eat chicken biryani. Moving forward, Shankar started to compile a list of one hundred things that she had always loved. Sanyukta helped him by surrendering her free will and tendency to take decisions independently, to Shankar's knowledge of her tastes and desires. After lunch, Shankar ordered pistachio kulfi for her. She relished the dessert and wondered how she could forget that taste. When they went home, Sanyukta retired to the bedroom to take a nap. She was still recovering and her body was devoid of the raw energy, she once had. Shankar watched her sleep. He noticed that when she slept, her facial muscles were more relaxed. In that state, the scars on her face almost looked hidden beneath her thick hair. The signs of that fateful night on the back of her neck and lower back also looked milder than ever. "The only positive part of her memory loss was that she no longer recalled any of it." He thought to himself before leaving from there.

While she slept, Shankar and Javed sat outside, talking.

"How is she doing?" Javed asked.

"I think there is improvement." Shankar replied

"Hmmm, what about her parents? Has she not asked about them? And don't you think it is wise to inform them? After all, they must know that their daughter is safe and well."

"You are right. I also thought about that. But, as I see it, right now our biggest priority is her safety. I don't know if we should disclose the information to her parents as I am not sure how tightly bound that information would remain. They would certainly come here to meet and possibly take their daughter back with them. In that case, her safety might be compromised. We also do not know who is behind all that has happened to her. Whatever we know is just a point of view. There is no evidence supporting our assumptions," Shankar replied.

"I understand what you mean. But still, I think we are snatching the right of a father and mother to meet their own daughter."

"I agree. That is why I have set up a timeline for everything. I want to give us a period of six months. For her parents, another six months means nothing since for them she is already assumed dead. They have already wept for her. If they come to know that she is alive but cannot recognize them, it will make them sad again. I do not think it would help the situation in any way. Moreover, I know for sure that whatever thin chances Sanu has of recovery, those chances are only with me. I will spend every second of the next six months with her and I promise you that she will be the same Sanyukta again." By the time Shankar finished, he had a lump in his throat.

"I am with you brother, as always. We lost her once but we will not lose her again. Don't worry about work or money or anything else. The martial arts center is doing great especially with our new self-defense program for women. Your part of the profit is getting deposited in your bank account. So, six months, it is." They both smiled and then Javed left. From that day onwards, as per his plan, Shankar spent every moment with Sanyukta. His unconditional love for her was visible in its most unadulterated form. They spent their evenings at India Gate, ate her favourite dishes in various places around the city, shopped for clothes, and took long scenic drives outside the city. Shankar took her for a long drive to Shimla. He drove her to the pristine Thar Desert and Jaisalmer. Sanyukta loved every moment and wondered how somebody else could know so much about her and then felt happy every time she added one more item to her list of favorites.

By now, the weather was changing. The trees had started shedding their leaves. Shankar and Sanyukta were blissfully happy for almost five months. Though the doctors still struggled to find a clear solution to her lost memory, Shankar's dedicated efforts never lost their steam, despite no signs of improvement. She did not remember anything and this made her more and more stressed when she considered it. She liked the time spent with Shankar but she felt, deep down, that she no longer felt the same love she had once, supposedly, felt for him.

PART 5

NEW BEGINNING

25TH AUGUST, 2018. THAT DAY, JAVED CALLED Shankar and told him about an invitation from an orphanage. He was to be the chief guest at their annual day function. He suggested that Shankar brings Sanyukta along. Spending some time with children might be a good change for her. Shankar agreed that the visit might be therapeutic for Sanyukta and followed his advise.

On the day of the event, Shankar was dressed in a lemon shirt and black trousers. He wore a pair of elegant light brown leather shoes that matched the color of his belt. While brushing his hair, he noticed his receding hairline and the grey at his temples. Time never stops, he thought to himself and smiled as he started whistling a song from a Raj Kapoor film: "*Kisi ki muskurahaton pe ho nisaar, kisi ka dard mil sake to le udhar, kisi ke waaste ho tere dil mein pyaar, Jeena isi ka naam hai...*" Sanyukta heard Shankar whistling and came out of the room, dressed in a red and white salwar kameez. When Shankar looked at her, she was already smiling. She looked dazzling. He noticed the reappearance of the sparkle in her eyes. They both left for the function, feeling uncharacteristically giddy.

When they reached the venue, a set of people rushed towards the gate to welcome them. It was a very different scene from what they had expected. The orphanage was set in a fairly large compound; more than fifty children were comfortably seated on the uneven grassy earth. The guests were expected to sit on a dais in an elevated part of the grounds, barely a few meters from the stage where the kids would perform.

They were ushered to the chief warden's office and made comfortable. While they waited for him, they gazed at the photographs of the children, arranged around the wall. Sanyukta's gaze rested on a picture and she gave a short laugh. A small girl, around four or five years old, was covered in thick mud, staring out at the viewers.

"Welcome, welcome both of you." Shankar and Sanyukta turned and saw a middle-aged woman entering the office.

"I am Geeta, the chief warden and the founder of this initiative," the woman introduced herself. "Pleased to meet you. It makes me so happy to meet people like you who are contributing so much to society." Sanyukta smiled.

"Thanks for mentioning that. I noticed you were looking at that picture." Geeta pointed towards the picture.

"Yes, indeed. I like it," Sanyukta replied.

"You know what, that is my favorite picture because it reminds me of the fact that children are so different from the grown-ups."

"Yes, children are certainly different but I am keen to hear your views on how you think this picture conveys that message," Sanyukta tilted her head curiously.

"Well, during the rainy season, this place is deluged. The narrow streets around it get clogged with muddy water, all movement stops, food supply is erratic, and everybody is forced to the upper floors. Diseases spread and so do the rodents. The sunlight brings relief for a day but then the sunlight starts the destruction too. The streets become more clogged with cars and mud, the buildings develop deeper cracks, the dust becomes stronger in the air and the tin roofs show big holes. Those two months are quite calamitous for us." Geeta paused for a while and then she spoke with a smile. "But this is just for us, the grown-ups. These kids, despite all the hue and cry, are least affected. The muddy water is like a splash pool and the raindrops are moments of happiness in their lives. They smile even during the toughest times, the same way you can see this little girl smiling in that picture."

"You are right. Children are so different. We can learn a lot from them." Sanyukta nodded in appreciation.

"Very well said. We will now move to the venue where the children are waiting to perform for us." Geeta led her visitors towards the ground.

Geeta was an elderly lady, widowed very early in her life. Post her husband's demise in a road accident, she had dedicated herself to the service of orphaned kids. After years of struggle, she realized it was rare that somebody came to see and understand how well she had contributed to the society. For the disinterested people, she would put on broad smiles and a conscious effort to charm the influential visitors who could possibly give a generous donation to the comfort of the orphanage. But Geeta was no sycophant; she was a strong character. She was neither offensive nor was she flattering; she respected herself. She was genuinely happy to see the compassion in her visitors' eyes and didn't try to conceal that happiness.

The kids sang a couple of songs. Then a group of six little girls arrived, dressed in colorful clothes to present a dance performance. The sparkle in their eyes was so delightful that Sanyukta felt a tear suddenly falling down her cheek. The emotions in their most nascent stage are like uncurbed horses. You don't know how to stop or control them; they just move and fly as per their will. There are only a few moments in one's life where the mind and soul of a person are aimed in the same direction, this is when the force of energy is at its acme and the body radiates the energy in the form of an ethereal light on the face which can't go unnoticed from the seekers. Shankar saw it. While he looked at Sanyukta, she was already drowned deep in the past and was staring at nothing. Suddenly she came out of her pleasantly aching thoughts and noticed the smile of one of the dancing kids. She broke out in excitement, "Oh, she is the one in that picture."

The little girl was in a pink frock. She had dimples on her brown cheeks, which had been reddened by the lip gloss that had been applied there. She had large brown eyes and long curls flipping on her forehead which she regularly tried to move back with a stroke from the back of her hands.

There were a couple of other cultural activities that included one more dance and one small play before the little girl returned to the stage with a poem. It was a confident recital about the great warrior queen, Laxmi Bai. The girl was an ordinary child with an extraordinary tone to her voice and sparkle in her eyes.

The function went on for almost two hours, after which both Shankar and Sanyukta returned to their home. Sanyukta looked very happy. When they returned, she told Shankar that she would like to re-paint their place. She insisted on doing it all by herself. The next morning, Shankar bought the paint and tools she had requested. He helped her clean the place and then whitewashed the walls. Sanyukta painted them a light chocolate brown. They painted one wall of the living room in brick red and put a large oil painting of a wild horse galloping across the grasslands. She changed the arrangement of the furniture and went on a shopping spree for the next three days. She bought a new double queen size bed, a study table, a revolving chair with an armrest and a twin-seater couch whose fabric matched with the color of the walls. After a week of work, Shankar and Sanyukta stood inside a beautifully redintegrated home. That evening, they went to a restaurant for dinner when Sanyukta said, "I know that I can never give birth to a child."

Shankar was startled by Sanyukta's statement. He didn't say anything. Sanyukta looked at him and then continued, "I have read my medical reports and I accept my fate. But I can still enjoy motherhood by adopting a child."

Shankar suddenly straightened up and looked at her. He had watched her expressions during the function in the orphanage. But he had not expected such a thought from her.

"Well, that is not a bad idea. I will support you completely," Shankar replied in an earnest voice. "I expected nothing less from you. Can we go and meet Geeta tomorrow? I wish to know the process," Sanyukta said.

"Sure my dear. We are on." Shankar matched her enthusiasm.

After making an appointment, Shankar and Sanyukta visited the orphanage the next afternoon. Geeta welcomed the idea wholeheartedly. She gave them a few documents and told them to see her after two weeks to discuss the path ahead. When they studied the documents, they realized that they did not meet the requirements for being parents. First of all, they were not married and second, they had no clear plans for their future and income.

"Well, it is a tough road ahead. I don't know how ready you are to get married to me. Also, it will be tough to bring up the child once our savings are consumed in the next three-four months. The martial arts school can support both of us but with an additional member, it would struggle." Shankar said.

"Hmmm, so in this case, let's address one problem at a time. First thing, let us get married." Shankar almost jumped from his seat on hearing those words and she laughed. "Do not worry, I am not marrying you just for the child but because I want to marry you. I believe that you love me and I feel protected when I'm with you. It may not be exactly the kind of love that people generally talk about, but the way I feel for you is certainly not anything less than that either." "Hey, did you just propose to me?" Shankar asked with a naughty smile.

"Of course I did. But don't you dare say no to me!" Sanyukta replied.

"No way, madam." He jumped forward and stole a kiss. Feeling shy about the unexpected kiss, she rolled her eyes and looked at Shankar. "Whattt?" at least now I should be allowed to kiss you. Been so long since I have stopped myself." Shankar smirked in a baffling tone.

"Is it?" She giggled as she saw him folding his hands.

"Yes, my darling..." Shankar came close to her.

She saw her image in his eyes so close to hers. The tenderness of ever benevolent love was once again spreading its aroma everywhere. In a moment, Shankar placed his lips on hers. She did not resist and after a moment started kissing him back. It continued for several minutes till their lips hurt. Then as the lips were unlocked, they felt the warmth of each other's breath and saw the red faces of each other. "Do you remember our first kiss?" Shankar whispered.

"No...but I won't forget this one." She replied.

"That sounds promising." He smiled and then he pulled back continuing from where they had just paused, "So, first things first, let us get married. I will call Javed and Mani Kaka. They will have to make the arrangements. Also, I believe it's time to meet your parents as well. We should visit them. Let me call them first."

Soon Shankar called her parents. Her mother answered the phone and took no time to recognize him. "I have to share something important to you, Aunty."

"I am listening, since you have called, it must be important." She replied in a bit curious tone. "We have found your daughter, Sanyukta."

"Whhaattttt??? How come... How is she and where is she?"

"She is fine and safe with us right now."

"Oh my god... bring her on the phone. I want to hear her voice..." Then she moved her mouth away from the receiver and called for her husband ecstatically, "Listen, Sanyukta's papa...come here fast."

"Aunty...wait a moment, there is one more thing..." His voice quivered.

"What is that Shankar?"

"She has lost her memory after the accident. She doesn't recognize anyone and doesn't remember anything."

"Ohhh no. So you mean that she doesn't remember even me?"

"Yes, aunty."

"I understand... well, at least she is alive and we remember everything about her. We will remind her of everything. Don't worry. Are you bringing her here or we should come over?"

"I will bring her. We can leave today if you are there."

"Very much here my son, very much. We are waiting. Come soon. I will cook her favorite food and will set up her room right now."

After disconnecting the phone, he thought to himself, "I should have called them earlier..." Then he looked at Sanyukta who stood beside him, "We should leave immediately."

"Sure. How are they and what did they say?"

"Ohh, they are super excited to hear that you are here. They just want to meet you immediately..."

"What happened? What is troubling you?" She asked as she picked up the defensive tone in his voice.

"Nothing much... uhh, actually, I want to make a confession Sanu."

"Go ahead..."

"After talking to your parents I realized that I should have told them much earlier. I don't know what was I thinking, Javed warned me a couple of times but I did not realize my mistake until now. Sorry about that."

"Hmmm...we will know how big the mistake is after we meet my parents. For now, let's leave." She said in a cogent tone.

In a couple of hours, they both were out on the road traveling to Sanyukta's parents in a rental car, Javed had organized for them. As the destination drew closer, strangely Shankar felt more nervous than her. Apart from the guilt of keeping them away from their daughter, he also felt sorry for them since he had recently felt the pain of having your most loved one completely failing to recognize you. He didn't want her parents to feel it. On the contrary, Sanyukta felt no such pressure. She looked in control and much better prepared to kick start her new life. "I can see the future clearly Shankar. I do not know what my aspirations were earlier but as of now, I see a family of my own. You, I and a little girl. I will know my parents now and through their eyes, I will know myself better... just the way in the past months, I have come to know about me through you." She said to Shankar when she saw him tapping his feet incessantly while sitting in the car.

"Hmmm, just so you know... you also had an elder brother. He died years ago in an accident." Shankar quickly briefed her hiding the details carefully.

"Ohh... I should have known that. Thanks for letting me know. What happened to him?"

"I... I do not know the details. Maybe, you should not even ask your parents. Some things are better if stay untouched."

"I understand... I will remember that."

After four hours, the car entered a street. When they looked outside, two people stood in the corner of the street looking at their car. The man in his early sixties, wearing a white Kurta Pyjama and the woman probably in her late fifties in a maroon suit, perhaps stood there for at least a few minutes. They perhaps had peeped into every car passing by, expecting their long-lost daughter. And now they looked at the white car with a bit of hesitation so as to not to fool themselves once again. Shankar, recognizing them from the distance, poked Sanyukta with the elbow, "Your mom and dad." As she realized, she immediately lowered her car window and waved her hand towards them.

"There they are." The man exclaimed.

The car came to a halt just in front of them. Shankar quickly got out to open the door for Sanyukta but she had already done that and come out to meet her parents. The warm smiles of them which had the scent of the long wait and an undeterred hope were extremely contagious. Sanyukta became a part of those hugs and assimilated into those emotional moments in no time. "And I forgot these hugs as well." An emotional Sanyukta thought. Realizing that she does not need him to sort out her likes and dislikes in that environment, Shankar took a sigh of relief and moved ahead to greet her parents. Her mom and dad who had suddenly started looking younger embraced the young man and then started walking to go inside the house with white walls and yellow boundary walls.

As they went inside, her dad, Mr. Kapil Bhatnagar asked them to be seated on the grand old teak wood Sofa. Sanyukta's mother, Mrs. Nishita Bhatnagar called their servant, Raju, to bring in water. Then she sat next to Sanyukta and took her hands in hers. She kept looking at her face, her scars, her eyes and her ears for some time. When her eyes got moist, Sanyukta pulled her forward and said, "I am okay, mumma."

"Yeahhh... as if I can't see that."

"No really... these are only the scars, they don't hurt anymore." She replied sincerely.

"I believe you...tell me, did you really forget everything once?"

"Once..?" Sanyukta sounded puzzled.

Sensing her confusion, her mother rephrased herself, "I mean, now since you remember everything, me, your dad, your home etc... did you really not once remember all of it?" "Maa... I...." As she struggled with words, her dad stood from his seat and came closer to his wife, "Nishi, bring her something to eat. Our daughter has come after so long and you are bombarding her with your questions... come on." As he forced her to get up from there, she stood and went inside the kitchen frowning a bit.

"Don't worry about your mother, you know how she is..." Her dad spoke loudly so that his wife could hear and then he winked at his daughter. When he saw his wife disappearing into the kitchen, he sat near Sanyukta and said, "I know how you would feel. She just doesn't accept that you have really forgotten everyone. I will make her understand. Don't worry and don't stress at all."

"I am not worried dad, just finding it strange myself that how could I forget such affectionate touch of yours and mom." She lowered her eyes as she found her eyes moist too.

"Don't worry, now when you are with us, we will make sure that we create beautiful new memories together which you will never forget again." He flustered his large hands through her hair and patted on the back of her head with a soft and gentle touch. He then turned to Shankar and said, "Thanks for bringing her back to us Shankar. We owe it to you."

"Not at all Sir. In fact, I am sorry that I took so long to bring her back." Shankar first time confessed to himself that he always felt a bit intimidated in front of Sanyukta's father. His large hands and his broad chest made him look like a landlord of some kind and his long-twisted moustache on his round face further made him look like a decorated army personnel, much different from his real occupation of a banker. Immediately then, Sanyukta's mother came in with a tray of *laddoos* in her hands. "Have this *beta*" The forever soft and gentle voice of Sanyukta's mother, on the other hand, always brought back his confidence which he had just lost in front of her father. It happened again. He took one *laddoo* and he suddenly felt relieved again. "Over to Sanu now." He thought to himself, then he looked at Sanyukta and smiled. She smiled in return.

They spent the next five days there together. They went to watch a Hindi movie, "Padmaavat" in the local theatre. They ate *kachoris, golgappas* and *samosas* from the street vendors. They went to Sanyukta's school and met the teachers there. While Sanyukta explored the house that once was her home, she found an old trunk. As she opened, she was pleasantly surprised to see a picture of hers, several years younger, lying inside. She ecstatically shouted, "Look at this dad. What have I found."

"Oh wow. My girl has found a lost treasure." He too rejoiced in the childish explorations of his grown-up daughter.

They together took out the stuff from the trunk to find out several of Sanyukta's old writings, her poems, her coin collection, pictures and several greeting cards. One very old poem which she penned at the age of 10, read:

"I am my papa's doll,

The whole world is just like a playground. With bhaiya the referee,

I am free to kick the ball anywhere around. With mumma in my team,

I can never lose my ground. This is my perfect abode,

Where love, laughter and happiness surround.

I Love my family

She read the poem several times and moved from one room to another with the paper in her hands. She laughed out on the innocence of those words of a very young girl. In a way, she was happy to know about her lost parts and that happiness, as infectious as it was, spread through the rooms and the walls of that aging house.

At the end of those five days, Shankar had discovered another dimension of his soon-to-be better half. The dimension that was always hidden from him, even in the older times. "Was it suppressed because of the haunting memories of her past or this part of hers can only open up in front of her parents?" He thought... "Whatever it is, it is great to see her happy. Happy, the way I have never seen her."

On the sixth day, in the morning, Shankar went to Sanyukta's room and woke her up. "What happened?" She asked still half asleep. "You had to talk about our marriage with your parents. When are you planning to do that?"

"Well, you should do that. Are you scared of my dad?" She giggled lightly

"Don't laugh. Decide soon. We have to then prepare for the wedding and then have to talk with the orphanage as well. Don't you remember?" He said a bit seriously.

"Ohh, don't be so serious Shankar. I will talk soon. I am having so much fun here, just can't stop it..." She gave that cuddly look to him and smiled.

"Okk, if you don't speak today, I am going to speak with your dad tomorrow. I am not scared of anyone." And he stood up after saying that.

From there, he straight went into the compound and started strolling there, thinking of the best way to broach the subject of their marriage in front of Sanyukta's parents, her dad in specific. A few minutes had passed when he saw Sanyukta's daddy approaching straight to him. He felt a bit nervous. A few moments later, Mr. Bhatnagar reached him and said, "Quite early today. Is everything okay?"

"Yes Sir. All is well."

"Hmm... I think it's time when you should stop addressing me "Sir" or "Uncle"."

"Umm...I didn't get you..." Shankar understanding what it meant, pretended to not have understood.

"Well, you both should get married soon now. I can see that you both love each other, then why is the delay? Do that so you can proudly call me Daddy as well." He answered in a convincing tone.

"Yeahhh...I guess, whatever Sanu says." He said in a relaxed tone.

"Wonderful, I expected that. I will speak with her today. Let me see what is cooking in her head." He winked.

"Sure, by the way... I just wanted to tell you something. There is a burden I am feeling and I want to share it with you." Shankar stepped up and for the first time, he initiated a topic to discuss.

"Sure, go ahead."

"I am guilty of not telling you about Sanyukta for so long. I just did not realize what I was doing. I am sorry for that."

Suddenly taken aback by this disclosure, Sanyukta's dad

stepped back a bit but then in a second, he came forward, put his hand on Shankar's right shoulder and said in a poetic way, "*Na tu galat, na main sahi.* Neither you are wrong, nor am I right. I am sure you would have a reason to do what you did. We can always take sides between "Right" and "Wrong" but, factually, the life dwells somewhere in between these two extremes. I am glad you spoke what you felt and I admire it. Just don't tell this to Mrs. Bhatnagar... Keep no grudge and prepare for the next chapter of your life."

"Thank you Sir... ohh, sorry, Dad..." Shankar smiled as Mr. Bhatnagar embraced him to his broad chest.

That afternoon, Sanyukta's dad suggested Shankar and Sanyukta get married in Bareilly itself. "It will be safer for you, my daughter." He almost concluded.

No one saw a problem in that, so the proposal was accepted by consensus. By the evening, the wedding preparations had started with a target date of 23rd September, just after 15 days. The date was finalized based on a high possibility of getting the date in the court for the registered marriage.

Though there were not many guests, contrary to how Sanyukta's parents had once dreamt of her wedding, there were still enough activities and charm to make the ambiance vibrant. They made the guest list that evening itself. Shankar suggested Sanyukta to reveal about her survival to her boss, Mr. Das and invite him to the wedding. "We have to carefully start revealing about her. Cannot keep it a secret forever. Also, the way Mr. Das had always worked with us and Sanyukta especially, I believe he also deserves to know about you. And you may not remember but you always lavished praise on him, Sanu." He put forth his argument. With no one to say against the argument, the guest list was soon finalized. Shankar called up Javed, Mani, Hanumant and Mr. Das himself and invited them formally. Mr Das., first shocked and then pleasantly surprised after knowing everything, happily gave them blessings. He, however, conveyed his inability to attend the wedding due to some prior commitments. Javed called up Girija as well, inviting him and his wife for Shankar's marriage. He however due to his wife's ill health, instead invited all of them to their home in the village after the wedding.

The shopping started the next day, that continued till the very last moment. Mr. Bhatnagar got the appointment for the registered marriage in the court as well, for the same day, as planned. Two days before the wedding, Mr. Bhatnagar's home was filled with omnipresent laughter and music. All the guests had reached their home. As a very private and concealed affair, no relative of Mr Bhatnagar's family knew about the wedding. The only select attendees were Javed, Mani with his family and Hanumant apart from the two next-door neighbors of the Bhatnagar family. Finally, the day came when the marriage was registered in the court of law, making Shankar and Sanyukta legal husband and wife. The wedding was followed with a lavish dinner hosted by Mr. Bhatnagar in Hotel Sapphire, the five-star hotel in Bareilly. Mani hosted the cocktail party the second night that was attended by all. Javed booked the honeymoon suite for the newlywed couple for 3 nights in the same hotel as the wedding. The celebrations came to an end with the cocktail party. People started to disperse leaving an aroma of their presence everywhere around.

After spending three days in the hotel room which Javed had booked for them, the couple reached Sanyukta's home to see the family one final time before they leave for Delhi. As it dawned upon them that the house will once again reek of the emptiness, both of the parents felt a lump in their hearts. While Mrs. Bhatnagar hugged them tightly as if she would never let them go, Mr Bhatnagar seemed to have saved the final words for the last moment. He came forward and gently touched Sanyukta's cheeks saying, "Never lose faith in yourself. You have never ever done anything in your life that could make us any less proud of you." Then he looked at Shankar and before hugging them both he said, "You will always take care of her, I know that."

The journey back to Delhi was the silent one. Both Shankar and Sanyukta were transiting from one phase of their lives to another. The two phases conjoined by several strands of memories and experiences in one phase, and the web of aspirations and desires of another. As they were about to reach Delhi, Sanyukta said, "The next on the checklist, to adopt the girl, is to work out a stable income for us."

"Right... by the way, sometimes I feel that you have married me only to complete that checklist..." Shankar spoke in a lighter vein. "Well if you say so... my darling" She raised an eyebrow and then gently put her hands on his cheeks.

"Whatever... I am happy." He smiled and then spoke in a slightly serious tone, "Mr. Das seems to have something for us. He texted me this morning."

The next hurdle, finding a stable source of income, needed much more planning and work. The next day, Shankar called Mr. Das. The man who had constantly supported Shankar's vision and Sanyukta's natural talent, asked them to meet him in Delhi. He planned to visit in a couple of days.

They met Mr. Das in a café, "Fairmont", in South Delhi, in the university area. Dressed in his quintessential khadi kurta, white pyjama and rectangular black spectacles, he shook hands with Shankar on meeting and congratulated for the wedding. Then he turned towards Sanyukta and asked, "Are you trying to recognize this aging face, Sanyukta?"

As if caught red-handed, she turned her eyes from his face and then not to embarrass herself anymore, she reached out for his hands and shook them while keeping a smile on her face. "Congratulations to you as well Sanyukta. I am very happy to see you finally." Mr. Das said. "Thank you, Sir." She replied.

They took a seat and Shankar ordered two latte coffees for himself and Sanyukta and one Long Black for Mr. Das.

"First of all, here is your wedding gift, Sanyukta." He took out a parcel and handed over to Sanyukta.

She accepted the parcel and opened it. There she found a bank's cheque book and some bank letters.

"What is this, Sir?" She enquired.

"These are your banking documents and investment documents. You had given the office address for the communication. You almost always took my suggestions when investing. I am sure after this long and with the recent rally in the stock market, your mutual fund investment would have been multiplied. This was anyhow your money. As the wedding gift, I have transferred you three months of salary as the joining bonus to once again start working with us. The offer letter is also sent to your email address."

"Ohh... that is a lot Sir... isn't it? I don't know how should I react..." She spoke with a mix of excitement and confusion in her tone.

"It is nothing Sanyukta. You deserve this. Moreover, as you both start a new journey now, I think this should be useful." Then he turned towards Shankar and asked, "What are your plans, Shankar? You have done great as well. I have always followed "Janadhikar Sangha". You are the biggest and the strongest pillar of the union. What a spectacular journey that has been... great job."

"Thanks for the kind words Mr. Das. But I am not that much associated with the Sangha now anymore. I think my role is over there." Shankar replied in a casual manner.

"Why do you say that? I don't know what is in your mind but I don't believe that you can ever take the Sangha out of you and nor can the Sangha pull you out ever." Mr. Das said persuasively.

"I differ from you. I think the Sangha has found the true pathfinder in the form of Javed. He now is the face of the Sangha." Shankar scratched his head by the thumbnail of his right hand.

"And you are the soul of that. And you, Sanyukta, Javed and Mani together are the heart. Anyway, I won't judge your opinion. You do what you think is right." He said and leaned back on his chair with a light frown on his forehead.

"I didn't want to offend you Mr. Das. You know that I respect you a lot." Shankar spoke defensively.

"And I admire you, Shankar... I have admired you like anything. Sanyukta also admired you for these qualities. Now she may not remember but she always spoke about you with her head held high. Also remember that the world does not fail when the incapable fails, it happens when the capable quit." Mr. Das spoke fervently and then he looked at the time on his expensive wristwatch.

"Okk, I agree with what you said. I also agree that I can't take out the Sangha from me. But in my current situation, I have to make a living, I have to earn money. I don't find it right to accept any money from the Sangha for any work I do for it. People have opened their hearts and wallets out to fund our activities. I can't use that money to buy my bread and butter."

"Hmm, that makes more sense. In that case, I have a proposal for you. In fact, the proposal is for both of you. Do you want to hear it out?" Mr. Das asked moving his right hand on his greyed hair pushing them back.

'Sure."

"I am starting a new venture in the world of Citizen Journalism. It is an online portal called "*Aap se Aap Tak*", short form "ASAT", where the normal citizens of India can join and contribute by telling their parts of the stories. The concept is still new in India but it has tremendous potential. Moreover, it can work as another arm to Janadhikar Sangha that communicates in the fast-growing digital world. Just imagine, the most under-privileged people getting voice through this platform. Also, since many of those people are not literate, the portal has an advanced text to speech conversion technology implemented. People will just speak and it will be converted into the text of their choice of language. The news stories will be moderated for any errors before publishing." Mr. Das finished and looked at both of them as if asking for their feedback.

"Wow, it sounds amazing. What do I need to do?" Shankar asked

"Not you alone, you both need to be prepared and jump in it. I can offer a great deal. You both can be on-board and hold equity in the venture. This can be big. Do not rush for anything. Just think about my proposal for a few days and then let me know."

They soon then finished their coffees and took leave from there. Shankar and Sanyukta could envision a new world in front of them. But often it happens that when life brings you an opportunity, it often accompanies another. Shankar and Sanyukta also had two opportunities in front of them and it seemed they could take hold of only one. They sensed that if they involved themselves with Mr. Das then it would be difficult for them to continue with their adoption process, their second opportunity to bring a meaningful change in their lives. That is where Javed came forward to their rescue. He offered to support them fully to take care of the child. "The girl won't have only two parents like everyone else, she would have three parents." He said supportingly.

They visited the orphanage to meet Geeta and the little girl. They updated Geeta about their plan, proposing to adopt the girl, formally within the next few months as the paperwork itself was expected to take a considerable amount of time. Mani also suggested that they should disclose the fact of Sanyukta's return to the other Sangha members. He argued that once she became active in the business world, it would not remain a secret any longer. At least this way, they would retain some control over her security and the measures they could take.

Everybody agreed and they revealed the news of Sanyukta's return. Sanyukta's complete loss of memory was also revealed as a measure for her safety so that the perpetrators do not have a reason to fear. In a week, ASAT started and along with started the long, and unending paperwork to adopt the girl child. Mr. Das told them that he was meeting a big investor in nine months and if Shankar and Sanyukta could help with the scaling up before that, then he could have a much better chance of gaining the financial backing. Both fully ready to make it big accepted the challenge, and started working day in and out. They wanted to utilize every second of the time till they become the full-time parents.

As the news of Sanyukta's return broke out, by then the promoted Sub-Inspector Hanumant Sharma, immediately stationed a constable in front of their residence for protection and extra safety.

While so much happened in the lives of Shankar and Sanyukta, the news of Sanyukta's return had made some people nervous. Ajay Singh, in particular, was extremely baffled.

"How could she survive such an accident? Both my men were killed that night but she is still alive. How is it possible? My boss will be furious when he knows this." Ajay Singh thought to himself as he was fuming to one of his accomplices.

"This is rather strange, I agree, but fortunately she does not have any memory of the past," the man with the dark brown skin standing in front of Ajay Singh said.

"How can you be so sure? They might just be playing some tricks." He raised his left eyebrow and questioned angrily.

"Sir, I have news of her medical condition. I have the details of her doctor and her medical reports. Moreover, she was released from the hospital about a year ago. If she remembered anything, don't you think they would have already done something against us by now?" The man said. "Yes, you are right. But I am not fully satisfied. I want you to organize a way to keep an eye on her activities," Ajay Singh emphasized.

"Don't worry, sir. I am sending my special men to keep a close watch on her. If anything seems suspicious, we will get to know." Ajay Singh felt relieved for the first time in the last twenty- four hours as he heard the man promising convincingly.

Ajay Singh belonged to a middle-class family from Uttar Pradesh. He was always interested in getting into the political arena, but the first time he stood in the college elections, he suffered serious injuries. The opponent was a distant relative of the state ruling party and that was when he realized that everything could be altered for personal gains through the use of power. The incident made him crave for power. He defied the strength of the opponents and stood once again in the college elections in the final year and arranged support for himself. His remarkable win over the much stronger opponent attracted many mainstream political wizards, but it was Devi Dutt who gained Ajay's loyalty. Devi Dutt, at that time, was already in his forties, but unmarried and devoted to nothing but politics. Ajay's loyalty for Devi Dutt was unquestioned and this had led him to the top rank in the party. He was an extremely confident man who trusted no one but himself.

On the other hand, far from the hue and cry of politics, both Shankar and Sanyukta worked with great enthusiasm. They worked day and night with the same old vigor and passion.

Their energies kept on increasing as the days passed and as the date of adopting the little girl came closer. They took the help of the Sangha to find stories for the venture. With thousands of eyes and ears helping them, they were soon loaded with many good pieces of information. With the quality of the information provided and the strategic marketing approach under the keen eyes of Mr. Das, the portal found its takers. The number of hits on the web-portal grew rapidly and consistently.

As the venture prospered, Mr. Das felt increasingly confident and certain that with the current statistics, any investor would be pleased to work with them.

Seven months passed like a whiff. The financial year had come to an end and all the reports were generated. On 27th April, 2019, much less than nine months from the date Shankar and Sanyukta were brought on board of the web-portal, the meeting with the investors took place and was a big success. The venture got good funding and Mr. Das declared bonus dividends for all the stakeholders. With strong financial support to back their plan of adoption, the last hiccup too got kicked out of their way. The rest of the paperwork was already completed. Both of them went to meet Geeta in the orphanage as per the schedule on 6th May. Geeta welcomed them warmly and started the conversation. "I am glad to see you both back. Many want to be parents remain in a dilemma regarding taking such a responsibility. Thankfully you did not."

"You are right. Being a parent is certainly not easy. We thought it over several times but it was Sanyukta's determination that brought us here today." Shankar spoke with a smile and looked proudly at Sanyukta.

"I am glad to hear that. So how do you plan to go ahead with this?" Geeta asked.

"Geeta ji, if you allow it, then we are completely prepared to take the little girl home," Sanyukta said.

"Well, I am convinced by your motivation. You should get your home ready now because we need to do an inspection before allowing our child to start living with you. You may take another couple of weeks to complete the preparation and then we will come for the inspection," Geeta replied.

"Sounds great," Sanyukta said cheerfully.

Both Shankar and Sanyukta came back with a lot of plans in their minds.

They spent the next two days with an interior design consultant. Shankar raced to the market to buy a whole list of toys, books and clothes. The work inside their home was in full swing, under the expert scrutiny of the consultant. The next week, Shankar started noting down the advertisements for the primary schools where they would have to send their daughter. Two weeks passed in a jiff and the orphanage staff reached the place as per the schedule.

The inspection was successfully done and received acceptance from the center. The house that had witnessed several timeless memories, which was once even devoid of life and enthusiasm, bore a fresh feeling of flowers blossoming in the spring. The walls had been painted sage green and the largest wall was covered from one end to another with pink base wallpapers bearing the fantastic images of Cinderella, Snow White, Thumbelina, and many more characters completely unknown to Shankar. The double bed in the smaller bedroom was covered with a beautiful bedsheet, which bore the images of many more animated characters. The cupboard's top two partitions were full of tiny dresses in a range of colors. The lower two partitions had loads of toys. Shankar made space on his bookshelf to give way to many picture books for his daughter.

Everybody has a right to start once and "the start" always comes with no prior experience. But parenthood is such a huge job that even without any prior experience, people must not forget that providing luxuries and facilities is never a big deal because those can be bought by money; the all-important task is to inculcate values and build character in the child, which reflects his or her own uniqueness and peculiarity. No money can do that, for it needs the strong force of molding thoughts which only a thinking parent can do. The soul of a child should be irrigated by the stream of positive and constructive thoughts. Shankar and Sanyukta were those concerned parents who stepped into the world of parenthood with a lot of thought.

On 21st May, 2019, the new parents gave a very warm welcome to the little girl in her new home. Well acquainted with each other over the period of the last few months, they now were starting a new life together under the same roof. The little girl, turning six in a month, stepped in cautiously into her new life. As she hesitantly moved around her new home looking at everything in her surroundings with curiosity mixed with awe, the new parents followed her quietly. When she reached the bedroom, specially decorated for her, she froze at the large pink wallpaper covering the whole wall with a beautiful picture of an animated character "Moana". She stood there stupefied while the parents watched her from the back. After a few minutes, the curious parents came forward and knelt down watching their daughter from the two sides. "What happened darling? Did you not like it? We will change it if it is so..." Sanyukta said in a slow hushed tone.

The girl looked at her and then suddenly wiped a tear that had just come out of her eyes uncontrollably. Surprised at the strength of such a young girl, Shankar asked, "Hey... You can tell us anything you want. We are your mom and dad, we will always take care of you and will never ever hurt you."

"Noth... nothing." She controlled her sob and gave a firm answer.

"Hey... no rush. We are now living together as a family and family is always there for each other. Whenever you want to talk, we are all ears." Sanyukta pulled the girl towards her and hugged her tightly. After a few hesitant moments, the girl melted into her arms and embraced her with her little arms. And then she said, "Geeta amma always said that someone will come one day and will take care of each one of us. All of us always believed her but never saw anyone coming over. You are the first one I saw who did what she made us believe in."

Shankar looking at them in the mirror on the opposite wall, had a warm smile on his face.

In the evening, when they sat on the dinner table, Sanyukta asked the girl, "Sweetie, is it fine if we change your name? We both think that a new name will also give you a fresh start of life and help forget all the bad memories of the past if you have any. Do you think so?"

The girl, a bit surprised on the question started rolling her forefinger in her curly hair. "Just like you" Shankar whispered to Sanyukta.

"If you do not want, then we won't do that. We also like your name Dipti." Sanyukta spoke again with a smile.

"It is ok. Whatever you decide." She answered smilingly.

"Excellent... let us ask your dad what is his favorite name. Tell me Shankar, suggest a beautiful name for our wonderful daughter."

"Well, you decide. I am fine with whatever you decide." Shankar replied shyly.

"No. Don't start running from the responsibilities, Mr. Dad." Sanyukta forced again with a naughty smile. The girl giggled on seeing the light-hearted teasing.

"Alright ladies... I will think of a beautiful name... in fact I am thinking now... and as I think.... One name that comes to my mind is Ar..."

He suddenly paused as he remembered Aria. He felt a bit uncomfortable as he realized that there is something about his past that Sanyukta was not aware of.

He thought of clearing the air first and thus took Sanyukta's hands in his and spoke softly. "There is one thing I must tell you Sanu."

"Hey, what happened to you?" Sanyukta was surprised at the sudden change in Shankar's tone. "Nothing much, I just thought of a name for our girl. And while doing so, a part of my past came before my eyes and I must share it with you. Otherwise, it will always bother me."

"Hey, blurt it out honey," she said warmly.

"When we believed that we had lost you forever, this place became unbearable to me. It was at that time I went on a journey to the Himalayas."

"Alright, that is fine with me Shankar. If you decide to become a hermit once again, just take me along with you." Sanyukta giggled

"Listen to me carefully please."

"Ok, sorry. Go ahead." Sanyukta tried to maintain a serious expression.

"During that time, I found a woman there and was briefly involved with her. Her name was Aria."

"Aria...that's a nice name."

"It is not about the name, I want to say something else, Sanu."
"I understood that. But I was not a part of your life then. So it doesn't have much meaning for me. It is ok. Just don't dare to pull that stunt now," she laughed.

"Wow, that was easy. Thanks for understanding."

"You are welcome, sweetheart. By the way, I like the name Aria... if that is what you meant?" Sanyukta winked.

"I do like that name. So are you fine with it?" Shankar asked again

"Oh yes. If she also likes it. What say, young girl?" Sanyukta looked at her and moved her eyes as if asking for her feedback.

"What does that mean?" the girl asked.

"It means lioness." Sanyukta answered with a roar.

"Okk, so you knew the meaning as well." Shankar asked with a surprise.

"Don't you think that it's only you who has a penchant for words Mister." Sanyukta cheekily replied.

"I am loving it already Mumma and Dadda." The girl replied and both looked at her as they heard those words for themselves first time in their lives. Thrilled, they planted a kiss on her slightly dusky cheeks and said, "Let her be Aria then, the Lioness."

After that evening, Sanyukta took a leave from the office for a few days and then opted for the work-from-home option. Javed became a regular once again in that home as he made sure that he did not miss at least one meal with Aria. He often would stay there after dinner to narrate her a story. Aria got the admission in a nearby primary school in grade one. She started her first day bit tentatively. Shankar picked her up from school in the afternoon. As he started driving back to the home, he noticed the queer silence on Aria's face. Curious to know about it, he asked, "How was your first day at school my doll?"

"Ok." She said.

"Did you make new friends?"

Aria did not reply to that question and just kept silent fidgeting with her blue necktie. "Hmmm...must have been a rough day then...am I right?" he asked again.

She looked up at him and then nodded slightly.

"I too had several bad days during my school days... you know I had no friends at all in my class."

On hearing that, she looked up in amazement and then asked, "Really?"

"Oh yes, then one day I met your Javed Chachu. It was difficult before I met him but after that... it was so easy." He smiled as he finished his sentence.

"But I have friends... they all are there with Geeta amma."

"Yes, you are right...you did make some great friends. So, you can do it again. We will also take you there on weekend so you can meet your old friends. In fact, after two weeks it's your birthday, we will celebrate that with your friends and will also celebrate here so you can make some friends here as well. Doesn't that sound good?"

She smiled and showed the thumbs up. From that day, it became a routine for them to visit the orphanage every weekend. She also made few friends in her class as well. On 22nd June, 2019, Aria's sixth birthday was celebrated in her school as well as in the orphanage.

Gradually, the visit to the orphanage came down to once a month. When Javed was not there, Shankar took charge to tell the stories. She took a special interest in the old mythological stories and as Shankar loved to play with words, Aria loved his versions of the stories. Slowly, everyone became a part of the system that each one of them enjoyed. With no threat looming on them after almost four months, Shankar asked Hanumant to remove the extra security. Javed too reduced the number of security people around the house especially for Aria to give her a normal childhood. After six months, as the winter had set in, one weekend Aria decided to stay at home and play with friends from her school instead of going to the orphanage.

During the day, she went out with her friends to play outside. A couple of hours later, Sanyukta came out to watch her daughter. When she came out, she noticed that Aria is trying to calm down another girl who seemed to be a bit older and bigger than all of them. Curious, she came closer to them and started hearing their conversation.

"I will surely throw her in the mud." The big girl warned

"As I said, she is my friend, you won't do that as long as I am here." Aria strongly opposed her "You won't be here always... you can't save her forever, silly." The big girl grinned.

Aria seemed to be thinking for a moment while another girl, of the exactly same height and perhaps the same age hid herself behind Aria. After a few moments, Aria stepped forward, "Ok, I have a solution. In place of her, why don't you do that to me..."

The big girl looked confused for a while but soon realizing an opportunity for her, she nodded and pulled Aria towards her from her arms. She then pushed her in the little mud pool on the ground and saw her getting soaked into that before leaving from the scene. Aria soon pulled herself out of it as the other three girls present there helped her. She started dusting off her clothes when she suddenly looked at her mum smiling at a few meters away from her. "Sorry, mumma." She said as she went to her.

"That is ok my child. What was it today?"

"Nothing, she was just trying to bully my friend."

"Hmm... come on now. Let's go upstairs. I will wash you properly." Sanyukta held her hands smiling at her. Realizing that there was no escape from her mother now, she waved goodbye to her friends. Sanyukta took her to the washroom, as her hands were caked with mud and her curly hair was wispy. After a bit longer session of showering, she made a hot chocolate drink for Aria that she drank sitting in the warm snuggle of Sanyukta. She had finally settled in her new environment.

LITTLE ARIA

ARIA, THOUGH SHE MISSED THE CHILDREN'S home initially, soon got used to her new home and surroundings. She noticed and observed everything around her with sincere curiosity. Slowly, everything settled into a rhythm and it seemed as if it had always been destined to turn out that way. Within six months, everything and everybody in and around the house had settled into their place. From Shankar's clothes, which were pushed to the top half of his cupboard to give way to the new toys and clothes of the little girl, to his bookshelf, that was moved to the living room and replaced by a new wooden shelf painted with metallic red, all the changes took place smoothly. The bathroom had a new shower and a translucent glass partition. The refrigerator was filled with fruits, vegetables, chocolates and milk cans while the small utility balcony had a washer firmly fitted with the cold water tap split from the main tap of the kitchen. The proud father took responsibility for getting his daughter ready in the morning, preparing breakfast and dropping her off at the school. Aria spent her morning in a perfectly protected learning environment best suited to kids her age. Later in the afternoon, Shankar would pick her up and drop her home before returning to his work. In the evening, he would spend quality time with her, Sanyukta and Javed before they all went to sleep. During his evenings, he had reignited his imagination so as to reply to hundreds of inquisitive queries from his daughter. In the evening, he often sat on the balcony with Sanyukta and they looked up at the sky, watching the clouds take different shapes while Sanyukta made evening snacks. Every new shape of the clouds led to a new story from Shankar. He told Aria about his mother and his upbringing in the Himalayan village.

Aria was a fussy eater who would inevitably contort her face during her meals. Her parents had to literally chase her around the furniture to push food into her mouth. And more often than not, this chase would lead to the three falling down onto the couch, roaring with laughter. Aria flourished in the protective and nurturing environment of her new home and willingly accepted the couple as her parents.

In no time, all of them became so fond of each other that they could not even eat alone. When they were together, the home exploded with laughter and gaiety and in the absence of one member, the others waited anxiously for those footsteps.

The first year of Aria in the new home passed quickly. Aria had successfully been promoted to the second grade in her school. Spring had ended once again giving way to the Sun to be illuminated at its full might.

Her seventh birthday was around the corner. One morning, Shankar and Sanyukta woke up with Aria looming over them. She was excited and her eyes were shining like moonstones. They sensed her glee and lovingly asked her why she had woken them up so early in the morning. She pointed towards the window and jumped off the bed, rushing to open the panes. As she opened the window, a gust of wind wet with rain lashed the inside of the room. A pleasant moist smell of water mixed with sand and dust filled the room with its sweet earthy fragrance.

Shankar rose and stood next to the window, feeling the rain on his face. Sanyukta too came, and stood by his side. It was still very early and the sun was not yet visible on the horizon, though the dark clouds had already paved a path for it. The sky's colors were constantly changing, and the flashing thunderbolt sporadically illuminated everything. Sanyukta felt happy to be awake to witness such a beautiful scene and picked up little Aria. The child was laughing at the noise created by the hammering of raindrops, the roaring of the thunderbolt and the other pleasant sounds emanating from the street. She was happy and laughing till all of a sudden she remembered something and fell quiet.

"What happened to you, my doll?" Shankar asked.

"Dadda...I had a bad dream... I saw you, and you were bleeding from your head." And then she started sobbing.

"Ahhh, don't worry baby. It's just a dream." Shankar laughed lightly.

"I wish so Dadda... but I have seen that several times, my dreams have come true... I wish, it doesn't happen this time." She sobbed again.

On hearing her, Sanyukta felt a shiver and she hugged Aria tightly.

"It's just a dream baby, just a dream. Do not take it seriously." Sanyukta repeated it in a soothing voice until the child fell asleep. The memories of the bad dream were quickly erased from everyone's mind but Aria. She somehow knew that something ominous is growing somewhere but decided to keep her feelings to herself.

Shankar and Sanyukta planned to celebrate their daughter's birthday in a grand manner; grand in terms of the number of attendees but devoid of any pomp and show as per their way of life.

Javed arranged the venue while Mani and Hanumant took care of the guests. Sanyukta organized catering of the choicest of food in the big community hall. Sanyukta invited all the children from Geeta's orphanage. Shankar made special arrangements to fetch them and make their evening special. There were a host of party games for the children as well as a table full of food. Aria was dressed in a pretty fit for a princess. She had pink ribbons in her hair and wore pink sandals. The highlight of the evening was Shankar singing the birthday song in his hoarse voice, and making everyone clap and laugh. The presence of so many children had given a special vibrancy to the evening. By the time Shankar got home with his family, it was late evening and they were tired but very happy. They fell asleep hugging each other with smiles on their faces.

THE VISIONS

THOUGH THERE WAS STILL NO SIGN OF improvement, the treatment for Sanyukta's memory loss continued. There were some brief moments when she suddenly had sporadic visions of some shadows from her past but they were too vague to make any sense to her. She had however gotten used to Shankar's care, the doctor's diligence & her medication that had become a part of her life. Her work life was stabilized as the digitized world gave her ample opportunity to easily work-from-home.

Aria was doing well in school and Shankar too was well settled in the job. Javed visited them almost every day and Mani met on a weekly basis. Sanyukta's parents had already visited them thrice within one year. Almost everything for Shankar had fallen into place and they seemed to lead a predictable and stable life. But as always, the road of life took a turn at the most unexpected moment.

Aria had started waking up regularly in the middle of the night. She had recurring dreams of Shankar getting badly injured. She initially resisted the feelings and tried to keep it to herself but her sobs were well heard and the shiver in her body was well felt by her parents whenever the dreams took place. Shankar and Sanyukta tried their best to allay her fears through positive talks, but nothing seemed to work and the nightmares continued. Shankar took her to a psychiatrist and though Aria slept better for a few nights after taking the medication he prescribed, she woke up crying again the night she missed her dose. Her parents were extremely worried. Mani suggested that they take a break and go on a holiday somewhere outside the city. Girija had already invited them to their home quite a few times. Shankar agreed with the suggestion and, with Sanyukta's consent, booked the journey to Chandan Nagar. The monsoon had set in due to which, the life had almost come to a halt in the city anyhow. Javed too joined them for a journey into his melancholic past. All of them set on their journey the next weekend.

Shankar had already informed Girija of their impending arrival. When they reached, Girija was waiting to receive them. Shankar and Javed touched the feet of the old man. Then Shankar introduced Sanyukta, "She is your daughter-in-law". She came forward and touched his feet. "And here is your grand-daughter."

"Excellent. So, the family is complete. I am so happy for you. What are your plans, Javed? Where is your life partner hiding?" Girija teased Javed in his classic light-hearted tone.

"Don't know myself, Guruji... And by the way, all the great politicians have remained unmarried, so let it be." Javed replied smiling.

"Correct, *Netaji*."

"Now you are making fun of me *Guruji*. You know Sanyukta, he is like my father. He saved me when I was a child and it is his home where I was brought up. I owe everything to him." Javed spoke in a somber and dignified tone.

"You don't owe me anything, Javed. You were a good boy then and you are a good man now. Just be good to others, that is the best way you can pay me back..." Girija replied with the same dignity he was always known for, then he looked at the little girl and said, "Come on let's go. Come Aria, hold my hand."

"Yes *Dadu*." Aria followed.

"As we walk, I will tell you many stories of your Daddy and your Chachu. The naughty boys as they were."

"Wow, even I will hear those." Sanyukta immediately came forward, interested in the words that were soon to come out of Girija's mouth.

On the way to his home, Girija told Sanyukta and Aria about the childhood capers of Shankar and Javed. Aria paid special attention to everything, unlike most other kids her age. They were taken straight to Girija's home; he had insisted that they stay with him rather than go anywhere else. Shankar and Javed could not say no to him. Girija's wife, the aging woman welcomed them whole heartedly.

By the time night fell, Aria had become very friendly with Girija. She called him *Dadu* and seemed to be very happy in his company. Girija was the perfect grandfather figure, talking to her, playing with her, and telling stories to her till she fell asleep in his lap. Aria's parents were extremely pleased to see the bond between them. They finally got some time for themselves after a very long time. Girija's wife made sure her guests enjoyed the excellently cooked food.

Replete and satiated, Javed retired to his bed sooner, while Shankar and Sanyukta talked through the whole night. It was a welcome change for everyone and they were thoroughly enjoying the start of the break, in their own different ways.

The next morning, 28th July, 2020, Shankar, Javed and Sanyukta planned to go out to take a tour of the village with Aria. Aria, however, wanted to stay with her *Dadu* as she enjoyed his magical stories more than anything else. So, while Aria stayed with Girija and his wife at home, Shankar, Sanyukta and Javed went out to roam around.

Girija took Aria for a walk and told her a story. The story was about a fairy who could make everything right for good people. Absorbed in the story, Aria looked at the sky for several long minutes after it was finished. Girija patiently waited for her to respond. Then after those minutes ended, she asked Girija, "*Dadu*, do you know that in real-world there are no fairies?"

"Ohh, okk. But how do you know that my girl?" Girija asked in a slightly broken voice.

"My friend says so. She is very good, still, her parents died so soon... And I have never ever seen a fairy myself."

A bit confused on how should he answer, Girija thought for a moment and then he said, "There was a fairy around her and around you as well... and you know her."

Surprised to hear that, Aria cautiously asked, "Who is it?"

"Your Geeta amma... isn't it? She always took care of each one of you. There are people who have the devil and the fairies in them. You can spot them easily. Now, for example, your mumma and dadda are just like your fairies and you are one favorite fairy of them. See the world of your parents. You have changed everything around them for the better."

Convinced on what she was told, she nodded slowly and then asked, "What if something happens to mumma and dadda?"

"Why are you asking such things, my baby? Your father is a strong young man and he has great friends like Javed Uncle around him. They can handle any danger, I have seen them both do so, and I know that they will always do it. Don't worry," Girija replied in a lighter tone.

"I wish, *Dadu.* But there are these dreams which trouble me. Moreover, I know that my dreams become real one day as always. I am afraid of them now."

"What dreams, Aria? What are you talking about?" There was this serious tone in Girija's voice, after listening to Aria.

"All kind of weird dreams, *Dadu.* I don't talk about them to mumma and dadda because they won't believe it. They always say it's just a dream. But every time I see my other dreams becoming a reality, I get scared." Aria spoke with such intensity that Girija got goosebumps.

"Okay, I believe you. Tell me what have you been seeing."

"I saw Mummy adopting me much before she actually did. Last night I saw *Dadi* with a wound on her forehead and blood dripping down from it." Aria suddenly stopped talking. Girija kept on looking at her and then Aria suddenly spoke. "Let us go home. Perhaps we can do something to save *Dadi* from the accident. She might get hurt."

When they reached the house they found Giriija's wife working in the kitchen. She seemed fine. Girija was so relieved and pleased that he went straight towards his wife and hugged her from behind and whispered, "You are my lifeline. I love you." His wife, soon turning sixty, clad in a brown saree, was happily surprised and then turned around to say, "What on earth has bitten you today, my husband?" And then she rolled her eyes and pushed him away. Girija stepped back and came to Aria. He picked Aria onto his shoulders and said, "Everything is fine, my little girl. Don't worry. Nothing bad will happen." As he finished his sentence, there was a loud noise from the kitchen. He quickly put Aria down and ran back inside to find his wife sitting on the floor with her hands on her head. Blood poured out between her fingers. The pressure cooker was lying on the ground. The safety valve of the cooker had malfunctioned and the cooker had burst open. Its lid had hit his wife right on the forehead, just above the right eye, precisely the spot Aria had mentioned.

Girija could not believe it. He remained in a state of shock and disbelief for the rest of the evening. When Shankar and company returned, they thought that it was the accident that was worrying him, but Aria knew it wasn't. Girija could not sleep the whole night. He looked older with the creases on his wrinkled face suddenly looking more prominent with worry.

The next morning, he rose and woke up Aria for a morning stroll. As they walked, Girija spoke, "My sweet girl, I believe in your visions. I can also understand your fears and I thought of your situation all night. I kept thinking, why has the Almighty given a small girl like you such a strange power? After all, it could ruin and torment a small life, and you must be a strong girl to cope with it." Girija pressed the tiny biceps of the little girl humorously as if to measure her strength and then both of them burst out laughing.

"*Dadu,* I don't want to know the future. Seriously, I don't. " Aria was suddenly very sad.

Girija held her hands firmly, then patted her back and said, "I know, my dear, I know. But you are a very special child. When one cannot change something, then you must learn to make the best of it. This is what we need to do now. Don't be afraid of your dreams, but try to see everything clearly and remember them. We might be able to learn in advance about the danger your papa might fall into. This will be a boon for us."

Understanding what she had been told, Aria felt a strong sense of responsibility and motivated to up her otherwise hunched shoulders "Ok, *Dadu.* I understand. I remember quite a few things from my dream. Do you want to know?"

"Oh yes. Tell me in detail. Tell me everything you remember."

"There was one dream in which I saw Papa running in the dark, followed by a few men. They had guns in their hands and their faces were covered." Aria said seriously.

Girija pressed her for more details. "Try and recall anything more," he said.

"I don't remember anything more about this dream, but a couple of nights back I dreamt that a man was searching for my mother in a train station, maybe a metro train station," Aria replied.

"Metro station? Which one was that? And who was the man?" Girija asked "I don't know, *Dadu.* I don't remember anything else," Aria replied.

"Ok, let me think about it. I might discuss this with your father," Girija told Aria and they walked home.

That evening, Girija, Shankar and Javed convened for a private discussion. Girija promptly asked, "Has anything ever happened to one of you in a metro station?"

Shankar and Javed were taken aback by the question and Shankar asked, "What is this in reference to, *Guruji*? Please tell us more."

"Leave it then," Girija suddenly stood, ending the discussion abruptly.

"What happened, *Guruji*? Please don't be offended, I am just trying to understand what this is in relation to. We have plenty of metro stations in Delhi and we have been to many of them on various occasions." Shankar tried to prolong the discussion but Girija was unaffected as he said, "I want to know any major incident that happened in your lives that might be connected to a metro station."

"Sir, there is one metro station where one of our party workers, Brijwasan, was found dead. We also have strong evidence for Sanyukta's presence in the same place, just before she disappeared. The evidence supported the involvement of the Chief Minister and we believe that Sanyukta was abducted from that point. We do not know anything else about the incident and there was not enough evidence to implicate anyone. But why are you asking about this now?" Shankar replied.

"After hearing your story, I think there is a strong connection between the metro station and your future. Tell me more about all the clues and the evidence, the police found there." Girija ordered.

Shankar and Javed told Girija about the Sangha, about Sanyukta's involvement in it, about the elections, Javed's escape from death, and the day Brijwasan died and Sanyukta disappeared.

"From what I have seen and heard from you guys of Sanyukta, she seems to be an intelligent and courageous woman. And I wonder if such a person, when in trouble, would not leave behind some proof. Especially as a journalist who knew the art of capturing the news, there is a possibility that she managed to gather some very important information on the day she was kidnapped. Don't you think that she might have managed to gather some proof and hide it somewhere before she was taken? I am just thinking aloud. At the end of the day, you know her better."

"*Guruji* might be right. It is quite possible. I remember Sanyukta always used her mobile phone for recording. We once recorded a session with a corporate investor during a fundraising meeting where the company asked us to accept money under the table and return a percentage to them through a legal channel. She was very smart in the manner she used her phone," Javed said.

"Yes, you are right. Hanumant Singh even found her mobile phone and the bag, but I remember that there was nothing in it," Shankar recalled.

"There might be a mistake, Shankar. Check everything again. You might get a clue. The danger hasn't subsided as yet and you must be very careful," Girija sounded concerned.

"Don't worry Guruji, we will handle it. But you didn't tell us how these thoughts came into your mind all of a sudden," Javed asked Girija.

"Do not ask. Some things must be left unanswered. Let's go inside. You might want to speak to your friend Hanumant... Just one thing more that I will say... Aria is a very special child. You are blessed to have her." Girija said and then turned back to go inside the house.

Shankar smiled back and saw Aria peeping out at them from the window. He was confused but decided to just let go and make the call to Hanumant Sharma.

Hanumant was out of town, so he asked for some time to relook into the matter. The days passed in the mountains very fast. Aria spent a lot of time with Girija as they spoke for hours. Shankar and Sanyukta often were surprised at the connection they had developed and then they thanked their stars as they got some quality time only for themselves after a long time. Aria stopped having any more nightmares and slept peacefully. Javed was usually on phone talking to Mani or the party workers about the work. When he did not do any work, he usually went for long strolls with Shankar on the outskirts of the village, to Shankar's home and near the banks of the river, exploring the old pathways they had once walked upon. It drizzled almost every day. Shankar and Javed too were drenched in the drizzle almost every day. "I can never forget these paths." One day Javed spoke to Shankar when they strolled towards Shankar's home.

"Never... remember how Sheru used to follow us?" Shankar asked as his eyes beamed with the memories of his past.

"Yes, and then you always tried to trick him by hiding on the tree ,but he as the perfect pet never could be tricked."

"Hahaa... and when Maa started cooking *rotis*, he could smell them from a distance and came running for it..."Shankar spoke as he was soaked into the memories of the past.

"Yes brother.. .and I could never forget that night when..." Javed suddenly stopped as he was about to utter something.

"One of us had to die that day... you saved me so the animal died."

"It was destiny Shankar... just the way we were destined to be together."

"Perhaps... but when you kill someone, even if by accident, a part of the killed one seeps into you becoming a part of you, haunting you for the rest of your life... and then you can never get rid of it."

"I can only try to understand brother, but I can always promise to be there with you." Javed patted his shoulder.

"Of course brother." Shankar patted back Javed's shoulder as they reached Shankar's home.

Ten days went by with all of them living the best times of their lives in each other's company. Javed's 38th birthday was celebrated with all of them together.

Around two weeks later, Hanumant called Shankar and told him that their earlier report was correct and there wasn't any new evidence or relevant data about the incident. Sanyukta's mobile had only a contact list and some messages. There was nothing else and, moreover, the phone didn't have enough memory to hold any photos and videos. Shankar was surprised to hear that. He knew how much Sanyukta had liked to keep space on her phone. He felt there was a missing piece somewhere. He discussed it with Javed and he had the same opinion. They decided to get back to Delhi quickly and sit with Hanumant and Mani. Thanks to the fresh air of the mountains, the village and the wise company of Girija, everyone seemed to be better prepared for the troublesome times ahead.

QUEST FOR TRUTH

THE RAINS WERE LASHING THE CITY. THE streets flooded with water and gave no space to the people to walk around normally. It was getting dark sooner for a normal day in August. Somewhere, at the same time, in a less illuminated room of a small house located on a similar flooded street of Delhi, a medium-sized man with fair complexion and short straight hair stood in front of Ajay Singh.

"They are coming back to Delhi, sir," the man informed Ajay Singh.

"Ok. What is the condition of the woman? Has she recalled anything?" Ajay Singh questioned menacingly.

"No, sir. I don't think that you have anything to worry about. She might never get her memory back," the informer replied in a confident tone thwarting any threat for Ajay Singh.

"You don't get to decide on that. Just keep a close eye on them," Ajay Singh barked.

"Yes sir. My men are always following them. None of their activities are hidden from us. Even their phone calls are being traced. Yesterday, Shankar called up that Sub-Inspector who was investigating this case," the informer said.

"I want to hear everything that they spoke about. Can't we get their phone calls recorded?" He asked brusquely.

"Not the mobile phone sir, but in their absence, we have bugged their home with tiny microphones and transmitters. Whatever they say in their home can be recorded and made available to us," the informer replied battling with the snarls confidently.

"Now, that sounds better. Update me about everything and come to me at once if you hear anything important," Ajay Singh commanded.

"I will do so, sir." The informer replied as he left the room. As he left, Ajay Singh took his mobile and dialed a number, "Yes Sir, everything is in control."

Shankar was still completely oblivious to these developments. When he reached home, he called Hanumant Sharma and asked him to meet him at a café. Javed joined them for the meeting.

Hanumant was not in his uniform. They were meeting after a long time and the atmosphere was as lively as it always becomes when friends meet. Hanumant hugged both of them and then sat down as they ordered some beer and roasted snacks.

"I can see that both of you had a very good time in the mountains. Your bulging tummies tell the tale well," Hanumant chuckled.

"You are right. It was marvelous to be home after so long. I really belong to my village," Javed replied.

"He is right. It was great to be there. I now know exactly where I will live when I retire. And yes, Javed did not stop staring at those beautiful village girls. I am sure he wants to be back there as soon as possible." Shankar chuckled while Javed was positively red-faced.

"Haha, Javed *bhai* is young and even younger at heart." Hanumant said emphatically.

"Yes, I am young and romantic. And you guys, instead of being jealous, should be more like me." Javed smirked while the others laughed even louder.

Hanumant noted that their order had still not arrived. He quickly turned around to search for the waiter and he froze when he spotted somebody. He immediately turned back and whispered, "I think we are being followed."

"What? Why do you think so?" Shankar asked.

"That guy sitting in the corner was behind you when you both arrived. I saw him driving in right behind you and he is now sitting in the café alone. He must not know that I already know him. He runs a small mobile shop in central Delhi and has been caught by the police a couple of times for selling stolen mobile phones. But every time he has been bailed out by a person in power. It is believed that he works for Ajay Singh." Hanumant looked worried.

"Hmm. So what should we do now?" Javed asked leaning a bit and watching the man surreptitiously.

"Nothing. Just behave normally. He should not realize that we have identified him. Don't look at him. We will talk slowly and then decide what is to be done with him." Hanumant ordered.

In a couple of minutes, the waiter reached their table with their order. Hanumant quickly took out a mobile phone and handed it over to Shankar, concealing it behind the waiter's body.

"As I said, there is nothing in the mobile phone. You can see for yourself," Hanumant said.

Shankar opened the mobile phone and saw that the multimedia card slot was empty. "I think the memory card is missing and that is what we must look for." Hanumant thought for a moment and started typing something on his mobile while Shankar spoke.

"But how do we find out where the card is hidden? We need to know of a starting point," he said.

"Why not start at the place where all of it happened?" Javed pointed out.

"I know what you mean. The metro station could be the place. But even if we agree that Sanyukta could have hidden the memory card somewhere in the metro station before being captured, it is still way too difficult for us to find a place where such a tiny object might be hidden in such a large area. And again, this is just a presumption. The memory card could already be lost," Hanumant said.

"This empty slot is clear enough evidence that the card has been taken out. If Devi Dutt or the culprit who so ever it be, had known of some recording then he would have taken the phone into his custody and destroyed it. This means that this was a deliberate act by Sanyukta to protect some information. And being the intelligent lady which she is, I am sure she must have found a place where the memory card could be hidden safely. The challenge is to find that place. The greatest probability is that the hiding place is somewhere in the metro station itself." Shankar stopped talking as he noticed Hanumant typing on his mobile and asked, "What are you doing on your mobile phone, by the way?"

"Shhh, do not talk so loud. I have summoned my assistant here and now he is sitting right next to our man in the café." Hanumant winked.

"Your assistant? Why?" Javed asked.

"He will follow the one who is trying to follow us," Hanumant winked again with a smile. "Oh, excellent. That is an ace over the opponent's king." Javed chuckled.

"Indeed. So, now that we know we have to search for a small memory card in a huge metro station, the question is, how do we do it?" Hanumant asked.

"Well, I think we should simply go there tomorrow evening and take a round of the area. It's *Janmashtami* tomorrow. The metro station won't have too many visitors as many offices will be closed. There could be many nooks where the card might be hidden. Let us just start the exercise?" Shankar said vehemently.

"Yes, that can be done. But we must be very careful. I am sure that by now the enemy will be monitoring our every activity and this means that you people are in constant danger." Hanumant sounded worried.

"I understand. But we will have to take our chances." Shankar tried to comfort Hanumant.

"Ok. So be it. I will join you at the metro station tomorrow. Message me the plan when you make it. But make sure that your family is always under somebody's supervision. I will also arrange a policeman for protection in a day or two. These festivals are a big headache for police." Hanumant sounded frustrated.

"Don't worry. I will ensure that someone is always there to protect Sanyukta." Shankar answered.

"I will also get my security around the house back." Javed said.

The three of them finished their beers and left the café. Hanumant waited for a while to watch the shadowy man quickly get up from his seat to follow Shankar. However, the man didn't know that he was being followed too.

The next morning, Shankar called Mani and told him everything. He asked Mani to come to his house in the evening so that he could stay with Sanyukta and Aria while he was gone.

The day crawled onward to a dusty evening. Shankar returned from his office, which operated every day including the festival holidays, in the evening. On his way back, he called up Mani,

Javed and Hanumant confirming the plan. When he got home, Aria jumped up to hug him. Sanyukta too came out of the kitchen and hugged her "equal half". The three of them walked into the house together. Shankar quickly put down his bag and went into the bathroom to change his clothes.

"Are you going somewhere?" Sanyukta asked.

"Yes, honey. Javed wants to meet me and discuss something. I will be back in no time," Shankar replied.

"Ok. Drink your tea first and then go. And yes, please drive safely. The roads have become mad these days." Sanyukta sounded miffed about Shankar's going out again.

"I am not driving, honey. I will take the metro. Javed will be in his car so he will drop me home. And yes, Mani Kaka will be coming. Ask him to wait for me. I will be back soon."

"Alright." Sanyukta gave a terse reply.

Shankar sipped his tea, said his goodbyes and quickly moved out of the door. He took out his phone and scolded himself for not charging it, but he kept moving towards the nearest metro station to catch the train.

"Oh, this mobile doesn't ever stop ringing. Aria, can you please answer it, baby?" Sanyukta called out to her daughter. Aria answered the phone. She immediately took the mobile to her mom as the voice on the other end demanded to speak to Sanyukta.

It was a worried Hanumant at the other end. "Hello, *Bhabhi.* I can't reach Shankar's mobile phone. Where is he?"

"He has already left the house. He said he was meeting Javed.

What happened? What is the matter?" Sanyukta sensed the urgency in Hanumant's voice.

"Nothing much. I just wanted to talk with him. Where is Mani? Has he not reached yet?"

"Not yet. But what is the matter? How do you know that Mani kaka was coming here? Please tell me. I am feeling extremely nervous," Sanyukta said.

"Bhabhi, I just got to know from one of my men who was following Ajay Singh's man that your house has been bugged with some tiny transmitters. Last night, when Shankar called up Mani kaka, everything was heard by them. This is not an auspicious sign. It seems that we are getting close to finding something which could lead us to our enemy. I must run to meet Shankar. Please don't go outside. Mani kaka will be coming there shortly and I will also send a couple of my men to your place." Hanumant spoke in a single breath.

"I don't understand. What did Shankar say to Mani kaka and how does it affect somebody else so much?" Sanyukta was completely zapped by now.

"Don't worry about it too much. Just understand that we might have a strong enemy known as Devi Dutt, who we suspect was the one behind your disappearance. His deputy, Ajay Singh, is behind all this, though he only follows instructions from his boss. Fortunately for us and unfortunately for them, we have survived. Just follow my instructions. I should go now. Will keep you updated. Bye." Hanumant put down the phone hurriedly, leaving Sanyukta gasping at the sudden disclosure of all the turbulence.

Sanyukta thought for a while and then she clenched her fist.

The next moment the doorbell rang. She saw Mani through the keyhole. She quickly took the car keys and opened the door to let Mani in. Then she spoke to Mani: "*Kaka*, I can't stay here just waiting for my husband to come back when I know that he is in danger. Please take care of my daughter for me." And then without waiting for a response from Mani, she moved out of the house. Mani had no option but to ensure the safety of the little girl.

IMMINENT DANGER

SANYUKTA DIDN'T REALIZE THAT SHE WAS being followed. She drove to the metro station at a fast speed. Although she had lost all her memories of the past, the feeling of losing her loved one had come back with a force that hurt her head. It is said that the intensity of love is never realized until the moment of separation. The mere thought of separation had made her extremely nervous and she drove, racing against time. It was almost a thirty minute drive, and the heavy traffic on the roads due to the festival shopping had made it harder for her to navigate through. In order to reach quickly she decided to take a short cut by taking various small and narrow streets. In her desperate rush, she bumped her car a couple of times against stationary vehicles but nothing stopped her. Taking a right turn, she looked into her rear-view mirror and noticed a motorbike behind her. The motorbike had two masked men riding on it. The man who sat on the back seat wasn't wearing a helmet. She suddenly recalled what Hanumant had said. She started noticing her surroundings. She kept a watchful eye on the movements of the motorbike behind her. After a couple of minutes, she slowed down to give way to the motorbike. As the motorbike sped past her car, she heaved a sigh of relief. She continued at the same speed for a few minutes and then increased her speed as she raced towards the destination.

Another few minutes passed as Sanyukta navigated the busy streets of Delhi to finally reach an empty stretch. It was a small stretch of around five hundred meters, crossing a small canal that flowed through an industrial area, where not many people were seen after office hours. That being a holiday, the area was totally devoid of humanity. It was also getting darker so she thought of turning the headlights on when suddenly a light flashed before her eyes. As she tried to see through the glow, the object carrying the light came very close to her car. She impulsively applied the brakes to avoid a collision. By the time she realized it was the same motorbike coming towards her, it was already too late. The man at the back had jumped from the bike and stood right in front of the car, staring at Sanyukta. His revolver was pointing straight at her.

LURKING SHADOWS

SHANKAR REACHED HIS DESTINATION, AND Javed arrived shortly after. He probed, “What happened to your mobile phone? Hanumant and I tried your number so many times.”

“Oh, the battery is dead. What is the matter?” Shankar asked cautiously as he sensed the tremor in Javed’s voice.

“We all are in danger. The man who followed Devi Dutt’s man heard him talk to somebody else today. They know your every activity as they installed transmitters in your house while we were away in Chandan Nagar," Javed said agitatedly.

"Oh God. Then I must inform Sanyukta and Mani. Give me your phone," Shankar said to Javed.

"Don't worry. We have informed Sanyukta and Mani kaka about this. Sanyukta now knows everything," Javed replied.

"Oh, ok. That's a relief as well as a point of tension for me. She will have so many questions by the time I get back home."

"I am sure. You better prepare yourself! But for now let's not waste any more time, let's start our search. Hanumant is almost there. He is meeting us at the front gate of the metro station."

While they walked towards the gate, Javed's phone buzzed. "Mani Kaka!" he said. There were some tense moments after the call was ended. Mani had told Javed that Sanyukta had left the house in search of Shankar. Javed tried calling Sanyukta but there was no answer. Hanumant reached them and as his eyes met Shankar's, he understood that the situation was dire.

"What should be done now? I should have told Sanyukta everything. She is now reacting impulsively and most importantly, she still doesn't know the gravity of the situation," Shankar said.

"The three men I had posted outside your house told me that they saw her leaving in her car. I asked two of them to follow her and keep her out of danger," said Hanumant.

"Oh, that is much better. Thanks a lot, brother." Shankar sighed, relieved.

"Don't thank me yet. The problem is, that somewhere along

the way, they lost track of her. They informed me and I ordered them to find her at any cost. They are assuming she might have taken a shorter route to avoid the heavy traffic on the main road."

Feeling helpless, Shankar proposed, "Oh, so in that case, we can't do much. I think that rather than wasting any more time, Javed and I should head out to look for her. You stay here in case she shows up."

"That is fine. I will wait here." Hanumant quickly gave his consent.

THE RESCUE

"THERE IS HER CAR," SHOUTED THE MAN riding the pillion on the motorcycle. Then he shouted again, "Some men have stopped her car, she is in danger."

The man driving the bike immediately accelerated and in the next five seconds their bike reached the spot with a deafening roar. The man with the gun pulled the trigger but Sanyukta ducked and remained low in the seat as the two men on the second bike jumped and rushed towards the shooter, pulling out their service guns. The shooter saw the two men approaching. He quickly stepped back, aimed and fired at them. The two men, who by now were obvious as policemen, threw themselves behind the car and returned fire. The accomplice of the shooter sensed the danger and quickly started his bike, and attempted to speed away. On seeing his accomplice flee, the shooter too stepped back to run but fell to the ground as he was hit by a bullet fired by one of the policemen. The cops came out from behind the car and found the man heavily bleeding, counting his last few breaths.

They reached Sanyukta's car and knocked on the door but Sanyukta gave no reply. She was still hiding, not realizing that the other two men were actually her rescuers. It was only after one of them spoke about Hanumant, that she looked up to notice their *khaki* uniform. She quickly opened the door and came out of the car. The policemen called Hanumant and updated him on the situation. Hanumant asked them to bring Sanyukta to the metro station. He then called up Javed and spoke with Shankar, informing him about Sanyukta's safety. Shankar was relieved and asked Hanumant to make arrangements to bring Aria and Mani to the metro station too. He didn't feel confident about leaving Aria at home without him around. He also decided in his mind that he would take his family to some other place until everything had settled down.

Hanumant informed of the situation to the police control room and asked to prepare for a contingency back up. "Finding the missing piece now becomes even more important, Javed. Until we find that, our lives will always be in constant danger." Shankar said to Javed and they both started searching for the missing memory card.

In another corner of the city, amid the raging heat of festival and conspiracy, Ajay Singh was having a chat with Devi Dutt while they doused their throats with liberal measures of Johnny Walker's premium scotch. Suddenly, Ajay's phone buzzed and as he saw a number flashing on the screen, he quickly disconnected the call. Devi Dutt raised an eyebrow but was soothed when Ajay said, "Call from my parents, Sir. They just want to convey their festival greetings." After another two minutes, he said he needed to go to the bathroom. When he entered the bathroom he quickly took out his phone and checked the received text message. A sudden gust of rage shook his body. He dialed a phone number and ordered the man on the other end in the coldest voice, "Finish all of them. Take your best men and complete the task. This is a war now." Then he came out and sat down next to Devi Dutt. There was no sign of anger on his face.

It was dark by then and the metro station was getting desolated. It is said that evil raises its head when godliness becomes predominant. After all, God and the Devil are nothing but two sides of the same coin. But somewhere between is the human who is the most capable, holding two swords called Destiny and Free Will. If both the swords point in different directions, which is more common than not, the person displays shades of grey. But if these two swords point in the same direction, then the person gains absolute power to go beyond the capabilities of The God and The Devil. Shankar and Javed, two people perhaps destined for something big in their lives, had started showing the courage to embrace the sword of free will early on. It was just a matter of time until the sword of destiny also gets aligned so that both pointed in the same direction. With the rise of the serpent head of evil, their destiny was marked with only one of the two options; stand tall or perish. To their good fortune, they had another fighter standing behind them giving them support and holding their hands in the middle of the storm, Hanumant. "I will take you to the exact spot where Brijwasan was found dead. Keep your car close to you for any emergency, drive to the backside of the station. You will find me there." He said while Javed and Shankar followed him.

They went about their task, not realizing that at least five pairs of eyes were following them. Behind the metro station, there was a large ground that was used for carnivals, fairs and events and could accommodate a fairly large gathering. On that day too, a large part of the ground was covered with tents for the carnival. As they moved closer to that side, the cacophony of music coming from loudspeakers, a chattering crowd, crying babies, screaming people sitting on the giant wheel and the calling of the numerous hawkers met their ears. They could smell the dust in the air. When their eyes adjusted to the haze, they saw Hanumant standing in front, rubbing his eyes to wipe it clean of the dust particles.

Shankar moved forward to help him. But as he moved forward, a light flashed from the right, followed by a loud sound. The next moment, he saw Hanumant kneeling and screaming in pain.

THE REAL FOE

SITTING ON THE BAR STOOLS, UNDER DIM light, with light instrumental music in the background, Ajay appeared a bit nervous as he finished his glass.

"I should go now, sir," He said. "No, it is too early. We must finish this bottle first." Devi Dutt spoke with authority.

"Sir, I am done for the day. Please let me go." Ajay tried to convince Devi Dutt but his words had no effect.

"What are you saying? You are an alcohol guzzler and I have

just ordered your favorite chicken tikka. Here is your large scotch on the rocks and here is mine. And now, bottoms up."

Ajay had no choice but to follow the order as he chugged down another glass of Johnny Walker. Devi Dutt filled the glass once again and saw Ajay down it in a hurry. Ajay was in a strange state as he was caught between the extremely dizzying effect of a large volume of spirits partaken in a hurry and an urgent need to stay attentive. The more he tried to stay awake, the more the spirits worked against him. He tried to keep his eyes open but then there was another drink waiting for him. He picked up the glass and started drinking but his body had given up as he fell back on the couch and the glass fell out of his hand to the floor.

Suddenly, his phone buzzed on receiving a text message. He tried to reach for his phone but could not find it. Devi Dutt stood up and handed Ajay his phone. Ajay took the phone in his shaking hands and as he entered the password to unlock the screen, Devi Dutt snatched the phone from him. Ajay tried to struggle but his body did not support his mind. Devi Dutt quickly read the message and then he started scrolling through all the text messages on the phone. As he kept reading, his eyes grew bigger and his breath became heavier. He quickly took out a pen and paper and started making some notes of the numbers and messages. He went through all the records of the phone and then took out his own device and dialed a number.

"Hello?"

"Hello Mani, Devi Dutt here." Devi Dutt quickly introduced himself.

"Why are you calling me, Devi? You have already done enough

to destroy our lives." Mani was fuming.

"What are you saying, Mani? I know I am a greedy man but I am not a murderer. I just called to tell you that that your lives are in danger. I have just come to know that my best man, Ajay Singh, was actually working for Hari Lal. The same Hari Lal who once conspired against you all. He is still operating from behind prison walls. Please guard yourself and help Shankar, Javed and Sanyukta. I hope I see you all alive tomorrow. Then I will show you the evidence that proves my innocence and Hari Lal's work. For now, Ajay Singh is in my hands. Good luck." Devi Dutt disconnected the call and summoned his boys to restrain Ajay Singh.

FINAL CONFLICT

SHANKAR AND JAVED CRAWLED TOWARDS Hanumant to pull him behind their car parked in the area. The bullet had entered his chest in the upper left corner and had just missed his heart and lungs. Hanumant was badly injured but he could probably survive if taken care of. Shankar pointed to his right and said to Javed, "I saw the bullet coming from there."

"They are not firing now. That means that either they are coming towards us or they are waiting for us to become visible. Clearly, we are not too visible in the dark and that is the only thing favoring us." Javed analyzed.

"Right. We can't wait for them to reach us. Hanumant's wound is quite large. That means the shooters are well-armed. We also have no idea how many of them are there. To understand their position better, let me do something." Shankar quickly opened the back door of the car and slipped his arm inside. He pulled out an overcoat. He picked up a small stick and hung the overcoat on top of it and then slowly raised the stick in such a way that it seemed as if a person were trying to sneak out from behind the car. Another shot was fired right through the overcoat and this time, both of them noted the position of the shooter. There was a truck standing almost three hundred meters away from them. The shots were being fired from the top of the truck.

Right then they saw the approaching headlights of another car entering the metro station parking lot. "That could be Mani Kaka's car," Shankar said. Shankar and Javed looked at each other and then as if at an unspoken signal, they slammed their fists together and sat on the ground to take their next decisive action. Then, in a series of orchestrated actions, Shankar took the revolver from Hanumant and fired it in the dark, in the direction where the shooter was expected to be. Javed pulled Hanumant into the car, jumped into the driver's seat, pulled the ignition and put the car into the gear. Shankar fired once again in the same direction, hopped into the car as Javed drove towards the gate of the station. As expected, Mani had heard the sound of the gunshots and hence he quickly turned the car around and came out of the parking lot.

When they were about to come out of the station gate, two

masked men appeared in front of Javed's car and started firing. Shankar and Javed ducked but their car veered and rammed straight into the right gate and became immovable, jamming the path. Mani's car also stopped right behind Javed's. The policeman inside the car, responsible for Aria's security, quickly jumped out of the car and started firing into the dark without realizing that the masked men were hiding behind the walls on the two sides of the gate. But these few moments gave Shankar and Javed enough time to come out of their car, pull out the injured Hanumant and get into Mani's car. Aria, scared enough to lie very low in the back seat, tightly hugged Shankar on seeing him enter the car.

"Let us go from here, Papa. Please let us go," she cried.

"I won't let anything happen to you. Do not worry; we soon will be out of this place," Shankar promised her.

The policeman had finished his round and while he reloaded his gun, the masked men came out of their hiding place and opened fire. The policeman was hit and fell on the ground, injured. Shankar fired from inside the car while Javed quickly got out and picked up the gun from the injured policeman. It had one round of bullets in it. Mani put the car in reverse and pressed the gas pedal, taking them back to the rear parking lot and away from the two men. As the car moved back, the two masked men came out into the open. Javed and Shankar spotted the best opportunity and the next two shots from their guns hit the vital organs of both the masked men and they dropped dead. The car kept on reversing at a high speed till it rammed into a motorcycle. The little girl was horrified but Shankar pressed her tight to his chest, trying to protect her. The handle of the motorbike had got tangled into the car's lower body and after a few attempts to free it, the car also came to a halt, immobile. Now they could do nothing but wait for another attempt from the enemy to locate their position without putting themselves in danger. Suddenly one more shot was fired from the direction of the truck but the sound now appeared to be much closer. "It seems the first shooter is still alive and is approaching us," Javed said.

"Yes, but his fire seems to have no aim. I think he is not able to see us clearly and thus firing to keep us from firing at him," Shankar said.

"You are right. In that case, if we fire at him then our location will be revealed. Instead, we should move out of the car and search for the best place to hide," Javed suggested.

They cautiously came out of the car one by one and scrambled towards the wall of the parking area. They hid behind it. Mani told Shankar and Javed about his conversation with Devi Dutt. Even Hanumant, only half-conscious, was astonished to know that Hari Lal was still active from behind the prison walls.

"I have just called my station. We should get some help soon. But if the enemy reaches us first then we won't be able to fight them. Our bullets are almost out and the enemy still seems to be at full strength." Hanumant, in pain, spoke laboriously.

"Right. Our only chance for survival is to enter this ground and then the carnival gates and make an exit from behind the stage. There must be a concealed exit through which artists reach the stage." Mani spoke, gasping heavily. He too was wounded on his left arm as a bullet had hit him when he drove the car. It was not life-threatening, but still very painful.

"This is correct. I will stay here and you must leave

immediately," Hanumant said.

"No, we won't leave without you. We will go together," Shankar snapped back.

"No way, Shankar. My man is lying here, injured. I can't leave him as well. Moreover, the police force will reach very soon and I must be here to guide them. I will keep the revolver with the last four bullets in it and return fire at the invisible enemy. While I handle him, you should be able to cross the ground and reach the carnival gate. Get to a safe place fast, you have a big morning tomorrow as everyone will see how a convict has been master-minding a conspiracy from behind the prison walls. Go ahead guys, Move." Shankar saw Hanumant speak with such authority that he could not refuse. Everybody else too fell in line as Hanumant commanded.

When Hanumant fired his first shot, Shankar, Javed, Mani and Aria started running towards the carnival gate. The loud sounds of the festival celebrations and the distant vehicles were clearly audible. It was dark and difficult to move nimbly and suddenly the girl struck her foot against a large stone. She opened her mouth to scream but Shankar instantly put his hand to her mouth. Then he held on to her foot and pressed down to dissipate the pain. She calmed down and Shankar lifted her up in his arms and started moving cautiously towards the carnival gate. They heard a shot from the back but fortunately, nobody was hurt. They turned and saw six shadows leaping towards them. They increased their speed. Another shot was fired close to their ears and Shankar and Javed understood that they had to take the situation into their own hands. So they prepared themselves and took positions. Shankar asked Mani to lie down on the ground and dropped

Aria in his arms. Javed stopped, turned back, and jumped on the man closest to him. His large and strong hands, together with the speed of the punch and the weight of his large upper body, struck a lethal blow to the man. The man fell to the ground and his head hit a pointed stone.

Shankar rolled towards the men approaching and in a moment, he grabbed the feet of one of the men. He struck hard with his right leg between the man's legs. As the man knelt down, Shankar jumped up in the air and punched his face. As the two men surrendered, Shankar and Javed took their weapons into their possession and opened fire.

Ten shots were fired in less than 10 seconds and four bodies collapsed. Two of them were masked men, and two were Mani and Javed. Shankar froze when he saw them. Then he screamed loudly and, in an instant, leaped towards the fifth man who held the revolver. He aimed and tried to shoot again but the empty barrel made a tapping sound. Shankar punched him hard in the face and when he fell, he smothered him under his knees. Shankar looked at the still bodies of Javed and Mani, and lost his self-restraint; he picked up a heavy stone and struck it with full force against the head of the man. It was complete mayhem; dreams were shattering, souls broke, memories lost, identities sloughed off.

There was a heavy silence. Looking at the sixth masked man who still held his ground and waited for him, he felt a sharp pain in his abdomen. Suddenly his mouth was parched. He touched down there, but his hand became wet. He glanced down and saw the hole made by the bullet in his stomach. Tired from the exertion, he thought for a moment and then clenched his fists decisively, and started running towards the sixth person like a steaming engine. With bloodshot eyes, a tempestuous heart and the roar of a warrior, he rammed straight into his opponent, who could not anticipate anything. The strike was so powerful that the broken sharp edge of the stone he carried speared into the stomach of the masked man. He removed the mask and screamed loudly, demanding to know where Aria was. When no answer came, he felt the stillness in his face and then he raised himself to look around. Groaning with pain, he screamed Aria's name and started looking for her.

There came a timid voice, and Shankar's feet halted. "Papa." The most melodious sound was audible; the prettiest face was in front of his eyes. She hugged him and time stopped. Her beatific smile filled Shankar's heart with love again.

Sanyukta arrived, escorted by the two policemen. One of them checked the pulses of Javed and Mani and declared, "They are still alive. Take everybody to the hospital quickly."

Sanyukta came closer to Shankar and whispered to him, "I will not let anything happen to you, my love." Shankar heard her speak but he realized that perhaps his time was done. He held her hand and took it to his chest. The thick fluid raced out of the body. She sensed the blood and her eyes opened wide with fear. One of those pieces of iron had put a hole in his rib cage. Suddenly, feeling numb and dehydrated with the loss of blood, Shankar fell upon the ground. Sanyukta tried to hold him but to no avail. Eyes closed, his life started moving before his eyes like a movie. In a few moments, he saw his soul turning into a white light and a glow of contentment reflected on his face.

His eyes were closed, and when he opened them he saw he was in a long white tunnel filled with white clouds. A red beam passed through the clouds, dispersing into tiny red molecules spread across the tunnel. He saw some other people were walking the path along with him. Nobody was looking at each other as if oblivious to each other's presence. They walked straight without moving their necks as if hypnotized by a grand force. He looked at the walls of the tunnel, trying to get a hint of where he was, but nothing was written on them. He tried to call out to somebody but he could not hear his own voice. He could not hear anything, neither his pulse nor his heartbeat. He tried again and started recalling his days in the cave. He felt nostalgic and then in the blink of an eye, he was transported to the cave. He could hear the water dripping from the roof. He saw the contorted bushes and weeds growing inside the cave and the small rodents finding shelter under them. Hc loved to be there, he loved every bit of the time spent on the beautiful earth. He cherished every moment, good or bad, that he had spent with his friends and family. He was in love once again with his past, with his present, with his surroundings, with his friends, with his family and with life. He wanted to live once again. Love is known to be the strongest force of all. It is known to bring life to the aridest places on earth.

Shankar was restless because he wanted to see his world once again. Suddenly, two ferocious eyes flashed in front of him. The eyes of the predator glowed and soon gave shape to the whole body of the dying leopard. "The curse still follows me..." He sighed heavily. Then he saw himself leaving the cave and suddenly he was back in the tunnel. He started to run back but his feet grew heavy as if in a quagmire. He was unable to walk but he tried to, persistent. He moved one foot forward and then another with greater force. He was getting drained but he kept on trying. Suddenly, his step touched no ground and he started falling in an endless abyss. He screamed as he fell freely and then all of a sudden, he was not falling any longer. He felt as if he were on a bed of clouds. He could feel his pulse and heartbeat. He could feel the arms of a woman around him. He opened his eyes and saw the angelic face of Aria, the woman from America who adored him. "But what happened to her? Why was she lying so exhausted in bed? And where am I? What happened to me? Which place is this? Why am I so small? Why are there so many people around me and why are they smiling. Why am I wrapped in towels? I am a grown-up man and not a baby, or am I a newborn baby? Oh, is it a rebirth? Who is my mother?" He started crying in frustration.

"Oh, my baby. Come to Mama." Aria cuddled him closer.

"Oh, so she is my mother. She is so lovely. Her touch has soothed me. But what happened to my family? How is my daughter, Sanyukta, Javed and Mani?" And he started crying again.

"Ohh baby. Don't cry. See, Papa is here with you." A man tried to make the baby smile. "So, he is my father. Well, I think this is destiny. I very much wanted to come back to this world, so here I am. Let me accept it now. I hope my family is fine." And then he fell into a deep sleep. When he woke up after some time, he had no memories of his previous life. Though few things still did not change. Aria had named him "Shankar" and her husband accepted it without any question.

THE LAST STRAND

SANYUKTA WOKE UP THE NEXT MORNING and found herself in hospital. She had fallen unconscious when Shankar died in her arms. But this morning seemed to be completely different. She looked at everything with curiosity. She called up the nurse and asked about the well-being of everybody else. She was comforted to know that everyone else had survived despite some serious injuries. They all needed time to rest and recuperate. She wanted to tell somebody that she was feeling different, that she remembered everything, everything she had once forgotten.

The night before she had gone through trauma for the second time in her life. But time is like the sea; it doesn't keep anything in itself. It throws everything it has taken back to the shore when it is least expected. While the first incident took her memories, the second one brought everything back. Her memory had returned to answer many questions.

When the nurse arrived, she asked for her mobile phone. Then she dialed the phone number of Ram Kishen, one person whom she trusted besides those who lay injured and asked him to reach the hospital as soon as possible.

Devi Dutt also arrived at the hospital to express his condolences. Sanyukta accepted his words and his promise for unconditional support for bringing the perpetrators of the crime to justice.

She was released from the hospital in two days. She immediately went to the metro station with Ram Kishen to search for the memory card which she had hidden a long time ago. She reached the spot where Brijwasan was found dead. Recalling everything she said slowly, "He was not a bad man." Then she looked around and started visiting the pillars that carried the whole structure on them. After looking at several of them, she suddenly stopped in front of one pillar. As if she had recognized something, she swiftly moved her hand around it and spotted a small aluminum shutter. She pulled that open. There was a small hole in the pillar that carried electrical cables and wires. It was one of the openings for the electricians to install and later troubleshoot the electrical faults. She peeped inside and then pushed her fingers inside looking for something. After a few moments, her hand came out of the hole while her fingers held onto something.

It did not take much time for Ram Kishen to realize that she had found the lost memory card. They soon checked the card and found the information still intact. She shared the information with Mr. Das who promptly published the video. With due support from Devi Dutt and the video as prime evidence, Ajay Singh was taken into custody while Hari Lal was sent to the high-security prison. All his communication with the outer world was severed.

By the time Javed, Mani and Hanumant were walking again, Ajay Singh was sentenced to life imprisonment by the Supreme Court. It was a high-profile case and the court had set a precedent to bring the case to a close as early as possible. It was not only a win for Sanyukta but a testimony of the fact that truth can never be bulldozed by the weight of lies; it just gets hidden somewhere for some time and then erupts out of the deepest of the pits at the right time.

Little Aria was growing fast. After the tragedy she faced, she became more silent. She matured so fast that it seemed as if a full grown-up woman was trapped inside a girl's body.

Shankar, the baby, had started crawling, readying himself to enter the world and bring the change he was destined to. This time he was not even seen as a misfortune by the people around him.

Javed was very lonely after Shankar left the world so he engrossed himself in the world of politics and accepted that it was his destiny. Different truths will have different paths. He knew that he was part of a filthy world but he had mellowed down to become a lotus that flourished in muddy water. His experiences gave him the wisdom to absorb the goodness from the ugliest forms of life and he moved forward, learning the lessons of life all the way.

One day, while flipping through some old diaries, Sanyukta found a name. She dialed the phone number written against the name and heard the voice message: "You have reached the message box of Aria. I am currently not able to take your call. Please leave your name and phone number so that I can get back to you."

Sanyukta left a brief message with her name and number and for the first time after the death of Shankar, she felt numb. The following morning, she received a call. The voice on the other side was a bit hesitant. Recognizing the discomfort, Sanyukta quickly said, "Hi Aria, Shankar had told me about you. I understand that you both shared a great bond, so I thought you must be informed."

"Informed... about what?" Aria sounded worried "Shankar is no more..."

There was a long pause before Aria spoke. "I hope he died for a cause... that is what he would have wanted"

"You are right... where ever he is, he must be proud of himself."

"I always knew that you would come back into his life one day..." Aria said slowly.

Surprised to hear that, she asked, "Did you know about me?"

"Oh yes... he loved you like anything."

"I am sure... but he perhaps loved you no less."

"Why would you say that?" she asked as her heartbeat ran faster.

"Well, he named our daughter after you. Her name is Aria."

Aria could feel the smile that Sanyukta has gladly placed on her face as she spoke with a person completely unknown to her, yet she felt so connected.

"Ahhhh... thankfully I don't owe to him anything now..." Aria smiled back "What does that mean?"

"Well, my son's name is also Shankar. He is six months old now." "Ohhh... that is exactly when Shankar died... life is a mystery and death..." "A bigger mystery..."

"Sure it is."

After that phone call, where they were initially hesitant to speak in detail, slowly, both women found solace in their many conversations. Once the threshold of the silence was breached, the two women confided in each other effortlessly. Geographically separate, their lives were connected by a last unbreakable strand. In each other's company, they found the joy of catharsis.

Years passed by, Aria was about to turn eighteen. That night she slept in her bed just like she always did. Suddenly in her deep sleep, she saw people drowning in water. The flood very soon reached her house and she felt her bed floating in the water. As she looked around for help, she suddenly saw the serene face of her mother she had loved the most, slowly disappearing in the deluge in front of her. "Maaaaaa..." She yelled in horror and suddenly woke up from her dream... *the story continues in the next part "And the Sun catches fire".*